The Mahoning Trumpet ©

A novel by

James Heathe

ISBN: 978-1-968403-29-4 (Paperback)
ISBN: 978-1-968403-30-0 (Hardback)
ISBN: 978-1-968403-36-2 (eBook)

Published by Red Rock Book Writer

Foreword

In the quiet corners of South Boston, a discovery lay hidden, waiting to explain history and destiny. **David Costigan,** in the simple act of opening a footlocker in his grandmother's attic, unearthed truths that would challenge his understanding of family, legacy, and self. This moment of revelation was not just a personal journey but a bridge connecting the lives of two families from Youngstown, Ohio, and one from Boston, Massachusetts.

The story takes us back to January 1944, a pivotal moment in history when the United States began its assault on Nazi Europe, with Italy as its target. The events of January 22nd, 1944, would forever alter the destiny of a city and its people. It is within this historical context that the fates of these families became connected, their lives forever changed by the echoes of war and the passage of time.

As you turn the pages of this book, you will journey through the connected lives of these families, discovering how a single moment in history can ripple through generations. This is a tale of discovery, of understanding, and of the enduring connections that bind us all. Welcome to a story that spans decades, challenges perceptions, and celebrates the unbreakable bonds of family and history.

Prologue

David could smell the fresh bagels from Kuppel's Bakery as he finished his tenth comfortable lap. It was miraculous to find this place, knowing so little about Brookline before moving here. So, it is different from the streets of South Boston where he was raised. "Southie," as it's affectionately known in Boston vernacular, had been home growing up. But with children of his own now, it felt cloistered and eccentric, albeit gentrified. As a boy, no matter which way one turned, the faces you saw were guaranteed to be Irish Catholic—most one hundred percent.

It was harder to breathe today, thanks to the unseasonably cold air rolling down from Canada. But it didn't matter. He had four miles to run, and he was going to finish all four. This was now his only isolated sanctuary, even though eight or ten others were running or walking the three-quarter mile dirt track that circled the Brookline Reservoir. The reservoir sits on the outer edge of Chestnut Hill, shared by Brookline and Newton. Brookline itself was affluent and ethnically diverse, with a significant population of Jewish and Chinese families.

In addition to wealth, the town's focus on education was almost unmatched nationally. Many families gave up larger homes and yards just to claim a Brookline address, so their children could attend the town's prestigious schools.

Coming from South Boston—and being married to Mary, who was born and raised in Scituate—Brookline had once seemed foreign. Newer generations of "Southies" had gained the economic moxie to leave the city within the city. Many moved south, along the lower Metro-Boston coast. Over two generations, towns like Scituate, Duxbury, Marshfield, and Cohasset became known as the Irish Riviera.

He was the heretic, of course. He had disappointed his father. Forsaking the family ironworks business, he went to medical school and chose not to raise his kids in Southie. Instead, he moved to Brookline, which his father referred to as *Coolidge Corner, UN*, a jab at its multi-ethnic demographics. His father softened, eventually—especially when his youngest son, Brendan, married Rachel Eisenberg, a nice Jewish girl from Swampscott.

His mother loved Rachel from the beginning, even though she wasn't Catholic. But being Catholic and being Irish Catholic were two different things. Despite their reputation from the busing crisis of the 1970s, Irish Catholics, in his experience, really did love everyone. They were among the most welcoming people he knew. That had certainly been true of his family.

His great-grandfather, Robert Oldeon Costigan, came to America while the Spanish-American War was being fought. With almost no money, he boarded an immigrant ship out of Liverpool and arrived in America via Long Island—the lesser-known sibling to Ellis Island. He had written ahead to his cousin Sean Murray, who had emigrated ten years earlier. Sean gave him what was a closet for a room.

Robert found work at Citron Iron Works, the company he would one day own. With a little cajoling, Sean put his own reputation on the line to get him the job. Robert had a head for business as well as metalwork. When the opportunity came to buy the business, he took the risk. He raised money from friends and family, and secured a small, manageable loan from a bank not typically disposed to lending to the Irish. Thus, Costigan Iron Works was born.

The wedding came at St. Margaret's Church in Dorchester. Robert Costigan married Nancy Donaghue—because back then, Irish married Irish, Italians married Italians, and so on. The company struggled at first, until westward expansion created demand for all manner of iron tools and weaponry. St. Louis may have been the gateway to the West and the hardware capital of the country, but men like his great-grandfather helped fuel America's growth—and its wars.

In 1920, Robert and Nancy welcomed David's grandfather Francis into the emerging Irish Catholic Dorchester. Francis had been born to inherit the Costigan Iron Works.

Or perhaps not.

Chapter 1

Francis Goes to War

That sleepy, cold Sunday morning felt no different from the dozen that came before. The Depression still lingered in memory, but under Roosevelt's leadership, America was stronger. The Dust Bowl was finally over, and the era of duplicative farming was now seen as a disastrous experiment. The American military remained a minimal shell, but it hardly seemed to matter. The nation felt isolated and secure. Europe's turmoil—the Spanish Civil War, the annexation of the Sudetenland and Austria, the invasion of Poland—was viewed as someone else's crisis. Even Hitler's campaign against the Soviet Union was little more than an occasional headline to most Americans.

Most—but not Jewish Americans, who had already begun hearing firsthand accounts of Nazi atrocities committed against their European families. France had fallen under the weight of its bloated, antiquated military. Now, only Britain and Russia stood against Hitler's sweeping domination.

Half a world away, Hitler's ally Japan was tearing through Manchuria and Southeast Asia, leaving behind a trail of plunder and brutality. North Africa was in the hands of the Italians—reluctant warriors dragged into conflict by Mussolini's ego and his allegiance to Hitler.

Still, America remained determined not to be pulled into another world war, despite Churchill's repeated pleas for support.

Dorchester was deeply Irish Catholic, and families like the Costigans had no love for the English. Even so, they shared a natural revulsion for what Hitler was doing to the continent.

In 1940, Francis married Elizabeth McGowan. Like the best Irish Catholics, she was soon pregnant. David's father was born ten months later, followed quickly by Uncle Tom. But then came that calm, cold December morning—the one that rewrote the life plans of millions of Americans in just a few short hours.

Robert, Nancy, and Robert's brother William sat in Robert's sitting room, listening to the president speak about a "date which will live in infamy."

During his youth, Francis had dreamed of a life outside the ironworks. He'd wanted to be a doctor, but those hopes had been met with ridicule.

"We're not doctors. You need to live in reality," his family would say. By twenty, Francis had accepted that he had no support for anything outside the family business. His future had been defined before he could walk.

But a week after the bombing of Pearl Harbor, he made a different choice—enlisting in the U.S. Army's Medic Corps. If he couldn't be a doctor, maybe he could at least be the next best thing.

Robert stood in the Victorian foyer, hands clasped behind his back, rocking on his boot heels. A tall man—six-foot-four and a solid two-fifty—he had the prototypical Irish face: pale, with red blotches and striking diamond-blue eyes. His thick, white hair sat like a crown, and his ever-present Virginia cigar dangled from the right side of his mouth.

Nancy came up behind him and rested a steady hand on his shoulder. An embrace would have been too much—a violation of their quiet, Irish restraint.

"He'll be safe, Robert," she said softly, her Boston twang gentle. "He'll be helping the wounded, not fighting."

"It's not our war, Nancy," he grumbled. "It's for the damn British and the Jews to deal with. We should've stayed the hell out of it."

"They attacked us," she reminded him.

"Please, Nancy." He chuckled, removing his cigar and blowing a puff of smoke against the icy window. "That son of a bitch Roosevelt pushed us into this thing. With his lend-lease scheme and Churchill buddy act. Screwed with Japan's oil supply just enough to provoke this. Do not kid yourself—this was his goddamn ticket out of the Depression."

Nancy tilted her head. "I hate to say it, but... isn't this good for the works?"

They always called it *the works*, never *Costigan Iron Works*. It wasn't just a business, it was identity. Legacy. "We're ironers now," the family used to say.

Francis came down from upstairs, duffle in hand, coat buttoned up, plaid skullcap tugged low. Shorter than his father, and darker like his mother, he still had the same black hair and sharp eyes.

"You're not just going to leave?" Nancy asked. "I haven't even had a proper goodbye."

"I know, Ma." He sighed. "But I've got to catch the ten-thirty out of South Station."

"You know you have plenty of family in Belfast," Robert said.

"Belfast?" Francis looked puzzled. "Why are you bringing up Belfast?"

"You could go there. Sit this thing out. Do something for your own people."

"My own people, Pop?" He laughed. "My people are the American people."

"Bullshit!" Robert barked. "This is the land of the free and the home of—"

"...all kinds. Blacks, Hebes, Pollocks. Not to mention the Guineas."

"This again, Pop? Do you forget 'Irish Need Not Apply'? All the drunk Mick jokes?"

"We kicked their asses, didn't we? Half the state legislature's Irish now. So are the cops and firemen. What about Joe Kennedy? He could buy half the damn Wasps in Boston."

"Pop, what does any of that have to do with what I'm doing?" Francis asked.

Robert turned slowly toward his son. Nancy's hand stayed on his shoulder. He puffed his cigar and paused to choose his words.

"Remember who you are. And where did you come from? In the War of Secession, they pulled Irishmen right off the boat and threw them into Gettysburg. This is no different. They'll use you—and kill you—if it suits them."

"Who's *they*, Pop?"

"Them. The government. The same parasites holding Churchill's and Stalin's balls."

"Robert!" Nancy gasped, crossing herself. "I'm not happy about this either, but I'm proud of our son."

"Proud?" Robert sneered. "Proud like sheep marching for their masters."

"Or Jews marching to gas chambers?" Francis said pointedly.

"Rumors." Robert scoffed. "Jewish rumors drag us into this war. Do you really believe people could slaughter others like that?"

"I don't know," Francis said quietly. "Ask the Indians."

"This is your doing," Robert said to Nancy. "This Calvin Coolidge, FDR liberalism—and the idiotic stories they tell make us act more like lemmings than men."

"Think what you want, Pop," Francis said, reaching for his mother. "I love you, Ma."

"I love you too, honey."

From behind them, Elizabeth and young Patrick entered the room. She wore that timeless expression known to every wife and mother whose men are heading off to war. Even if this was only basic training, it marked the beginning of a long, anxious, uncertain journey.

Elizabeth and Francis met in 1932, at the Coconut Grove nightclub, thanks to a blind date arranged by friends. Elizabeth always spoke fondly of "The Grove," and mourned the terrible fire and tragic loss of life that followed a few years later. But that first night had been magical.

"Francis Costigan stood out in a crowd like a steeple," she often recalled. "That coal-black hair and sapphire-blue eyes could melt the steel off an automobile."

Their courtship lasted just over a year, though her parents vehemently disapproved of Francis. Her father, Bryan McGowan—an Anglican and a physician—saw Francis as nothing more than a steel man. Ironically, those very qualities may have drawn Francis in. Robert, for his part, had even less tolerance. Protestantism—particularly Irish Protestantism—was, in his eyes, a betrayal of heritage.

So, in true Francis Costigan fashion, he and Elizabeth slipped away to Provincetown, found a justice of the peace, and married. Nancy insisted they make it right by marrying in the Church. They were remarried in 1933, but in St. James Episcopal Church in Cambridge—just a stone's throw from Harvard Square.

Robert all but disowned his son. Only through Nancy's insistence they'd eventually sanctify the marriage in the Catholic faith. They did eventually marry in the Catholic Church and would later raise their sons Catholic as well.

Now, Robert and Nancy stepped aside, making room for Elizabeth and their grandson—even if, to Robert, the child was a Protestant one.

"Do you have everything you need?" Elizabeth asked, her palm resting gently on Francis's cheek.

"I think so," he replied. "The Army'll fill in the gaps, I imagine."

"This doesn't make you a doctor, son," Robert interjected. "It may keep you safer, though."

"Safer?" Francis chuckled. "I'll be treating men while bombs are blasting around me."

"Frank!" Elizabeth scolded, nodding toward young Patrick.

"Tommy?" Francis asked.

"He's napping, honey," she said. "I can wake him if you want."

"He's too little to know what's going on."

"We'll make sure he knows, dear," Nancy said.

"I know you will, Mom."

The gray bus pulled alongside the guard shack, waiting for clearance from the MPs. The driver exchanged pleasantries and paperwork with the guard, then rolled through. Fort Riley, Kansas, was drab and brown flatter than the top of a glass table. Even inside the self-contained camp, the horizon stretched endlessly in every direction.

Francis stepped into the crisp January air, only to be immediately confronted by the NCO waiting beside the bus. He was wiry but strong, his jaw shadowed with stubble though freshly shaven. He barked at orders as soon as the men's boots hit the dirt.

"What part of *line up* don't you sissy boys understand?" he hollered. "Make a line! Didn't your mommies teach you what a line is?"

The recruits shuffled and jostled until they were aligned shoulder-to-shoulder.

"My name is Arnie Edelstein," the sergeant barked. "I'll be your mother, nursemaid, and general ass-whacker for the next six weeks. My job is to turn you soft-bellied dreamers into something resembling soldiers—though I'd have better luck turning a jackrabbit into a lion."

As Edelstein continued his tirade, Francis leaned slightly toward the man beside him, trying to shield himself from the abuse.

"Francis Costigan," he whispered.

"Joe Brady," the man replied.

"I'm from Boston."

"Youngstown. Ohio, ."

"I know it—Steel City."

"Yeah. What kind of name is Costigan? English??"

"Irish."

"Brady's a Mic name if I ever heard one."

"Yeah—but not Catholic," Brady admitted.

"I am," Francis said, and the two men shook hands quietly.

"So, we've made some acquaintances, have we?" Edelstein growled, walking over with a sarcastic smirk. "You with the black hair—get down in push-up position. And you—smiley—sit on his back. Twenty crisp pushups, then you trade places."

Francis dropped to his knees, then onto his belly. Brady climbed aboard, trying to avoid pressing all his weight.

By the sixth push-up, Francis was visibly struggling.

"All right, all right," the sergeant barked. "Maybe smiley over here is stronger than—what's your name, boy?"

"Francis Costigan."

"And you?"

"Joseph Brady."

"Well, my two fine lads, I'll be watching you closely. Don't cross me. I'll make soldiers out of you yet. You see, the damn Huns are killing my people over there—and you fine gentile boys are going to help stop it."

Edelstein was an anachronism for his time. Raised in Chelsea, Massachusetts, he worked two years after high school, then attended LSU in Baton Rouge. He didn't resemble the few Jews Francis had known back home—he didn't hide his identity, nor did he fit any stereotype. As hard and abrasive as he was, there was a strange goodness about him. He wore that uniform like it belonged to him alone, and yet he felt completely out of step with the world around him.

That evening, after some running and stretching, the recruits were issued clothing—pants, shirts, tees, underwear, socks, and a heavy pair of Army boots. They were also given blankets and pillows, then guided through a maze of aluminum prefab buildings to the makeshift barbers.

Francis, like the other seventy-odd men who had arrived that day, entered one of the four chairs and had his hair shaved off in seconds.

Inside the newly constructed barracks, Francis grabbed the bottom bunk and started making his bed.

From his blind side, a figure appeared—and shoved him onto the mattress.

"Who said you could have that bunk?" the now-visible recruit demanded.

He was stout, heavily bearded, with a dark Mediterranean look.

"I thought it had first come, first serve?" Francis replied, sitting upright.

"Yeah—first to those with the balls to take it. What kind of idiotic accent is that?"

"Boston," Francis said evenly. "Boston, Massachusetts."

"I know where Boston is," the swarthy man snapped.

"Wasn't sure. And you're from…?"

"Jersey City," he replied, with a thick New York–New Jersey accent.

"I thought so." Francis gave him a small smile. "What vowel does your name end in?"

Before the man could respond, another recruit stepped between them. Tall and pale as milk, he spoke with calm precision.

"You best mind your own beeswax," the darker recruit warned.

"Or?" the pale one said with eerie confidence. "Or you'll be sleeping outside tonight, my Jersey friend."

The confrontation escalated quickly. The dark recruit stepped in, throwing a fist—but the pale kid dodged it cleanly and returned a sharp knee to the gut, followed by a punch to the face.   The darker man stumbled against the bunk frame, only to be met with another blow. He dropped to his knees, then face-first onto the floor.

"Much obliged," Francis said, offering his hand.

"Henri Vachon," the pale kid said.

"Vachon. French. But that accent…"

"Struthers, Ohio," Henri said. "Families from Quebec. One of the few non-Italian families there."

Francis laughed.

"I'm serious," Henri insisted.

"Quebec to Struthers, Ohio—wherever that is."

"Stone's throw from Youngstown."

"Youngstown?" Francis perked up. "There's a guy I met; he's from—"

"I know," Henri chuckled. "I saw your push-up exhibition, remember?"

"Oh yeah."

That evening, the men lined up for mess. Francis found Joe Brady and Henri Vachon. They sat together that night, and as many 1st Infantry veterans would later recall, "after that, you never saw the three of them apart."

Boot camp passed quickly. Just enough time to toughen them before joining the fray alongside the last free powers in Europe: Britain, her Commonwealth, and the Soviet Union. Britain had managed to repel the Nazis in the air in 1940, but politics complicated strategy. Roosevelt and Marshall favored striking Europe directly. Stalin wanted relief on the Eastern Front. Churchill pushed for securing North Africa to protect the oil fields. The Allies won there, having already rescued the front from the crumbling Italians. Now, with Italy defeated and occupied by the Nazis, the Italian campaign was next—and Francis was going.

With him: Sergeant Arnie—now affectionately named—Brady, and Vachon. But first came some R&R… and Thanksgiving.

Francis invited the Ohioans back to Boston. It would be their first trip to "Beantown."

Nancy set the table, nervously adjusting everything twice. She wasn't sure if her jitters came from seeing her son after months or being judged by two strangers who might compare her cooking to their own mothers'.

Still, everything was impeccable—right down to the jellied cranberry and sprigs of mint.

A knock, followed by the familiar squeak of the door.

"He's home!" Nancy cried, drying her hands on her green-and-white apron and rushing to the hall. "Franky!" she called—a name she rarely used.

"Mom!" Francis laughed, wrapping her in a hug. Soldier or not, in that moment he was still just a kid about to see carnage beyond imagination.

"Well, well. If it isn't the conquering hero," Billy said, rounding the corner. "Good to have you home. And these fine patriots?"

"Mom, Billy—this is Joe Brady and Henri Vachon."

"Vachon, good Irish name," Billy chuckled, shaking their hands. "Thought we beat those bitching Huns in the last war, it looks like my brother'll have to bail out the French and Brits again... no offense."

"None taken," Henri replied.

"You boys like turkey and stuffing?" Nancy asked. "Recipe goes back to my great-great-grandmother in Galway."

"Sure thing, Mrs. Costigan," Joe said. "Army food's just about run its course."

Nancy moved swiftly between kitchen and dining room, setting plates and silverware with practiced grace. Billy poured water into crystal glasses. Then Elizabeth entered with little Tommy, just waking from his nap.

"Sorry to keep you waiting," she said. "Tommy enjoys his sleep."

The boy bolted from behind her and into his father's arms.

"Hi, sweetheart," she said, smiling as Francis embraced her. His hug was warm, genuine—but not desperate. Brady and Vachon exchanged a glance that said more than words.

"Liz, this is Joe Brady and Henri Vachon. We went through basic together."

"I've heard a lot about you," she said, handing Tommy to Nancy. "I trust you'll keep Francis safe and bring him back to me and his sons?"

"We'll make sure this lace-curtain fool doesn't get himself killed," Brady said with a grin. "Excuse me, I didn't mean—"

"Don't worry, son," Robert chuckled from the hallway. "Lace-curtain's a step up from what those Brahmins call us."

Elizabeth just smiled.

For a while, the only sounds in the mahogany dining room were the soft clinks of silverware on China. Not unusual for the Costigans—too much talk often led to conflict, and no one wanted a repeat performance in front of guests.

Still, some silences begged to be broken.

"I've been thinking about what I'll do when the war's over," Brady said, finally.

"Aren't you getting ahead of yourself?" Robert said dryly. "You haven't even shipped out yet."

"Dad," Francis warned.

"It's all right, Frank," Brady smiled. "It's just how I get through it. If I don't think I'm coming home, I might not."

"That's very wise," Nancy said. "I think you should think like that too, Francis."

"I would," Francis replied dryly, "but I'm not even sure what 'that' is."

"The Iron Works," Robert declared. "It'll serve this family for a hundred years."

"That's *your* dream, Pop." Francis grimaced, thrusting a forkful of food into his mouth.

"That's my dream *for you*, boy."

"And what if that isn't—"

"That's enough!" Nancy interrupted. "It's a holiday, and who knows when we'll be together again. I will not spend it bickering. Just get yourself back safely. The rest will take care of itself."

"Yes," Robert added more calmly. "That—and get this medicine stuff out of your head."

"So, my dreams are just garbage?" Francis snapped, throwing his napkin onto the table.

"Your language, young man," Nancy warned. "I won't have that in this house."

"Sorry, Ma," Francis muttered.

"Franky, the Iron Works is a better place for you," Elizabeth offered gently. "My father will tell you about medical school."

"Your father doesn't talk to me, Liz. And mine doesn't listen."

"Maybe *you're* the one who should listen," she said, trying to stay serene. "This is your heritage."

"Heritage?" Francis laughed bitterly. "To be a greasy steel monkey until the day I die?"

"To do something honest and honorable," Robert said. "There's nothing wrong with an honest day's work. And this—this you'll inherit."

"I don't mean to intrude," Henri Vachon interjected, "but why is it so terrible for Francis to want what he wants?"

"And what will *you* do after the war, Henri?" Billy asked.

"I'll go into the family business. But that's because I want to.

"And that is?" Robert asked.

"Real estate and importing," Henri replied.

"Real estate and importing?" Billy snorted. "That's like us being in steel and lingerie."

"Bill Costigan!" Nancy barked. "Apologize this instant."

"I'm sorry, Henri."

"No worries," Henri said with a wave. "But still—why is Francis' dream so terrible?"

"It's not who we are," Elizabeth replied. "Francis has these illusions of being a medical man, but he'll come to his senses."

Henri folded his hands under his nose and glanced toward Joe Brady, who had silently put down his fork. He then looked at Francis, who sat bending his fork between his thumb and index finger.

After dinner, the men moved to the living room while Nancy and Elizabeth cleaned up. Robert opened a cabinet and withdrew a square wooden box. He placed it on the rustic coffee table and lifted the lid to reveal rows of neatly wrapped cigars.

"Gentlemen," he said. "Since you're off to save our democracy, I think a cigar and a little brandy are in order."

"That'd be great, Mr. Costigan!" Joe said with enthusiasm.

Henri and Francis exchanged a look.

"These cigars are hand-rolled by—"

Robert paused, then said with a grin, "by good Southern hands down in Virginia. Not much else for them to do up here, but they sure know their way around cotton and tobacco.

Brady's smile faded as he took the cigar, noticeably less enthused. Francis glanced at Henri, whose jaw had stiffened.

"You know, Mr. Costigan," Henri began carefully, "I—"

"Oh, come on now," Robert cut in. "Are you going to lecture me? They get paid. Lazy anyway—what else are they gonna do?"

"Maybe earn a decent wage and have a shot at some dignity," Henri said, holding his ground.

Francis looked at his friend with renewed admiration. Henri wasn't just principled—he was bold enough to speak out.

"So, you're one of *those* who thinks they're just like us?" Robert asked.

"They *are* just like us," Joe interjected.

"Really?" Robert scoffed. "They'd still be swinging from trees in Africa if—"

"If it weren't for our generous kidnapping and auctioning them like livestock?" Brady snapped. "Wow. Real heroes we were."

"You must be a goddamn Democrat," Robert muttered.

"As a matter of fact," Joe grinned, "yes."

"C'mon boys," Francis said, attempting to cut the tension. "Let's smoke. Politics won't win the war—we're here to stop the Nazis and the Japs."

"Why not medical school?" Henri asked Robert, steering the topic back.

"You heard what was said. We're steel men, not—"

"I never said *girly* men," Robert corrected. "It's just not who we are. This life—this *company*—it's good. And we'll do well during this damn war, if there's one silver lining."

"I still don't understand," Henri pressed. "If Francis—"

"Now you're stepping a bit over the line," Robert said coldly. "We are who we are. Costigan men have worked with their backs for 500 years. Francis may not care for tradition, but I do. Even his wife understands this fantasy is just that."

Joe lit his cigar, then lit Henri's and Francis's. "To our safe and profitable return," he said, raising his glass.

They all drank—though only some of them smiled.

As their brothers in arms contended with the Japanese in the Pacific, the three "brothers" engaged the Germans in North Africa. The British already pushed the Italians out of the war. The Soviets were pressing for a second European front, to pull German forces out of the East; but Rosevelt and Churchill believed North Africa was first. Much of the world's oil came from beneath those deserts, so capturing and commanding them was critical. Roosevelt and Churchill understood, The Germans had virtually no natural resources. Hitler knew where those resources were and if lost, Germany would be plagued by a shortage of oil and thereby Petrol.

Francis had always imagined Italy as warm and sun soaked. Mid-January on the Italian coast proved otherwise. Cold and wet, the beachhead assault was brutal. The Germans, now occupying their former ally, counterattacked Mark Clark's Fifth Army in one of the bloodiest campaigns prior to D-Day.

Francis, Brady, and Vachon slogged through freezing rain and mud, advancing toward Rome. First came Sicily. The British struck from the east while German Field Marshal Kesselring—a shrewd and battle-hardened commander—mounted fierce resistance. Victory was inevitable, but the cost was steep.

Word was, Rome would fall within the week—a symbolic prize following the Allied triumphs in North Africa and Stalingrad.

Combat, some soldiers said, was like being drunk. You could describe the symptoms, the disorientation, but you could never truly *know* it unless you lived it. Francis, Brady, and Vachon came to understand. They endured the torrential Italian rains, the unending mud, and the ceaseless thunder of German artillery. Still, Francis found something rare amid the carnage—not a love for war, but a quiet satisfaction in his role as medic.

It tore at him to see boys—eighteen, nineteen—crippled, disfigured, dying. But this was as close as he'd ever got to practicing medicine.

And in that, there was meaning.

One morning, after a brutal enemy attack and a sleepless night tending to the wounded, dead, and dying, the postmaster finally arrived with mail—nearly three weeks behind. With the freezing weather and the relentless German resistance, letters had dropped to the bottom of the priority list.

In his last message home, Francis had written to Elizabeth, declaring that once he was stateside again, he would pursue his life's passion.

Now, he held a letter in his trembling hands. Inside was a photo: his family, standing at the bottom of L Street, holding a handmade sign that read, *Come Home to Us.*

The image hit him like a blow to the chest. He swallowed his tears, unwilling to show weakness in front of the others. But the truth was—they were all just boys. In another world, they'd be playing baseball or swimming in a pond. Instead, they were fighting, killing, and dying. The war aged them in ways no clock ever could.

Except for the fresh replacements—whose life expectancy was measured in weeks, these were no longer boys. These men had crossed North Africa, seen death on an unfathomable scale, and now slogged through Italy. And they knew: after this came the rest of Europe, and the Japanese in the Pacific. The tide was finally turning, but the war was far from over. And much dying still lay ahead.

Francis let out a quiet sigh. Not quite enough.

"What is it, Frankie?" Henri asked. "Bad news from home?"

"Bad news *for* me," Francis muttered.

"Everyone all right?" Joe asked, squinting.

"Here. You read it." Francis handed him the letter.

Joe and Henri leaned together, reading silently.

"Christ," Joe muttered. "This part about your 'passion being foolishness' brutal."

"Did you finish it?"

"Not yet. Not sure I want to."

They read to the end. Joe folded the letter neatly and handed it back.

"I just don't get it," Henri said.

"Get what?"

"Why are they so against you wanting to be a doctor? And why do you go along with it."

Francis gave a crooked smirk. "Not sure you'd understand."

"Try me," Joe said, opening his hard tack ration.

"Me too," Henri added.

"It's part of the Irish way," Francis began. "There's this deep self-loathing. A belief we can suffer anything. Misery's like... Irish fuel."

"What the hell does that have to do with not becoming a doctor?" Joe snapped, chewing on the brick-hard food.

"It has *everything* to do with it," Francis said. "From the moment I was born, I was expected to fall in line. Even Liz buys into it."

"Wouldn't she rather be married to a doctor?" Henri asked.

"I never said it made sense. It's just... the way it is."

"So, this—being a corpsman—is the compromise?" Joe said, half-laughing.

"Close is better than never," Francis said.

"I'm not so sure about that," Henri replied with a faint smile.

The next morning, two brigades were called up to break a German stronghold and rescue the trapped troops of the 5th, holed up in caves outside Anzio.

Rain fell steadily, turning the ground to muck. The soldiers slogged through ankle-deep mud. At 6:00 AM, the battle began. By 9:00, Francis and the medics were waist-deep in blood, sinew, and death.

Joe rushed up beside Francis, mortar blasts shaking the earth around them.

"Keep your head down!" he shouted through the chaos. "Now'd be a hell of a time to get yourself killed!"

Francis, hunched over a wounded soldier, looked back. "I don't plan on it!" he shouted back with a grin. "Maybe tell that to the Krauts!"

Joe gave a curt nod. "Let's get it done."

Joe, Henri, and the rest of the brigade pushed forward over a gravel hill just south of the German line. Francis followed close behind, scanning for anyone struck by bullets or shrapnel.

As he reached the crest, Joe turned back—just in time to see a mortar shell explode at the top of the hill.

"Frank!" Joe cried out, slapping Henri's shoulder. "Francis!"

They scrambled back toward the mound. Climbing to the top, breath heaving, they looked across the smoking, ravaged landscape.

"Francis," Joe said again, slinging his rifle over his shoulder.

Chapter 2

Generations

The automatic doors parted. A stretcher rolled in, flanked by two paramedics in dark blue uniforms. The one on the left held an oxygen mask over the unconscious patient's face, while the other pushed the bed briskly through the emergency room bay.

The ER stretched in both directions from the ambulance corridor. From the right, and around the nurse's station, a doctor jogged over—stethoscope bouncing against his chest. He was in his thirties, tall, classically handsome. Jet-black hair, sapphire-blue eyes: unmistakably Black Irish.

"What do we have here?" he asked, arriving at the stretcher.

"Broadside car accident—Comm Ave, just off Babcock," the right-side paramedic reported. "Shallow breathing, reduced heart sounds."

"Internal bleeding?"

"All signs point to yes."

"Let's prep for O.R.," the doctor ordered. "And get X-ray down here. I want a full picture fast."

The paramedic handed him a clipboard as nurses moved in to ready the patient. The doctor glanced at the name tag on the paramedic's chest and smiled.

"Jesse, huh?"

"Yeah," the paramedic nodded.

"Jesse?"

"Miller."

"And you?"

"Costigan. David Costigan."

"Cool name," Jesse said.

"Irish."

"Black Irish, right?"

"Exactly." David grinned. "Well, thanks, Jesse. This woman might not have made it without you."

Later that evening, David turned onto Beacon Street, still thinking about the woman from earlier. No signs of foul play, but she'd be lucky to survive the night.

The porch light was on. His mother's car sat in the driveway. David loved his mother, but after a long shift, he wasn't in the mood for company.

"Daddy!" rang through the house as soon as he stepped inside.

Two children came barreling down the paneled hallway, launching themselves into his arms.

"Whoa—whoa!" David laughed, catching them both.

"How was your day, Daddy?" asked his five-year-old daughter.

"How do you *think* it was?" his seven-year-old son replied dryly. "Daddy helps people with their arms and legs cut off."

"Not always, James," David chuckled. "Sometimes it's just broken bones."

"And how was *your* day?" he asked, smiling at both. "What about you, Jacqueline?"

"Really good," James grinned. "Nannie got me a new game."

"Video game?" David asked.

"Yeah—*Call of Duty!*"

"Perfect," he said wryly.

Still holding Jacqueline, David walked into the kitchen where his wife and mother sat at the table, sharing coffee and stories.

He bent awkwardly and kissed his wife. "Mom," he said with a glance at his mother.

"That's not much of a hello," Anne replied.

"Hi, Mom," David said, more properly. "Didn't expect to see you here."

"Well, we never see *you* at home," she said. "I wanted to spend time with my grandchildren."

"You know how busy I—"

"Please, David" She cut him off. "No one is *that* busy. I wish this thing with you and your father would just stop."

"He's the one always judging," David said. "He doesn't treat Brendan that way."

Anne Costigan—born Anne Marie Hassell at Cardinal Cushing Hospital—was Boston Irish through and through on her mother's side and Dutch on her father's. Raised in Quincy, along the South Shore——she grew up with Catholic school discipline and tightly held traditions.

She'd met Patrick Sean Costigan through her brother Mike, who'd been friends with Patrick since youth. Patrick, apprenticing at the Iron Works, was being groomed to take over the family business when Robert and Billy Costigan retired.

Like many Irish Catholic men of his generation, Patrick dragged his feet about marriage—until Anne gave him an ultimatum: a ring, or the road. He chose the ring.

Anne became pregnant almost immediately. Nine months later, David was born. Two years after that, Brendan arrived.

From the start, it was clear: the two boys were opposites. David, intensely curious and emotionally stubborn, much like his father. Brendan, more laid-back, hands-on, and in many ways, Anne's mirror image.

Where Brendan cried easily, David withheld emotion—refusing even as a child to let his father see him break. It became a contest of will between father and son, a slow-burning battle of pride and silence.

"You sound like you're nine," Anne scolded now, sipping her coffee. "It's like I've got three boys refusing to grow up."

"Mom, I—"

"I blame your father too," she said. "You're both too damn stubborn."

Mary Costigan, born Mary Allison Mahoney, was Boston Irish as well raised in West Roxbury. She graduated from Central Catholic High and became a nurse after attending the University of Massachusetts. It was there, in the infamous Southwest dorms at UMass Amherst—surrounded by chaos, drugs, and 24-hour parties—that she met David, a sharp, quiet pre-med student.

Despite the insanity of their environment, David and Mary steered clear of it all. Their focus was on each other—and on their goals. To the deep displeasure of both families, they moved in together before marriage, unwilling to compromise their path for tradition's sake.

Mary worked at Worcester City Hospital while David entered med school. They married in a quiet ceremony at St. Thomas Aquinas in Springfield. When Mary became pregnant earlier than planned, they adjusted. James was born just as David began his residency at South Shore Hospital in Weymouth.

After maternity leave, Mary took a part-time position at the same hospital. With help from both grandmothers, they made it work. Their apartment in Quincy kept them close to her family, to the hospital and not far from South Boston—home to the rest of the Costigans.

Halfway through residency, Mary became pregnant again—this time with a girl. A lifelong admirer of the Kennedys, Mary had always dreamed of naming her daughter after Jacqueline.

And so, Jacqueline Costigan came into the world, loved and cherished.

James was loved, too—but like many Costigan boys before him, he was treated as a man-in-training from the very beginning. Maturity and responsibility weren't just expected, they were assumed.

The Costigan women may have adored their sons, but they didn't always *nurture* them.

David opened the refrigerator, grabbed the orange juice carton, and poured himself a glass.

"Maybe you're right, Mom," he sighed. "Both of us being stubborn just keeps this going. And poor Bren—he has to listen to Dad whine about me."

"Why don't you do something special for your father's birthday?" Anne suggested, braiding Jacqueline's hair.

"That's a splendid idea," Mary added with a smile. "What do you think he'd like?"

"I…" but then interrupted himself. "Actually, I know. His dad's Army jacket. The one they brought back after... well, you know."

"What about it?" Anne asked, intrigued.

"Have it pressed. Maybe mounted. He always talks about his father—what a hero he was."

"He died in Europe, didn't he?" Mary asked.

"Italy," David replied. "He was a medic. Killed during the invasion of Sicily."

"How old was your dad when it happened?"

"Younger than James is now."

Anne nodded. "It was really Granny Elizabeth and Uncle Billy who helped raise your dad and Uncle Tom."

"So, he never knew his father?" Mary asked.

"No. He was just a toddler. That always haunted him," Anne added softly. "Only two years ago, he finally went to Italy to visit the grave."

"He's buried there?" Mary asked.

David nodded. "Same with a lot of guys—Italy, France, Belgium. They didn't always come home."

"I had no idea you knew so much about the war," Mary said.

"You can't be a Costigan and *not* know about the war—or my grandfather."

"His name was Frank, right?" she asked.

"Some called him Frank, " Anne said. "But his name was Francis. Most people called him that."

David's phone buzzed in his pocket. He pulled it out and glanced at the screen.

"Costigan," he answered. "Yes, I remember. Hello, Jesse."

He paused, head dipping slightly.

"Thanks for calling. And the little girl, you said..." He was cut off. "Oh boy. I'm sorry to hear that. What's that? Yeah, I'll be in all day."

He hung up and slipped the phone back into his pocket.

"What's wrong, honey?" Mary asked gently.

"The woman from this morning—car accident—she just died."

"Oh, sweetheart, I'm sorry," Anne said, reaching for his hand. "Who was that on the phone?"

"The paramedic who brought her in—Jesse."

"Why would he call you?" Mary asked.

"I guess he thought I should know."

"But why you specifically?" Mary pressed.

"I told him earlier that he saved her life. I was wrong."

"I'm not sure you were," Mary said, taking his other hand. "She might've died even sooner if not for him."

"She had a three-year-old daughter," David said, his voice tight. "And no one else."

"What do you mean?" Anne asked.

"Just that. A three-year-old girl is now an orphan."

"I think that's tragic," Anne said sincerely. "But you did all you could."

"Past tense, Mom," David said, voice raised. "The girl is only three."

"And?" Mary asked cautiously.

"Look, I'm not *saying* anything," David replied, clearly frustrated. "You made me go to Mass, be an altar boy, walk in Christ's footsteps—you taught me to care."

"That I did, honey," Anne said, softening. "You were always bringing home lost kittens and injured birds."

"We're not talking about a *bird*, Mom!"

"So, what is it you want to do?" Mary asked calmly.

"I don't know. It's been a long day. I'm not thinking straight."

Anne patted his hand. "Back to your dad—what did you have in mind?"

"Well... he bleeds Boston sports, but I keep coming back to his father's GI jacket."

"Why don't we all pitch in?" Mary offered. "Some Sox tickets for the three of you, and we'll get the jacket restored. I don't even know what kind of shape it's in—it's been in the attic forever."

Mary paused, clearing her throat.

"Well, of course, that includes you and Rachel, dear," Anne added, reaching across to touch Mary's hand.

"Thank you, Mom," Mary replied with a warm smile.

Rachel—Brendan's wife—was a North Shore girl and Jewish. In Boston, marrying outside your neighborhood was often considered tabooer than marrying outside your faith. But Patrick and Anne, both deeply Irish, had taken Rachel's faith and background in stride.

They'd been raised to remember—Jesus was Jewish, too. Patrick, a convert to Catholicism, cared more about cultural identity than doctrine. And bigotry? That bothered him more than most.

For much of the 20th century, South Boston had been an Irish enclave. The North End was Italian. Until the '60s, the West End was Jewish, while Roxbury housed Boston's growing Black community. The Jewish population, once dominant in Roxbury and Mattapan, gradually migrated north to Winthrop, Swampscott, Marblehead, and Peabody as demographic tides shifted. The Italians and Irish had dug in, fiercely protective of their turf. The Jews chose to move out.

"Granny Elizabeth never liked us going into the attic," David said, rubbing his chin. "That was always a hard no."

"Just go next time you're over," Anne said matter-of-factly. "She's an old woman. You're a grown man."

"You think that'll matter to her?"

"You're not ten anymore," Anne smiled. "That rule was to keep you boys safe. You're a doctor now."

"She's right," Mary added. "No more boogeymen."

"I know," David said. "She was just... always intense about that attic."

"You're a grown man, honey," Mary said, standing from the table. "Like your mom said—just go do it."

Elizabeth Costigan's home was a classic New England Victorian—oak pocket doors, twin staircases, window seats tucked into corners. The attic wasn't just a crawlspace; it was a full third floor, complete with rooms and windows.

Now and then, David and Brendan had snuck up there—only to face Granny Elizabeth's fury.

She was usually sweet and unassuming, except when it came to two things: talking about her late husband, and the attic. Her refusal to discuss either became part of her mystique—an eccentricity the family had grown to accept.

Even Billy, her brother-in-law, avoided the topic of Francis's death. Patrick, her son, accepted the silence. But Tom—Francis's younger son—had always wanted to know more about the man who'd died before he could remember him.

When pressed, Elizabeth's reply was always the same: "He was a good provider, husband, and father—and he died for his country." If anyone pushed further, she'd tilt her head and fix them with a stare that made it clear: the matter was closed.

As kids, David and Brendan called her "The Medusa" behind her back—because when Granny turned that stare on you, you froze.

They used to say, "She's like two people," they used to say. "Kind and sweet most of the time… and then suddenly, the other one."

Anne and Patrick had always told the boys: *It's her privacy. Respect it.*

"The Irish keep secrets," Anne would remind them. "To the world, we're the Brady Bunch. What happens behind closed doors— that stays behind closed doors."

On the surface, the Street hadn't changed much since he was a boy—but in truth, everything had. Boston, and South Boston in particular, began its gentrification in the late 1980s. By the time the new millennium arrived, Southie was no longer the Irish Catholic stronghold it had once been. Three-family homes that had housed generations of working-class families were now carved into expensive condominiums, well out of reach for most Irish descendants. In their place came white-collar professionals, sweeping through what had once been a sacrosanct enclave.

Still, a handful of holdouts remained, Elizabeth Costigan Costigan among them.

David didn't knock. He never had to. The heavy oak door with its leaded glass inlay squeaked comfortingly as it opened. He didn't call out. He knew Granny Elizabeth was at his Uncle Tom's house with Great Uncle Billy.

He moved quickly, climbing the broad front staircase to the second-floor landing, still covered with the Persian rug laid long before he was born. Crossing the hallway, he passed the closed bedroom doors and reached the attic door, the one that had always made its own peculiar creak. He pulled it open and began climbing.

The stairs rose straight at first, then turned sharply right. Each wooden step groaned under his weight, now much heavier than it had been when he was a boy.

At the top of the final step, David paused. It had been at least a decade since he was last up here. He drew a deep breath through his nose—and with it came the scent of his childhood. A flood of memory washed over him.

He stepped into the first, smaller room. It was still and dim, interrupted only by the distant drone of planes overhead from Logan. The room, surrounded by multi-paned windows, was lined with boxes of Christmas and Easter decorations. A thick layer of dust coated the pine floorboards. Cobwebs draped from corners, like delicate curtains no one had disturbed.

Walking to the east-facing windows, David looked down on the street. He smiled faintly. The view hadn't changed—but the people, the pulse of the neighborhood, had.

He wiped a finger along the sill, lifting a streak of dust. He stared at it, then blew it away. His smile faded.

He moved across the creaky floor into the larger room. It was darker—just one small window let in light. This space had never been meant for living. It was for stashing life's leftovers.

Two trunks sat in the far corner, end to end. In the middle of the room, a single chain dangled from a light fixture overhead. It swung slightly in the still air, disturbed only by his presence.

He pulled the chain. The light flared on, too bright at first.

The leftmost trunk was dark blue. He opened it—unlocked—and found mostly women's clothes, including what looked like Elizabeth's wedding dress, delicately wrapped in an old linen sheet.

He closed it gently and slid to the reddish trunk on the right. The clasp was caught in a small padlock looped loosely around the latch. Not secured—more for show or forgotten over time. He slid the lock free, unlatched it, and opened the top.

The hinges creaked, but the musty smell he expected didn't come. The air was still, faintly metallic. Inside: carefully preserved artifacts, all from his grandfather's short military career.

He lifted two small leather boxes and stacked them. Opening the first, a surge of emotion struck him. A five-pointed Silver Star lay inside. He opened the second—this time, a greater jolt. The Purple Heart.

He ran his index finger gently along its edge, reverently.

After a long breath, he placed the medals back where he found them.

Toward the rear of the trunk lay a collection of black-and-white photographs—clearly from the 1940s, likely North Africa or Europe. Most featured the same three men in various levels of Army uniform.

One photo stopped him. Three men stood arm-in-arm in front of a tent marked with a red cross. One was unmistakably Francis Costigan.

They weren't just posing, they were grinning, wide and unfiltered. That kind of joy only close friends share.

He turned the photo over. In faded script:

Joe

Henri

Frank

Tripoli, 1942

David stared at the names. Joe. Henri. Frank. He had never heard those names spoken. Not once. Yet here they were—his grandfather's best friends. He ran his finger over the writing. A woman's handwriting, he guessed.

He flipped through the stack. One photo stood out—a local shot, taken at the bottom of L Street, near the famous Brownies' swim spot. His grandparents stood side by side, younger than he'd ever seen them. Behind them, his father and uncle were boys. His grandfather wore his uniform. It must have been taken during a brief leave, early in the war.

He flipped the photo—no date, no caption. He turned it back over and stared.

"Smile, would you," he whispered.

He noted the contrast. In Tripoli, his grandfather had beamed. In this one—he looked like he had already changed.

Placing the photos back carefully, David peeled away a few layers of fatigues. Beneath them, the dress jacket. He lifted it with both hands, holding it out as if examining something in a department store.

It was pristine, thanks to the cedar lining of the trunk. The insignia and patches were all still sharp and intact.

"Grandpa," he said quietly, realizing just how little he truly knew about the man everyone called a hero.

He started to stand when something caught his eye—just the corner of an envelope peeking out from beneath a layer of clothes. It didn't belong. He crouched again, brushing aside the fabric.

As soon as he pulled it free, he knew exactly what it was: a FedEx envelope. Old, weathered—maybe twenty years—but unmistakably modern. It didn't belong in a trunk filled with artifacts from the 1940s.

He pressed the clothes down to create a flat surface and turned the envelope over. Out spilled twenty or thirty smaller envelopes, some deeply yellowed, others only slightly aged.

He picked one up addressed to *Mrs. Elizabeth Costigan.* The paper felt brittle, so he opened it carefully. Medicine had taught him to be gentle with fragile things.

The letter read:

Dear Elizabeth,

I hope this letter finds you and the children well. It is uncomfortably hot here, and that makes treating these poor wounded boys that much harder. Still, we manage to get through the days and the battles. Everyone here is anxious to get done here in the desert and get into Europe. The Germans are only here because the Italians really had no stomach or heart for this. I have never seen a group of soldiers so happy to surrender and be done with this. The Germans are a different story. They are tough, and their will and capacity to fight is frightening. It is as though they were born to it. The devastation to these young bodies is tragic, but I must admit, I was born to heal.

Your husband,

Francis

David reread the letter, expecting something he missed. But it wasn't there—no warmth, no tenderness. It felt impersonal. A dispatch from a medic, not a husband. He imagined his grandmother reading it for the first time, and his chest tightened.

He slipped the letter back into its envelope and opened another, less yellow. The structure was similar: a polite inquiry about her and the children. But this time, it ended simply:

Frank

No mention of love. No title. Just a name.

David looked again at the neat stack of letters. *How did she feel, reading these?* he wondered. He knew how deeply she loved—how much affection she gave everyone in her orbit. These letters must have landed like cold stones.

Realizing he was short on time, he made a quick decision. He tucked about fifteen of the letters into the inside pocket of his jacket. He'd return them later. The rest he carefully slid back into the FedEx envelope, replacing it as precisely as he could.

Then he closed the trunk, stood, and made his way down the stairs.

At the second-floor landing, Elizabeth Costigan stood waiting. She had heard the steps. Her nails dug into her palms, and her breath caught in her throat. A flicker of panic flashed through her mind—*a stranger?*—but only for a moment.

David flinched as he opened the attic door, startled to see her there. For a long moment, neither spoke.

Her eyes dropped to what was in his hands.

"What is that?" she asked, voice low and tight.

"It's Grandpa's army jacket," David said, instinctively bracing.

"And it's in your hands… why?"

"I can explain," he said quietly. He suddenly felt ten years old.

"I don't think you can, David"

"We wanted to do something special for Dad's birthday. We thought—"

"No. You didn't *think*, young man!" Her voice sharpened. "If you had, maybe you would have asked. Instead of violating my privacy, *my home*. It astonishes me you function as a doctor, let alone an adult."

David blinked. The weight of her words stung more than he expected.

"Granny, I'm sorry. I didn't—"

"Didn't what?" she snapped. "Didn't care how I'd feel? Didn't think I deserved the courtesy?"

"Granny, don't you think—"

"Don't I *think* what?" Her voice rose to the edge of a scream. "That I'm overreacting? That I'm making something out of nothing? This is my home. Those are *my* things—not yours, and not your father's!"

David's tone changed.

"My dad?" he said, taken aback.

"Now look here—"

"No, Granny. *You* look here." His voice was calm, but with a firm tone she had never heard from him. "I'm sorry. I should've asked. But I'm not a child anymore. I'm a grown man, with a family and a career. Be mad at me, but don't talk to me like I'm still nine."

Her eyes turned to stone. The Medusa—the figure he and Brendan had joked about—was here. But now, for the first time, David saw the pattern clearly. The Medusa only appeared when Grandpa Francis was involved. It wasn't just pain. It was something deeper. Maybe even something buried.

"If you think you can come into my home and speak to me this way…" she began.

"That's your right, Granny," he said, softening again. "If you want to forbid me from coming back, you can. But I think that would hurt both of us. I won't do it again. All I ask—please don't punish James and Jacqueline."

Her eyes wavered. Then, slowly, they softened. Tears welled in the corners.

"Okay, then, David," she whispered. "Maybe I do get too emotional. But you haven't lived my life."

The Medusa was gone.

He stepped forward and wrapped his arms around her.

"I love you, Granny," he said, his voice thick.

"I love you too, my darling." She squeezed him tightly. "Now… let me see that jacket."

She held it in front of her, just as he had done in the attic.

With a deep breath, she let out a wistful sigh.

"Oh, how he looked in that uniform," she murmured. A faint smile touched her lips, fragile but warm. "That black hair, those blue eyes. *Lord, he was gorgeous.* So… what are you going to do with it?"

"We thought we'd have it framed. For Dad's office."

She nodded, still studying the jacket.

"That's a thoughtful idea," she said quietly. "We've spoken so little about your grandfather. And your father—he's the perfect Irishman."

"Granny?"

"We're a private and suffering bunch," she said with a soft laugh. "I imagine your father wanted to talk about him—about your Uncle Billy too—but he just... knew the Gaelic way."

"Gaelic way?" David asked.

"Plenty of Irishmen would rather endure any amount of misery than actually deal with anything."

"Really? Even our family?"

She gave him a wry smile. "Why do you think we have so many rugs, sweetheart? So, we've got somewhere to sweep everything under."

"Even Grandpa?"

She walked slowly to the far window seat, sat down, and patted the cushion beside her.

David joined her. She took his hand gently.

"This stays between us?" she asked.

"I promise."

"We're not big on regrets in this family. It's part pride, part heritage. But there's one I'll carry to my grave."

"Okay."

"Did you know your grandfather wanted to be a doctor? More than anything."

"I think my mom mentioned it once. Maybe twice."

"That was his dream, David Just like it's yours."

"Then if he hadn't died—"

"No." She shook her head. "That's not what stopped him."

"I don't understand."

"Things were different then. You were born what you were born—it was like an unwritten caste system."

"How does that apply to Grandpa Francis?"

"His father wouldn't support the idea. My father—a doctor himself—thought it was foolish. And worst of all… I agreed with them."

"Why, Granny?"

"Because we were raised that way," she said, eyes clouded with something deeper than regret. "He was an Irish Catholic boy from a working-class family. You didn't reach too far above where you came from. Why do you think our family's full of cops and firemen?"

"I thought they just wanted to follow in their father's footsteps."

"It's more complicated than that. When it's all you know, to want something more feels like disrespect. Especially to your father. Or to his father."

David sighed. "So, Grandpa died with that dream still inside him?"

She nodded slowly. "Most men of his generation did. Regret was their inheritance. Your father's generation—*your* generation—was the first to really chase their dreams."

David looked down. "Is that why my dad seems to hate that I'm a doctor?"

"Hate it?" she laughed gently. "Your father is so proud of you, it practically hurts him."

"Could've fooled me," David muttered. "You've seen how he talks to me. Like he can barely tolerate me."

"When you were a kid, of course he wanted you and Brendan to take over the business. When it became clear that wasn't happening… Well, Brendan stepped in. You didn't."

"Then why—"

"It's not about the business anymore," she said. "It's *you*. You're just like him—stubborn, willful. That's what he's proud of… and what irritates him the most."

David chuckled. "Oh my God, Granny. Sometimes I just want to *shake* him."

She smirked. "And now you know how *he* feels."

"I don't know. He just seems disappointed."

"He loves Mary like she's his own. He adores grandkids. And he loves *you*." She stood, resting a hand on David's head. "But here's a little Irish secret."

David looked up.

"He wants to feel like you *need* him. But the truth is… you never really needed anyone."

David hadn't talked to Mike Donovan in a few years. Mike and Brendan had been best friends in high school—best men in each other's weddings. David trusted him more than most.

It was a last-minute lunch at La Paloma in Quincy, but David needed someone to confide in the letters. Someone who might have access to details he didn't.

Mike had once been an all-state offensive tackle at Pope John High—one of seven towering Donovan brothers. He'd turned down a full ride to play college ball at UNH, instead joining the Suffolk County Sheriff's department. Three years later, he took the postal exam and had been with the USPS ever since. Twenty years on, he was already eyeing retirement. His path had always puzzled David who couldn't understand why someone with Mike's physical gifts would turn down college ball.

Quincy was its own paradox: part industrial city, part suburban haven. Bluebloods and new immigrants. Old brick factories alongside trendy cafes. It felt like the past and future trying to live side by side.

The two men hugged, then sat down to margaritas, chips, and salsa.

"Shit," Mike said, laughing. "Haven't seen your crazy brother in a while. How's he? How are the folks?"

"Everyone's good," David said, eager to get to the point. "Dad and Bren are doing great with the business. How's the PO?"

Mike grimaced. "Not what it used to be. Used to be able to do thirty years and spend half your shift in the can with *The Globe*."

"Tough break," laughed.

They talked about old times. About Southie—how it had changed, how it hadn't.

Then David pulled the stack of letters from his jacket. "So, I found these in my grandmother's attic."

"Letters?"

"From my grandfather. During the war."

"That's cool," Mike said, glancing at his drink.

"C'mon—don't you think this is amazing?"

"You think just because I work for the post office, I'm obsessed with mail?"

"I, uh…"

"I'm messing with you," Mike grinned. "Lemme see."

He took the stack, carefully flipping through. He opened one or two but didn't read far—clearly uncomfortable invading what felt private. He slid the letters back into their envelopes, then began to return them.

But stopped.

He pulled the stack back toward himself.

Then slowly flipped each envelope over, studying the fronts. One by one, he laid them down on the table. His brow tightened with each.

He picked them up again. Then again.

David watched, curiously. "What is it?"

"These are all from your grandfather?"

"Yes. To my grandmother."

"Really?"

"Yeah, really," David said, eyebrows raised.

"How?"

"What do you mean 'how'?"

Mike laid three envelopes side by side. Pushed the chips and soda aside.

"Look at the postmarks."

David leaned closer. "One says USO… and the others… Youngstown, Ohio?"

"Yep. And now the dates."

David looked closer. "They're different. From different years…"

He trailed off, suddenly uncertain.

Mike leaned back in his chair.

"David… Are you *sure* all of these are from your grandfather?"

"C'mon David, the year! "David leaned in and squinted.

"1944... 1953... 1961?" He looked up, puzzled. "That doesn't make any sense."

"That's why I asked if they were *all* from your grandfather."

"They're addressed to my grandmother and signed by him." David waved a hand. "They *have* to be."

Mike leaned back and took a sip. "I thought your grandfather died in the war?"

"He did. At Anzio," David said, firm. "Buried there. My dad and Uncle Tom even visited the grave."

Mike raised his eyebrows. "Then I can only think of three possibilities."

"I don't think I want to hear this," David muttered, gulping his margarita.

"Someone was pretending to be him... this is a *Twilight Zone* episode and he wrote from heaven... or—"

"Or he didn't die in Europe," David interrupted, eyes narrowing.

Mike set his glass down. "Either way, it's pretty damn twisted."

David stared at the envelopes, tapping his finger against his glass.

"Wait—the return address," he said suddenly.

Mike looked down. "Two of these say Boardman, Ohio. Same P.O. box."

He flipped through the rest of the envelopes. "Every letter after 1944 is from the same box."

"I don't get it." David leaned back. "Nobody in my family's from Ohio. I don't know a single soul from Youngstown."

Mike traced a finger across the envelope. "Well, someone there clearly knew your grandmother."

He paused. "You remember Gus O'Grodnick?"

"Sure. Didn't he marry your cousin Emily?"

"Yep. They've got eight kids."

"Good Irish Catholic," David chuckled.

"You're not kidding," Mike laughed. "You know what Gus does?"

"Not a clue. I haven't seen him since your wedding."

"He's a captain in the State Police. Forensics."

David raised an eyebrow. "And?"

"His specialty is handwriting analysis."

David sat up straighter. "Seriously?"

"Yeah. What if I ask him to look at the letters? See if the same person really wrote them?"

"They *look* the same to me," David said.

"Oh, I forgot you were a certified handwriting expert," Mike deadpanned.

"Also…" David hesitated. "Can you find out who owns that P.O. box?"

Mike winced. "Come on, David. You know I could get fired for that. I've got almost twenty years in. Not trying to throw that away."

"I get it," David nodded. "But this might be… important."

"I'll see what I can do. No promises."

Causeway Street was jammed—Bruin's game traffic mixed with rush hour chaos. Even after the "Big Dig," downtown Boston's one-way streets still refused to make sense.

But Patrick Costigan didn't mind. He *loved* driving into the city.

"God, I miss the old Boston," Patrick sighed, fingers tapping the wheel. "You could smell the cannoli in the North End, grab a spucky from a dozen little joints… it was real then."

"Yeah," muttered from the passenger seat. "Back when Southie was all Irish and Black folks were shoved into Roxbury or Dorchester."

Patrick bristled. "Don't put words in my mouth. When have you ever heard me say anything like that?"

Brendan leaned forward from the back seat, poking his head between them. "Do you two *ever* get through a hockey game without bickering?"

David turned toward the window; eyes narrowed at the neon glare of the Garden.

"Easy for you to say," he mumbled. "You've always been his favorite."

"Oh, for Jesus' sake," David groaned. "You're a doctor, David. Not a preschooler."

"So now I'm a *preschooler*?" David snapped.

Patrick threw his hands up and slapped them back onto the steering wheel. "For the record, I have *two* favorite sons. I love you both. But I'm too old and too set in my ways to turn into some Hallmark-card dad. I stopped coddling you when you ditched diapers. I love you, David. I hope you love me. But I'm your father, and nothing's ever going to change that. Cowboy up."

David said nothing.

Physically, father and son were nothing alike. Patrick was stocky, with light hair and deep brown eyes, Elizabeth's features through and through. David was tall, lean, black-haired, and sapphire-eyed like Francis Costigan. But temperament? Identical. Both possessed that notorious Black Irish stubborn streak, and a relentless drive to succeed.

David glanced at the traffic. "Do you think we could've picked a *worse* way to get in?"

"There *is* no other way," Patrick muttered, keeping his temper on a short leash. "We need to park, don't we?"

"This whole night's a waste, "Patrick grumbled."

"You mean taking you to a Bruins game *for your birthday*?" David fired back.

"Apparently so."

"Do you two always have to go at each other?" Brendan cut in, exasperated.

"Watch your mouth, son," Patrick warned. He wasn't one for profanity.

Brendan Costigan was the family paradox. He looked like his dad, had his mother Anne's calm temperament, and sharp instincts. Not the highest academic achiever, but deeply capable and well-liked. His fuse was long—but when it ran out, you'd better run.

Back in high school, Brendan played football at Pope John alongside Mike Donovan. Mike was an all-conference lineman. Brendan, smaller but lightning quick, played defensive end. They led their team to a Catholic League championship and a near-win in the Super Bowl against Everett High.

But Brendan's true grit wasn't on the field. Senior year, he snapped. Dickie O'Brien, a bully since middle school, tripped Brendan in the cafeteria. Brendan spilled food and drinks on himself and two others. Something broke. Dickie got the beating of his life— three teammates had to pull Brendan off him. The bullying stopped. Dickie kept his distance. And Brendan gained a reputation in Southie that stuck laid back, but *not* to be pushed.

They finally parked and made their way inside. Their seats were just behind the Bruins bench.

Patrick played some hockey in high school, even a short stint in the old AHL. Hockey was *his* game. He loved all sports—but this? This was his soul. And he'd passed that love down, whether his sons liked it or not.

"Now *these* are good seats, David," Patrick said, offering a rare compliment to his eldest son.

"You don't turn sixty every day, Dad," David smiled, handing over the foil-wrapped hot dogs he'd grabbed on the way in.

"How about a few beers?" Patrick asked.

"Sure," David said. "I can get them."

"No, you boys have spent enough. I'll go. Don't want to get up once the game starts."

He excused himself, shuffling down the row toward the steep stairs that led to the concessions.

"Dad really appreciates this," Brendan said, taking a bite of his hot dog. "By the way—what's going on with his army coat?"

"It'll be ready Saturday," David said, the shift in tone hinting he had something else on his mind.

"Great. Then Sunday at Granny's?"

"Yup. Um…"

Brendan looked at him. "What is it?"

"I have to tell you something."

"All right," Brendan said, setting his food down and giving his brother his full attention.

"When I was picking up the coat, I found some letters. From Grandpa Frank to Granny Elizabeth."

"Cool."

"Not really."

"Huh?"

"I had lunch with Mike the other day."

"Donovan?"

"Yeah."

"How is he? I should call him."

"He's good. But he noticed something… strange about the letters."

"Strange, how?"

David glanced toward the stairs. "Those lines are a mile long—he'll be a while". Okay. So, some of the letters were postmarked from Ohio. And some were dated into the 1960s and 1970s."

Brendan's brow furrowed. "That doesn't make sense."

"Nope."

"Grandpa Frank died in the war. Dad and Uncle Tom saw the grave."

"I know." David nodded. "But still…"

"Did you ask anyone about it?"

"Are you kidding? Ask Granny? or Dad?"

Brendan tilted his head. "Fair point. That'd go down like a lead balloon."

"There's got to be an explanation," he added after a moment. "Maybe someone else wrote the letters?"

"That's what I thought. Mike's giving them to Gus O'Grodnick."

"The cop?"

"Yeah. He's a handwriting expert."

Brendan leaned back, thinking. "What if it *is* Grandpa Frank's handwriting?"

"I don't know," David muttered.

"What about the Ohio connection?"

"Mike said he'd see if he could find out who rented the P.O. box."

"In *Ohio?*" Brendan blinked. "Youngstown?"

"Yeah."

"Like in that Springsteen song?"

"I guess? I don't really know his stuff."

"You always had terrible taste in music," Brendan grinned. Then he spotted movement. "There he is."

Patrick reappeared, carefully balancing three beers in a cardboard carrier. He passed them down, then stood a moment, eyeing his sons.

"Jesus, you two look like the cats that ate the canary. What's going on? You can stop with the birthday surprises."

"Dad…" David said, trying to keep his tone even.

"Don't bullshit me, boys," Patrick said, lowering himself into his seat. "You think I don't know you?"

"Let it go, Dad," Brendan said, lifting his beer. "Just be happy with whatever we do."

Chapter 3

Changes

David looked over the chart, then at the nurse, and finally the patient—sitting upright in bed, wincing as he shifted.

"You know," David said, "that's why bikes have handlebars."

The twenty-something gritted his teeth, clearly in pain from his stitched-up leg and hairline fractures.

"I don't want to sound like my father—or yours—but you're lucky you weren't killed."

Dressed in a full Celtics satin warmup suit, the man clasped his hands in front of his face, nodding slightly. The nurse, a young brunette, offered a confirming glance at the doctor's words.

"The guy had a stop sign," the man muttered.

"And that matters how?" David asked.

"He should've fucking stopped."

"Watch your language," David replied. "Just because you were reckless doesn't mean you have to prove it in every sentence."

"Sorry," the man said quickly.

"It's okay," the nurse added with a small smile.

"So—he hit you?" David asked.

"No, I hit him."

David exchanged a glance with the nurse, both suppressing a smirk.

"You were coming out of Lars Anderson?"

"Yeah, I was coming down the hill at... well, you probably wouldn't know it."

"Don't be so sure. I live in Brookline."

The man's eyebrows lifted. "Oh. You sound like..."

"Southie?"

"Yeah. Or Dorchester. Charlestown, maybe."

"Born and raised in Southie," David said. "I decided to raise my kids in Brookline."

"I was raised in Brookline. We live in Allston now."

"We?"

"My wife and I have a daughter."

"You've got a kid and you're still doing this?"

"I've always been a biker," the man shrugged.

"Do me a favor," David said, handing the clipboard to the nurse. "Be a *smarter* biker, will you?"

"Thanks, Doc."

Another nurse approached. "Phone for you, Dr. Costigan."

"Thanks. I'll take it in Consult Room Two."

David entered the small room, turned on the light, and shut the door behind him. He picked up the phone.

"Hello?"

"Hey man," came the familiar voice. "It's Mike."

"Hey. What's up?"

"Well... I've got good news and bad news."

"Start with the good."

"It's all the same."

David leaned against the wall. "Go ahead."

"O'Grodnick called. The handwriting—all the letters—same person."

David was silent for a moment. "Okay... what else?"

"I tracked the P.O. Box. Opened January 1944. Closed May 1990."

"Who leased it?"

"A woman. Jennifer Goodearl."

David blinked. "Jennifer Goodearl? You think my grandfather was having an affair?"

"Could be. It's in Youngstown, Ohio."

"You're kidding."

"Nope. Still lives there, apparently—with someone named John Goodearl."

"Her husband?"

"Unless she's a seriously spry cougar, no. He's in his late fifties."

David exhaled. "Thanks, Mike. I owe you."

Mary and the kids were setting the table. Typical night—except David's expression was distant, locked in thought. Mary stirred her ham and bean soup, stealing glances at him.

"Tough day?" she asked gently.

David didn't respond. His gaze was fixed somewhere beyond the kitchen.

"Our son James," she said, placing a glass of milk before him, "has decided to take an internship in Alabama. Or Mississippi. Somewhere in the bayou."

Still nothing.

She slammed the glass back on the table.

"What?"

"You're not listening."

"I found something," he said quietly.

"Found?"

"In my grandmother's attic."

Mary sat beside him, her hand over his.

"What is it?"

"You know how we were always told my grandfather died in the war? In Italy?"

"Of course," she said warmly. "He was a hero."

"Well... I'm not sure he did."

"What do you mean?"

"I mean he might not have died at all. At least, not like we thought."

Mary stared at him. "Where is this coming from?"

He pulled a few envelopes from his breast pocket.

"Letters. From him. To my grandmother."

"So?"

"Look at the postmarks."

She flipped through them, brow tightening.

"Youngstown? Ohio?"

"Exactly."

"Do we know anyone there?"

"Nope. No family ties I've ever heard of. I don't even know where it is."

She turned back to the dates.

"These are from the 60's and 70's. David—that's impossible."

"Unless he didn't die. Or someone else wrote them."

"Then...?"

She was cut off by the clatter of their kids entering the room.

"We'll talk after dinner," David said.

The chime rang out in its familiar three-tone harmony. Elizabeth Costigan heard it loud and clear despite her fading hearing.

She folded the afghan she'd been knitting, pushed herself up from the leather chair, and shuffled to the door. Through the aged lace, she spotted a familiar face.

"Billy!" she smiled, opening her arms.

He stepped inside and returned the hug. "You're not in the middle of a party, are you?"

"I hid the Chippendales in the coat closet."

Billy laughed, stepping inside as she closed the door behind him.

"Something to drink? Eat? I've got roast in the fridge."

"Just water, thanks. I grabbed lunch at Five Corners."

"Oh yeah? Where'd you go?"

"Oh, Chuck Nolan, Gary O'Malley and I went to Bertucci's," Billy said.

"Good pizza," Elizabeth smiled. "And I like that dough they give kids to play with. What an idea."

They both laughed.

"So, what's the occasion, Billy?" Elizabeth asked, settling back into her chair and picking up her knitting.

"No occasion, Liz. I was in the neighborhood."

"I thought you said you were at Five Corners?"

"Well, actually…"

"C'mon!" she teased. "What's really going on?"

"What do you think about this party for Patrick?"

"Not every day a man turns sixty. He's worked hard in his life. He deserves recognition."

"But this whole thing with Frankie's army coat… Is that necessary?"

"My grandson thinks it is," she said plainly, with the tone of someone stating a weather report. "Why? Do you have a problem with that?"

"I just don't know if dredging up old wounds is a good idea."

"Whose wounds, Billy?" she shot back, her tone sharpening. "I just wish he'd asked me."

"Asked you what?"

"About the coat."

"I'm not sure I…"

"He just took it," she cut in. "I found him coming down from the attic with it slung over his shoulder."

"He went into the attic. He went through the trunks?"

"He didn't find a headless corpse," she said with a laugh. "Just the jacket."

"Did he say anything?"

"Just that he was sorry for not asking."

The nurse handed David the clipboard for review. He scanned the first sheet with his pen, then the next.

"This looks fine, um…"

"Tracy Langham," she said. "I transferred here from OB."

"You left OB for this chaos?" David asked, leaning back.

"It's just a different kind of insanity," she smiled. "I'd been there fifteen years. Time for a change."

"You'll get change. Not much sleep—but change."

He handed the clipboard back. She started to leave but hesitated and turned back.

"What is it?" David asked.

"That woman from the other night—the car accident. She died."

"Yes, I know," he said, trying to keep his tone clinical.

"What's going on with the little girl?"

"Do I look like Social Services?" he snapped, then immediately regretted it. "Sorry, Tracy. Long night."

"I understand, Doctor. I was just wondering."

"Not a problem." He paused. "What was her name?"

"The mother?"

"No—the child."

"Her name is Veronica," Tracy said softly.

"And you have no idea…"

"I can find out," she offered, placing a hand gently on his arm.

The warehouse was pure noise: clanging metal, hissing steam pipes, shouted commands. It would drive anyone mad who wasn't used to it. No one spoke in normal tones—everyone yelled or gestured. With the weather still mild, the giant steel door was left open. The men appreciated the air. Even the toughest among them couldn't stand the relentless smell of solder and burnt steel for too long.

Brendan ranked third in the hierarchy. His father, Patrick, was the boss, and his uncle Billy served as foreman. Patrick wasn't just good with tools—he could fix anything. But more importantly, he was the only one who could sell the kind of high-ticket jobs that kept the shop afloat. Tom, Patrick's younger brother, worked there mostly because Patrick's mother and uncle had asked for it.

Patrick also had a sixth sense for Boston's political machinery. He'd cultivated relationships with everyone from local union bosses to city mayors. A friendship with former Mayor Joe Scanlon proved especially beneficial. Scanlon was admired by the city's powerful—both legitimate and otherwise. But Patrick kept his distance from the more shadowy figures. Later, his friendships with Mayors Torpelo and McCaulley continued even after they left office.

The shop's biggest growth spurt came during the infamous "Big Dig," Boston's massive infrastructure project to bury its inner-city highways. Originally budgeted at a few billion and three years, it ballooned to fourteen years and $17 billion. Amidst scandal and corruption, Costigan Iron Works remained clean—supplying precision steel without taking a dime in bribes.

Brendan laid out blueprints on the main drafting table, waiting silently. His father never liked to be rushed. For Patrick, values like honor, respect, and honesty weren't buzzwords; they were the code he lived by.

"So, what've you got?" Patrick finally asked, approaching the table. "This for that Hull railing?"

"Yup," Brendan said. "I think you'll like it."

Patrick traced the blueprint with his finger. Brendan watched closely, hoping he wouldn't reach for his pencil—but he did.

"This is good work, son," Patrick said, smiling. "But you'll need stronger grade steel here, for the weight-bearing points. This lighter stuff won't hold up in winter."

"I hear you, Dad," Brendan replied, pulling a calculator from his pocket. "We had to bid low to land this job."

Patrick pressed his palms to the table and leaned in. He traced the page again, pausing at stress points.

"What if we used lighter alloy on the crossbars? Less pressure on them. What does that do to the margin?"

Brendan calculated quickly. "About a six percent margin. Barely worth it."

"But we don't lose money, right?"

"No, sir. We'll net around twenty-two grand."

"They're building that new park next summer," Patrick said. "Joel Kramer mentioned a decent chunk of wrought iron in the spec."

"You gonna bid on it?"

"No—you are."

Brendan blinked. "Dad, I don't—"

"You've got to get under center sometime, Brendan. Joel's wife loves your mother's boiled dinner. Drop one by."

"That seems… contrived."

"It is. And Joel knows it. But if you don't do it, someone else will."

"So that's how we get the deal?"

"No. That's how you let him know we took a loss on this one as a favor. You don't ask for anything. Just drop it off."

"You think he'll get it?"

"He's in public procurement," Patrick chuckled. "He knows damn well he may need a favor someday."

Brendan hesitated. "Is that… ethical?"

"Ethical?" Patrick asked, his tone edged with disbelief. "We want a fair shot at bidding a good price for a high-quality job. Ethical doesn't mean milk toast."

Brendan rolled up the blueprint. Patrick returned to his work. At the door, Brendan reached for the handle but paused—his hand resting on the cool metal, unmoving.

"Do you ever think about your dad?" he asked quietly.

"My father?" Patrick said, still rolling a pen between his thumb and forefinger. "Sometimes. Why?"

"I was just wondering… do you remember him?"

"A little," Patrick replied. "I was pretty young. Your grandmother says I get my style from him."

"Style?"

"I've never had trouble talking to people or selling them on an idea. I'm told your grandfather was the same. Why the curiosity?"

Brendan hesitated. "What if he hadn't died in Italy?"

"But he did."

"I know, but what if—"

"I don't play those *what if* games," Patrick cut in, sharper now. "We're dealt a hand, and we play it. Wasting time on hypotheticals doesn't build anything. This will be your business someday, Brendan. Daydreaming won't keep it alive. I've tried to teach you both that."

"And you have, Dad," Brendan said, stepping closer and placing a hand on his father's shoulder. "Look at David. He's a doctor, for Christ's sake."

"Watch your mouth," Patrick snapped, not harsh but firm. "Yes, your brother is a doctor."

"And aren't you proud of him?"

"Are you?"

"Of course. He's the first doctor in our family."

"That he is," Patrick said quietly, returning to his work without looking up.

Chapter 4

Ode to the Rust Belt

On September 19, 1977, Youngstown, Ohio, went from a thriving industrial center to a virtual ghost town in a single day. Jennings Lambeth, the CEO of Youngstown Sheet & Tube, announced the closure of the Campbell and Struthers plants. This decision triggered a rapid downward spiral that immediately cost five thousand people their jobs and ultimately sent more than forty thousand into unemployment and poverty.

The collapse, driven largely by greed and the rise of cheap imported steel, shattered not just the economy but the very spirit of the community. The Mahoning Valley, once a proud contributor to America's industrial growth and war efforts, found itself gutted just before Christmas, with families praying for their neighbors instead of celebrating.

Though the economic fallout spread from Pittsburgh to Toledo, Youngstown suffered uniquely. Unlike larger cities like Pittsburgh or Cleveland, Youngstown lacked both the size and the infrastructure for reinvention. Trapped between two major metropolitan hubs and burdened with irreparable industrial pollution, the city also bore the stain of deep-rooted political corruption and organized crime. Without visionary leadership, revival would be nearly impossible.

Yet, something remarkable endured. Ethnic communities—Croatian, Italian, Slavic, Jewish, and Greek—refused to vanish. They leaned on their traditions, their faith, and sheer willpower to survive. While cities like Boston and Pittsburgh eventually rebounded, they did so at the cost of their working-class neighborhoods. South Boston, once the heart of the Irish Catholic community, became gentrified and unrecognizable to the generations who built it.

David leaned back in his chair, rubbing his eyes. He'd known nothing about Youngstown before, nothing about steel, nothing about the devastation. But it struck a nerve. His family's business, small as it was, supported a hundred men. Men who depended on Costigan Iron Works the same way Youngstown workers once did. There was loyalty there. A weight.

He stood, stretched, and picked up the phone. He dialed Brendan's number.

"Hey, hermano!" came the familiar voice.

"Hey Bren," David replied. "How are you doing?"

"Can't complain. Business is solid, Rachel's not yelling, and the Pats are winning."

"So, what do you think about a little road trip?"

"Road trip?" Brendan asked. "You mean like... Miami?"

"Actually, I mean Ohio."

"O-fucking-hio? What the hell is in Ohio?"

"Youngstown."

"This again? With Grandpa Francis?"

"Did you think it was going away?" David asked. "Don't you want to know what this all means?"

"The truth? Not really. I like my version of things. We're Irish, David—we sweep everything under the rug. It's kind of our superpower."

"Okay, James Joyce, but are you coming with me?"

"How long is this trip? What the hell do I tell Rachel?"

"The truth won't work. Tell her we need brother time. She might actually believe that."

"You do remember who I'm married to, right?" Brendan snorted. "So, we're talking about what—leave Friday, back a few days later?"

"Day's drive there, maybe three or four days in town, day back. Yeah."

"What about Dad?"

"He won't love you taking off work, but he's all about brotherhood. He thinks you're a good influence on me."

"What, because I drink and swear less?"

Mary sat on the edge of the bed, scrolling through an AAA trip ticket on her new iPad. David stood nearby, leaning on the bureau, arms clasped behind his back like a kid waiting to be scolded.

"Several days?" she asked, still looking at the screen.

"Friday to maybe Tuesday."

"And you have to do this?"

David pushed off the bureau and sat beside her on the bed.

"What would you do?" he asked, watching her expression.

Mary turned to him, her smile warm despite the concern in her eyes. She loved him more deeply than a wife who loves a husband. She believed, truly, that he was her angel.

"I'm scared for you," she said softly. "I can live without you for a few days. That's not it. But this thing... whatever you're opening up, you don't really know where it leads."

"I don't think there's any danger. I—"

"Oh honey," she sighed, brushing his cheek with her hand. "You can be so innocent sometimes."

"What?"

"If any of this is true—if someone made a choice to disappear—he probably wanted it to stay buried. I don't know what kind of man does that."

"So... you think I should be scared?"

"I think you should be smart, David," she said, her voice calm but firm. "If this goes where you think it might, there are secrets someone went a long way to protect. Don't be naïve. You have a family."

Chapter 5

Where Are We?

A profoundly difficult question to answer is: which is worse, I-84 or I-90? For David Costigan, the question was academic. Both roads were long and dull, though I-84 took one through the most decrepit cities in Connecticut. Driving for some nine hours, they were at least beginning to see signs to Pittsburgh and Youngstown.

"I need to piss," Brendan said, waking up from a sixty-minute slumber. "And I could use a bite to eat."

"There's an exit a couple of miles up. I'll take that."

"Youngstown?"

"It said Liberty, whatever that is."

David veered the car off the road, looking for a place to stop, relieve themselves, and eat. Looking left and then right, he turned left and assumed they would find someplace.

"What about that place?"

"Which?" Brendan asked.

"Station something or other."

"Fine, or I'll just piss in their parking lot."

"And you wonder why people hate Bostonians," David laughed, exiting the car.

Mary opened the door, apron on and her hair looked more like she'd been skydiving than cooking.

"Dad?" she said, surprised to see her father-in-law. "This is a nice surprise."

"Cut the crap, Mary, but it is nice to see you," he said, kissing her on the cheek.

"C'mon in. Can I fix you a cup of coffee?" she asked, only to be polite.

"Black," David said, not one to mince words. "Kids at school?" he asked, settling into a chair at the kitchen table.

"They are. I'm trying to get some dinners made for the week. It's always easier to get them made in advance," she said, realizing she was babbling.

"So, my two sons have taken a little holiday?" he asked.

"They wanted to spend some time together," she said. "I think brothers should do that."

"Really?" Patrick smirked.

"Yes, well don't you think so?" Mary asked, trying to plan her next comment.

"I suppose I do, Mary, but what's all the urgency and cloak-and-dagger?"

Mary took a breath, closed her eyes tightly, reopened them, and turned toward her father-in-law.

"Look, Dad, this was an impromptu thing. I think they had been talking about it for a while, but neither did anything. I think David had enough of talking and decided to do it."

"Do what? Where?"

Mary looked at him, recognizing this as a pivotal point in the conversation. She felt a spark of anger toward both her husband and father-in-law for putting her in such a compromising position. Mary too was Irish in almost every way, save the mountain of secrets that plagued much of the Costigan family.

"Just a road trip, Dad," she said confidently. "They got into the car and just started driving. They'll stay in hotels over the next several days, see the sights, yuk it up I'm sure, and then come home."

"Look, I'm just asking, Mary. It's not like Brendan to just take time off out of the blue. Also, with his Jewish mother-wife, it is damn amazing she let him out of the house."

"Rachel isn't that bad," Mary protested.

"When was the last time he visited when she didn't call him every three minutes? Tell me."

"Okay, she can be a little persistent."

"Persistent? She's a damn stalker, that one."

The conversation settled down to talking mostly about James and Jackie, as Patrick referred to her, and he and Anne's solid, though sometimes tepid, relationship.

He finished his coffee and stood. The two embraced each other with sincere affection and respect. She walked him toward the door as he zipped up his jacket.

"Thanks so much for stopping by Dad. You know you're always welcome."

"I always feel out of my element in Brookline. Too touchy-feely for me."

"Okay, Dad."

He turned and stepped out onto the stone stoop, then turned and smiled at the daughter-in-law he truly loved.

"You are the best thing that could have happened to David, Mary," he said. "But you are one crappy liar."

"Dad?"

"Road trip? What a crock. I don't want to get you in the middle, and David should be ecstatic you cover for him — though I know no one who hates to lie as much as you."

"Dad?"

"Not to worry, honey." He laughed. "This isn't on you. Since they were little, I always told them: I may not know at that moment, but I will always find out. They're still my boys."

"The GPS is stuck," Brendan said in frustration.

"We're looking for Indianola."

"This place is rough, bro," Brendan said, fiddling with his phone. "There it is. It's recalculating now."

"I've been reading about this city. Did you know its economy collapsed in just one day?

"Collapsed? How?"

"Basically, the core industry here was steel."

"What happened?"

"They closed it down. Laid off thousands of people."

"Not everyone could have worked for steel companies," Brendan said.

"Steel companies, or companies that catered to steel companies or steel workers. You don't have to be an economist to understand the dominoes."

"Well, that was a long time ago. Why haven't they fixed this?"

"Hell, if I know."

"Here, make a right at the next street, and then your first left," Brendan instructed.

David guided the car around both turns and slowed down, looking for the right address.

"There," Brendan said. "That gray house."

David pulled the car in front and turned off the engine. He gazed around him. The gray house was Tudor in design and in pretty fair condition compared to most of the houses on the oak tree-lined street. Chipped paint, overgrown lawns, partially boarded windows — the street was clearly depressed. Still, it was obvious this had once been a nice, upper-middle-class neighborhood, likely inhabited by some affluent people. Now, it was a mere ghost of what once was.

"Hey," David said. "There used to be a big amusement park not far from here."

"How do you know that?"

"I read," David scolded. "You should try it sometime."

"I assume it's gone now," Brendan said.

"Pretty much gone the way of Nantasket and Revere."

"Nantasket and Revere aren't beat up like this. This is like fucking Roxbury used to be."

"Let's go," David commanded.

The two men exited the car and made their way up the cracked walk, more weeds than concrete.

"What the hell do we say?" Brendan asked.

"We tell them who we are, and why we're here."

David pushed the unlit doorbell; nothing. He pushed it again with the same result.

"Of course, this damn thing doesn't work."

Brendan knocked.

A few seconds later the door opened, and they were cautiously greeted by a middle-aged, balding man in a dilapidated blue robe. He was unshaven by a matter of days, and there was a familiar, albeit sour, odor.

"Yes?" the man asked.

"Hi, my name is David Costigan, and this is my brother Brendan," David said.

"Honestly, boys, we don't get many people knocking on our door. If you look around, you can see why."

"We're not salesmen," David said.

"We already got religion."

Brendan snickered.

"That's funny?" the man asked, not amused.

"My brother can be a tad immature. We are neither. It's a personal matter," David explained.

"Okay?" the man said, clearly confused. "I'm not sure I understand."

"Well, to make a long story short," David started, "there was a PO box here that letters to my grandmother from my grandfather came from."

"What does that have to do with me?"

"The PO box was opened by your mother."

"My mother? Why?"

"That's kind of why we're here," Brendan interjected.

"Look, why don't you come in? My mother is napping on the couch, but she's due for her medication."

David and Brendan stepped into the foyer. A different, though equally unpleasant, smell hit them instantly. They looked at each other, Brendan making a scowl.

"Smells like shit à la gin," Brendan whispered.

The house was filthy—clearly untouched by cleaning efforts this decade. A noticeable layer of dust and dinge covered the vintage, flowered furniture, and the floor was barely visible beneath piles of old newspapers and magazines collected over many years.

The man turned, cinching his robe.

"There was a guy here, oh maybe a year ago, also asking strange questions about people my mother may have known seventy years ago."

"Man?" Brendan asked.

"He was from the government, I think," the man said.

He looked at David and Brendan and smiled. His teeth were a rancid yellow, with one in the front broken and crooked. David and Brendan exchanged a look out of the corner of their eyes—volumes without saying a word.

"Wait here. I think I have a card," he said.

The man exited into the kitchen. He returned a few moments later and handed a bent and torn business card to David.

Lemuel R. Covey

United States Marshal

United States Department of Justice

"What did he want?" David asked.

"The only thing I remember was, he told me to call him if anyone contacted me about my mother and questions about the 1940s."

"Fucking strange, excuse me," Brendan said.

"Come in, gentlemen."

An old woman, dressed in a housecoat and nylons rolled down to her ankles, sat sleeping on a dusty old sofa covered in magazines. Her head, encased in parody netting, was tilted to one side, her legs splayed awkwardly.

"Nice," Brendan muttered.

"Momma," the man said, gently nudging her. "Momma, wake up."

The old woman shuddered, startled. She sat up, a flatulent squeak accompanying a burp better suited to an NFL lineman. David looked at Brendan, his face a blend of whimsy and terror.

"Momma, this is Brendan and David Costigan," the man said.

"Costigan?" the old woman echoed, clearly struck by the name. "Did you say Costigan?"

"Yes, ma'am," David responded. "We've come a long way to see you."

"Why?"

"It's about a post office box you opened in the forties. My grandmother received many letters over the course of at least thirty years from it. Are you Jennie Goodearl?"

"I am her. What is it you want to know?"

"Did you know Francis Costigan?"

"Know him?"

"Yes, ma'am."

"No, I can't say I know him, but I do know the name. Elizabeth, isn't it?"

"Yes," David replied. "My grandmother."

"Oh, I see," she said, still trying to wake up.

"The post office box was opened in your name. It's the return address on the letters to my grandmother," David explained.

"I know. I mailed them."

David and Brendan looked at each other, pleasantly surprised.

"So, why the PO box, and my grandfather didn't open it?" Brendan asked.

"Where did you say you're from?" Jennie asked.

"Boston, ma'am," David answered.

"You've come a long way. What are you looking for? Your grandfather?"

"I guess ultimately yes, but we're just trying to understand why the post office box—and why you?"

"Now that is a terrific question. Dom, would you make us some tea? Do you boys use milk or sugar?"

"We're fine, ma'am," David said.

"Nonsense. My son may force me to live in a pigsty, but he can't make me ignorant."

The robed man left the room, and the old woman patted the couch, urging David and Brendan to sit.

"I know it's dusty. Lay some papers down," she laughed.

David brushed the couch and arranged the papers so they could both sit.

"You wouldn't know it to look at me, but I was something in my day," she smiled.

David and Brendan exchanged glances again.

"Here, you—the young one—go get that picture on the right side of the mantle and bring it here."

Brendan did as he asked and walked over to the cracking red-brick fireplace. He picked up the frame and blew the thick dust off of it. He looked at the picture and smiled. It showed a woman in her twenties in a long, white satin wedding gown, flowing to the floor. Her brown hair fell to her shoulders, and a small tiara rested atop her head.

"God, is this you?" he asked.

"Nineteen thirty-eight. My wedding day. Lord was Slappy McGillucutty's father was a looker. The man is rolling in his grave over his "unachieving" son."

"He passed away?" David asked.

"Oh my, yes," she sighed. "In 1973. After his death, Dom asked if he could move in and help me for a while. His wife had just left him, you can see why—so I thought it would be mutually beneficial. 'Mutual' was the wrong word. He's blown through the tidy sum his father left, and now it's just Social Security and welfare. Frankly," she bemoaned, "I can't wait to move on, but the good Lord has his own timetable."

"What's your son going to do when, well… you know?" Brendan asked.

"I don't mean to sound crass, young man, but I really do not give an old lady's shit what he does. Anyway, you didn't come all this way to hear an old woman whine."

The dirty man re-entered the room carrying a large tray with three mismatched coffee mugs and what looked to be Oreo cookies. He set it down on the heavy cedar coffee table.

"Very classy, Dom," she said with embarrassment.

"It's all we had, Momma," Dom replied.

"Why is that?" she said rhetorically. "So, there's only so much I know, but maybe this will help. Please, enjoy."

David and Brendan each picked up a cup. David instantly noticed the dried coffee drips down the side and made an indiscernible gag but held the cup politely.

"I had a bit of an admirer in those days—just before the war. I would've never acted on it, but a woman loves to know she's beautiful. You understand?" she asked.

The brothers nodded.

"Daniel, my husband, was a very secure man and knew it was all innocent. In those days, people weren't jumping willy-nilly in and out of each other's beds. Not like today. Right, Slappy?" she said to her son.

"One day, someone came to the door and asked if I could do him a huge favor."

"Favor?" David asked. "My grandfather?"

"Lands, no. One of the Vachons—Henri, I think."

"You never told me this," her son said, shifting uncomfortably, his modest package now very visible.

"I never told you a lot of things. And put that ugly thing away," she scolded.

"You were saying, ma'am?" David prompted.

"He asked me to open a post office box—very discreetly—and mail letters when they came."

"Letters from whom?" David asked.

"Letters between Francis and Elizabeth Costigan," she said as though they should have known.

"I'm not sure I understand," Brendan added, distracted by Dom Goodearl's still-exposed manhood.

"Close those goddamn legs, Dominic!" Jennie shouted. "Not like you have anything to show off, you faggot."

The brothers held back their laughter.

"Ma'am?" Brendan said, regaining focus.

"They were on my stoop—always in such a pretty card box," she reminisced. "In those days, Slappy's father kept that stoop, and everything else, pristine."

"And so, you mailed them?" David asked.

"Oh, always the same day. I think it annoyed Daniel a bit, but he never made a fuss. What a darling of a man. What the hell happened to you?" she snapped at her son.

"Momma!"

"Jesus Christ, a fifty-five-year-old man calling his mother *Momma*. I can hear him in his room at night. You know, that wet squishy rubbing?"

"Momma!"

"Oh hush, Dom. It's not like you have any pride anyway."

"So, you found them on your porch?" David asked.

"They were there, yes."

"So, you never knew who actually put them there?" Brendan asked.

"No, I knew exactly who put them there. That's what I'm trying to tell you boys. Darn, I thought you Bostonians were smart."

The brothers looked at each other, unsure how to respond. They said nothing.

Jennie took a sip from her mug and smiled. "Gotcha!" she laughed. "Forgive an old lady for some fun. Of course, you don't know."

"Ma'am?"

"His name was Joseph Brady," she said.

"That name is familiar," Brendan replied.

"Well, I don't know anything about that, but old Joe is still alive."

"Alive? Where?" David asked.

"Go get me a pad and pen, you lazy sack of shit," she told her son.

Dom went to the kitchen, thankfully closing the door on his revolting exhibition. He returned a minute later with a legal pad and pen.

"My boy wonder expects I'll be writing you boys a letter," she muttered as she began to write. "He's in a convalescent home in Girard. Funny thing," she continued, "I lost touch with him until I received an anonymous call one day."

"What is Girard?" Brendan asked.

"It's a small city North of Youngstown. Happens to be where he lives now.," she replied.

David and Brendan looked at her blankly.

"Whoever had called me and gave me Joe's contact information. I reached out. I've been to see him, you know. I took a cab—because SACK-A-Jawaja over here lost his license after his fourth arrest. It's about twenty minutes from here to Girard."

She tore the yellow-lined page away and handed it to David. He took the paper, glanced at it, and folded it neatly.

"He still has those eyes," she said, clasping her hands and exhaling. "He's not gone completely bonkers, either. You'll be able to talk with him. My Daniel was a ripened tomato by the time he passed."

The brothers set their cups down, untouched.

"Well, boys," she said, placing her own cup down. "I have to see a man about a dog. Dinsdale will let you out."

"Thank you, ma'am," David said, standing.

"Help me up!" she barked, her son springing across the room.

Taking a moment to steady herself, she grabbed her three-legged cane and began to shuffle across the dingy floor.

"Good luck, boys, and Godspeed. I hope you find what you're looking for."

Patrick opened the door of his mother's house and called out.

"I'm in the kitchen," Elizabeth replied.

He walked down the quaint, creaking hallway and entered the vintage 1990s kitchen.

"How are you, Ma?" he asked, kissing her cheek.

"You just missed your brother Tom," she smiled. "He brought me some fresh halibut. He was up in Kittery yesterday with his kids."

Like most families, the Costigans had blind spots when it came to their children. Patrick Costigan was the dutiful son, who not only took on the family business but grew it by more than five hundred percent from what his grandfather had built. Tom, on the other hand, was the one Elizabeth doted on and expected little from. He was her baby—smaller in stature than his elder brother, albeit with the same edgy Costigan Black Irish looks.

For a time after their grandfather's death, Tom and Patrick tried to run the business together. It wasn't long before it became clear that Tom had neither the business sense nor the work ethic to be successful. Moreover, Elizabeth demanded that Patrick watch out for his brother and provide him with a livelihood at The Works. Patrick could be as tough and pragmatic as a martial arts fighter, but he loved his brother and had watched over Tom since they were kids.

"So, I understand the boys have gone on a boys' weekend?"

"They have," Patrick said.

"Where did they go?" she asked.

"According to Mary, they're on the road and will stay wherever they are when they get tired."

"Really?" Elizabeth laughed, setting down what she was doing. "Your son David is just winging it?"

"According to his wife."

"And that sounds reasonable to you, Pat?" she asked.

"Well, remember—his brother is with him, and planning to Brendan is like minimum wage to a Republican."

"That may well be, but I've seen David grow up. The idea of just taking off without a plan would drive him insane. Don't you think so?"

"Ma, they're having a weekend together. I don't think we need to overanalyze it," Patrick said, pouring himself a glass of milk. "I think we should be happy about it."

"You've always been naïve, Patrick Sean Costigan," she said— another casual insult.

"They're up to something. And if I were you, I'd find out just what."

"Why do you always think there's something nefarious going on?" Patrick asked.

"Experience."

Chapter 6

Breadcrumbs

The two men showered, had a quick breakfast at Bob Evans, and made their way to Market Street, which is Ohio Route 7. Ohio 7 was the original road that connected the Ohio River in the south to Lake Erie in the north. Ohio 11, a proper highway, now connects the two, bypassing many of the towns and cities that Ohio 7 still winds through.

Brendan fiddled with the GPS on his phone while David paid attention to the signs.

"Look for Girard," Brendan said, not removing his eyes from the display.

"AOK," David replied. "This place doesn't look half bad from the highway."

"I hope so," Brendan said, still staring at his phone.

"There it is—one mile." David merged into the far-right lane.

They passed through another run-down section of the city before arriving at their destination.

It was a convalescent home; all right dilapidated like everything else they'd seen. It was once clearly maintained with pride, but those days were long gone. The building was now in critical disrepair.

Inside, things weren't better. The wallpaper—older than the brothers—was torn, stained, and yellow. The wooden floors were dull and chipped. There was a foulness in the air.

A woman in an immaculate white dress, just to the knee, came around the corner, clearly approaching to greet them. She extended her hands.

"Rachel Nilson. I'm the director here. What can I do for you?"

"We're here to see an old friend of the family," David said. Brendan glanced sideways at his brother, silently clocking the lie.

"And does this old friend have a name?" she asked.

"Joe Brady," Brendan interjected. "He was very close with our grandfather."

"Mr. Brady is not well," she said. "I'm not sure he'd understand anyway."

"Please, Miss Nilson—" David began.

"**Mrs.** Nilson," she corrected with sharp precision.

"My apologies. Mrs. Nilson, we've come a very long way to see him."

She didn't reply immediately. She stared at them, calculating. Then she nodded slowly—not to agree, but to show she was processing. She glanced around, her posture suddenly stealthy.

"I could be fired for this, but... What's your name?"

"I'm David, and this is my brother Brendan. Costigan. Our name is Costigan."

"Maybe fifteen minutes, okay?" she said. "He's just down this hall."

They followed her. Other employees straightened when they saw her approaching, offering anxious grins or waves. No one looked her directly in the eye. They made a show of being engrossed in their work.

"This is what you get when you pay people eight dollars an hour," she quipped, without caring if the staff heard her. "This is his room."

She pushed the door open. It creaked like something out of a haunted house.

Inside, an old, frail man sat in a black vintage rocker, gazing out the barred window to his right. David noted the chicken wire covering the outside.

The nurse crossed the room without hesitation and placed a firm hand on the man's shoulder gentle as a bull rider.

"Joe?" she said, her voice full of patent disrespect. "You have some visitors."

"Visitors?" he asked, turning slightly.

"Yes. Two men from... Where'd you say you're from?"

"Boston," Daid said.

The old man turned his head as best he could and smiled at them. Most of his teeth were gone. His face was white with a two-day beard. His beige robe was stained and frayed. Fragile didn't begin to describe him—it was a mix of age and neglect.

But his eyes still had something. David had seen that look before in his patients: resignation edged with a flicker of memory.

"I like Boston," the old man said with childlike softness.

"I'm David Costigan. This is my brother Brendan. May we sit with you for a moment?"

The old man's expression changed. The blank sweetness vanished. He raised a trembling hand and beckoned them closer.

"You can go," he said to Nilson.

"I really think I should stay, Joe," she said. "We wouldn't want you to—"

"I asked you to leave, Nurse Ratchit." He barked. "I may be old, and maybe even daft, but I don't need you snooping on my conversations."

She glared at him. Her nostrils flared, eyes narrowed. She nodded curtly to the brothers and left in a huff.

"Sit down, boys," the old man said. "I'd offer you something, but I'm lucky if I get one good meal a day."

"Thank you for seeing us, Mr. Brady," David said, pulling up a torn vinyl chair.

"You said your name is Costigan, right?" Brady asked.

"It is," David replied.

"So, what brings two young men from Boston to see an old dying son-of-a-bitch like me?"

"We're hoping you can help us. About our grandfather," David said.

"Your grandfather?" Brady squinted. His unkempt eyebrows shot outward like brittle wires. "What makes you think I can help you with that?"

At that moment, Nilson re-entered the room, her displeasure radiating off her like heat.

"I think that's enough for today, gentlemen," she said, savoring the interruption.

"Goddamn it!" Brady snapped, breaking into a cough. "I—"

"Excuse me, Mr. Brady—maybe I can help," David said, standing to meet Nilson. "I'm a doctor." He pulled out his wallet and flipped it open to his license. "Mr. Brady is doing just fine."

"Well, you're not *his* doctor," she said.

"Then have *his* doctor call me. I'll explain the situation. If he's concerned, he can come here himself."

She stood shaking, visibly indignant.

"Now get your fat ass out of my room," Brady said with a grin.

She stormed out.

"There'll be hell to pay later, boys," he said, still grinning. "But that was worth it. So—where were we?"

"You knew our grandfather. You served together in World War II. In Italy."

"Frank," he said softly, eyes dropping to the floor. "He was a hero, you know."

"Mr. Brady—"

"Joe."

"Joe," David said. "We've figured out he didn't die in Anzio. He sent letters to my grandmother from here for years after the war."

"You know his grave is over there," Joe replied.

"We know there's a grave," Brendan finally spoke, "but we don't believe he's in it."

"So, you've got letters. Maybe someone was playing a cruel trick on Elizabeth."

"You knew my granny's name," David said, narrowing his eyes.

"Like you said, son—we were friends. Liz Costigan… She was a looker."

"Granny Elizabeth?" Brendan asked, half choking.

"She's your grandmother. Let's not go there," Joe muttered with a grin.

"Please, Joe," David urged. "Please help us."

"Why? Why do you need to know anything?" Brady asked. "Wouldn't leaving well enough alone be the right thing to do?"

"There's a truth out there," David replied. "Something at least part of our family doesn't know. We have a right to it."

"Right?" Brady scoffed. "Who exactly gave you that right?"

"The truth is the truth," David said. "It's black and white."

"Is it now?" Brady chuckled. "What about the truth of why Italy and not France? Or the grassy knoll? The Bay of Pigs? Is that all black and white to you?"

"He died or he didn't," Brendan snapped. "It's not complicated."

Brady turned toward them, his expression hardening. "Do you boys even understand honor? A sacred bond between friends? Promises made and kept?"

"I'd like to think we do," David said evenly.

"I'm not so sure," Brady muttered. "I don't think your generation has the first goddamn idea about honor or character."

"I promise you, I do," David replied. "But the question still stands."

"I made a promise," Brady said, shaking his head. "And I intend to take it to my grave—just like I said I would."

"Then we came here for nothing?" David asked.

Brady didn't answer. Instead, he lifted his frail hands. "Help me up."

David and Brendan moved quickly, each taking an arm and lifting him to his feet.

"Take me to the window. I want to look outside."

Brendan pulled back the dusty navy drapes. Despite the broken-down building, the view was beautiful. The rear of the facility overlooked a sweeping valley of farms and trees. Rolling hills dipped and rose in the distance. A scene right out of a Currier and Ives painting.

"Look down to your left, son." Brady said.

Brendan strained his neck doing what Brady asked.

"What do you see?"

"I don't know. Hills, trees, rust." Brendan answered.

"That rust was the lifeblood of this area and the country. Steel mills stretched as far as you could see. From Warren to Youngstown. The air was always brown like hamburger grease, but this area, this economy thumped with industry twenty four hours a day."

Brady stared off or almost through Brendan. He was old, frail, weak, but he was sharp. The pain on his face spoke volumes. He wasn't just talking about factories and smog. He was talking about the heart of a city-a community. It was all gone in a flash.

Between Youngstown and Girard on the Mahoning River, the land was striking—lush, rugged, quiet. Even Brendan, skeptical as he was about Youngstown, had commented on how beautiful the terrain was outside the city. Even this close.

"It's peaceful, isn't it?" Brady asked.

"It is," Brendan said, glancing at his brother as they steadied the old man.

"I lived with pride and honor, boys," Brady said. "Never thought I'd die like this."

"You've still got life in you," Brendan said, not quite joking.

Brady chuckled. "Barely enough for a few good dumps, I'm afraid." He paused, suddenly solemn. "This isn't how a man should die."

"Maybe we can help each other," David said gently.

"Help? How?"

David met his eyes. "I'm not asking you to break your promise. But if there's anything you *can* say—anything at all—I might be able to help get you out of here."

"I don't have any money," Brady said.

"Evidently," Brendan muttered.

"I'm dying, not deaf," Brady snapped.

"Sorry," Brendan replied, eyes down.

Brady stared out the window again, licking his lips, lost in thought. But there was no confusion in his gaze, just contemplation.

"There's an attorney in Youngstown. Go see him."

"An attorney?" Brendan asked, instantly impatient. "What's his name?"

"Rushton. John Rushton. You'll have to find the address."

"Will he know why we're coming?"

"No."

"Then what do we tell him?" David asked.

"You'll have to figure that out," Brady said. "You know why you're here. Make him understand."

"But if he doesn't even—"

"I've said enough," Brady cut Brendan off. "I've done all I can. Please respect that."

He looked at David with something deeper than reluctance, maybe guilt, maybe hope.

"A man has to trust in the character of others sometimes," he said.

"I haven't forgotten what I said," David replied softly. "You don't belong here."

They helped him back to his stained bed, tucked him in, and David laid a hand gently on his forehead. Joe Brady was already asleep, worn out from the rare company and the weight of memory.

The brothers exited the room and started down the corridor.

"The door's this way," Brendan said, pointing right.

"We have business first."

They turned left and arrived at the sorry excuse for a nurse's station—a pair of mismatched desks buried in papers and food wrappers. Three middle-aged women sat gossiping.

In the center, Nilson sat with practiced indifference, clearly aware of their presence but refusing to acknowledge them.

"You can ignore me," David said calmly, "but you need to listen carefully. If that man is mistreated, even slightly, because we visited—there will be hell to pay."

Nilson finally looked up, her face tight like a scolded child holding herself in a tantrum.

"You're not in Boston, gentlemen," she snapped. "Don't threaten me."

Brendan leaned over the desk, palms flat, voice low but dangerous. "I'm not threatening you. I'm telling you this place is a disgrace. That man in there gets clean sheets, a bath, and new clothes. We'll be back to check."

"What's he to you?" she scoffed. "His daughter's in Illinois. Calls maybe once every year. She doesn't care."

"He's a World War II veteran," Brendan replied coldly. "To let him rot here is shameful. Fix it. Don't screw with me."

"You've overstayed your welcome," she hissed, standing like a ruffled cat. "I'll call the police if you don't leave."

"Why don't you?" David smiled. "We'd be happy to involve some other departments—state reps, maybe the VA?"

Nilson froze. Her fists unclenched. She took a breath, recalibrating.

"I'll see to it Mr. Brady is given a bath. Clean sheets and towels and clean pajamas."

"Thank you," David said, guiding Brendan toward the door.

It felt good to be outside, away from the smell of the home. David turned and looked back through the filthy windows, his view distorted by layers of grime. He reached into his pocket for the car keys just as a vehicle turned onto the street, heading their way. Neither brother thought much of it—at first.

As the car neared the nursing home, it slowed to a crawl. Brendan, always more street-smart than David, instinctively stepped in front of his brother. The brand-new green Jeep Cherokee slowed even more. Brendan noticed the rear passenger window rolling down.

"Get down!" he shouted, yanking David to the ground beside a parked sedan. He crouched low and peered through the car's windows, just in time to see the muzzle of a gun poke out.

He threw himself onto David as the first shots rang out.

The windows of the sedan exploded, spraying glass over them. More shots followed, bullets thudding into the car's frame like fists into meat.

"What the fuck, David?" Brendan gasped. "We don't even have a fucking weapon!"

"If they get out," David said, "we go after them. I'd prefer not to die face-up like a fish."

Two more shots. Two more thuds. And then—silence.

Shards of glass trickled onto the pavement as the brothers slowly got up.

"Holy shit," Brendan muttered. "What the fuck was that? Someone just shot at us. Jesus Christ!"

David pulled out his phone and dialed. Ring. Ring. Ring. On the fourth, a soft click.

"Lem Covey," a calm voice said, faintly Southern.

"Lemuel Covey, my name is David Costigan. Do you have a minute?"

"I do. Just call me Lem," he replied, the Southern drawl now more distinct.

"Okay. I was told you might be able to help me."

"Help you how?"

"Well… a woman in Youngstown gave me your card."

"Jennie Goodearl?"

"I don't—"

"It's okay," Lem cut him off. "It had to be Jennie. I told her to call."

"Someone just tried to kill us."

There was a pause. "Kill you? Why?"

"I have no idea."

"I'm in Erie.. I can be in Youngstown tomorrow night. Want to meet for dinner?"

"Yes, but I don't know the city."

"Ask someone or use your GPS. I'll meet you at the Inner Circle Pizza at 7:30. That work?"

"We'll make it work. Thank you, Mr. Covey."

"Call me Lem."

The brothers reached their car. David quickly started the engine and pulled away.

"This is some shit, brother," Brendan sighed, wiping his face with his sleeve.

"We definitely hit a nerve with someone."

"You going to call this Rushton guy?" Brendan asked.

"Let's talk to Covey first. He might be our best chance."

Mary answered on the second ring.

"Hello?"

David smiled at the sound of her voice.

"I was starting to worry," she said. "I hadn't heard from you."

"It's been… an interesting day," David replied.

"Good or bad, interesting?"

"I'm not sure yet. We got a couple of leads. We spoke to a man named Joe Brady—he knew my grandfather from the Army."

"Did he help you, honey?"

"He gave me the name of someone who might."

"In Youngstown?"

"Yes."

"How long do you think you'll be gone?"

"Miss me already?" he teased, trying to keep it light.

"I do. But your dad and grandmother are starting to ask questions."

"What kind?"

"They think this road trip is… odd."

"They're not wrong. I'll be home by the weekend."

"I love you."

"Love you too."

Brendan sat on the bed, flipping through TV channels. He looked over at David, who stood by the window, lost in thought.

"I noticed you didn't tell Mary someone tried to kill us," Brendan said.

"You think?"

"What the hell are we even doing?"

"We're getting to the bottom of this," David replied, slipping his hands into his pockets.

"You mean before someone gets us killed?"

"Ideally."

Route 224 stretched across the Mahoning Valley like a commercial artery—from Central Indiana to Western Pennsylvania. Locally, it connected Canfield and Poland, running through Boardman Township, lined with fast food, retail, car lots, medical offices, and the tired Marcel Vachon Plaza.

Once a booming strip, Vachon Plaza was now a shell of itself. Built in the 1980s by Henri Vachon, it struggled as Youngstown collapsed. But while the city fell, its suburbs—Poland, Canfield, Boardman—grew and adapted.

The Mahoning Valley, part of the original Western Reserve, had once been surveyed by George Washington himself while he was still a British officer. The valley ran from Warren in the north to Lisbon in the south, with Youngstown, Canfield, and Poland tucked between.

In 1797, the city of Youngstown was founded by John Young, who saw the geographic value in the junction of the Mahoning River and Mill Creek. It was a place built for purposes now worn thin with time.

David turned into the Inner Circle's parking lot and found a space near the front. The brothers stepped inside the bustling foyer. Several couples and families were waiting. David added their name to the list; the hostess told them it would be fifteen minutes.

They moved to a quiet corner near the wall, watching as tired families and gray-faced men came and went. On the walls: old photos, local sports memorabilia, memories from a town that had seen better days. Football helmets from local high schools sat on corner shelves.

"This place really does breathe football," Brendan muttered. "Isn't Namath or Marino from around here?"

"Pennsylvania," David replied. "Butkus, I think, is from Ohio."

The door opened again. Cold air spilled in.

Another couple left.

The door swung open once more. This time, a man stepped in alone. He wore a wrinkled, striped blue suit and scanned the room. He looked like he was in his late fifties, maybe early sixties. Messy white hair, and a mustache-and-goatee combo that made him look like Colonel Sanders—if the Colonel had seen some shit.

"Mr. Covey?" David asked, taking a chance.

"David Costigan?" the man smiled. "Lem."

"Lem, this is my brother Brendan," David said.

"Pleasure," Covey nodded.

The hostess called David's name, and the three men followed her to their table.

They sat as she laid out three sets of napkins and silverware. She took their drink orders, and none of the men spoke until she walked away.

"Any luck?" Covey asked quietly, his dignified Southern drawl smooth and measured.

"Some," David replied. "We met with an old Army buddy of my grandfather's."

"Joe Brady," Covey noted.

"Yes. How did you know?" Brendan asked, eyes narrowing.

"It's my job."

"Someone tried to kill us," Brendan revealed bluntly.

"What?" Covey exclaimed, his eyebrows raising. "When?"

"Tonight," David said. "Coming out of the nursing home. They shot at us."

"You're not hurt?"

"No, but it makes this even more fucked up," David muttered.

"Well, you listen to what I say, and we'll all get through this."

"All?" Brendan asked. "Who is 'us'?"

Covey smiled—one of those I-know-what-you-don't smiles, lightly patronizing.

"There are very powerful and dangerous people not happy about your inquiries. You've now had a taste of how far they're willing to go."

"People? What people?" Brendan pushed. "And why are *you* so invested? Why would a guy like you come all the way up from D.C.?"

"As I said, there are things in play here that go far beyond your family history or your grandfather," Covey replied calmly.

David and Brendan exchanged a cautious glance. They weren't sure if they were being helped… or handled.

"So, you're with the Justice Department?" Brendan asked, blunt as always.

Covey leaned forward, pulled a worn wallet from his back pocket, flipped it open, and laid it on the table.

"I've been a Marshal a long, long time," he said, tapping the badge. "As you can see from my aging carcass."

The brothers leaned in, examining the ID and badge catching the pendant lamp's glow above them.

"Have either of you been to Youngstown before?" Covey asked, sliding the wallet back into his pocket.

Both brothers shook their heads.

Covey settled into a short lecture. He described Youngstown from the 1920s onward. It had once been a steel titan—a Mecca for industry—and home to one of the most infamous crime families in America: the Vachons.

Marcel Vachon, great-grandfather of Aiden Vachon, the current head of Vachon Enterprises, made his fortune bootlegging during Prohibition. He partnered with none other than Joe Kennedy and Frank Nitti. Covey explained that Prohibition, "one of the most idiotic laws ever passed," gave birth to organized crime in America. And though the business would eventually expand into gambling, prostitution, and drugs, its power came from liquor distribution.

Marcel's son, Henri Vachon, enlisted in the Army after Pearl Harbor and later took over the family business, giving it a wisp of legitimacy.

"Car bombs and cookie tables, boys," Covey chuckled.

"Car bombs and what?" Brendan asked.

"Ask anyone."

Covey then laid out the industrial and criminal roots of the city—how James and Daniel Heaton had built Youngstown's first blast furnace in the early 1800s, triggering a steel boom that fueled both global war efforts and economic might. The Mahoning Valley became a melting pot: Slavs, Croatians, Lithuanians, Bulgarians, Jews, Ukrainians, Italians, Greeks—all chasing opportunity in iron and fire.

Coal from Appalachia fed the furnaces. Unions grew. And with the unions came organized crime. Car bombs settled disputes. Loudly. Permanently.

And yet, amid all the violence, Covey pointed out another tradition—one that outlived many of the people who practiced it.

"The cookie table," he said, smiling. "An Eastern European or Italian wedding tradition. Dozens of relatives and friends all bring trays of homemade cookies. It spread to every church and synagogue between here and Pittsburgh. Weddings here are sugar-fueled bloodlines."

"You need to keep a low profile," Covey warned. "There is no depth to which that bunch won't sink."

"But all we want is the truth about our dad's dad," David said. "We're not looking to mess with the Vachons or anyone else."

"Just go back to your hotel after dinner and stay there until I call you," Covey insisted.

After dinner, David and Brendan returned to their Canfield hotel as instructed.

"There's something squishy about that guy," Brendan said as he opened the room door.

"He's a government guy, "David replied. "His job is to be squishy."

"I don't know," Brendan said, collapsing onto the bed. "There's something not quite right about that KFC son of a bitch."

"Yeah, did you see that hair? The mustache? That beard?" David added.

"Clearly no one's told him how ridiculous he looks."

"Maybe he doesn't believe in mirrors, "David laughed.

The next morning David looked up John Rushton online. He found an address and plugged it into the GPS.

"I thought Covey told us to stay put," Brendan said, smirking.

"Yeah, right," David replied with a shrug.

They headed toward Youngstown, turning onto Ohio Route 11. As they drove, David noted how the city reminded him of Boston's own urban renewal, the long, dirty path from forgotten to functional.

They exited the highway and followed signs for Federal Plaza and downtown Youngstown.

On the way, David called Rushton's office, telling the secretary he was only in town for a few days and that it was an emergency.

She informed him she could squeeze him in for forty-five minutes—no more.

Just as David hung up, his phone rang.

"It's Covey," he said, recognizing the number.

"Call him later," Brendan said. "He doesn't need to know where we are."

Federal Plaza is Youngstown; Ohio's downtown business district located at the intersection of Market and Federal Streets. Decades ago, while Youngstown thrived on steel, Federal Plaza was a bustling commercial hub, much like many downtowns before suburban sprawl and indoor malls reshaped American life. But the collapse of the steel industry—and the rise of the Vachon Plaza and Eastwood Mall up north in Niles—turned Federal Plaza into an urban ghost town.

A slow, sputtering renaissance began in the 1990s. Today, there are businesses, condos, and a handful of upscale restaurants, but it's far from what it once was. One gem that endures: the DeYor Performing Arts Center in Powers Auditorium. Founded by the famed Warner Brothers. It's the oldest of their theaters and still draws international acts—more recently, also a sought-after wedding venue.

The lobby of 300 Federal Plaza could've been in any major city. Marble floors intersected by walnut pillars gave it more of a Boston feel than a Rust Belt one. A small but upscale coffee shop sat tucked into a corner of the otherwise opulent space.

David ordered three coffees, signed himself and Brendan in at the security desk—also walnut-finished—and stepped into the elevator to the fifth floor.

Upstairs, the floor was carpeted in a rich burgundy pattern— fitting for a law firm. The same warm walnut finish lined the walls, and the floor-to-ceiling French doors were etched in silver:

Hoglith, Greenstein and Rushton, LLC.

David tried the doors, but they were locked—intentionally. No one was just dropping in on this firm.

Inside, a stunning African American receptionist in a teal business suit looked up from her work with limited interest.

"Yes?" she asked, pressing a hidden button beneath her desk.

David spotted the intercom next to the elevator.

"David Costigan. I have an appointment with John Rushton."

"Oh. The emergency," she said dryly.

"Yes."

A buzz. A soft click. The door swung open.

The brothers stepped into the reception area. The phone rang. The receptionist held up an index finger to them while answering it. She hung up and scribbled a note.

"Mr. Rushton will be right with you. Can I get you something to drink? Coffee?"

"Bass Ale," Brendan grinned.

She didn't even blink.

"Some water would be great," David said.

She returned with the water just as a man entered the room— white dress shirt, sleeves rolled, suit pants that weren't bought at Macy's. He had straight black hair, sharp features, and neon-blue eyes that stood out like LEDs.

"Mr. Costigan?" he asked, voice tinged with that Northern Ohio twang.

"Mr. Rushton," David replied, standing. "This is my brother Brendan."

Rushton nodded. "Will it be the two of you?"

"Why don't you two go on," Brendan said, staying behind.

David followed Rushton into a spacious corner office. The lawyer closed the door behind them.

"Have a seat," Rushton offered, gesturing to the leather chair opposite his desk. Just outside the window, the word 'Vindicator' hung vertically at the corner of the old newspaper building.

David sat and looked out across the faded downtown skyline.

"Shame it looks like that," Rushton said. "A lot of us are trying to find ways to revive this city. But it's not easy."

"It's really run-down, "David said. "Parts of Boston used to look like this when I was a kid. But that's all gone now."

"Great city, Boston," Rushton smiled. "My JD is from BC."

"No kidding?" David chuckled. "Where'd you live?"

"Just off Cleveland Circle. With a bunch of Southie townies."

David leaned back and frowned.

"Oh boy," Rushton muttered. "Southie?"

"Born and raised," David said. "Though I don't *think* I'm a townie."

Rushton laughed softly. "So how can I help?" David hesitated, then cleared his throat.

"My grandfather's name was Francis Costigan. He died in Italy in 1944—or so I was always told."

"And?"

David rubbed his thumbs together. He leaned back, unsure how to explain why he was really there.

"Does the name Joe Brady mean anything to you?" he asked.

"It does. Why?"

"Well…" He cleared his throat again. "He suggested I come and see you."

"You talked to Joe Brady? Ninety-something Joe Brady?"

"I did. I went to see him."

"Where is he?" Rushton asked, suddenly concerned.

"That's another thing we probably ought to talk about. He's in a despicable nursing home. A place called Girard. It's a disgrace."

"As you say, we'll talk about that. But why did he send you to me?" Rushton asked.

"I'm not sure," David admitted.

"Then how do you think I can help you?"

"I'm not sure about that either."

Rushton leaned forward, pressing his elbow on the desk and his forehead into his palm. He rubbed his face and closed his eyes.

"Mr. Costigan—"

"David," he interrupted.

"David. I'm a lawyer. I deal in facts and get paid by the hour. This conversation produces neither. I'm not sure—"

"Give me five minutes to explain."

Rushton nodded. "Okay."

David launched into the entire story—from the letter at the Post Office, to meeting John and Jennie Goodearl, to being shot at, and finally to the involvement of Lemuel Covey.

"Goodearl?" Rushton asked, suddenly typing something into his laptop. "Jennie Goodearl?"

"Yeah."

Rushton looked up, face darkening.

"She was murdered."

"What?" David froze.

"She was killed yesterday morning. An apparent break-in. Her son—her *derelict* son—slept through the whole thing. Poor woman had nothing."

David's jaw dropped. His eyes widened.

"Don't you think that's a bit of a coincidence? David asked. "Brendan and I get shot at, and she gets killed?"

"It is a bizarre coincidence. I'll give you that. But you already have that Covey guy, and it's the Youngstown Police—not me—who should be investigating this."

"But Brady sent me here for a reason."

"He didn't say why?" Rushton asked.

"He said something about being bound by honor and some kind of promise," David explained. "He said he was already crossing the line just giving me your name."

Rushton pushed his chair back and stood. He turned toward the window and ran a hand through his hair.

"Tell you what," he said. "You seem very sincere, and you've got a compelling—maybe even Hollywood—story. When you get to the point where you need an Ohio attorney, I'll be the one. Fair enough?"

David stood, disappointed by the outcome.

"I'm not crazy," he said. "I'm a doctor, for Christ's sake. Something is wrong here."

Rushton turned and gave a faint smile. "No doubt."

The two men shook hands, and David turned to leave. As he reached the door, something on a shelf caught his eye. Framed family photos. He paused, staring.

"Your kids?" David asked.

"Yes. You have kids?"

"Yeah—boy and a girl. Like you, evidently."

"Yes. Nine and eleven. My son is the eldest."

"As is mine," David said. "Your boy?"

"What about him?" Rushton asked.

David turned back and walked to the desk. He pulled out his wallet and took out a photo. He looked at it, hesitated, and then placed it carefully on Rushton's desk.

"What?" Rushton asked, his patience wearing thin.

Anne Costigan was as content as a wife and mother as any could be. She loved her husband and her sons, and unlike many of her friends, had little to complain about. Patrick Costigan wasn't the most romantic man, but he was a good one—decent and loyal. He was affectionate enough with Anne, though far less so with the boys. She understood that this came from his views on manhood: real men didn't get babied, and showing physical affection could "stunt" a boy's growth into that role.

Anne didn't challenge her husband's ways. Instead, she softened them quietly, offering warmth where he held firm.

Her relationship with her mother-in-law, Elizabeth, was respectful—sometimes even close—but Anne always sensed a hardness in the older woman. She figured it stemmed from Elizabeth losing her husband so young, with two small children to raise. Still, Elizabeth doted on her grandsons, and that cured many of Anne's concerns.

"Hello, dear," Anne said, opening the door. "Rachel and Mary are already here," she added in a whisper, as if sharing a secret.

"I knew they were coming." Anne smiled.

"Hello, Mom!" Mary said, standing to greet her.

"Hello, Anne," Rachel chimed in, not looking up from her *People* magazine.

"Hello, girls," Anne said, not taking Rachel's eccentricities too personally.

"I made a scrumptious stew," Elizabeth called from the kitchen. "It's getting frigid out there—perfect day for it, don't you think?"

Anne sat at the table while Elizabeth plated the food.

"Need help, Mom?" Anne asked.

"No, you girls sit and visit. You don't get enough girl time together."

"So… have you heard from the boys?" Anne asked.

"They're in Ohio," Mary replied, choosing her words carefully.

"Can you believe they just took off and left us?" Rachel grumbled. "Why did we get married, again?"

"You know the brothers need this time together," Anne said.

"My sister Janet's in New Hampshire. You don't see me running off anytime I like."

"It's different with boys," Mary said.

"It really is," Anne agreed. "They're just not as strong as we are."

The three women chuckled.

"I know," Rachel said, laughing. "Give them some football time on Sunday and a secret drink from the orange juice container, and they think they've gone to heaven."

"What are you girls laughing about?" Elizabeth asked, ladling stew into bowls.

"Men, Mom," Anne said with a grin.

"Men," Elizabeth echoed, her eyes locked on the cabinet in front of her. "They are unfathomable to me."

"To all of us, Granny," Mary said dryly.

"Mary… they were in Ohio two days ago," Anne whispered. "They're still there. What are they doing?"

"Mom, I have no idea what they're doing. They should be home by the weekend," Mary lied.

"You don't have to tell me girls," Anne said, glancing at both, "but Elizabeth and my husband can both sense something's up. Uncle Billy too."

"Mom, they'll be home soon enough," Mary replied.

"I just hope they get this out of their systems," Rachel muttered. "I'm not putting up with this again."

"Oh, Rachel…" Anne smiled knowingly.

Elizabeth joined them at the table and dipped her spoon into the stew. Anne and Mary followed her lead. Rachel didn't lift her eyes from her magazine.

"Eat, Rachel," Elizabeth suggested. "You're not starving, but you don't want it to get cold."

Rachel looked up, offered a faux smile, and returned to reading.

"She'll eat, Mom," Anne said. "Won't she?"

"I'm just letting it cool a bit. I'm sure it's delicious," Rachel replied without making eye contact.

"So, what about the boys?" Elizabeth asked. "Where are they? What are they doing?"

"They're traveling," Mary said. "Spending brother time together."

"Oh," Elizabeth said flatly. "Brother time."

"Yes," Mary replied, already feeling the vexation Elizabeth so expertly stirred.

"I don't like being lied to, young lady," Elizabeth said. "I understand every good Irish Catholic family has its secrets, but this is a little extreme."

"I'm not—"

"She isn't lying, Mom," Anne cut in. "She really doesn't know. Maybe sometimes a duck is just a duck."

Elizabeth shook her head and dropped her spoon a little too loudly into the bowl. "Philosophy, dear?"

Anne smiled. She'd been a Costigan long enough to know exactly how to navigate Elizabeth's jabs.

"Cell phones, I-Pops, and all sorts of toys connect you all 24 hours a day," Elizabeth continued, "and you don't know what they're doing? Or where they are? Do you at least know they're alive?"

"Of course, we know they're alive," Mary said. "We—"

"Then how can you sit there and tell me you don't know what they're doing?" Elizabeth interrupted again.

"Ma!" Anne interjected, raising a hand gently toward her mother-in-law. "The boys went away for a few days. They don't spend enough time together, and it's not an issue for their wives."

Rachel glanced over at Anne, eyes narrowed.

"Why is this becoming such a huge issue?" Anne continued.

"Why?" Elizabeth repeated, voice sharp with suspicion. "Who in their right mind picks *Ohio* as a destination?"

The three women stared at her—silent, unsure how to respond.

"Look at you," Elizabeth said, clearly savoring the moment. "Like deer in headlights. Strike a nerve, did I?"

"Mom?" Anne asked, her tone half-warning.

"Don't 'Mom' me, Anne. What are they doing in Ohio?"

"David, I get the sense of your story and your family," Rushton said, leaning forward slightly. "But this sounds more like a case for a private investigator than a lawyer. I don't know why Joe Brady sent you to me—but I can't help you."

David studied him from across the desk, searching his face. For a fleeting second, he wondered if this man, too, was part of some dark conspiracy. But all he saw was a sincere expression… and a kind of helplessness.

"I'm not crazy, you know. I understand how this might all sound."

"I don't think anything," Rushton replied evenly. "But it does seem like your family's reality may not be what you were raised to believe. I get that. And I'm sorry."

Rushton tore a page from the yellow legal pad on his desk and began to write.

"Here," he said, handing it over. "A couple of PIs I've used. They're both talented. Maybe they can help. Like I said—if you ever find yourself in need of actual legal services in Ohio, I'll be here."

David took the paper and glanced down at the names. His arm dropped to his side as he slumped slightly. Rushton didn't know this man from Boston—but he knew the look of quiet defeat. David Costigan looked drained. Beaten. And while Rushton prided himself on being pragmatic and logical, he wasn't without compassion.

"I've taken up enough of your time," David said, reaching for a pen from Rushton's desk. "Here's my cell. I'll be in town for another couple of days. If anything crosses your mind… if you want to talk, call me."

"I told you—"

David stepped into the reception area, where Brendan was waiting.

"You, okay?" Brendan asked.

"Yeah, "David said, though it didn't sound convincing. "He's the one with the headache."

Brendan pushed the door open just as David turned back at a sudden voice.

"Costigan?" Rushton called from his doorway.

David stopped. "Yeah?"

"Let me think about how I *might* be able to help," Rushton said.

David tilted his head. "Why the shift?"

Rushton paused. "I don't know. Something about your story… It intrigues me. But in the meantime, call one or both of those PIs."

David gave a single nod. Brendan held the glass door open as they stepped into the hallway.

David's phone buzzed. He pulled it from his pocket and smiled when he saw the name.

"Hi, honey," he said, buttering a piece of bread.

"It's not good here, David," Mary sighed. "Your grandmother knows something is up. She knows you're in Ohio."

"How the heck does she know that?"

"I have no idea—but she *knows*. You need to get home."

"Just one more day, baby," he pleaded. "I've found more."

"Your grandfather?"

"Yes," he said, handing the butter to Brendan. "How are the kids?"

"They miss you. Are you eating?"

"At a Red Lobster with Brendan."

"Red Lobster?" She gagged playfully. "Don't *ever* let your mom hear that."

"I'm in Ohio," he whispered. "Not like they have Anthony Hawthorne's here."

The elevator doors slid open and David stepped into the lobby, greeted by a wash of morning sunlight through the glass façade. He'd slept surprisingly well—thanks to the wine.

As he had had the past two mornings, he strolled past the registration desk and into the hotel's breakfast area. It wasn't home, but the spread—waffles, scrambled eggs, fruit, and breads—was decent. Pulling out his phone, he scrolled through messages: mostly work, except one from a name that stirred something in his memory.

J. Miller

Little Veronica Polino is being moved into permanent foster care. Thought you should know.

David frowned. "Why the fuck is he sending this to me?" he muttered under his breath.

So distracted, he didn't see the woman standing right in front of him.

"Oh! I'm so sorry," she said, startled. Her hands were under the hem of her blue skirt, as if adjusting something.

David blinked. She looked to be in her mid-twenties. Her blonde hair was perfectly cut just above the neck, styled with a subtle inward curve. Green eyes, porcelain skin, and just enough makeup to look sharp and professional. Her blue suit was crisp, her white blouse pristine, and a string of pearls rested in three elegant rows just above her chest.

"Sorry again," she said, recovering. "I was supposed to have an important meeting here, but wouldn't you know—two of them came down with the flu."

"That's too bad," David replied awkwardly.

"Yes. A shame," she smiled. "Well—you win some, you know?"

"And lose some?" he offered, trying for humor.

"I guess," she said, amused but unsure.

"I suppose I should eat. Would you like to join me?"

"I, um…"

"I *know* you're married," she laughed. "It's harmless. What do you think—I'll seduce you?"

"How'd you know I'm—?"

"The gold ring," she smirked, pointing. "Dead giveaway."

"Oh. Right." He lifted his hand, staring at it like he'd just remembered he wore it. "Stupid question."

"I've had stupid-er." She grinned and gently took his arm. "Buy a lady some breakfast?"

David hesitated but followed her toward the buffet, already feeling guilty.

It would be easy to rationalize—*no real harm done*. But the truth of the matter sat heavy in his chest. He didn't mention his brother, sitting just a few tables away.

They found a table with three chairs. No mention of Brendan. They sat for a moment before rising together to scan the buffet. David returned with a modest plate—socially acceptable portions. So did she.

He still didn't know her name.

David unfolded the thick paper towel and placed it on his lap. She followed suit.

"How rude of me," she said, sipping her cup of black coffee. "Esther Chase."

"David Costigan," he replied.

"Costigan? Irish?"

"Very. You're not Midwestern."

"How do you know I'm not from here?" she asked.

"With that accent? You're a Boston boy as sure as shooting. Right?"

"Actually, yes."

"And let me guess." She shook her head. "Black Irish, Boston; I bet you're a Southie guy."

"Very good." He smiled, now beginning to enjoy this little duet. "You?"

"Baltimore." She smiled. "I was raised in Fairfax, but I am not crazy about Virginia, you know?"

"I don't really know…"

"Whacko." She interrupted, taking a bite of toast. "You cross the Potomac; it's like another country. Well, maybe it is."

As they conversed, she slid her chair closer to his; then a few inches closer, and then again, until her leg was touching his. David never once contemplated being unfaithful to Mary—not even when they were first dating. Now she was his wife and was the one who held down the proverbial fort, including all the bills, cleaning, and of course, the kids. He wondered how he could ever violate that, but the feeling of Esther's warm leg against him sent a wave throughout his body. He stabbed at a sausage link on his plate, looking for any reasonable distraction.

Then his phone rang, and he was relieved and disappointed at that moment. He took the phone from his pocket and looked at the display.

"Your wife?" Esther asked.

"No, my brother." David replied.

"Southie?"

"No, upstairs. Hello?"

Brendan told David he was going to check e-mails and take a shower. He also told his brother not to wait on him for breakfast.

He hung up the phone and returned it to his pocket.

Esther sat with her elbow on the table, fork bouncing between her thumb and index finger, and she stared right through his eyes.

"Well?"

"He's not going to make it to breakfast." said, a small grin on his face.

"Oh, that's a very good thing." She laughed and began to eat again.

She wiped her mouth slowly and with great dramatic effects. It was not lost. David stared at the motion, hypnotized by her red lips.

"So, your brother is delayed, my meeting has sunk. What would you like to do?"

"I still have things to do, you know." He quipped nervously. "I don't have all that much time."

"You look like a fifteen-minute man to me." She laughed, her hand finally finding its way onto his knee.

"I am married, you know." He spoke. It was more for him than her.

"I am aware." She smiled, squeezing his knee, causing him to jump.

The few lingering patrons turned, as he re-settled himself.

"Now that's…"

"Shhhh." She whispered, placing her free index finger over his mouth. "Let's not spoil this. Let's not say anything, except thank you when you're done with me."

David, not knowing why, followed Esther into the elevator. Both stared ahead at their exaggerated reflections in the metal wall. David squeezed his fingers into his palms, the image of his family running through his head.

"Until I get to her room, I haven't done anything wrong." He thought, trying to convince himself.

The elevator bell chimed, signaling they had reached the third floor. Esther stepped out of the elevator, glancing back to make sure he hadn't changed his mind. He too stepped off and followed behind, both making their way down the narrow hotel hallway. Reaching into her purse, Esther withdrew the plastic hotel key card. She stopped in front of the next door to her left, inserted the card in the appropriate slot, and opened the door. She stepped inside. David stopped before reaching her room. Two or three seconds passed, and Esther's head appeared out of the threshold. She smiled at him.

"Don't be shy now." She insisted. "Thinking about us in that bed has me going. You're not going to leave a girl hanging?"

David walked ten feet or so and passed her into the room as she held the door.

"I have some Pepsi and pretty good rum." She said, removing her jacket.

"That would be great, actually." David said.

Esther poured the liquids into the plastic cups from the bathroom and handed one of them.

"What shall we toast to?" she asked, being almost annoyingly cliché.

"To Youngstown?" He suggested shyly.

"Youngstown?" She laughed. "This pit. No, let's drink to great orgasms."

David gulped and then took a mouthful of the strong drink. He g "Too strong, she asked. I have plenty of Pepsi" and took another mouthful, standing still in one spot.

"Now you sit down here." She said, leading him to bed. "You're going to watch first. Then you'll be fucking me."

David complied.

Esther moved directly in front of him, though there was only a couple of feet between the bed and dresser. She began to move her hips and swayed from side to side. As she did, she started to unbutton her blouse from the bottom. In a few moments the blouse hung open, revealing inner edges of her blue laced bra. She reached around her back, and David could hear her skirt zipper moving. She pressed down on the top of her skirt, and it slid easily to the floor.

"You like?" she asked.

"Uh-huh." He stammered, taking another sip.

She leaned against the dresser, arching her back toward him. She carefully caressed her breasts and slid one hand down to her panties.

"I want you to watch me cum." She said, rubbing herself over her panties.

She began to softly moan, her hips pulsing as she rubbed. She slid her panties aside, revealing her well-shaved vulva. Sliding her index finger between her now shiny lips, she moaned a little louder. David could feel the excitement within and wanted her.

She looked at him as she pleasured herself, seeming to be even more excited by his voyeurism.

"Beats running around after some old mailbox, hey?" She said.

He raised the cup again but stopped. He looked at the floor and closed his eyes for a moment. Esther did not stop touching herself, though she took note of his distraction. She stopped rubbing.

"You know women have egos too. You seem less interested."

David finished the drink, stood, and reached around her, placing the cup onto the dresser. He stood arrow straight, looking down into her eyes.

"What is it?" she asked nervously.

"Mailbox?" He asked.

"Yes. You told me your story at breakfast."

"I said nothing about a mailbox." He said.

"You did, you…"

"No, I didn't!" He interrupted angrily. "I never talked about anything like that. I made no reference to a mailbox."

"I don't know then," she said, placing her hand onto his chest. "Lucky guess or just logic."

"Nice try, but why don't you tell me the truth," David insisted.

"David, I…"

"I nearly betrayed my family," he said. "What is this? Are we being recorded?"

She didn't answer.

"Jesus Christ," he said, turning toward the door.

"David, wait," she said. "I'm sorry."

He stepped back toward her. She moved back, seeing the anger in his eyes.

"I'm not even interested in why," he said, "though I probably should be. Someone hire you to set me up? Ruin my marriage? Who are you really?"

"I am really Esther Chase."

"So, what is all this? Why the whole fucking seduction thing?"

"Kind of a directive I was afraid to turn down."

"Directive? Who?" He laughed. "Fuck up my marriage and my family as a request?"

"I can't say," she said.

"Of course not," he said, throwing his arms into the air.

"No, I really can't, David. I could if I would."

"Ah well, that makes sense," he said sarcastically. "What do you care about my family? Would you have actually gone through with it?"

"No. I didn't have to. This was already enough to create the leverage he needs."

"Who needs?" David asked.

"I work for the government," she said.

"What, as a civil service hooker?"

"No, as a Justice Department investigator."

"Investigator?" He laughed. "You investigate people by fucking them?"

"No. I don't—I... it is an extraordinarily difficult and complicated situation."

David laughed, looked down at the floor and shook his head. "Famous last words. *Complicated* is a code word for "I don't *want to talk about it.*"

"I can't talk about it!" she scolded. "You have absolutely no fucking idea what you've set in motion here."

"Well, I'm out of here," David said, moving back toward the door. "What was the point of this setup?"

"Absolute cooperation," she said.

"You mean blackmail?" he asked.

"Incentive."

"What, do what you want—for my wife to find out?" David asked angrily.

"Leverage," she said.

He turned back toward her but held his position.

"You have no ethical problem with this? No issue with maybe ruining someone's life?"

"You don't understand," she said. "There are powerful people in this world who get what they want."

"There are no boundaries. No lines that can't be crossed. What the hell is it you need my cooperation for anyway?"

"I can't say."

"Oh, you can't," he protested.

"I mean it. I don't know. I was asked to set you up—get the pictures—and I was done."

"And you just agreed?" David asked.

"I've said too much already. As I said, you haven't the vaguest clue."

"What?" He laughed. "I am no one. I am a guy from Southie, who was smart enough to wangle my way into medical school, marry a dream, and get the hell out of that ghetto."

"You wouldn't be the first person to learn things that are enormously dangerous and not even know it."

"What things? This is about my grand—" He stopped.

"David?"

"Someone shot at my brother and me a day or so ago. What is it you are trying to protect?"

"You seem like a nice guy. You should go home. You need to be careful, David," she said. "There are things in play here above my pay grade."

David turned and stepped closer to her. He put his hands into his pockets and rolled up and down on his heels.

"You seem like a very smart woman. I suggest you learn to say no."

Esther stared at him, emotion welling up behind her eyes.

"Your wife hit the jackpot with you," she said. "You are a good man."

"Not that good, Esther. I shouldn't be here."

"Where have you been?" Brendan asked, as David walked into the now cleared breakfast area.

"I got hung up."

"Huh?" Brendan said, shrugging his shoulders.

David walked over and sat down next to his brother. He looked at him the way a father might look at his child.

"I think we're in a dangerous situation," David said. "I'm sorry for getting you into this."

"Sorry? Fuck them. They don't realize who the Costigans are."

"Might be, but we don't know either."

"Maybe you should call that Covey guy. He might be able to help us even more," Brendan suggested.

David did not hesitate. He pulled his phone from his pocket and dialed. He looked at his brother as the phone rang once, twice—then an answer.

"Mr. Covey, it's David Costigan."

Brendan watched as his brother shook his head.

"We were tied up," David said. "Yes, I saw Rushton. How did you know?"

David listened, as Brendan looked at him anxiously.

"Okay, we'll see you at seven-thirty."

David placed his phone back in his pocket and sat back in his chair. The elevator bell rang, and Esther stepped out as the door opened. She looked over at the brothers, smiled, and proceeded to the front desk, her suitcase in tow.

"What the fuck," Brendan laughed. "You still got it, brother. Did you see the way she looked at you?"

"I really didn't notice," David said.

The desk clerk handed Esther the receipt, and she tucked it into her purse. She turned, looked at David again, and walked out of the hotel.

The MVR restaurant is a Youngstown staple. Very casual and on the outer edge of the Youngstown State University campus. Known for its simple menu and the largest indoor bocce court outside of Pittsburgh, it had served generations of "Youngstowners" during and after the steel industry collapse.

David parked, and the brothers walked into the crowded restaurant. Almost instantly, he saw the white-haired Marshall sitting in the far corner. He waved at Covey, as the older man waved back.

"Right on time, boys," Covey said in his drawl. "I like that."

"What's good here?" Brendan asked.

"Just order a sandwich," David instructed.

"What did Rushton have to say to you?" Covey asked. "More importantly, what did you have to ask him?"

"If he had any knowledge of my grandfather?" David replied.

"And?"

"No, it was pretty much a waste of time," he said, feeling uneasy about trusting anyone. "Why?"

"We've had our eye on that practice," Covey said. "I'd be careful with him."

"How so?" Brendan interjected.

"He has ties in some rough places," Covey said. "Remember, someone tried to kill you."

David's phone rang. He recognized the Three-Three-Zero number on his display.

"I have to take this," David said, standing from his seat.

"Important?" Covey asked.

"My wife," David lied. "Doesn't get more important than that. Hold on," he said into the phone as he walked outside the restaurant.

Outside, he looked around cautiously.

"Mr. Rushton?"

"I think we're past that, David," the voice said.

"What's up?"

"I still don't believe I can help you, but I did a little digging on your grandfather. It's a little squirrely," John said.

"How so?"

"Can you come to dinner tomorrow night? Leesa, my wife, is a good cook."

"Sure, but it's my last night. Where do you live?"

"I'll text you, my address. You have GPS?"

"Yup."

"I'm in Canfield. Say six-thirty?"

"Sure," David said, placing the phone back in his pocket.

David sat back down at the table, where Brendan was chomping on a plate of stuffed peppers.

"No need to wait for me, Bren," David chided.

"Hey, I'm hungry."

"Everything all right at home?" Covey asked.

David smiled, thinking about all the books and movies about the government and the technology they had. Had his people listened in on David's conversation? Did he already know that it wasn't Mary on the phone? David felt very anxious and questioned whether he should have lied.

"Pretty much. It's always something with kids."

"Sure is," Covey replied. "Are you familiar with the name Vachon?"

"They own one of the MLB baseball teams, don't they?"

"As a matter of fact—one of their few legitimate enterprises."

Marcel Vachon was a second-generation American. Born at the turn of the century, his father emigrated to Youngstown from Quebec forty years earlier. Scraping by doing a variety of manual jobs, Marcel decided this was not the life he wanted to lead. Not intending to exploit the vacuum left by Prohibition, he soon learned his family back in Canada was an asset in his early days of illegally importing liquor into the United States.

It was a small operation, requiring Marcel to make the five-hour drive to the border, pick up what he could carry in his relatively small truck, and transport it back to Northeast Ohio without being arrested. The Federal Bureau of Investigation was a fledgling organization at the time; their focus was on the crime syndicates popping up in Chicago and New York.

Youngstown was a shift town at the time; the steel industry was not yet at its peak. There was a market, however, for all manners of liquor, particularly for the mill workers changing shifts before going home. Though a small enterprise, it was not so small as to escape notice from men like Capone, Siegel, and Moran.

At first, Marcel was concerned they wanted him out of the way—to take over the Youngstown illegal liquor market. Preparing for the worst, Marcel Vachon quickly built his own syndicate, fully prepared for a war if it came. In two years, he had almost seventy loyal thugs whom he paid very well for the day.

In truth, neither Capone nor Siegel wanted to overextend themselves into Youngstown, and in 1929, Bugs Moran was eliminated in the infamous St. Valentine's Day Massacre. Instead, the two syndicate bosses offered Vachon a piece of the broader enterprise for a fair cut of his business. It was the manifestation of honor among thieves.

Vachon concluded it was a much safer proposition not to have these men as enemies. They could—and did—help him also open the door to both prostitution and gambling. Other, smaller crime elements began to pop up all across Central and Northeast Ohio, and his alliance with both Capone and Siegel made quick work of snuffing them out. It was not unusual to see a corpse or two floating down the Mahoning River, the unfortunate consequence of competing with Marcel Vachon.

This was the world Henri was born into and groomed for. Unlike his father, however, Henri saw the future and the need to transform the syndicate into as legitimate an enterprise as possible. With Al

Capone's arrest and imprisonment, Henri realized even more that the days of that kind of organized crime were coming to an end.

Once Marcel retired and became ill, Henri set out to become both legitimate and respectable. With the acquisition of the then-Washington Senators and the building of a reputable real estate empire in Ohio, he almost achieved that objective. Old habits die hard, however, and giving up prostitution, gambling, and the emerging drug market proved to be too attractive to abandon.

Nonetheless, the Vachon family contributed greatly to Youngstown, and many argued that without them, the little life Youngstown had after 1977 would have been extinguished.

"The name is somewhat familiar," David said.

"That family has tried to pawn themselves off as respectable. Even MLB wouldn't play that game, and they have other questionable owners as well," Covey said.

"What does any of this have to do with us?" David asked.

"Rushton is connected at the hip to them," Covey said. "That's why I was concerned about you contacting him."

"We can take care of ourselves," Brendan interrupted.

"You have no idea who you're dealing with here, son," Covey lectured.

"But you do?"

"Yes, I do," Covey said as the waitress set their food onto the table. "I have been chasing them for more than twenty years." He took a bite of the sandwich. "Some of my JD compatriots think I'm crazy, but I will get the bastards."

David looked over at his brother and, at the same time, took a bite.

"I am not interested in the Vachon family," David said. "This is way over our pay grade. This is strictly family."

"Yet Aiden Vachon, Henri's grandson, is obviously not happy with your digging."

"And what do you want out of this?" Brendan asked.

"Justice," Covey said indignantly. "I started this twenty years ago, and as God is my witness, I am taking them down."

The three men continued eating, David trying to have as little conversation as possible.

"I am here to protect you," Covey said, wiping his mouth with a napkin. "I am your guardian angel."

David's phone rang again. He looked at the display but did not recognize the number. He sent it to voicemail.

"Wife again?" Covey asked.

"No, hospital administration," David lied.

"Not that important?"

"If it is, they will leave me a voicemail. I can call them back."

A few minutes later, the phone rang again—the same unknown number.

"I probably should take this," David said. "They are obviously trying to track me down."

Again, David said, "Hold on," as he made his way through the crowded restaurant.

"Hello?" he said, stepping outside.

"David, hi. Esther Chase. Please don't hang up."

"How'd you get my number?"

"Please," she laughed.

"What do you want?" he asked, trying to run from his indiscretion and guilt.

"I thought about today." She paused.

"Yeah?"

"I need to make a change. I can't rationalize everything through my job."

"That's great, but why are you telling me?"

"I wanted to give you one more piece of information," Esther said.

"Okay."

"The agent who asked me to do what I did today—I want you to be careful. If he contacts you, I'd at least like you to be forewarned."

"I guess I appreciate that. You have to know—I'm married, and I want to stay that way. Today was a mistake, and I won't make it again."

"I know that. I'm sincere. That's not what this is about. I'm on my way to be with my husband and daughter."

"That's a good thing, Esther," David said.

"So, his name is Lemuel Covey, and—"

"What?" David interrupted. "Lem Covey?"

"You know that name?" she asked.

"My brother and I are with him now."

"God, David!" she exclaimed. "Don't give him any indication you know anything about this. He is a very dangerous man."

"Then why did you agree to do this?"

"My boss is a spineless bureaucrat, and he's afraid of Covey. A lot of people over here are."

"Why?"

"He's one of those men who have no limits or governor on ambition. I think his days are numbered, but right now, you know? He gained a lot of power in both the Bush and Reagan administrations but is seen as a dinosaur."

"What does he want with me?" David asked.

"One thing. The only thing he's ever cared about—the Vachon family. He sees taking them down as his ticket into the FBI or Homeland Security leadership."

"Esther?"

"Yes?"

"That slip at the hotel about the PO Box—a pretty big mistake."

"I don't make mistakes," she said.

David hung up and walked back into the restaurant. He took several deep breaths and manufactured a phone conversation in his mind.

"Everything all right?" Covey asked.

"They're very shorthanded at the hospital," David said. "I was trying to help them fill some gaps."

"You'll be back there soon enough, right?" Covey asked.

"We'll be home this weekend."

"Is something wrong, David?" Covey asked, watching him closely.

"I'm just tired," David said, wondering how he was going to make it to the Rushtons' undetected.

"Getting back to what we were discussing," Covey said, his eyes no longer fixated on David. "Somehow, this quest of yours overlaps with the Vachons. So, we have mutual interest in the outcome."

"What are you saying?" David asked.

"Simply—we can work together to achieve our mutual goals."

"But we don't care about this Vachon family," Brendan said. "We just care—"

"Yes, yes," Covey interrupted. "The thing is, here we are—and I represent the power and reach of the United States government. What do you represent, son?"

"Don't call me son," Brendan chirped.

Covey smiled and took a bite of food. He chewed slowly, almost dramatically. He took a small sip of beer and smacked his lips in an exaggerated way.

"So, this is what we'll do," Covey smiled. "We'll check in once a week. Whatever you know, I know. Whatever you find, I know. Whoever you talk with—I know. Do we understand one another?"

"You know!"

"We understand," David said, interrupting his brother. "Maybe we do have a shared interest here."

"That's the spirit," Covey said. "Make sure not to placate here. That would really chap my ass."

Covey stood, pulled a roll of bills from his pocket, and counted out some amount. He picked up his glass of beer from the table, took a final drink, and slammed the glass back down.

"You said you were our angel, here to protect us. This doesn't feel like that," Brendan said.

Covey smiled at Brendan's naïve comment.

"I'll be in touch, boys," Covey said, and walked out of the MVR.

David opened the door at the rear of the hotel and looked both ways carefully. The blue Youngstown cab pulled alongside the door as David had instructed.

This may not fool anybody, he thought, *but maybe I'll just get lucky.*

He gave the taxi driver the address, to which the driver grumbled due to the short distance to John Rushton's house.

Heading south across Route 224, it was only a couple of turns and one traffic light to the destination.

Canfield, Ohio, is not terribly dissimilar to most upper-middle-class Midwestern communities—a conglomeration of high-end suburban housing and farms. There's not a whole lot in between. Born as an agricultural community and home to the famed Canfield Fair (held every Labor Day since 1846), Canfield borders Youngstown, Salem, and Boardman. It boasts affluent and highly rated schools but has miles of open land and farms.

Canfield is also a prestigious sports community, having won regional state championships in football, baseball, girls' and boys' soccer, and tennis. Similar to Brookline, Massachusetts, Canfield had become one of the Youngstown area's destinations for people wanting to "move up," along with Poland and South Range.

Having the foresight to purchase a bottle of wine earlier, David rang the doorbell of the colonial red-brick home. The chime was a single, low tone and classical. Canfield, as much as anything else, was traditional and classical. Innovative, contemporary, and unusual were not synonymous with Youngstown architecture.

A moment later, the door opened. A young girl stood in front of him, surrounded by the familiar bedtime accoutrements.

"Hello," David said, smiling down at her.

"Are you Mr. Cost?" she asked.

"Well, yes, that would be me—Costigan."

"My dad knew you were coming, you know," she said with sincerity.

"Well, I'm glad he did," David said, still standing on the stoop.

"Abigail?" a woman's voice rang out from somewhere in the house. "Please ask Mr. Costigan to come in."

"His name is Cost-e-gann, Mom!" she screamed back into the house.

A moment later, John Rushton appeared from the other room and picked his daughter up, kissing her on the cheek.

"Well, Mr. Cost-e-gann, I'm glad you could make it," Rushton laughed.

"Me too. She's a sweet little girl," David said.

"I'm not sweet," Abigail insisted. "I'm smart."

"I bet you are," David said, realizing how much he missed his family.

The Rushton house was large, with open ceilings extending more than twenty feet, and only a few walls separating the spacious first floor. The kitchen was about twenty feet from the foyer, but the view was unobstructed. A woman, small in stature, stood on the far side of the kitchen and waved to David as he entered the house. David waved back, assuming she was Leesa Rushton.

"C'mon in," John said, motioning David into the house. "Just put your coat over any of those chairs."

There was an evident warmth and casualness to this home, though not noticeable in either the décor or its immaculate condition. David thought of his own home—with the same kind of warmth—but a home where children clearly lived. He immediately noticed nothing was out of place and thought perhaps this was akin to the ordered mind of an attorney.

"Hello, David," the woman said as he entered the kitchen. "I'm Leesa Rushton."

He took her hand, still wet from the dishes.

"Excuse my wet hands. John is always yelling at me about getting a dishwasher, but I guess I'm just traditional that way."

"Very nice to meet you," David said.

"Now Dad has to meet with Mr. Costigan, honey," John said, putting his daughter gently down onto the floor.

"Cost-e-gann," Abigail whispered, correcting her father.

"Yes, Cost-e-gann," John smiled.

John kissed his wife for no other reason than he did and then kissed his daughter. David smiled—not out of envy—but recognizing how different families were. He loved Mary and the kids with all he was, but random affection was not the Irish way. Kissing hello, goodbye, and goodnight were all part of his life, but random displays of affection weren't something he was accustomed to.

"Let's go into my office," John said, walking out of the kitchen. David followed, rubbing the top of Abigail's head as he passed.

His office was just what David expected: traditional mahogany walls, the smell of cedar, and all manner of historical items including eighteenth-century world maps, sextants, a vintage replica of the

Declaration of Independence, and of course, pictures of Youngstown at the height of the steel industry.

John sat down in one of his desk-side chairs, instead of behind the desk. This gesture was not lost on David, who, as a doctor, was sensitive to human interaction. David sat in the chair next to him and took a breath.

"So, I looked into Francis Costigan. Everything I turned up suggests he died in Anzio in 1944 and was buried there."

"I know that's what the record shows, but I have a stack of letters that says otherwise."

"Well, that's the thing," John said. "I'm not disputing the letters. Have you considered them being written by someone else—as a kind of grift?"

"Sure, but it isn't. The letters, handwriting, and tenor are the same pre- and post-1944.

John nodded. David wasn't sure if he agreed or was just acknowledging his point.

"Why are you helping me?" David asked.

"I'm not entirely sure," John replied. "I feel badly for you, I guess."

"I don't need pity," David declared.

"Oh, it's not pity. I can't imagine how I'd feel if I learned my grandfather wasn't who I thought he was."

"You knew your grandfather?"

"Yes. He was a great man—a doctor who helped this community until the day he died."

"You're lucky," David said.

"Indeed I am."

Leesa Rushton entered the office carrying two glasses of burgundy liquid.

"The wine you brought," she said, handing each man his glass.

Both men thanked the gracious and polished woman, and she left the office immediately.

The two men compared notes about growing up in Boston and Youngstown and the challenges of raising children in our technology-laden society. It was a pleasant conversation, but both men were clearly trying to get a deeper read on the other.

"Tell me about the Vachon family," David asked, watching carefully for John Rushton's reaction.

"What about them?" John replied, not seeming anxious about the question.

"Maybe the question is your relationship with them," David clarified.

John uncrossed and re-crossed his legs and set the nearly empty glass on the corner of his desk.

"The Vachon family is one of two or three philanthropic Youngstown families. I played summer league basketball and Pony League baseball with Aiden—the head of that family since his father died about fifteen years ago."

"That's not really what I meant," David said.

"I see Aiden socially now and again, and he and I are on a couple of boards together. I've represented both him and the Vachon Corporation on a few occasions. Why do you ask?"

"I was warned that our looking for information about my grandfather has alarmed him."

"Warned by whom?"

"A federal marshal named Lem Covey. Does that name mean anything to you?"

John thought for a moment and then shook his head. "Can't say it does. Why is a federal marshal involved here?"

"He has this obsession with the Vachon family, I guess."

"He told you that?"

"Sort of. There's this Justice Department agent, a woman, he coerced into setting me up."

"Setting you up how?"

"She was supposed to seduce me—well enough to get some pictures. Agent Chase said—"

"Esther Chase?" John interrupted.

"Yes. How on Earth do you know her?"

John explained that in addition to representing Aiden Vachon and the corporation, he helps by being a bridge between the Justice Department and the Vachon family. Though fundamentally legitimate now, the Vachons were still well connected to some of the most important people in the world—including the Italian, Russian, and Chinese syndicates. Esther Chase was most often the Justice Department's designee for obtaining critical information. For that, the Vachon Corporation was given the room to move toward complete legitimacy—though not quite there yet.

"I have to tell you, John—I'm still surprised every day. There's so much about this that's royally fucked up... oops, can I say, 'fucked up'?"

"This Covey business is ugly and dangerous," John sighed. "If Aiden believes you're a threat to him, that could be worse than this Covey fellow. Now, tell me the story again."

David proceeded to recount the whole story—not just since the letters—but the story of the Costigans from the beginning. He talked about his great-grandfather, and what a hard, cold man he could be. About his grandfather's unrealized dreams. He talked about his own father and the strained relationship with him—and about life since the discovery.

Feeling as though any reservation would be unproductive, he reiterated everything about Covey and Esther Chase.

John poured both of them another drink and pulled his teak humidor from the bottom shelf. The two men drank and laughed, fumbling the cutting of the cigar—not from alcohol, but from laughter. David thought about how long it had been since he laughed like this.

The laughter subsided, and John Rushton became serious, almost sullen.

"If the Vachons are trying to kill you, that's not good."

"Oh, you think?" David replied, and the two men fell back into another uncontrolled fit of laughter.

A knock came at the door as Leesa opened it. She was very small in stature, with an evident eye for fashion. Her hair was shoulder-length, and her face, for some reason, reminded David of Mary.

"Given what you boys are talking about, I didn't expect belly-slapping laughter," she said.

"I'm sorry, honey," John said.

"Can I get you something, boys?" Leesa asked.

"I'm fine," David said.

"How is your family?" Leesa asked. "John tells me you've been away from them. You and your brother?"

"Yes, I'm down here with my brother Brendan."

"You have a close family, David?"

"By Boston Irish Catholic standards, very close," he laughed. "Yeah, I think we're close. I know I miss my wife and kids like crazy."

"What are their names?"

"My wife's name is Mary. My son is James, and my daughter is Jacqueline."

"Beautiful names. I thought Irish families were partial to juniors, saints' names, and such."

"They are. We are. But I didn't want that for my kids."

"John is English-Scotch, and I'm German English," Leesa laughed. "My parents are a little taken aback by our public displays of affection."

"I think it's nice," David said. "Maybe that's what my family needs."

"Maybe," she said, closing the office door.

John rose and walked over to the far window. He opened the wooden blinds and took a puff of his cigar.

"You have it going on at both ends," he said. "This Covey guy on one end, the Vachon family on the other, and Esther Chase in the middle. Maybe it's Chase and I who are in the middle."

"Just wonderful, isn't it?"

David talked about how he felt the first time he realized his grandfather likely didn't die in Anzio—how it felt when Mike Donovan showed him the postmarks from the fifties, sixties, and seventies. He talked about protecting his father and grandmother from all these horrific revelations.

"That's why I came to Youngstown," David said. "I'm trying to find out what the real story is—without blowing up my family."

"So, they don't know any of this?"

"My grandmother must know something. The letters I found went on for thirty years. They're addressed to her."

"You think she was a party to what seems to be unraveling here?"

"I don't know anything, John," David sighed, taking a large sip of his drink. "I found a stack of letters indicating my grandfather was very much alive after the war and living in Ohio. The letters were in my grandmother's chest, and I assume she put them there. She's also been over the top my whole life about us going up into her attic. It always seemed a little excessive to me."

"I don't know," John said. "I don't have the emotional connection to all of this the way you do."

"I'm not sure it's the government," David said, puffing on his cigar.

"I thought you said Covey is with the Justice Department?"

"He is—but how Esther Chase characterized him…"

"You mean the whole lone wolf thing?" John asked.

"More than that," David replied. "It was more of an obsession, and how people in the government are afraid of him. He also pretty much told Brendan and me that."

"So, he thinks he can get to Vachon through you," John thought out loud. "How long did he say he's been chasing him?"

"I think he said more than twenty years," David said.

"And nothing, right?"

"I guess. He didn't say that, but obviously he's one frustrated old man." David laughed.

"You a Pats fan, David?"

"Oh, die-hard," David laughed. "Browns?"

"Hell no. I'm Black and Gold all the way. Chuck Noll was my idol. Cowher—not too bad. But Tomlin, damn…" John sighed. "You understand the notion of playing not to lose?"

"As opposed to playing to win?"

"Yes!" he exclaimed. "You get it."

"What about it?" David asked.

"Ducking for cover and fumbling in alleyways is playing not to lose," John explained.

"And playing to win?"

"Vachon. Straight up. We take this to the holy grail."

"You remember he tried to kill Brendan and me?" David asked.

"I remember," John said. "The timing has to be right, and I'm not sure we're there yet."

"I guess I hadn't thought about it like that," David said.

"Think about it like that," John suggested. "Every other approach has your back to them. I'm in it," he half-laughed. "Besides, I'm here in Youngstown, and this will likely inevitably roll up on me anyway. Don't you think it's better to see it coming than take it in the back?"

"I guess. But taking it at all is not all that attractive," David said.

John laughed. "So, what are your plans?"

"I have to get home Saturday," David replied. "My wife will divorce me, and the hospital will start recruiting for an ER doc. Funny how much our families are alike."

"How so?" John asked.

"We each have a son and a daughter. Both our grandfathers were notable, though for very different reasons. And we both have strong and lasting marriages."

"Yes, but you're Catholic. I'm not. Your family comes from Ireland, mine from Canada. And I don't have Lemuel Covey looking to castrate me."

David froze and vexed John over his comment. Both men stared at one another—barely a blink or breath. Then John let out a thrust of air and started laughing hysterically.

"What's so funny?" David bemoaned.

"Not having nuts would suck!" John screeched.

"Maybe that's part of all this," John said. "My grandfather was considered a great doctor here. When I was a kid, he told me being a doctor was like breathing to him."

"I don't know…"

"What about your dad?" John asked.

"My dad? He's a paradox. He's smart, business savvy, and politically astute. But he considers himself a blue-collar guy. It's almost a kind of guilt that prevents him from putting on a suit full-time."

"And you becoming a doctor?"

"Oh, he hates it," David smiled. "It's a kind of betrayal to him. Brendan—now he's the loyal one."

"So, you're the educated one, and Brendan is the good son?" John laughed.

"What? Oh no, that's not it. Brendan went to Bowdoin on a hockey ride and was summa cum laude. That's what I mean about my dad being a paradox," David said, puffing on the stub in his mouth.

"Does your dad get it now that you're a doctor?"

"He accepts it, mostly," David said. "Loyalty and tradition are very important to us Irish Catholics. I'm his heretic son. Truth is, we're very much alike, so we butt heads. Your dad?"

"He died when I was sixteen," John said. "My grandfather was more like a dad to me. He was a loving and giving man."

"Well, that's wonderful," David complimented. "You're very lucky."

"You know, the mills were mostly Italian and East European, but there were a fair number of Irish," John explained. "My grandfather would single the Irish out and say, *'Thing about those Irish Catholics—they'll work themselves to death, and there's always another generation to take their place.'*"

Chapter 7

Collision

The fog smelled good rolling in over the harbor as they entered the Ted Williams Tunnel. It had been a long drive, stopping only once for a "tonic" and a bite to go. David wanted to get home as fast as he could, wondering if everyone would have been better off if he had left this all alone.

He planned to drop Brendan off first and then get out of there before he had to talk with Rachel. He was also anxious to get home to Mary and the kids. He dropped off his brother and made his way back into the tunnel, heading west toward Brookline.

The traffic was agonizing. Not because it was heavier than normal, but because he so wanted to get home—and he was reminded Youngstown had nothing resembling real traffic.

He pulled into the driveway, grabbed his suitcase, and ran toward the front door. Before reaching the first step, the door opened. James ran out, followed closely by Jacqueline and Mary.

"James!" David shouted, scooping his son up and kissing him.

"Daddy!" Jacqueline screamed, clad in her favorite purple "feety pajamas."

"C'mere you little Stinkles!" David exclaimed, grabbing her up with his free arm. "God, you two aren't babies anymore."

"What about your old, tired wife?" Mary said, dressed more for a night out than just being home.

"Come here, wife." He said, kissing her passionately, holding onto both the kids.

"We missed you," Mary said, wrapping her arms around her family. "I am not used to you being away like that, nor do I want to get used to it."

David opened a bottle of Cabernet and poured two glasses. He handed one to his wife, now sitting on the edge of the bed, and took a probative sip of his own.

"Pretty good," he said, smacking his lips.

"That's not all you're going to like, unless of course you got some in Ohio." Mary joked.

"Oh yeah, from Brendan," he replied, trying to push the Esther Chase thing out of his head.

"Well, I am at least better looking than your brother."

"That's a fact."

Mary took David's glass and set it—and hers—on the nightstand. She ran her fingers down the back of his head, fiddling with his earlobe, something she knew he couldn't resist. She ran her hand down his back, then over his thigh and back up to his crotch. She repeated the movement a few more times, finally leaving her hand on his manhood. She rolled her fingers with the finesse only a woman can, as she leaned in and kissed him wet and strong. He kissed her back, knowing full well no one had ever kissed him like that, and no one would again. Still, the nagging guilt about the hotel crept back into his mind, as hard as he tried to push it away. Nothing had happened between him and Esther Chase, but he did go back to her room, the most inappropriate thing he had ever done.

Still, he thought, *relieving his conscience would only cause Mary pain— and for what purpose?* This was the first and only significant secret he'd kept from her, and that alone made for tremendous anxiety and stress.

She pushed him back onto the bed, straddling him with her toned Stairmaster thighs. She sat upright, crisscrossed her arms, and pulled her nightgown over her head. David ran his hands up her outer thighs, over her buttocks and waist, and up to her breasts. He always thought Mary had perfect breasts, though she had a very different opinion.

"You're wearing panties," he said, running his thumb under the thin waistband.

"I know how much you like that," she said, leaning over, inserting her tongue into his mouth.

They kissed hard, as she ground herself into his excited crotch. She moaned as she pressed into him. She slid down his torso, now lying prone between his legs. She reached up, sliding his boxers only to his knees, and took him into her mouth. Mary's mouth and hand worked in precise unison, as David began to gyrate his hips, moans now coming from him.

Making sure not to bring him to orgasm—something a wife learns only after years of marriage—she climbed back up onto him, bypassing his erection, and finally came to rest on his face. She gasped as his tongue found all of her, and she became wetter and wetter.

Mary clutched the walnut headboard as her body shook and her sighs exploded. David felt her juices running down his cheeks, and he lost all thought or sense of Esther Chase.

Mary slid down his torso, reached back, and inserted him into her. Usually, needing a few moments to accept him, Mary instead thrust herself down onto him and began to push up and down with a kind of passionate rage. Not since their dating days had she screwed him like this—but he had never been away from her so long.

He held her hips, giving additional power to her thrusts. He could feel himself building and anticipating his explosion.

"Can I cum, baby?" he asked.

"Cum in me!" she cried.

"Jesus!" he shouted, his thrusts growing stronger and higher. "I'm cumming, baby!"

"I love you David," she said, leaning down to kiss him again.

"I love you too, Mary."

David walked out of exam room five, still reading and signing the chart. He handed the clipboard to the nurse, smiling in a familial way. He walked in and out of rooms again and again, a variety of issues ranging from the flu to gunshot wounds. Being a Level One Trauma Center, the hospital was the first stop for both initially diagnosed critical issues and the transfer of critical patients from surrounding community hospitals and nursing homes.

He entered the lounge, poured a cup of coffee, and sat for the first time in seven and a half hours. He sipped on the thick, tepid liquid, more interested in the cardiovascular impact than any particular flavor. A moment later, the door opened and two EMTs walked in, winded and sweaty. One was Jesse Miller.

"Hey Doc," he said, opening the refrigerator and taking a small orange juice container. "How's your day? It has to be better than mine."

The other EMT also took a juice container and sat down silently.

"What's going on?" David asked.

"Domestic shit," Jesse said, taking a big gulp, finishing the juice. "Guy decided to beat his wife with his thermos because the coffee wasn't sweet enough."

"I better get out there," David sighed, taking another mouthful of coffee.

"Wouldn't rush, Doc," Jesse said, going for another juice. "She expired on the way here."

"What?" David asked, rubbing his eyes.

"Cracked her skull in at least two places and knocked out her right eye. There was no coming back from that."

"What about the husband?" David asked.

"Oh, he was crying for his wife when BPD dragged him away. So full of shit."

"Getting cynical, Jess," David said.

"Cynical, Doc? I'm lucky I have any faith in people at all, with what I see."

"It's not all like that," David said. "It's the job."

"Na." Jesse sighed, taking another drink. "Cruelty and deceit and pain. That's what's out there."

"No, it's not just that."

"Oh, no?" Jesse asked, tossing his juice container as if shooting a basketball. "You know that little girl, Polino? The one whose mother died in the car accident?"

"Yes."

"She's being moved into a foster home in Allston. More of a way station. Women got quite a little business going. Little Veronica will be the sixth kid in. Not bad at a grand a month a head."

"Can't save them all, Jess," David said.

"It would be nice to save one, Doc. Just save fucking one. We gotta go. See ya."

"See ya, Jess."

David tapped the coffee cup on the table, tilting his head back toward the ceiling. He drew in a deeper-than-normal breath and exhaled with equal power. He stood, rinsed his cup in the sink, and washed his hands. He exited the lounge to find nothing had changed or slowed. The same general frenzy persisted as he walked down the hall to the nurse's station. Reaching the bustling desk, nurses and doctors were involved in a chaotic dance only they could construe. David waited for the administrator to finish the phone call she was on.

Mary Louise Murray was a lifer. Twenty-five years earlier, she graduated high school and landed her first job at Boston Medical Center. This was only her second job in twenty-five years, the first being a pseudo-orderly slash candy striper. Armed with only a high school diploma, Mary Louise—as the staff called her—was asked to fill in for the administrator who was ill. She took to it the way Tom Brady took to throwing a football. It was one of those strange things you cannot teach. She just had a knack for it. One of the other ER docs once said she was the "Radar O'Reilly" of this operation—and she was. She just knew where everything was, how to get it when needed, and how to predict what each member of the ER might be asking for.

Mary Louise was heavyset, with a reddish face and deep hazel eyes. She was innately pretty, but of course, her attractiveness was offset by her weight. She was married, however. Jack Murray worked as a short-order cook at two local eateries. Combined, they made little money, but both seemed happy to have found each other.

Mary Louise hung up the phone and smiled up at her favorite doctor.

"Doctor Costigan. We missed you around here," she said. "What can I get you?"

"You know the Social Services folks, don't you?" he asked.

"Every one of them." She smiled.

"Can you track one of them down for me?"

"Sure, which one?" she asked.

"Well, I'm not sure," he whispered, trying to be very discreet. "A couple weeks back, a woman was brought in. A car accident. She died. She had…"

"Polino, right?" she interrupted.

"Yes."

"What a shame. And no family to take the little girl. I… wait, you're not thinking—?"

"Can you find who has that case? I understand she's being moved to foster care in Allston."

"Sure, I can," Mary Louise said compassionately. "There are some good people in the foster system, but there are also a lot of slugs."

"Can you also get their phone number?" David asked.

"I'll have it for you in thirty seconds, okay?"

"I'll wait."

Mary Louise fingered through her meticulous file drawer, magically pulling a file from a row she rapidly fanned.

"Okay, here it is," she said, opening it on her desk. "Let's see… Looks like Kathy Scheinfeld has the Polino case. Once they leave here, we don't have any more paper."

"Do you have a number?"

"I'll write it down," Mary Louise said.

David ordered two coffees from the Au Bon Pain counter in the Downtown Crossing food court. The apex of Boston's Downtown Crossing is the corner of Summer and Washington Streets. Growing up, it was the place people would go, not only for shopping but for experiencing the holidays and socializing. Just down the street from

the Boston Common, Downtown Crossing was for many years
anchored by the two area gargantuan department stores: Jordan
Marsh and Filene's. Filene's, of course, was also world-renowned for
Filene's Basement, where many a tale was told of women undressing
in the aisles, men fighting over a thousand-dollar Saks suit marked
down to one hundred dollars, and where every Bostonian could—
and did—boast of the greatest bargain of their lives.

The Downtown Crossing "T" station was embedded in the
second level of Filene's Basement. During the holidays, whole troops
of people from all parts of the city and accessible suburbs would
make the trek, sprinting into the store the moment the train doors
opened.

There were also Gilchrist's and Woolworth's, but they were not
the icons Filene's and Jordan's were.

"Are you Doctor Costigan?" the short, blonde woman asked.

"Kathy?"

"Yes. Sorry I'm late. Coffee for me? You're a mensch."

She took the cup and then a big gulp—certainly not a woman
overly concerned with decorum or image. She was pretty, with big
blue eyes and a definitive, though cute, Jewish nose.

"My sister-in-law is a mensch," David said, exceedingly proud of
his Yiddish acumen.

Kathy laughed loudly. "My family would call you a *shagitz*." She
laughed.

"A what?"

"A gentile woman marrying a Jewish man is a *shiksa*; a gentile
man is a *shagitz*. Kind of derogatory but not really meant to be."

"Oh," David said. "You learn something every day."

"Well, also—only a man can be a *mensch*. I'm guessing your sister-in-law is Jewish?"

"Eisenberg," he laughed.

"She's *mishpacha*," Kathy laughed.

"Mish-what?" David laughed.

"Like Italian people would use *paisan*."

"Oh," David laughed. "So, thank you for meeting with me."

"Glad to," Kathy said. "Gets me out of the office to someplace other than these homes that would make you puke."

"It's that bad?" David asked.

"You have no idea," she said, no longer using levity. "Kids sleeping on pee-stained, bug-infested mattresses—if they're lucky enough to have a mattress. Roaches crawling over babies. Diapers' hours passed due for changing. Men hanging around the kids they barely know. That's all before the abuse and neglect."

"Sounds like a mess," David sighed.

"It is. And sad. The kids become part of this cycle of abandonment and abuse. It's no wonder gang membership is out of sight. It's the only stable family some of these kids have. But you didn't want to meet for a sociology lesson."

"No," David said, sipping his coffee. "It's about one girl in particular."

"One of mine?"

"That's what they said at the hospital."

Kathy pulled her iPad from her briefcase and turned it on. She tapped her finger on top of the device, waiting for it to activate.

"There we go," she said, punching in some information. "Okay."

"Her name is Veronica Polino," he said, not even sure why he was doing this.

"Polino. That sounds…" She paused. "The car accident. Her mother died. Very sad. What about her?"

"I was told she is going into the foster system," David said.

"That's information that is sealed. I can't divulge any of it."

"I'm not looking for any proprietary information."

"Then what are you looking for? This is a three-year-old girl," Kathy said.

"What if I wanted to help her?" David asked.

"Help her? You mean financially?"

"Not exactly," David stammered, knowing full well he had discussed none of it with his wife or children.

"Maybe we should speak plainly, Doctor," Kathy suggested. "I'm a nice Jewish girl from Winthrop. I don't do subtlety well."

"What if I wanted to adopt her?" he asked.

"What? Do you even know her? Did you know her mother?"

"I pronounced her mother dead. That was it. I thought you said the system was a disaster?"

"I did," she said sternly, "but there are processes and protocols. This isn't it."

"Look, I understand," David said. "I'm asking you to help me help a little girl. I thought maybe we could figure out how to maybe traverse the bureaucracy."

"Bureaucracy is the reality. I wish that wasn't the case, but…"

"Did you ever just have a chance to do the right thing? To make a difference?" David asked.

"We all do what we can," she said.

"Who do I need to call? What are these protocols?" he asked.

She stared at her iPad, again tapping her thumbs against the sides.

"I have to tell you—this is a first," she said. "I don't even see relatives express this kind of concern. Why this girl?"

"I can't say exactly," he replied. "There's a lot going on in my family that, well… I guess got me thinking. Then there's the paramedic."

"Paramedic?"

"The one who brought the mother in. He was at the medical center a couple of days ago and mentioned the Polinos to me."

"Yeah, but why you?"

"I'm not sure. He's mentioned the daughter Veronica to me a couple of times," David said, taking a sip of coffee.

"Have you expressed an interest in adoption to him?" she asked.

"No, I expressed concern over this little girl who evidently has no one."

She looked at him, trying to assess this man she had just now met. The two looked at each other, neither saying anything—both saying volumes. Kathy moved back and forth from the iPad to David, obviously contemplating this unusual conversation.

"I'll tell you what," she said. "Let me talk with the head of DSS. She is a childhood friend of mine. We were pretty good friends in high school, and both ended up at Northeastern." She laughed. "My boss and her boss hate the fact Elizabeth stops by my office every now and again just to chat. She's always telling me I can come to her when and if the red tape gets more ridiculous than normal."

"It would mean a lot to me, Kathy," he said.

"I don't know," she sighed. "Maybe I've been doing this too long—getting numb, you know?"

David walked out of the Boston Medical Center; another fourteen-hour shift behind him. It had been a typical night of either complete craziness or abject boredom. All he really wanted was to go home and go to bed. He walked to his car, half dazed by the long night. The cold air skipped in off the harbor, stinging his face as it cut by him.

He clicked the automatic opener and starter. His car engine turned over, and the headlights illuminated the parking lot.

"David." A voice came out of the darkness, causing him to jump. Placing his back against the car, he fit the keys in between his fingers.

"Covey?" he asked, squinting at the silhouette emerging from the shadow.

"Who else?"

"What do you want? What are you doing here?"

"The second question is irrelevant," Covey said, reaching the idling car. "The first—well, making sure you know what I expect."

"What you expect?" David sniped. "I don't work for you."

"And I thought we were becoming friends," Covey laughed. "And you turning down my sweet Esther—that's no small feat, son. She is a handsome woman, wouldn't you say?"

"Okay, I'm tired. I just want to go home," David said, rubbing his eyes.

"Let's get in. It's cold out here," Covey sneered.

Grudgingly, David complied and got into his car, Covey climbing into the passenger side. David turned up the heater fan, feeling the warmth against his face and feet.

Covey reached inside his left breast pocket and withdrew a small manila envelope. From his belt, with the opposite hand, he pulled an automatic pistol.

"Now, we can either have this," Covey said, holding up the envelope, "or this." He held up the weapon. "Your call."

"What is all this? Is this the Vachon business?" David asked.

"Of course, it is—and you're going to help me."

"How can I help you? This is not what I am doing. I am just trying to find out about my grandfather."

"Oh, boo hoo," Covey said, pretending to wipe tears from his eyes. "Do you think I give a damn, or am playing here?"

"What is it you want me to do? I don't…"

"I want you to keep doing what you were doing."

"What was I doing? Fumbling around, looking for scraps of information about my grandfather?"

Covey smiled, as though delighted at David's epiphany. He raised his white, unkempt eyebrows and smirked.

"You are going back to Youngstown, and you're going to keep digging," Covey said.

"And if I don't?"

"Vachon will find you—or kill you. Either way, he'll be out of his rat hole."

Covey's eyes were wide now and sparkling.

"He thinks he's legitimate. He passes himself off as a straight-up guy—building malls and statues of his scum-sucking grandfather.

Legitimate. That's a laugh. You, Mr. Costigan, will be the end of him."

"Why would I agree to that?" David asked, fear turning to anger.

"That pretty wife of yours—not to mention those two sweet kids. That's why."

Covey tapped the pistol against his temple. He leered at David, looking for any sign he had acquiesced. Then he placed his pistol back into its holster, buttoned his coat, and stepped out of the car. He leaned in, his head just inside the window.

"Don't screw around here," he said in his drawl. "I know everything you do."

He smiled at David, slammed the car door closed, and walked away into the darkness. David sat frozen, feeling like this was a bad movie with a bad script. It wasn't a movie, however. People like Covey did exist. He took a breath and told himself he had to think— had to keep his head. But Mary, Jackie, and James... This was out of control, and he was out of his league.

As much as David had no interest in the ironworks for himself, he still loved the sounds and smells there. It reminded him of his childhood, when he and Brendan would visit his father and Uncle Tom. He entered through the side utility door, but several of the long-standing employees recognized him and gave him a resounding hello. This was not lost on either Brendan or David, from the office that sat directly above the main factory floor.

Brendan motioned for David to come up. David was hoping to get Brendan to come down, but it was too late for that.

He climbed the thirty or so metal stairs and walked across the short steel connector into the office. He opened the door, stepped in, and the deafening sound from the factory floor faded into a modest roar.

"Well, my prodigal son has returned from his rust belt excursion. To what do we owe this honor?" Patrick said sarcastically.

"I'm not in the mood, Dad," David replied.

"Oh, you take my number two away for the better part of a week, and…"

"All right!" Brendan interrupted. "Can we have a temporary armistice, please?"

"Can I talk with you for a second?" David asked his brother.

"You two talk," Patrick said, throwing his pencil down onto the drafting table at the center of the office. "I'll check on the crew."

Patrick exited the office, making sure the slamming door sufficiently conveyed his mood.

"What's up? I thought you'd be working straight through till next summer," Brendan said.

"Covey came to see me," David said.

"Here?"

"Outside the hospital. He was waiting for me last night after my shift."

"What'd he want?" Brendan asked.

"To make sure I understand I have no choice but to help him."

"With that Vakon, Vak…?"

"Vachon. Aiden Vachon," David said.

"To do what exactly?" Brendan asked.

"Drag him out of his rat hole, as Covey said," David replied.

"How exactly do you do that?"

"By digging into stuff like before," David sighed. "Covey thinks that will force Vachon to come after me."

"By being a staked-down goat?" Brendan asked.

"Pretty much."

The brothers walked across the factory floor, their conversation well masked by the industrial noise. Almost every worker stopped for a moment to acknowledge David. Though he was not technically part of the business, the workers liked him, and most had known him so long, their pride in his career was more like uncles than coworkers.

At the far end of the floor, Tom Costigan stood jotting something on the clipboard he was holding. Tom was the apparent antithesis of his brother. Certainly not stupid, Tom was regarded as the classic underachiever by most of his family. He had little, if any, interest in running the company, growing it, or its overall success. Instead, Tom wanted an eight-hour-a-day job without the stress and responsibility Patrick embraced.

Without their father pushing him, Tom looked to his big brother for security and retirement. In the family, folks knew from the beginning that Tom was not well equipped to share the reins of the company, so this arrangement benefited both him and his younger brother. Tom was still a Costigan and possessed many inherent traits from his father and brother. So, for both familial and practical reasons, Patrick made his brother shift supervisor during their busiest time of the day. Fortunately, Tom actually did a good job, making Patrick's decision palatable to the company at large.

"Uncle Tom," David said, extending his hand.

"Well, Dr. Costigan!" Tom laughed, pressing his nephew's palm. "To what do we owe this honor?"

"Just came by to say hello," David replied.

"You picked the busiest day in a while, so I can't hang out too long," Tom said.

"I didn't want to intrude, Uncle Tom," David said. "But I didn't want to come by without saying hello."

"Glad you did."

The brothers continued walking, finally reaching the side access door. Brendan opened it, and the two men stepped out into the quiet cold.

David blew his breath, as if exhaling a puff of smoke.

"Cold day," he said, trying to recalibrate the conversation.

"So, what the fuck are you going to do?" Brendan asked. "You're not going to do this?"

"What choice do I have?" David asked. "Maybe if he gets what he wants, he'll leave me alone."

"Are you fucking crazy?" Brendan shouted. "Vachon already tried to kill us. You think you'll beat the odds and he'll miss again?"

"Then what the hell do you suggest?" David appealed to his brother.

"I don't know. Go to the authorities. Go to Dad."

"Dad?" David laughed. "And tell him what? His father didn't really die; he wasn't a hero? He decided to abandon his family and become someone else? That ought to be a great conversation."

"Don't you think we're a little over our heads?" Brendan chided.

"We? What we?" David asked. "I…"

"I was with you in that stupid Bocci place in Youngstown. Do you think Covey has forgotten that?"

David let out a breath and took a deeper one in. He placed his hand on the outside wall of the factory, leaning his weight onto it.

"I'm sorry, Bren," David sighed. "I am just worried."

"That's why you have to ask Dad for help. He's the most grown-up I know."

"Not yet," David said softly. "I just can't yet."

"Don't make him bury his son," Brendan demanded. "I'll kill you if you do that."

Brendan described convincing Rachel to let him go back to Youngstown as something that made the Israeli Palestinian problem seem simple. He had to tell her the truth, and what was at stake. Even Rachel Costigan couldn't argue against resolving this crisis.

The drive down Eighty-Four and through Scranton and west on Eighty seemed even more painful than the first time the brothers traversed it. With nothing resembling a plan, the brothers made their way into a situation they were unequipped for and scared to death about.

They spent the hours driving and compared each other's Boston sports acumen. Obscure questions about various sports personalities filled the time and generated much laughter.

"So, who kicked the field goal in the Nineteen-Eighty-Two snowplow game?" Brendan asked, certain his big brother wouldn't have a clue.

"Hmmm, think you have me?" David laughed.

"I don't think you have the foggiest idea."

"Would he have anything to do with 'Wheatabix'?" David smiled.

"You son of a bitch!" Brendan screamed, punching his brother in the arm. "You know!"

"Of course I know, you idiot," David laughed. "I've been a die-hard since before you could even spell football."

David was, of course, referring to the English soccer player turned American football player, John Smith, who kicked the game-winning field goal against the Miami Dolphins in the infamous snowplow game. At the time, there was no explicit rule about adjusting the field due to weather. The game was played in a certified blizzard, and snow had rendered the field and its markings invisible. Then-coach Ron Meyer summoned a small plow onto the field so Smith could manage the field goal. The plow did, and Smith did as well. The rule was soon changed. John Smith was also hired as the endorsing athlete for Weetabix crackers and soon became synonymous with the brand.

Oddly, coming through Liberty on I-Eighty was familiar to them—familiar in an uncomfortable way.

After checking into their Canfield hotel, David repeated his previous stealth, sneaking out the rear door, but this time making his way only to the restaurant just a quarter mile away. Assuming his cell phone conversations were no longer private, he told the restaurant hostess his cell wasn't working and that he had an emergency. She was a petite and friendly young woman, who didn't think twice about letting him use the house phone. There was only one number he thought to call.

David entered the restaurant carefully, almost neurotic about seeing Covey in every corner. He let the heavy door close as a young, tall man approached him—well-dressed, groomed, and mannered.

"Welcome to Michael Alberini's," the man said, stopping two feet from David. "Will you be dining with someone?"

"I'm waiting for someone."

"Would it be Mr. Rushton?" the man asked.

"As a matter of…"

"He called ahead," the man said. "He'll be a few minutes late. He's a regular with us."

The young man seated David at the far end of the second level. The restaurant was appropriately dark, making David feel a bit safer. The man brought David a glass of water and left two menus on the table. A few moments later, the heavy door opened, bringing sunlight dancing into the restaurant. John was greeted by several of the restaurant workers, followed a moment later by a man who appeared to be the owner.

The same young man looked toward David, motioning to where he was seated. John followed him up the three steps to the second level until reaching the table. Patrick stood as John extended his hand.

"Welcome back," John smiled.

"Call me a cop," David replied sarcastically.

The young man looked at David, seeming to understand the inside humor between the two men. He excused himself, indicating he would soon return to take their order.

John took a sip of water. "Sorry I'm late. I had a very needy client."

"No worries. Thanks for meeting me."

"Of course. How often do you get to Youngstown?"

David brought John up to speed. He described his encounter with Covey in Boston and what Covey was demanding of him. John sat and dutifully listened, as any good attorney would. David expressed his fear to John, and his regret for involving him in this situation.

"No regret, David," John said. "It's like blaming the rape victim for what the rapist did."

John told David about growing up in his family in Youngstown. He described his world, and his grandfather in it. Ernest Rushton was a kind and certainly benevolent man, expecting character and achievement from those around him but also understanding the plight of many through no fault of their own. He was, for much of his life, a community or neighborhood doctor. Before the advent of expanded health insurance—and even before Medicare and Medicaid—Ernest Rushton was a familiar sight in the East and North Sides of Youngstown. House calls were his standard, and children were his passion.

Though always drawn to help sick and chronically ill children, this passion was amplified after the calamity of 1977. He saw the fate of the children of the thousands who lost their jobs as both a crime and a sin.

"Did you bring a suit with you, David?" John asked.

"A suit? Yes, but how does this help with Covey?"

"It has nothing to do with Covey," John explained. "This is more personal than that."

"Okay."

The waiter returned and took their food orders. The restaurant was still very quiet, as it was more a dinner than lunch destination.

"Tomorrow night, meet me at my house at six-thirty. Okay?" John asked.

"Sure. Where are we going?"

"Stambaugh," John replied.

"What's Stambaugh?" David asked.

"Stambaugh Auditorium," John said. "You'll see. This will be a great time."

"What about Covey?" David asked.

"Let me think about that a bit," John said, as their food arrived. "I have an idea, but I need to noodle on it."

Brendan lay across one of the queen beds as David tussled with his tie.

"I always hated these fucking things," he said, pulling at the silk.

"Where are you going?" Brendan asked.

"Some auditorium in Youngstown."

"For what?"

"John said it would be meaningful. Beyond that, I don't know."

"Do you want me to go with you?"

"I'll be fine. Besides, you can't go like that."

David stared out the window as the SUV, as they wound around the perimeter of Mill Creek Park.

In 1891, the famous Youngstown attorney Volney Rogers bought options from more than ninety Youngstown landowners to begin the creation of what is now Mill Creek Park. The second-largest city park in the United States—larger even than Central Park in New York— Mill Creek runs from the northern tip of Canfield all the way to the South Side of Youngstown. Covering more than 2,600 acres and twenty-one miles of roadways, Mill Creek is a lake-filled oasis, much of it abutting the destitution that arose after the collapse of the steel and associated industries in the Mahoning Valley.

"This is Fifth Avenue," Leesa said, turning around to David. "Look at these homes. It's such a shame. There was a time the homes around Wick Park rivaled any in the country."

"This is all from the steel industry fiasco?" David asked.

"Pretty much," she said. "When all that happened, it also killed the hundreds of businesses that fed it. That was almost every business in the Valley."

"Do you think it will ever come back?"

"Hard to say," she sighed. "Some say our whole generation has to go before the will to embrace real change can happen."

"This was a pretty big crime city too, wasn't it?" David asked.

"Yes," she said, pointing to an open space across from the auditorium. "We were a big union town. That—and the geography— made it ideal, I guess."

"Geography?" David asked.

"Halfway between Cleveland and Pittsburgh. It was a perfect location to control the Ohio Valley."

"I remember studying that in school," David laughed. "Wasn't Washington instrumental here?"

"Surveyed a lot of it when he was a British soldier," John interjected. "The Ohio Valley was the frontier at one time. Can you imagine that? It was called the Western Reserve."

David and the Rushtons climbed the steep concrete steps up to the entrance to Stambaugh. All the way up, and into the beautiful early 20th-century foyer, people greeted John with a "Hi, John," or "Hi, Mr. Rushton." It was clear he was well known in this community and looked more like the mayor than just a respected attorney.

"So, you're going to let me in on what this is about?" David asked.

"Look," John said, pointing to a large poster resting on a black, oversized easel in the corner adjacent to the bustling open bar.

"The Mahoning Trumpet Thirty-Sixth Commemoration Banquet," David read aloud. "What is the—"

"You are an impatient Irishman," John interrupted. "Let's get a drink, and we'll go find our table."

"It's a wonderful event," Leesa smiled, extending her arm to David.

Leesa, dressed much like the other hundreds of women, wore a tea-length black dress, sporting a black shawl against the winter air. Most of the men wore tuxedos, but there were enough suits to make David feel less out of place.

They ordered their drinks and made their way to the second-story lobby, set up as a banquet hall for the event. At the far end of the lobby, a six-piece orchestra played soft classical music from their velvet-covered makeshift stage.

John led Leesa and David to the table closest to the stage, a card sporting the number "1" at the center of the perfectly set table.

They took their seats, David gazing about the crowded lobby, painfully curious about this mystery event. A few moments later, another couple took their seats, greeting the Rushtons as old friends. John introduced David, and the two men exchanged politically appropriate pleasantries.

Two more couples joined, and then a third. When the third couple arrived, the other men stood, greeting the man with a reverence that separated him from the others. It was hard for David to hear over the sextet. He watched the man as he acknowledged the other couples at the table. David was struck by the man's sharp features, his sculpted face looking like many of the celebrities seen at the Emmys or Academy Awards. He was ruggedly handsome and commanded a kind of respect familiar to David, reminding him of the politicians his father would entertain. The man's wife was also classically beautiful—golden blonde hair, a low-cut red dress, and diamonds sparkling from her ears, neck, wrists, and fingers. *Royalty* was the word David thought, watching the two.

Sensing the greetings were concluding, David rose, anticipating the coming introduction.

John motioned toward David as the couple turned toward him.

"Aiden, Marie, may I introduce David Costigan from Boston."

"David Costigan?" the man said. "I've been looking forward to meeting you."

"I'm sorry?" David replied.

"David, this is Aiden and Marie Vachon," John said.

"Come."

The voice came from inside the office as Esther Chase opened the door.

"Come in, Esther."

Mark Lockland rose quickly through the Justice Department ranks, finding that perfect blend of ability and savvy. Esther liked him personally, though she found his acceptance of dysfunctional politics diminished him. He was young, just thirty-two—one of the youngest department heads in all of Justice.

"Sit down, Esther," he said.

"This sounds ominous," she said.

"Not at all," Lockland said. "You're the best field agent I have."

"So, is this a commendation?" she laughed.

"Well, not exactly. How are you? How are your husband and daughter?

"They're fine, Mark," she said impatiently. "Look, can we get to it? We're both busy."

"You've really got to learn the art of schmoozing, Esther," he said, closing the hard-sided planner on his desk. "It'll hold you back otherwise."

Esther looked at him but didn't respond. She had long ago accepted the limitations Mark's critique identified—but she also accepted who she was.

He stood from the desk and stepped to the window behind it. His office sported a perfect view of the Washington Mall, and a first-edition reproduction of Mort Künstler's rendition of Chamberlain's Gettysburg charge hung just to his right. Esther was deeply trained and experienced in reading people from every possible perspective: how they talked, how they carried themselves, what they wore, and what they surrounded themselves with. She knew from their first meeting who Mark Lockland was, what level of ambition he had, and what he valued. He fell far short of being a politician, he was far too ethical and committed for that. Still, he knew the game and how to play it. At some level, Esther appreciated Mark doing it, so she didn't have to.

"I received a call from Undersecretary of State Cooper this morning," Lockland said.

"And?"

"It seems our friend Mr. Covey wasn't all that impressed with how you handled your assignment."

"You know, Mark, I—"

"Wait, Esther," Lockland interrupted. "I owe you an apology."

"Apology?" she asked.

"Sometimes I even get caught in the politics," Lockland said. "Covey is well connected, and it's given him a kind of impunity. So, I went along with his plan." He sat back down in his chair and crossed his hands. "You are not an unattractive woman, Esther, and that was the primary driver behind Covey picking you. I'm embarrassed I didn't tell him to shove it up his ass. I'm sorry."

"Well, thank you for saying that, Mark," Esther said. "But what are you going to do about him? He's evidently off his Virginia rocker."

"He's not the only one with connections," Lockland said, sitting back. "It's not a terrible thing to have an in with the Attorney General. First cousin, actually."

"You're going to talk with him?"

"Already did," Lockland smiled. "I don't think we'll be bothered by that son-of-a-bitch again."

Esther looked down pensively, calculating both her thoughts and words. She looked up and stared at her boss.

"What about David Costigan?" she asked.

"Costigan? You mean the guy you were supposed to set up in Youngstown?"

"Yes. How will we get him out of Covey's sights?" she asked anxiously.

He rubbed his lips with his thumb and forefinger, also calculating his words.

"Look, Esther," he started. "I can only do what I can do. I stopped Covey from meddling in this department. I don't have any influence out there."

"We're the fucking Justice Department," Esther scolded. "What do you mean we *can't* help him?"

"This is interdepartmental stuff, Esther," he said with conscious calmness. "There's already a belief Covey is a problem. The AG would have to take a more aggressive action, but frankly—it's bad politics."

"Bad politics?" she smirked. "Costigan only wants to find out the truth about his family, and we let Covey do what he wants?"

"Look, we only have so much authority here. Besides, if Covey really does get Vachon through this—well, not such a bad outcome."

Esther looked across the desk at her boss. Though it troubled her, she understood the political and practical reality of the situation.

"I just feel for the guy," she said. "He's a decent man. Not too many of those around these days."

"Then send him a Christmas card, Esther."

Aiden Vachon sat down in his seat, not taking his eyes off David. stared back in kind.

"I've wanted to meet you, Mr. Costigan," Vachon said.

"You have?" David asked. "Well, haven't you?"

"Excuse me?" Vachon said, with just a whisper of indignation.

"This is not the time or place," John whispered to David.

"I've wanted to meet you as well, Mr. Vachon," David said, an insincere smile on his face.

"David. Call me Aiden."

"Okay, Aiden," David said, elongating the name.

"Tell you what," Vachon smiled, not a man ruffled by much. "Will you be in town tomorrow?"

"I will."

"Are you here alone?" Vachon asked.

David smiled. "No, I'm here with my brother."

"Excellent." Vachon nodded. "Why don't the four of us have lunch at my club? John knows where it is. Say, twelve-thirty?"

"I think that would be fine," John said. "David?" he snarled.

"Sure. Twelve-thirty would be great."

Several awards and presentations were given over the next hour. David and Vachon traded sarcastic smiles and stares throughout the proceedings, while John quietly refereed the tension he had underestimated.

A short, balding man in an ill-fitting tuxedo climbed onto the platform, taking a position behind the podium. The man tapped on the microphone and cleared his throat. Gradually, the cacophony of voices and pinging China gave way to silence. David and Vachon continued to trade stares, though David fully understood he was far out of his league.

"Good evening and thank you for coming out on this cold night," the bald man started. "I am Mike Mortello, your host this evening."

Mike Mortello expressed his appreciation to the community and the board for the privilege of being chairman for the past three years.

"I'm told we have some out-of-town guests with us tonight, so a bit of history," Mortello said.

In 1977, after the collapse of the steel industry in the Mahoning Valley, a handful of community leaders identified a crucial need among many. This need was related to the children of families tragically impacted by the dissolution of thousands of jobs and their inability to provide adequate healthcare, nutrition, and yes, even Christmas presents to their families. In cooperation with various churches and synagogues in the valley, The Mahoning Trumpet was formed to provide just these things.

"There are many people to honor and thank, but two men especially," Mortello continued. "We are fortunate to have their grandsons on our wonderful board of directors—and I am, of course, speaking of Henri Vachon and Ernest Rushton. John and Aiden, would you stand?"

The two men rose, and the applause was deafening as the gathering also rose to their feet.

"John Rushton and Aiden Vachon are not only respected members of this community," Mortello said. "They are active members of this board, neither losing sight of the vision of their respective grandfathers." He continued, "It is not an exaggeration to say these two families have impacted the children of the Mahoning Valley more than any other."

David sat and listened to a story that transcended one, two, or ten families. This was a story that had impacted thousands of families and children, at a time when need was never greater.

Dinner concluded, and the crowd took to the dance floor. John and Leesa and Aiden and Marie were no exceptions, and it made David think of Mary and wish she were here.

Returning to the table, Aiden Vachon retook his seat, but Marie Vachon remained standing.

"Would your wife be terribly bothered if you danced with me?" she asked David.

David looked over at Aiden, eyes open and eyebrows raised.

"Don't look at me," Aiden laughed. "Totally your call."

"I'm sure she wouldn't mind," David said, standing and courteously taking her hand.

The two walked a few feet to the dance floor. David placed one hand on her hip and, with the other, clasped her hand. The band played *What a Wonderful World* and assumed the lead with his dance partner. The dance area had cleared as dessert was being served. David, taught by his father to be a good dancer, swept Marie Vachon across the floor with ease.

"Wow," she laughed, feeling his guidance as she followed. "Where did you learn to dance like this?"

"My father," he said, feeling his answer sounded ridiculous.

"Your father taught you to dance?"

"Not literally," he said apologetically. "He believes being a good dancer is one element of a man being a man."

"That's different," she said.

"I'm not talking about ballet," he laughed. "He says a man needs to be able to take his wife out dancing and not look like an idiot doing it."

"I guess there's a certain streetwise romance to that," Marie smiled.

David glanced over at Aiden Vachon, who seemed content—if not disinterested—in the dance floor. Aiden Vachon was never in a non-working state of being, so his wife's dancing with another man was inconsequential to him. There was also an evident understanding between the couple regarding Marie's role as Aiden's wife. She, too, had a job to do.

"Have you been married long?" she asked him.

"It's been a while," he said. "But we're happy and have two great kids."

"Boys? Girls?" she asked.

"One of each," he smiled, thinking about them.

"We have a daughter. She's grown—and two beautiful grandchildren. You know, my husband is a powerful man, but he's a good man."

"Are you telling me—or yourself?" he asked.

"I already know he's a good man. But he can't afford to be a boy scout."

"I guess we can all rationalize doing what we know to be wrong."

"That's a very simplistic way of looking at the world," she said. "Sometimes all we have are two wrongs, and we have to pick the lesser of the two."

"Really? And you believe that, truly?" he asked.

"Look around, David. There is so much good here. There were some questionable practices that made this possible. How can you argue with that?"

"I'm not a Machiavellian, Mrs. Vachon," David chided.

"Then you simply haven't been confronted with that reality yet. But you will at some point."

"You mean, I will choose between two evils? Unlikely," he said confidently.

She stopped dancing but kept hold of David's hand. She looked over at her husband and then about the ornate lobby.

"Sometimes the only choice you have is that" she said. "My husband means you no harm or bears you any ill will."

"I'm not sure what you mean," he said.

"Yes, you do," she said.

"What—that he tried to kill my brother and me?"

The song ended, but the two dancers had not moved. Aiden glanced over at them and smiled. Marie had no misconceptions about her role.

"*Try* and kill you?" she laughed. "David, my husband doesn't *try* to do anything. He *does* it. If that was what he intended, we wouldn't be dancing."

"So, he didn't shoot at us?"

"You're having lunch tomorrow, yes?"

"Evidently," David said.

"Talk with him. He is not your enemy."

The two dancers walked off the floor, returning to their seats at the table. Marie kissed her husband as she sat—not an obligatory or utility kiss, but a sincere show of love and devotion between two people.

The remainder of the night was less intense, and David began to feel comfortable enough to have a drink or two. He danced again with Marie Vachon and then with Leesa Rushton. It struck him: these people were unknown to him a few short weeks ago, yet here he was at an event he had no previous knowledge of.

It was, in the end, a very good night.

"C'mon, bro," Brendan said, shaking his brother over the bedspread. "We're supposed to be at your friend Rushton's house in less than an hour. You need a shower, man."

David coughed as he rolled onto his back. He pushed the hair off his forehead, looking down and realizing his shirt and tie were still on. He lifted the covers, only to see his bare legs.

"Well, I managed to get my pants off," he laughed.

"You did," Brendan smiled at his brother. "It took you almost ten minutes of hopping around the room."

"What, and you didn't help me?" David asked.

"And spoil that great show? Fuck no. Now let's go."

The brothers picked John up right on time, as he directed them out of his neighborhood to the Juniper Country Club just a few miles away.

"Did you have a good time last night?" John asked.

"I did," David said. "I think I had a little too much there toward the end."

"You hummed *Danny Boy* all the way back to our house," John laughed. "Leesa thought you might spend the night at our place."

"Why didn't I?" David asked.

"Let's just say, you were a bit indignant at the offer."

"Oh. Sorry about that."

The driveway rolled up a hill and wrapped around the front of the country club. It was a brick, almost gothic architecture, the snow-covered golf course visible at the sides of the main building. Though it was winter, there were a significant number of cars parked adjacent to the circular drive.

John pulled the car to the front door, as the valet attendant was already making his way to the vehicle.

"Mr. Rushton," the teenager said, opening the driver's door.

"Teddy," John said, exiting the vehicle.

Brendan and David were already out of the car when the boy made his way to their doors. John climbed the two or three steps to the entryway, and the brothers followed.

Inside, it was just as David imagined: old but immaculate red carpeting, walnut-finished walls replete with all manner of golf memorabilia, an open wood fire burning in the center fireplace, and the Christmas tree and associated holiday ornamentation covering a large portion of the main rooms.

A middle-aged man dressed in a jet-black suit approached the men as they pulled off their coats and gloves. He approached John first. The two men shook hands as John gave him some quiet directive.

"Gentlemen. Mr. Vachon has reserved our Poland Meeting Room for lunch," the man said, taking each of their coats. "Would you care for something from the bar?"

"Beer, any kind," Brendan answered immediately.

"I'll have a martini, dry," John replied. "You know my taste."

"Yes, sir," the man said.

"How about a ginger ale for me," David said.

"David made a bit too merry last night," John laughed.

"Yes, sir," the man nodded.

"Here we are."

The man pushed open the beautiful oak door, the three men proceeding into the classically decorated room.

Walnut paneling covered the bottom half of the walls. The top was painted hunter green, and the two contrasting coverings were divided by a two-inch-wide cherry chair rail, providing even greater contrast. Vintage clubs, shoes, and golf bags lined the room, and the walls displayed golfers from the 1920s and '30s.

The table was heavy oak, and the chairs were high-backed and leather, giving the feel of a boardroom or academic institution.

The three men sat down, each withdrawing their respective smartphones, and presumably catching up. Just a few moments later, the door opened again, and Aiden Vachon stepped into the room. The same man entered just after him and handed out four leather pads, each holding a newly printed paper menu.

"Please, gentlemen," Aiden said. "I'm required to spend so much money a month. John, you know—I'm not even close to my quota."

"The gnocchi are the best in Youngstown," John said.

"What the… I mean, what is gnocchi?" Brendan asked.

"It's really Pugliese cavatelli here," John smiled.

"You mean pasta," Brendan said.

"Just order it and eat it!" David scolded. "So, all these wonderful pleasantries aside, you don't like us being here."

"I have no issue whatsoever with you being here," Aiden commented. "In fact, I'm delighted you could come. You're just digging into some information that, let's say, creates issues for all of us."

"Why you?" Brendan interjected. "I—"

"Bren, enough," David said. "You have to forgive my brother. He tends to be cranky when he's hungry."

"Hmmm." Aiden smiled. "My father and grandfather taught me, the loser in any situation is usually the first to lose his head. You have evidently learned that as well."

"Working in a high-volume emergency room forces that lesson. But back to my question."

"That seems an unproductive conversation," Aiden said, getting up and pouring himself a glass of water. "Why don't we get to what it is you want?"

"Well, you *not* trying to kill us would be a nice start," David said.

"Yes, Marie told me you and she touched on that. I will confess to being a bit too melodramatic, but I wanted to get a clear message across."

"By killing us?" Brendan again interjected.

"You were never in any real danger—well, at least not from me. It was only meant to dissuade you from continuing to poke around."

"And now?" David asked.

"I asked you what you wanted. You never answered me."

"I am only interested in finding out the truth about my grandfather. Your dealings and business are of no interest to me," David insisted.

"He's telling the truth, Aiden," John said.

"And you, John?" Aiden asked.

"Well, given how little we know, a little truth would probably make me happier also."

The man in the suit reentered the room and took the four lunch orders. He asked if there were any other drink requests and left the room again.

Aiden stood and walked around to the far end of the table. He opened a cabinet that was part of an elaborate built-in shelf and cabinet system. He knelt down and pulled a plaque from one of the inside shelves. He laid it on the table.

"Take a look," Aiden said.

The three other men stood, so as to see the plaque lying flat on the walnut table.

The Annual Youngstown Benefactor Award

Presented on This Day

April 9th, 1979

To

Ernest Rushton, MD

For Service to The Neediest in our Community

"So, this is who Ernest Rushton was," Aiden said, running his fingers along the outer edge of the plaque.

"That's not what I mean," David said, trying to get back to where he wanted to be.

"What else is there? This is who the man was."

"Can you tell me anything about Francis Costigan—my grandfather?" David asked.

"Anything?" Aiden smiled. "There are some things, yes.."

David sat down, trying to calculate the best way to talk with a man like Aiden Vachon. He looked across the table at his host, determining the less said, the better.

"Well?"

"He found his way to Youngstown while the war was still raging in Europe," Aiden said. "Turns out, Youngstown was ideal—with the steel mills and all."

"I was under the impression my grandfather wanted no part of steel or iron," David said.

Aiden ran his fork around the edge of his plate, never taking his eyes off David and Brendan. David didn't know this famous—or even infamous—man, but he could see Aiden Vachon was mentally agonized, struggling to find the right words. Then, almost imperceptibly, Aiden's demeanor shifted. So subtly, in fact, that Brendan kept right on eating, and John was too focused on David to notice.

John wiped his mouth and, in a fluid motion, noted the time on his watch.

"I appreciate the lunch, Aiden," John smiled. "I'm glad I was able to connect you, David, and Brendan. If anyone can help them, you can, Aiden. David, Brendan, I'll leave you in good hands. Aiden, if I don't see you sooner, I'll see you at the Max Scheinfeld Golf Outing."

John pushed his Aiden, looked up at him and rubbed his palms together.

"You should sit, John," Aiden suggested.

"Aiden, I'm falling way behind at the office. You don't need me to hold anyone's hand."

"No, that's true," Aiden said. "Sit anyway". Aiden carefully folded his hands onto the table and reset his fingers a couple of times.

"I'm talking to all of you," Aiden said.

He flexed his lips and wrinkled his nose.

"All right then."

Aiden Vachon described the early life of Francis Costigan more compellingly than anyone in the Costigan family could have retold it. He told them of a man burning to fulfill his dream in medicine but confronted by the attitudes and mores that made that impossible. He described the friendship between three Army buddies who would, in almost every circumstance, gladly give their lives for one another. He described a man in tremendous pain—caught between his duty as husband, father, and son, and the agony his family refused to acknowledge. He spoke of a conversation between Henri Vachon and Francis Costigan, presenting an extraordinary option that took Francis weeks to come to terms with. He described his great-grandfather as the ultimate architect of the strategy that allowed Francis to escape his torment, without completely betraying his family. He described a man ceasing to exist—and another being created.

"So, it's true?" John said. "Francis Costigan didn't die in Italy. He came here."

"Certainly, yes. My great-grandfather made arrangements through his Sicilian partners to smuggle Francis out of Italy and back to the U.S. Francis, my grandfather, and Joe Brady had to figure out how to 'kill him off.' John involuntarily nodded, neither shocked nor saddened by the story.

"And they did?" David asked.

"That was the easy part. They put Francis Costigan's dog tags on a casualty. The night of his alleged death, the men my grandfather trusted took him. That was the end of Francis Costigan."

"I never knew any of this," John said. "Did David's grandfather fade into some obscure life?"

Aiden took a sip of water, set down the glass, and motioned to someone at the far end of the restaurant. David glanced over, noticing the restaurant host acknowledge Aiden's gesture and move out of sight.

David's heart began to race, his mouth going dry. Was this a setup? Is Youngstown so utterly corrupt that they could be murdered right here—and no one would ever know what happened.

David shot up from his seat. "I have to leave."

"Please sit down, Mr. Costigan. No one here means you any harm. Least of all me."

"Like Jennie Goodearl?" David snapped.

Aiden casually wiped his mouth with his napkin and cleared his throat.

"You came here to learn the truth about your grandfather. That is what I'm prepared to provide. And I had nothing to do with Mrs. Goodearl's death. She was loved by my family. It wasn't me who murdered her."

"Covey?" David asked.

Aiden tipped his head slightly forward and stared at it. No words were necessary.

A moment later, a large man—*huge*—approached their table. He was NFL large: clad in black trousers, a black sweater, and a black sport coat. His hair was cut to a stubble, and his facial shadow was dark and ethnic. He sauntered toward them with the grace of a dancer or a skater. His smooth style seemed antithetical to his sheer physical size.

As he reached the table, David slid his chair back, ready to jump and run if needed.

"Hello, Rocco," John said, reaching out and shaking the giant's hand.

"Mr. Rushton."

"David, this is my associate, Rocco Donofrio. Rocco has been with me twenty-five years," Aiden said.

The man extended his hand toward David. A random storm of thoughts fired in David's head. *Was John Rushton part of a sinister conspiracy? Was this Rocco here to execute David and Brendan? Were Covey and Vachon part of the same conspiracy?*

David reached for the man's hand. It dwarfed his own—as he had once dwarfed his children's hands at their birth. The strength in Rocco's fingers was significant, yet David felt no malevolence in his grip.

"Mr. Costigan, I've looked forward to meeting you for some time," Rocco said, releasing his hand.

David nodded.

"My apologies for frightening you. We didn't know why you were snooping all around."

"I thought you were just shitty shots," Brendan quipped.

Rocco smiled. David did not.

"Sit down, Rocco," Aiden instructed. "Maybe you can help me in providing Mr. Costigan with the truth about his grandfather."

Brendan looked at Rocco as he sat, following his movements with tactical curiosity.

"Is there a problem?" Rocco asked Brendan.

"Remind me not to do anything to piss you off. I appreciate the use of my legs," Brendan said.

John, Vachon, and Rocco all smirked simultaneously.

"I guess there's an inside joke here," Brendan chided.

Aiden sat up at the table and raised his hand. "No disrespect intended, gentlemen."

"Did you graduate from the Rocco School of Broken Bones?" Brendan mocked.

Rocco's demeanor tightened. Aiden reached over and placed his hand on Rocco's forearm.

"Actually, Rocco is a Stanford graduate—both undergrad and Master's. He was also their three-year starting right tackle."

John moved his arms to gain everyone's attention. He succeeded, as the full attention of the table was on him.

"Aiden, David and Brendan have come a long way. Maybe you could sort of cut to the chase about their grandfather," John suggested.

"It's a bit trickier and more complicated than that, John," Aiden explained. "I'll try."

Aiden continued to describe Francis Costigan's journey to Youngstown and how Marcel Vachon orchestrated everything. He described Francis' arrival and Marcel Vachon's help in obtaining his enrollment at the University of Pittsburgh Medical School. He recounted how Francis could not simply abandon his family, and how Marcel—and Henri upon his return from war—warned Francis that continued contact was very dangerous.

"Wait, wait," David protested. "This is going too fast. So, my grandfather fakes his death, with the help of his friends and Marcel Vachon; comes back to this area; goes to Pitt Medical School; and keeps contact with my grandmother? Then Francis Costigan didn't cease to exist after all?"

Aiden drew in a contemplative breath and folded his hands atop the table. A moment later, two waiters returned with varying dessert orders. The plates were circulated around the table until each man had a taste of mousse, spumoni, and tiramisu.

"No need to wait on protocol, gentlemen. Dig in," Aiden instructed.

John cut a small piece of Veal and slid it into his mouth. After a few chews, he restarted the conversation.

"So, if Francis Costigan ceased to exist, where did he go?" John asked.

"Well, he stayed right here," Aiden replied.

"Right here?"

"John, where is your grandfather from?" Aiden asked.

"A little town just outside Halifax, Nova Scotia. I've visited there."

"I'm afraid he didn't. I hoped never to share this with you."

"Aiden, we're not here to talk about my grandfather. We're here to talk about David's," John instructed.

"That's what I'm doing, John. Your grandfather isn't from Halifax. Your grandfather is from Boston."

"Boston, huh?" John pondered. "No, no, wait…"

"My great-grandfather understood that to be successful, an entire history needed to be created—complete with birth certificates, military papers, and a specific town or city from where he hailed. A new human being was invented and born."

"What new human being?" John asked.

Aiden stood and drank some water from the glass. He seemed anxious and troubled. Though Aiden Vachon's insight and planning skills served him remarkably well, he never once anticipated this eventuality.

"Aiden, who did Francis Costigan become?" John inquired.

"Francis Costigan ceased to exist in July of 1944, and Ernest Rushton was born."

John was frozen. His breathing stopped, and his eyes dilated many times their normal size. His bottom lip fell away, and his chin dropped to his Adam's apple. His eyes bounced about in their sockets, signifying a kind of panicked disbelief.

"Wait, wait," John contemplated. "My grandfather is Francis Costigan?"

"No," Aiden said. "Your grandfather was Ernest Rushton, to be precise. Francis Costigan died in Italy."

Brendan snapped out of his seat and stumbled backward a few feet. Instinctively, Rocco shot up and positioned himself between Aiden and everyone else.

"Whoa, everyone!" Aiden insisted. "Now do you see why I was slow in putting this out there?"

John and David sat quietly, paralyzed by Aiden Vachon's proclamation.

Brendan tipped at the waist, until his head was close to his knees.

"Are you alright, Brendan?" Rocco asked.

"Are you telling us Francis Costigan and Ernest Rushton were the same fucking guy?" Brendan asked, still bent like a clothespin.

"My great-grandfather invented John Rushton, his Canadian family, his heritage, and every piece of governmental documentation—including his military deferment to permit his medical school attendance."

David stood with surprising restraint. He slid both hands into his pants pockets and walked over to the window overlooking the Juniper Golf Course.

"This is nuts and fucking bullshit!" Brendan announced, now standing upright.

John remained frozen in his seat. David turned and surveyed the room.

"It makes perfect sense. And it explains a lot." David affirmed.

"My grandfather was Irish?" John sighed.

"That's the biggest problem for you, John? Is it?" David scolded. "You 're that offended over learning you have Irish blood?"

"Get real, David," John replied. "It's not about being Irish or French or French Poodle. It's about a revelation that just tipped my reality on its head."."

"Welcome to the party, John," David said., a sly sarcasm in his voice. Aiden sat back in his chair and pinched the bridge of his nose.

"Did you take note of anything last night?" Aiden asked. "Look around you. Look at what my grandfather and Dr. Rushton accomplished. Look at the lives they touched."

"And what about my family?" David asked angrily. "They were— we were—just casualties?"

"Casualties?" Aiden laughed. "Did he ever abandon you? Did he ever not support you?"

"What—you think money makes it okay? My father grew up without a father. What about him?"

"Your grandfather felt he hadn't a choice. He did the only thing he believed he could. My great-grandfather helped him."

"And what was the price?" David asked.

"Price?"

"What did my grandfather have to pay for this transformation?" David asked again.

"I don't understand," Aiden said.

"C'mon, you create a ruse that fakes his death and invent a person he becomes. You're saying your great-grandfather did that for free?"

"He did that because my grandfather loved him and would have died for him. Cost? The only cost or expectation was that Ernest Rushton would be the best doctor he could be—and be the personal physician to my family if he wanted to."

"That's it? That's the whole deal—with all the intrigue and lies?" David asked.

"What is it you want?" Aiden asked. "A little sci-fi and some government conspiracy?"

"It just shouldn't be that easy to erase a life and create one out of thin air," John said.

"Easy? Who used the word easy?" Aiden said. "There was nothing easy or inexpensive about it. It was difficult, and it has been carried through three generations. You met Jennie Goodearl."

"We did," David said. "If I hadn't..."

"Stop," Aiden said. "You have to learn—bad things often happen to good people, and it's not always our fault. You had no idea that would happen."

"So, my grandfather sent checks to Boston for...?"

"They still go," Aiden said. "That is part of his trust and wishes."

"Who sends them?" David asked.

"This isn't the forties anymore. That is all automated."

"Then someone in Boston gets those deposits," John said. "Who is that?"

"David's grandmother has always been the recipient. That has been since the beginning—both the checks and the letters."

"So, she's always known, David?" Brendan asked.

"I don't know, Bren," David sighed. "But that would explain her neurosis about the attic—and her very split personality."

"And she's had to live with her husband bailing on her for all these years?" Brendan asked.

"Evidently," David said.

"Wait, wait," Aiden interrupted. "He never bailed on her, as you say. He made sure your family was supported."

"This is the second conversation I've had around money making things okay," David said.

"You tend to interpret, David," Aiden said. "I said he never left his family. I never said it was okay."

"What about Dad?" Brendan asked.

"Dad? Dad has no idea—and can never know."

"Granny Elizabeth has kept this from everyone all these years?"

Aiden shot up in his chair, laughing almost uncontrollably. "Your grandmother is called *Granny Elizabeth*?"

"We're Lace Curtain Irish," David laughed, easing the tension of the moment.

"You know, David, Brendan, John… Your grandfather did a lot of good in this community. He is a hero to many."

The three men looked at each other, none of them having fully digested all of it.

"David" Aiden started again. "I understand you have another problem."

"If you mean Lemuel Covey—yes. It is a big problem. And it involves you."

"He wants to get to me through you."

"He has basically tasked me with, well… you know." David stammered.

"No, tell me."

"He, uh, told me to bring you out of your rat hole."

"So, our Mr. Covey had you come back and ferret me out of my lair. How are you going to do that?"

"Look, Aiden, I'm no spy. I asked him the same thing."

"And he said?"

"Just go back and start digging around. He told me you'd come after me again."

"In other words, put yourself at risk?"

"He threatened his family," John interjected. "He referenced David's wife and two small children."

"He also set up a woman at the hotel where we were staying—to get me to cheat on my wife," David added.

"That day I didn't come down to breakfast?" Brendan asked. "I knew you were acting weird."

"And did you?" Aiden asked.

"I didn't. But the truth is—it was close."

"He has been relentless for twenty years. We have been an obsession with him."

"That seems apparent," David said.

"What are we going to do?" John asked. "Do you think he's bluffing about David's family?"

"I wouldn't think so," Aiden said.

"Then what?" Brendan asked.

"Then you do what he asked you to," Aiden said.

"What?" David asked.

"You went to the event last night, and I seemed anxious when you talked with me," Aiden said. "I told you to go home."

"And I just go home? Just like that?" David asked.

"It's Mr. Covey we want to bring out of *his* shit hole," Aiden said.

Chapter 8

Decisions

David stepped out through the large glass doors, the cold air waking him from a long and grueling night. There were no major traumas, but a myriad of broken bones, cuts requiring stitches, and one man with a rodent carcass needing removal from his anus. Those were always the cases that made him question his career choices.

He gazed around, always anxious about Covey, and where he might be. It had been two weeks since his meeting with Aiden Vachon. As far as Covey was concerned, David hoped he believed David was following through.

He walked toward his car and was relieved upon reaching it. He climbed in and started the engine. His breath was a thick stream of white steam, due to the extreme cold. Giving the engine a few moments to warm up was always a good idea. Then he spotted a plain white envelope, the size of a small holiday card, wedged into the slit where the shifter rested. He opened it and found a neatly folded piece of paper and a small gold Italian horn—the kind that had gone out of style in the 1970s.

Anxiously, he unfolded the paper, gazing at the parking lot as he did:

Trying to keep you safe,

Your Peanut Bridge Angel

In Downtown Youngstown, as you travel into Federal Plaza on Mahoning Avenue, you cross over the Mahoning River on a steel bridge featuring the "Planter's Peanut Man." There is no commercial significance to the emblem. It was something the bridge builders decided to do. From then on, the bridge has been affectionately called the Peanut Bridge. Any Youngstown native knows exactly what "The Peanut Bridge" is. It is as embedded in the fabric of Youngstown, as "The Dorchester Gas Tanks" are to the citizens of Boston.

At first, he thought this was a joke, but there was nothing at all funny about his situation. He was well over his head in whatever this Vachon business was all about, and then there was still the elephant in the room.

He flashed his pass against the garage exit sensor, and the gate rose, letting him pass. The roads felt slippery to him, so he decided to take the back streets home. Cutting through the city, he made his way across Dorchester and Southie, then up Mass Ave.

Kenmore Square was awash in Christmas ornamentation, stretching from the Storrow Drive off-ramp to the convergence of Beacon, Brookline, and Commonwealth Avenues. Halfway through the square, David realized he had no conscious recollection of how he'd arrived at this junction. Hundreds of Boston University students and commuters flooded the crosswalks, heading to their respective destinations.

Commonwealth Avenue was also decorated with the holiday spirit, and David floated back to the hundreds of times he'd made this drive—free from the current anxiety now forced upon him. He turned onto Babcock Street, glancing at T. Anthony's Pizza. On impulse, he turned into the parking lot just after the restaurant, feeling as though a slice of pizza might be good medicine.

The counter was three-deep when he entered the shop, filled mostly with patrons much younger than him. As he moved closer to the counter, he noticed a man to his right who seemed very much out of place. He was older—a short and stout man; Italian in his complexion and features; sporting a long black trench coat and a rumpled gray hat.

David glanced in the man's direction. The man casually smiled and then looked away. This interaction repeated several times, as both men reached the counter simultaneously.

David ordered a slice of pepperoni, paid the clerk, and stepped off to the side. The Italian man also stepped away from the counter, taking a spot adjacent to David. For a minute or two, the two men did not acknowledge one another, though David could not escape the feeling of strangeness—not fear.

"Cold night," the man finally said.

"Yeah, and getting colder," David replied in the customary manner.

"Good pizza here?" the man asked.

"Really good," David said. "Never been here?"

"Nah, I'm from Youngstown, Ohio," the man said.

David turned, staring at the man. Though there was a clear toughness about him, he was very calm and poised, though he had to know his answer was provocative.

"Youngstown, huh?" David asked.

"Ah huh."

"And you're in Boston because?"

"Because you're here," the man said, without the slightest hint of emotion.

"Who are you?"

"I'm the Peanut Man," the Italian man said.

"Like in the note," David asked.

"Like in the note. There are people trying to look out for you."

The clerk called David's name, and he reached over, taking his small plate. A moment later, "Dom" was called out, and the Italian man took his slice.

"You want to find a table?" the Italian man asked.

"Might as well."

The two men found a table in the corner, under several pictures of BU athletes who went on to successful professional careers in the NFL and NHL.

"Pretty good," the Italian man said. "But I'm not sure it has anything on Wedgewood."

David took a bite, not taking his eyes from the Italian man's face. He took a sip from his bottled water and wiped his hands.

"So, what is this all about? The Peanut thing, all of it?" David asked.

"Mr. Vachon is concerned for you," the man said, leaning forward onto his forearms. "He wants to make sure you and your family are safe."

"In other words, he wants to make sure I don't give Covey any information."

"No, that's not it," the man said. "What is it you could tell him? What do you know? The only value you have to Lemuel Covey is getting Mr. Vachon to make a mistake. That won't happen."

"So, you're here to protect me—is that right?" David asked.

"Yes," the man said, taking another bite of his pizza.

"You know, my life seems to be a series of lies and half-truths. Why should I believe this?" David asked.

The Italian man smiled as he rolled some latent flour with his fingers.

"What choice do you have?" he said, shaking his head. "Would you prefer Covey?"

David pushed his elbows over the back of his chair, shaking his head as he thought. He rubbed his forehead, not really sure how to respond.

"I think everyone has their own self-interest at heart. What happens to me and my family—well, so what."

The man leaned in toward David, resting his chin into his open hand. His eyes were calm and focused as he watched David intently.

"I am Rocco Donofrio's uncle," Dom said. "Aiden has no interest or patience for games. He sets out to do something, and he does it." Dom paused. "I can shoot the center out of a Kennedy half at a hundred yards. I would have to be unconscious to miss you and your brother by ten feet."

"And what is the point?"

"He means you no harm," the man said. "Furthermore, your grandfather was important to him."

"You knew him?" David asked.

"Sure, of course," Dom smiled. "I knew him well."

"And he was what they say?" David asked.

"You know, you can break the world down to two kinds of people: givers and takers. Ernest Rushton was a giver. He changed people's lives in ways we can hardly calculate."

"You cared about him," David said.

"Yes, I did. And I cared about Jennie Goodearl."

"So, it's not just business for you?" David asked.

"You have to stay calm and centered," Dom replied. "You can't let emotion cloud thinking. But no—it is not just business anymore. Jennie Goodearl isn't dead because it was necessary. She's dead because he enjoyed it."

David stopped chewing and stared across the table at a man who so much more acutely understood the world around him, could be demonstrably calculating and cold, but who also possessed a kind of moral compass—something likely demanded by his employer.

"So, what then?" David asked. "You just stay here indefinitely?"

"Our Virginia friend is desperate," Dom said. "Our sources suggest he has been advised to cool his jets on this. That won't sit well with him. Rats in corners get vicious."

"So, my family and I are basically fucked."

"We don't always make the situation. We can only manage within it," Dom said. "You're not fucked. Not if you're smart." He leaned in toward David, pointing in an instructional way. "Covey decided, in his own twisted mind, you were somehow his ticket to getting Aiden Vachon. As crazy as it might be, that's the way it is. We must deal with the world as it is, not the world we wish it was."

"You sound like my father," David said.

"Not surprised. Your grandfather taught me that," Dom said, smiling.

"How the hell did you find me?" David asked, taking a cautious bite of the savory pizza.

"I didn't. I followed you," the man said.

"But you were here before I was."

Dom laughed. "If anything, you were looking for Covey, not me."

Dom wiped his hands with the thin paper napkin. David, who believed he needed to be more observant, watched him closely. The man wiped his mouth and sat back in his chair.

"It's okay, David. It is pretty cliché, I suppose. Rocco Donofrio is my nephew. My full name is Dominic Stagno."

"Sit down," Mary said, pulling the tin-foiled casserole dish from the oven. "I tried your mother's red beans and rice."

"Isn't it just red beans and rice?" David laughed. "I didn't know my mother had a patent on it."

Mary set the dish in front of her husband, poured him a glass of cold milk, and sat down beside him. He blew on his fork as he tasted the Cajun delicacy.

"Now this would make my mother jealous," he laughed.

"Glad you like it. So, what's going on?" she asked.

"You mean Youngstown?"

"I mean all of it," she said sternly. "I took a call for you today."

"A call? From whom?" he asked, taking another bite.

"A woman from DSS. Scheinfeld was her name."

"Oh, with everything going on, I didn't have a chance to…"

"David," Mary interrupted. "I get the thing with your grandfather, but why the hell would you talk with someone about adoption, for Christ's sake, without consulting me?"

"I know. I was wrong," he said apologetically. "This poor little girl—she has no one."

"You realize you have two kids of your own you already spend too little time with," she said.

David put down his fork and pulled Mary onto his lap. She looked at him, trying to maintain her frustration and anger. It was hard for her to do. David took a breath and told Mary everything. She stared at him with anxious eyes as he recounted his trip to Ohio, the meeting with Aiden Vachon, and the man, Dom, at T-Anthony's. Mary's eyes opened ever wider as he told her about Lemuel Covey and what he demanded of her husband. She reached over and took a large mouthful of the milk she had poured for him.

"And this Scheinfeld woman?" she asked.

"I obviously wasn't going to do anything alone," he said.

"You already did."

She kissed her husband and pushed herself off his lap. She opened the cabinet behind him and pulled out an open bottle of Merlot. She poured the burgundy liquid into the appropriate glass, took a sip, and returned to the table.

"Sometimes you just need a drink," she said, half-joking. "I get you, David. I always have. I never questioned your integrity or values, but the world is not your personal game board."

"Do you remember the song they put in my profile at the hospital?" he asked.

"It was Pink Floyd, wasn't it?"

"Yup. 'On the Turning Away,'" he said.

"Oh yeah. That's a good song."

"It's about responsibility and duty. It's about things not always being someone else's problem. No more turning away from the pain and downtrodden."

As frustrated as she was, she knew her husband was all about doing the right thing and living by a defining set of principles. He would often tell his children, character is the only real measure of a person, and the measure of a man's character was his word. She knew that—but would often joke about her husband's communication skills, or lack thereof.

She listened intently to what David was relating to, astonished at the various personalities he was revealing. One of the characters was Esther Chase.

"So, these people will go so far as to destroy your family and your marriage?"

"I don't think there's much they wouldn't do."

"And this woman Esther—she was attractive?" she asked.

"She was."

"And did you want to be with her?" Mary asked, her eyes welling up.

"No, I did not and do not," David said without hesitation.

"Then why would he try and tempt you like that?"

"I don't know. I'm a guy?"

"What did she look like?"

"I don't know, Mary," David said, really wanting to drop this part of the conversation. "Blonde hair, kind of pretty."

"Kind of pretty," she said, shaking her head. "'Kind of,' meaning prettier than me."

"No, of course not," he said. "Nothing happened. I wouldn't allow it."

"Something happened," she said coldly. "It was enough that you feel like you have to tell me."

"I don't like keeping secrets from you," he admitted.

"Secrets?" She pretended to laugh. "If nothing happened, then there isn't a secret, is there?"

David crossed his hands on the table and rubbed his thumbs together. He comprehended the hole he had dug but also understood there was far more at stake here than an indiscretion that didn't even happen. Still, he knew additional care must be taken in what he said and how he said it.

She began to talk again, but he put his hand on her shoulder. She stopped.

"Mary, I love you, and nothing happened between Esther Chase and me," he started. "That isn't what this is about. This is about extortion and threats and my family in danger—because I just couldn't leave well enough alone.

She took another mouthful of Merlot, taking her time swallowing the oaky liquid.

"I'm not sure I'm that thrilled you told me all of this, but I love you too, and I know you will always tell me the truth. The thing about it is," she said, rubbing the back of his neck, "you didn't do this. Your grandfather did. This was his decision. It would be like blaming the GIs who found the concentration camps in Europe for the atrocities against the Jews. You always say the truth is the truth."

"I love you, Mary. I love you more than my life. You know that."

"I do know that, but you are up to your Irish ass in alligators." She smirked.

"You know who you need to talk to," she said.

"Mary, I can't. He's the one—"

"Do you trust me?" she interrupted.

"Of course, but—"

"Sparing your father has dropped to a distant second here," she lectured. "Your family, your children are at risk. That genie is way out of his bottle."

David took a sip of milk, staring into his wife's eyes.

"Mary, I'll think about it."

"No, you won't, honey," she said. "Listen to me. Thinking time is over."

John stared out his study window, the snow whipping around like a white tornado. The warm air from the Gulf, combined with the cold air coming off Lake Erie, made Northeast Ohio weather both unpredictable and often dangerous. It turned unusually cold, even by Northeast Ohio standards. Canfield's geography, as part of the Mahoning Valley in the center of hills to the south and east, created a wind tunnel effect that lowered the ambient temperature several degrees.

He walked back to his desk, sat down, and turned his laptop back on. The same page he was reading yesterday appeared on his screen. It was an article written by Kurt Staley, a well-respected columnist for the *Vindicator* in the sixties, seventies, and eighties. So well respected, it was common to see his work in the Cleveland and Pittsburgh papers—and on several occasions, Boston and Buffalo.

The article was written in 1982; a tribute of sorts to a man who saw a region in need—the children of the families most affected by the shutdown of an industry that served an entire region and provided the country with the steel it required in the most urgent of times.

Staley described Ernest Rushton as a visionary and a hero. He outlined in detail the birth of *The Mahoning Trumpet* and the man who was characterized as more savior than mortal. John read the article before and even spoke about it at a myriad of Ohio Valley events. Reading it now, however, was somehow different.

Was the genesis of *The Trumpet*, as it was called, diminished by the new truth of his life? Would the families and children served by it think less of him—or it? Other than his own need to cope with this and his own identity, what material difference did it all make? He was, after all, John Rushton—community leader, father, husband, and successful attorney. If he looked into a mirror, he would see the same man he did before the advent of David Costigan and Lemuel Covey.

So, did it really matter? To him, it did. He was, after all, the progeny of the Rushton tree and not the Costigan lineage. But now the truth has changed it all. It changed his heritage, legacy, and even his very ethnicity. He was not English-Scotch after all. He was of Irish descent—a consciousness far and away different than that he had known his entire life. Instead of Cornwallis and Montgomery, it was Joyce, Bobby Sands, and the IRA.

He wondered: what if a Jew learned his grandfather was a Gentile German, rather than a Jewish survivor of Auschwitz? What would that mean? Would he think the Holocaust less cruel and less terrible? Would he suddenly feel a greater affinity for German people and be more forgiving of their complicity in the near annihilation of a people?

He was neither German nor Jew, but the difference between English and Irish was just as dramatic—and was perceived quite differently by each. Then there was the Boston element. Irish and Irish Catholic was one thing; Boston Irish Catholic was something else entirely.

And what of his children? They too now had the reality of their ancestry. Would he change that? Would he reveal this to them, or would he deprive them of the truth and this new family?

He picked up the phone and dialed. A moment later, he heard the ringing.

"Hello?" a familiar voice answered.

"David, it's John Rushton."

"Hi John," David said, clearly happy to hear from his Youngstown friend. "What's up?"

"I guess I just needed to talk. I have been sitting here reading about my grandfather."

"You mean Ernest Rushton?" David asked.

"Yes."

"What about him?" David's tone changed.

"All the good he did," John said. "How do I look at this? How am I supposed to feel about him?"

"What's the real issue here, John?" David asked. "Is it finding out you're really Lace Curtain Irish?"

"No, it's not about that," John protested.

"Then what's it about?" David asked.

"Who I am. Where I come from."

"You're John Rushton. Nothing changes that. You've made your own life and your own success," David encouraged.

"I was his grandson," John sighed. "That gave me some privilege I probably wouldn't have had otherwise."

"You're selling yourself short. I'm Patrick Costigan's son. I still made my own way," David said strongly.

"And what about my kids?" John asked.

"I can't tell you what to tell them," David said. "They're young. They have new relatives no one knew about. The rest can come when they're old enough to understand."

"I don't know," John said rhetorically. "It's a mess."

"Why is it a mess?" David asked. "It's different. It's not what we thought it was, but it's just different now."

"It's not the same for you," John insisted.

"Why's that?" David quizzed.

"You are still who you thought you were. The difference for you is your grandfather didn't die in Italy after all."

"And how's that different?" David asked.

"You know," John said.

"No. All I know is, turns out your grandfather was Irish. That seems to be the problem here."

"It's not about names or religion. It's about who you believed you were."

David paused, thinking about his next words.

"I think you need to really look at what's bothering you," David started. "If I were English, would this be as hard for you?"

"David…" John sighed.

"It's okay, John. It's a lot to deal with, and how you feel, however you feel—is legitimate. But don't delude yourself. Besides, we Irish have made a science of suffering. It helps us get through just about anything, and anything we can't deal with, we sweep under that big Celtic rug."

John laughed, and his laughter made David laugh, and the two fed off each other's cackling. It was, in that moment, as if they had known each other all their lives—and this laughing fit was somehow consistent with a life lived.

David turned the corner at the nurse's station; his eyes focused on the chart he was studying. He signed the paper and handed the chart to the secretary. Several nurses intercepted him, each giving him specific patient updates and looking for his direction.

As he finished with the nurses, the secretary handed him a piece of folded note paper. He stepped away from the desk and unfolded it.

Call me: Kathy Scheinfeld 508 444-6767

David told the nurse he was taking a short break, turned, and walked out of the emergency room. He walked down the long hallway to the main foyer and pushed his way through the side door into the biting chill outside. He pulled out his cell phone and dialed the number on the paper.

"DSS," an unfamiliar voice answered.

"Hi, this is Dr. David Costigan. I am—"

"Ms. Scheinfeld has been waiting for your call, Doctor," the voice interrupted. "I'll connect you."

There was a short beep, and then elevator music piped through his phone.

David watched his breath condense in the cold air as he blew out a silent whistle. His hands were already cold, so he tucked his left hand into his pocket. He felt impatient—mostly due to being out in the uncomfortably cold air, and the east wind spinning in off the harbor.

"Dr. Costigan?" a female voice came through.

"Kathy?" he asked.

"Yes, it's Kathy Scheinfeld. I have some news for you."

"Is it about Veronica Polino?" he asked.

"Yes. There is still investigative work to be done by Children's Services, but your application has been approved."

"Approved?" he asked, thinking about his conversation with Mary.

"Yes, you know—adoption. Do you remember the food court at the crossing? Is there a problem, Doctor?"

"No, no, of course not. I am at the hospital, and it has been a rough day."

"Now, I will need to schedule an appointment with you and your wife initially; and then your whole family," Kathy said pragmatically.

"My kids, you mean?" he asked.

"That would constitute your whole family, yes?" she laughed. "Maybe we should talk later. You seem very distracted."

"You see a lot of suffering here," he spoke. "Things are never really what you expect."

"I suppose not," she said.

"You have this image of your life and world, and what is right, wrong, and true. Then it all just gets blown up."

"Are we talking about the same thing?" she asked.

"It all seems so simple and real," he said, staring out toward Quincy Bay. "They tell you a story about your world and history, and you just assume it's so." He grimaced against the icy wind. "Then you find something that just rips it into pieces and changes everything."

"Are you all right, Doctor?" she asked.

He pulled his hand from his pocket and wiped his face.

"Yes, I am fine, Kathy," he said more confidently. "Whatever we need to do to move this forward, let's do it."

"Will you and your wife be available next Monday?" she asked.

"I think so, but I need to check my schedule. Oh, and please start calling me David."

"Can you let me know, David?" she asked.

"I will call you later today."

He walked back inside the warm hospital and made a note to call Kathy Scheinfeld on his smartphone. He arrived back at the emergency room to find an ambulance just arriving. The EMTs jumped from the van as several nurses ran to meet them. Opening the rear door, they pulled the gurney from inside, taking care not to disturb the IVs in place.

As they entered the room, David prepared himself and what he had been—

"What happened?" David asked, starting to evaluate the patient.

"Gunshot," the EMT answered. "Right in the gut, close range, and high caliber. He's lost a shitload of blood, and I think the bullet tore through his liver.

"Let's get the portable X-ray into Five, stat," David shouted, as they hoisted the blood-soaked man onto the bed.

The nurses finished tearing off the man's shirt and cleaning the bullet area so David could see the status of the wound.

"Jesus," David said, evaluating both the entrance and exit wounds. "He is torn to pieces inside. I'm not sure why he's still alive."

"Doctor?" one of the nurses asked.

"Let's get some plasma going. I also want to look at brain activity. There's a tremendous amount of blood loss here."

It was absolute chaos—the only way to be effective in an ER situation. Nurses seemed to run around in a haphazard way, with a myriad of barks and orders from every corner. It was, however, a finely choreographed dance, and every one of the players knew his or her job precisely.

The door burst open, and a young woman was trying to pull her way into the room, held back only by a security guard gripping her arm. She was screaming, evidently related somehow to the dying man on the table.

"Jimmy!" she screamed, as the guard pulled back on her.

"We'll do everything we can, ma'am," David shouted, "but you need to wait outside."

"Jimmy!" she screamed again.

David looked back over to her, was about to insist she leave, but then it hit him. He knew this girl. She was his Uncle Tom's niece—Meaghan Kelly.

"Meaghan," David shouted. "Is this Jimmy McGough?"

"Yes!" she screamed. "He told me to wait in the car, and he ran into the Cumberland Farms for cigarettes."

"You have to go with the guard, Meaghan," David said. "I need to focus here."

The automatic doors opened as David stepped out into the waiting area; his scrubs soaked in blood from chest to knees.

Meaghan Kelly was sitting on a couch against the wall, her mother holding her head against her chest. Mothers are never more vital than at times of trauma. As he approached, Meaghan's mother noticed him first, her eyes signaling caution in whatever way he had to communicate. David shook his head in the negative. She knew exactly what that meant. She rubbed her daughter's head and whispered something into her ear, then made the sign of the cross.

Meaghan lifted her head; her face lined with melted mascara. She looked at David but said nothing. David too remained silent, but their communication was prolific. She began weeping loudly again, her agony clear and profound.

From David's left, a uniformed Boston cop approached him. David nodded and the officer acknowledged him.

"Officer," David said as he moved to the opposite side of Meaghan.

"Bad situation, Doctor," the officer said. "The whole thing is senseless."

"It always is," David replied.

"No, I mean even as a crime, it makes no sense."

"What do you mean?" David asked.

"This guy waited for McGough to get into the store and then gunned him down."

"I don't…"

"It wasn't a robbery. The clerk said the guy bought a pack of gum and paid for it. Then McGough walks in, buys a pack of cigarettes and goes to leave. This guy pulls his piece and fires one shot. He had to know where he was shooting."

"What do you think?" David asked.

"I ain't a detective, but I think Jimmy McGough was a target. I don't think this is random."

"He's just a kid," David sighed.

"Yeah. Class valedictorian and a great kid at that."

"You're right. It doesn't make any sense, "David said.

Mary finished putting the dishes into the dishwasher, closed the door, and turned it on. She walked over to the kitchen table, where Jacqueline was sitting on David's lap.

"Why don't you go play with your brother," Mary said, sitting down next to her husband. "I want to talk with your dad."

Jacqueline did as her mother requested. Mary leaned forward, placing her hand over David's.

"You seem even more stressed than usual," she said, rubbing her thumb over his hand. "What can I do?"

"You know Meaghan Kelley—Uncle Tom's niece?"

"Yes, sure. She's engaged to… what's his name?"

"McGough. Jimmy McGough," he said.

"That's it."

"He was shot to death earlier today," David sighed. "Meaghan was there. It was a mess."

"Oh my God. What happened?"

"I'm not sure. It was in the Cumberland Farms in Southie, on Broadway. The guy just shot him. He didn't rob the place or hurt the clerk. The cop at the hospital thinks the guy was gunning for McGough from the get-go."

"Why?"

"No idea," David said. "Like I said, it's a mess."

"What else?"

"Remember that young girl? The one whose mother was killed in the accident?"

"Yes… and why don't I think I'm going to like this conversation?" Mary said, only half-joking.

"She needs a home, Mary. She needs a family—a mother and father," David implored.

"I'm sure she does," Mary said, working to remain calm. "That doesn't automatically translate into our family."

"I know that. But remember the Pink Floyd song?"

"We do what we can, David," Mary said, placing her hand onto his face. "You can't save the world by yourself, honey."

"I'm not talking about the world," he said sternly. "I'm talking about one little girl."

Mary stood, walked over to the refrigerator, and pulled out a carton of orange juice. She poured two glasses and returned to the table. She took a sip and set the small glass onto the table.

"What is it you'd like to do?" she asked. "You want her to magically become part of this family?"

"No magic, Mary. I have no illusions about how hard this can be."

"You have no earthly idea, David," she smiled. "You've always had that Jesus syndrome of yours. It's part of why I love you—but even David Costigan has limitations."

"We have to do something, Mary," David said. "I don't know why, but we've been called to this."

"Called by who—God?" she asked. "There are thousands of orphans. Why this girl?"

"I don't know, Mary," David said, squeezing his wife's hand. "I just know this is what we're supposed to do. Have I ever felt this way about anything?"

"Being a doctor," she said.

"This is just as strong," David sighed.

"What about Jacqueline and James?" Mary asked.

"They'll adjust—and maybe learn something about giving and sacrifice."

"Look, David," she started. "You just have to give me some time to absorb this, even conceptually. This is not like buying a new car."

The intercom buzzed. John answered.

"There's a man here who says you'll want to see him, Mr. Rushton."

"A man? What man? Does he have an appointment?"

"No, but he said he only needs ten minutes, and you'll want to talk with him."

"Who is he?"

There was a pause, as the intercom was not active.

"He says his name is Covey," the receptionist said. "He…"

John rose from his chair and pulled open his office door. The man in the reception area turned and smiled at him. He wore a long winter coat and gloves. His white hair and goatee contrasted brightly against his coat and felt hat.

"Mr. Rushton," he said in his mid-Virginia twang. "I thought you might have a few minutes for me."

"Hold my calls for fifteen minutes," John said, letting Covey pass him into the office.

John closed the door and walked around behind his desk. He sat and took a deep breath.

"I won't take up much of your time," Covey smiled. "I seem to be having some difficulty gaining Mr. Costigan's attention. I thought we might talk about that."

"Why don't you talk to him?" John asked.

"Because I'm talking to you," Covey said, sitting down in one of the wooden side chairs and removing his hat. His thick, curly white hair fell out, the back bouncing down past the bottom of his neck. He reached inside his coat pocket, withdrew a folded newspaper page, and placed it on John's desk. John looked at him, then at the paper. Covey motioned with his head, and John picked up the periodical. He unfolded it and laid it flat onto his desk.

John read the headline and the story. He stopped and looked up at Covey, sitting perfectly still with a quintessential shit-eating grin on his face.

"All right, a shooting in Boston. What does this have to do with me?"

"Did you know the unfortunate man's fiancée is related to our David Costigan?"

"How would I know that?" John asked.

"Well, if our mutual friend had connected any of the dots, I imagine you would have heard something from him."

John leaned back in his chair, picked up the paper with two fingers, and tossed it toward Covey.

"Now that is a mite uncouth, don't you think?" Covey asked.

"Are you trying to intimidate me?" John asked angrily. "I don't even know what you want."

"Yes, you do. You both do. Now, this time, someone is not terribly close to either of you—well, you know. Next time, maybe it won't be such a stranger."

"Mr. Covey," John started.

"Call me Lem."

"Mr. Covey, why don't we talk plainly? What do you really want me to do? All this dark back-closet stuff is not very illuminating."

"I want Vachon. I don't care how or what I get him for. I just want him gotten."

"What does that have to do with me or with Costigan?" John asked. "You seem to think we have some kind of inside track on him. We don't."

"It's not easy to get his attention—but you have," Covey smiled. "I want some admissions here. I want to hear Vachon talk about his business—and some of the more illicit parts of it."

John looked at Covey, disbelieving both the conversation and the man. This was assuredly a bad movie, with an even worse script. If not so serious, John thought, this could almost be comical.

"Let me connect with David," John said, knowing the most important thing was to get Covey out of his office and buy some time.

"I am neither patient nor foolish," Covey replied, crossing his legs and leaning back in his chair. "You do that. You connect with David Costigan. But know this—you have no secrets from me."

John stood, knowing a man like Lemuel Covey understood strength and could see weakness through any façade. He walked around the desk, stopping just astride Covey and looking down on him.

"I have clients," John said, turning and opening his office door.

"That's fine," Covey said. "I am not a man to be underestimated or trifled with, Mr. Rushton. I hope you can see that."

"I'm sure we'll talk soon," John replied.

Not twenty seconds after the elevator door closed, John picked up his phone and dialed David's cell phone. David answered on the second ring. John described Covey's visit in detail and without editorial descriptions. David listened intently, his anger bubbling. Lemuel Covey was rogue and undeterred by law or hierarchy.

Covey proved three things: an unrestrained government was an extraordinarily dangerous thing; obsession, like addiction, had no limits or boundaries; and now, no one was safe. Covey exceeded what, by any standard, were normal limits and created his own rules. If the government itself was unable to manage this 21st-century Melville character, what could John or do?

The only possible option either man could conceive was to seek help from the very target of Covey's obsession. Neither law enforcement nor the law itself had any obvious quarter with him. Only another who lived on the edge of the legitimate and illicit could possibly know how to deal with this situation. And more importantly, Aiden Vachon was the only one who could protect them.

The conversation with Mary was difficult, but she—more than anyone else in the family—knew everything, now even about Esther Chase.

"Try and cover for me," David said, pulling the zipper around the backside of the suitcase. "If you can. I don't want to get you any more in the middle."

Mary picked up David's thigh-length brown leather coat from her makeup chair and extended it toward him.

"Since I met you, you've been a master of bad timing," she smiled.

He took the coat from her and slung it over his shoulders, sliding the right arm into the sleeve and then the left.

"Timing?"

"Me in the middle," she laughed. "How much more in the middle could I be?"

He stepped into her and pulled her tightly into his chest.

"That's right—charm me," she laughed, reaching around his torso and clutching him.

"You know me. Always the charming one."

"Do whatever you have to do," she said with a sharp seriousness. "Finish this thing of yours before you get yourself killed."

John closed the car door and looked back at Leesa, standing in their doorway. He waved to her, and she blew back a kiss. Unlike Mary, she did not know the full extent of all this—but she knew her husband well enough to know it was both serious and dangerous.

She watched the car turn out of the driveway. She began to cry. John was her whole life, and he had, in some measure, rescued her from the perils of a Youngstown blue-collar life. After high school, Leesa attended a local two-year business school. A year later, she went to work for a prestigious Warren law firm. That job brought her and John together for the first time in the late '90s. John was representing a family stricken by several forms of lymphoma arising from a Superfund site in Struthers. Leesa's employer was representing the Hockland Company, whose years of pollution led to the myriads of carcinogens that ultimately crept into the groundwater and into dozens of families in the area.

From the beginning, Leesa saw John's passion and compassion— qualities that transcended any and all financial concern. He wasn't trying that case for money, though money was the only practical legal remedy. He was trying the case because it was right, and because he truly loved the city that gave so much to a nation and was easily forgotten by it.

They dated for almost a year before deciding to marry. Ernest Rushton loved Leesa from the beginning, and his wife, Lauren, treated Leesa more like a granddaughter than a granddaughter-in-law. It meant a lot to Leesa that Lauren saw the birth of her great-grandchildren, though Ernest died before they were born.

John's parents were also good people who loved their son, Leesa, and their grandchildren. John's father, also a successful attorney, decided to move his practice to Chardon, but died just before John's sixteenth birthday. Following in his father's legacy, John attended Ohio University in Athens and then the University of Michigan Law School. He spent a year interning in Ann Arbor, returning to Youngstown and joining a growing firm in Poland, Ohio.

Within three years, John bought into the practice as a partner and was instrumental in moving it from Poland to downtown Youngstown.

David turned onto Route 224 and drove the few miles across town to the Vachon estate. John called Aiden earlier that day, so they were expected as they reached the outer gate. A few seconds later, the gate swung open automatically, and the car drove forward onto the sprawling Canfield property.

Walking across the massive stone patio was Rocco Donofrio, clad in black trousers and a black sport coat over a black sweater. For a man of his size, he moved with a kind of graceful elegance, more akin to a dancer or skater.

John and David exited their vehicle and started toward the towering man. As they neared, he raised his hands chest high.

"I have to make sure you're not armed," Rocco said apologetically. "It's just protocol—one hundred percent of the time."

"Really?" David asked.

"Just cooperate, would you?" John suggested.

The two men raised their arms, and he patted them from shoulder to ankle.

"Good to see you again, David," Rocco said. "I understand you met my Uncle Dom."

"Yes. We had a slice of Boston pizza together."

"You had second-rate Boston pizza together," Rocco laughed.

John looked at Rocco, then back at David. "I need to try and keep up," John grimaced.

"He's expecting you," Rocco said.

Rocco escorted them to Aiden Vachon's study, where Aiden himself was already pouring three drinks.

"Well, well," Aiden smiled. "If it isn't the kissing cousins."

"Very funny, Aiden," John said. "We have a big problem."

David looked over at the corner of the room. Rocco was like a cat. He had made his way to the corner and was already seated. *How?* David thought.

Aiden handed David and John their drinks and walked over to the plush leather chair just in front of the steel and glass table he used as a desk. He crossed his legs and sipped his drink.

John and David sat in the two smaller leather chairs on either side of Aiden. They too sipped on their glasses of Tanqueray.

"So, what is so urgent, John?" Aiden asked more seriously.

"This might be better in private, Aiden," John said.

"You know Rocco and his relationship to me. There are no secrets here."

John reached into his breast pocket and pulled out the folded article from the *Boston Globe* describing the McGough murder. He handed it to Aiden, who unfolded it and skimmed through.

"I'm aware," Aiden said.

"How?" David interjected. "A random Boston murder? How could you possibly know?"

Aiden folded the article and handed it back to John. "It's my business to know everything I can about people who mean to fuck me."

"Lem Covey killed him to make a point?" John asked. "He wants David and me to both know he can get to anyone—even people closest to us."

"Covey has turned up the gas on this obsession with me. He found a useful stooge. No offense," Aiden apologized.

"What the f—"

"David," John scolded.

"Not meant as a personal affront," Aiden explained. "He is a man without limits—and no bottom."

"Should I be afraid of you?" David asked.

Aiden sipped his drink, placed it onto the glass table, and rose from his seat. He walked over to the built-in bookcase at the center of the study and pulled a thick, white, hardbound book from one of its center shelves. He walked back toward the table and placed it at the center. **Vachon Family Bible** was printed in gold lettering across the front. Aiden opened the Bible about halfway. He pressed down the pages to keep it flat and slid a letter-sized envelope from within. He withdrew a folded piece of paper from the envelope, unfolded it, and handed it to David. David took the paper and began reading.

    Dear Aiden,

    You must know I am sick, and my days are limited. Your great grandfather, grandfather and father have been as dear to me as my own blood, and you know even that is complicated.

    As I prepare for the next chapter, whatever that may be, I am troubled by one thing. I have two families I have and continue to care deeply for. One is far away and the other here. They are both my blood and I fear for both in this hard and hateful world.

    There are those who would do great harm to your family, and I fear that someday may involve mine. I ask you but one favor as you live your life and do great things for this city and this region. I ask that you watch over my two families and help and protect them if that need should arise. It may not, and things can remain as they are. If, however, that need does in fact arise, my secret is far less significant than their safety and well-being. My son Patrick has two sons, David and Brendan. I ask that you consider them no differently than my Youngstown family if that is what is required.

I ask you this as a man who owes his very life to your family.

With my sincerest love and pride.

Grandpa Ernest.

David finished reading and handed the letter to John, who also read it in detail. John finished reading and handed the paper back to Aiden. Aiden carefully folded it, placed it back into the envelope, and ever so respectfully returned it to the Bible. For a solid minute, the three men remained silent, none making eye contact with the other.

Everything David and John uncovered up to this moment seemed almost insignificant in comparison to this. The brief and impassioned letters were part love, part testament, and part edict. If John Rushton retained any doubt or confusion, that was swept away now. Ernest Rushton clearly understood the nature of the Vachon empire, his relationship—and by extension his family's relationship—with it. He understood it could and might be both the source and solution to what he feared most.

It was almost uncanny. He seemed to predict, or at least sense, this extraordinary convergence precipitated by his Boston Irish grandson and the implications and dangers from it. He understood power—and the use of power—for every conceivable outcome. He knew the genesis of the Vachon power, and the awkward marriage between the legitimate and the illicit that was almost common knowledge.

John already understood the good Ernest Rushton had done through his own volition and through his infinitely close relationship with the Vachon family. John knew the reality about the empire and its sometimes nefarious activities; but he also knew the Mahoning Valley—and Youngstown itself—may have descended into an even darker pit had it not been for the Vachon family.

Did all this spiraling revelation change any of that materially? Was his grandfather not instrumental in the creation of *The Mahoning Trumpet*? Shortly after its inception, Cardinal Michael Murray of the Youngstown Diocese said of these men: *"If ever we are weak of faith or the goodness that often lives camouflaged in men, let us look at these two saintly men who have quite literally changed the lives of thousands of men, women, and children in this valley."*

Michael Murray was not naïve to the realities of the Vachon family and empire, but he, like John, understood we do not live in a perfect world—and there are few absolutes in the game-board of good versus evil.

"So, I have a question," David said, almost laughing. "Does this make us cousins, stepbrothers, what?"

"I think probably cousins," John smiled. "Anything closer would be awfully weird."

"And our kids?"

"Cousins," Aiden interjected. "They are cousins—but mostly, they are family."

"So, when my—our—grandfather wrote that, he understood we might need protection one day? How?"

"Both my grandfather, father, and your grandfather were realists," Aiden said. "I wouldn't go so far as to call them pragmatists, but they understood we live in the world as it is—not the world we wish it was."

"What did you say?" David asked, sitting up in his chair.

"That they—"

"No, I heard it. My father says that often," David said.

"As did mine," John added.

Aiden placed the Bible back into its place on the bookshelf and sat back down in his plush leather chair. He folded his hands and rolled his thumbs over each other. He leaned back and clasped his hands behind his head. He looked up at the ceiling and clicked his tongue onto the roof of his mouth. He straightened himself, his hands now resting on his desk.

"Our mutual Virginia friend has been a busy boy and has caused grief for us all—not to mention that poor McGough kid." He rubbed his chin. "So, he wants me—and to get me through you."

"He's given us both the ultimatum," David said. "He doesn't like 'no' or 'we need time.'"

John shook his head but sat quietly. Aiden continued to rub his chin, his eyes moving in every direction as he contemplated the conversation. He stood and walked over to the waist-high credenza in the corner between the bookshelves and the floor-to-ceiling windows. The credenza was clearly old—mahogany top and sides, with inlaid stained glass adorning the two parallel doors on the front.

He bent down and opened the doors. Reaching inside, he pulled out a crystal decanter half-filled with a caramel-colored liquid and three small glasses. He set the glasses on the desk, pulled the stem out of the decanter, and poured each glass halfway. He picked up two of the glasses and handed one to each man. He picked up the third and raised it chest high.

"To Lemuel Covey," Aiden said, taking a sip of the pungent liquid.

"Lemuel Covey?" David asked.

Aiden looked over at John, just finishing a sip. John smacked his lips and nodded to Aiden in the affirmative.

"To his great success," Aiden continued. "People sometimes should be careful what they wish for."

Brendan kissed his wife hello and asked her to sit down at the table where he was seated.

Brendan told her everything he could recollect. He told her about their first encounter with Lem Covey, their conversation at the MVR restaurant in Youngstown, Jennie Goodearl, John Rushton, and the Vachon family. She sat mesmerized, staring at him as he recounted a story suited for a Hollywood drama—not the kind of things real life is made of. He told her how scared he was—his big brother was in Youngstown, caught between a government "whackjob" and a family with a very checkered history.

"This is so far out of either of your leagues," Rachel said. "What are you going to do?"

"I don't know," he said. "Wait for David to get back on Friday."

"And if he doesn't get back?" she asked.

"Don't talk like that."

"You're the one telling me how dangerous this is."

"I—" The phone interrupted Brendan's thought.

Rachel picked up the receiver anxiously, her new reality already sinking into her life.

"Hello? Oh, David. I'm glad it's you. Fine—he's right here."

Rachel handed Brendan the phone. He held it still for a moment and then moved it to his ear.

"David?"

"Hey, Bren. I don't have much time, but wanted to at least touch base," David said.

"You, okay?" Brendan asked.

"I'm hanging in, but there's something important I need to tell you."

"Okay."

"John and I have made a decision to give Covey what he wants."

"You mean Vachon? How are you going to do that?"

"John does a chunk of the legal work for the family. He knows where a lot of the bones are buried."

"I don't know shit about being a lawyer, but isn't that a violation of client confidentiality? Kind of like a priest?"

"So?" David asked.

"Can't they disbar him for that?" Brendan asked.

"Bren, Covey is going to destroy us—or worse. He doesn't care about us. He wants one thing. If we give it to him, he'll be done with us."

"Jesus, David!" Brendan exclaimed, pounding on the table. "What if Vachon finds out? Him killing you or Covey—does that much matter?"

"What fucking choice do we have, Bren?" David asked.

"I don't know. When will you be home?"

"Friday," David said. "Mary and I are meeting with that Children's Services gal."

"You're going through with that?" Brendan asked. "Mary went along with it?"

"Look, I don't want to talk about all this on the phone. We'll talk when I get back."

"Okay, brother," Brendan said. "Talk to you later."

Brendan stood and hung up the phone. Rachel poured herself a small glass of orange juice and sat down at the table.

"What did he say?" she asked.

"I can't believe it," he said.

"What?"

"He and John Rushton decided to give Covey what he wanted."

"Isn't that all he wants?"

"I guess. In theory. I just can't see a guy like that leaving loose ends, you know?"

"Your brother isn't a stupid man. He's a Costigan, for God's sake."

Brendan shook his head, as a slight, smirkiest grin opened his face. Rachel was taken aback by his reaction, shaking her head in the negative as she grimaced.

"What…?"

Brendan put his index finger to her lips, as he placed his other index finger on his own. He shook his head from side to side and then raised both hands in front of him. For a few seconds, whatever utterly baffled Rachel it was Brendan was trying to tell her. Then a smirkiest smile came across her face as well.

David pushed open the door to let Mary enter the office. It was an old, musty building at the junction of Franklin and Devonshire Streets in Boston's financial district. A thirty-something woman dressed in a paisley skirt, clearly from the TJ Maxx dome rack, greeted them as they entered the dank office. The wallpaper around the reception area was a faded brown pattern, probably hung in the early 1960s. The furniture also looked like something from a Salvation Army dome. An old, bad faux-leather couch, torn in several places; a rickety coffee table on which sat year-old magazines, discarded by their original recipients; and a floor lamp, repaired many times by all manner of duct and electrical tape.

The receptionist's desk was right out of the original *Twelve Angry Men*, her chair acquired from the same source as the couch and lamp.

"Hello," the woman said as they entered the room.

"Hi, David and Mary Costigan—here to see Kathy Scheinfeld," David replied.

"She's running a bit behind, maybe ten minutes," the receptionist said. "Can I get you some water—*watah*?"

"Water would be great," David said, as the woman retreated into the area behind her desk.

A moment later, she re-emerged with two bottles of Evian water and handed one to David and the other to Mary.

"She should only be a few minutes," the woman said.

David and Mary sat down on the couch, each twisting off the caps to their water bottles. David took a large gulp, while Mary sipped delicately. They sat for ten more minutes silently looking at the office. Finally, Mary sighed, as if to secure David's attention. David looked at his wife and shrugged his shoulders.

"This is one of our more stupid ideas," Mary said, sipping more of the chilly water.

"It's not stupid," David replied. "We talked about having a third."

"Our own, or a baby," Mary argued. "Not someone's orphan."

David looked at—or more accurately, through—her; his eyes tearing at her like cat claws.

"All right, which was uncalled for," she apologized. "But you make me so mad. We barely talked about this, and here we are

233

seriously considering the adoption of a girl whose mother just died in a car accident."

"What child could be more in need, Mary?" David asked.

"Jesus, David! Watch TV any night. There are a billion."

David clasped his hands over his knees and leaned forward onto his thighs. He thought for a moment and then placed his hand on his wife's knee.

"Mary, what do you tell people about us?" he asked.

"That we are a crazy family?"

"I'm serious, Mary," David insisted. "What do you tell people about our meeting each other?"

"That's different," she argued.

"It's not. Now tell me."

She sighed, as if trying to avoid having to say what they both already knew.

"I tell people God brought us together, and we are a miracle."

"What else?"

"That it was always our destiny. It was meant to be, and we both knew it from the first second."

"This is the same. I know this as sure as I know I love you," David explained.

"But how do you—?"

"I just do," David interrupted. "I know this is right and what we are meant to do."

"How? How do you know?"

"How did you know about me?" he asked.

"Oh." She smiled. "I knew it from the second I met you."

David laughed and sat back on the uncomfortable couch.

"What did your sister say when you told her about me?" he asked.

"Well, I waited five days."

"What did she say?"

"That I was crazy, and you can't possibly know that in such a short amount of time."

"Right. And was she right, Mary?"

"No, baby. She was wrong."

"That's how it is here."

"But we have two kids to think about," she said cautiously.

"God, Mary." He laughed. "You've raised them to believe in goodness and charity and selflessness. You don't think they'll get it?"

"They're just used to——"

"This isn't about getting used to," David interrupted. "This is about being presented with a choice and doing the right and charitable thing. What do you think they'd tell us?"

"They're children," Mary reminded him.

"Yes, they are—but they'll be adults in a blink."

"Is this a crusade of some sort for you?" Mary asked.

"No, Mary. It is one little girl who needs a family, and we are here."

A moment later, the outer door opened, and Kathy Scheinfeld stepped through, a clump of manila folders tucked under her arm. She acknowledged David and Mary with a slight nod but proceeded straight to the dour secretary's desk. The two conversed quietly about several of the folders. She turned, composed herself, and approached David and Mary, now rising from the couch. She was dressed in a gray skirt suit, complete with a white blouse and the compulsory pearls. She looked good, and David worried how Mary would take to her.

"Mrs. Costigan, I'm Kathy Scheinfeld. It's a pleasure meeting you finally."

"Pleasure is mine," Mary said in her usual style.

Kathy escorted the couple through the inner doors to an office, which was considerably different from the waiting area. It was painted in a light shade of green, with a walnut chair rail around the circumference of the room. An assortment of diplomas hung on the wall just to the right of the windows, and two contemporary paintings hung on the opposite wall. There was no desk in this office, only a round, inviting table in the center of the room.

The three sat down. Kathy pulled a folder from her briefcase on the floor and opened it on the table.

"Those are very different paintings," Mary said, admiring the artwork.

"My cousin Marcy in New York is an artist. If you like her work, she has a studio at a hundred forty-fourth."

"Interesting," Mary said.

"So, let's start with something that's oftentimes a huge issue in these cases, shall we?" Kathy said.

David and Mary nodded.

"Very good. Many times, couples come in here, and it turns out they are either not on the same page, or their perspectives are materially different. Does it make sense?"

Again, the two nodded.

"So—is this something you both really want?" Kathy asked.

David refrained from speaking. Instead, he looked over at his wife, wondering if this was already the end of the process. Kathy looked at David, then at Mary, and back at David again. She was very patient and understood how profound and important her question was. In fact, Kathy preferred a thoughtful answer to a quick one.

Mary cleared her throat and looked at David. At that moment, and in that place, the myriad reasons she loved him and married him rushed into her head. Sitting there, she could honestly say—for the first time—she understood.

"We both want this very much," Mary said, David's head turning in disbelief. "This little girl was put in our path by whatever force has guided David and me from the start—God, Jesus, Buddha if you like. There has always been a kind of mystical quality to David and my relationship, and this is part of that."

Kathy stared at her, digesting words she had never heard before.

"And your children—do they know anything about this?"

"No, not yet," David answered, "but that won't be a problem."

"How can you be sure until you put it out there?" Kathy asked.

"Love, charity, selflessness—these aren't just biblical parables in our family," David continued. "These are the values we have demanded from ourselves and our children."

"I believe James and Jacqueline would be horrified if we turned our back on little Veronica," Mary said.

Kathy looked at the prospective adoptive parents, using her questions and her instincts to evaluate them appropriately. Over the years, she had become an extraordinary judge of character and was seldom fooled by any manner of charlatan. She studied prospective parents, as she was trained to do. David's hand rested comfortably atop Mary's, but their physicality was not so overdone as to seem counterfeit. Every few moments, they would look at each other, for what seemed more for assurance of solidarity than flirtation.

"You understand your children will have to be interviewed, and your house duly assessed," Kathy said.

"Home," Mary interjected.

"Pardon?" Kathy asked.

"You said house. I said home," Mary explained. "The house is not as picked up as I'd like, and some of the rooms could use paint—but our home is amazing. Imperfect, but amazing."

David stared at his wife, struggling to contain himself. He dragged Mary into many aspects of their lives—Brookline, his career, this whole drama playing out around his grandfather, and now this impending adoption. She didn't mind, however. She knew David loved her, and there wasn't anything he wouldn't do for her. He stood up to Patrick, both in terms of career choice and domicile, and Mary knew the meddling in-laws were never going to be an issue in their marriage. She also knew his motives here were genuine and pure. She knew he believed this was a calling for them, and there was no option or plan B. Veronica Polino was destined to be part of the Costigan family, and that was that.

The next morning, Kathy Scheinfeld arrived at the Costigan home with an associate who would help with the details of the evaluation. This was not—and never is—a proverbial slam dunk. There was a seriousness about this process that would be valuable in those instances where undesirable pregnancy was involved. Granny Elizabeth often said, "Any idiot can get pregnant. That doesn't make you a decent parent." He always knew his grandmother was right, and this process was essential and necessary.

"This is my research associate Peter Ralla," Kathy said. "He is the investigator who evaluates the home."

"You were very forthright about the process, so we are happy and ready to help you any way we can," David said.

Peter Ralla was a Malden-born, prototypical government employee. It had nothing to do with his effort or the seriousness with which he did his job. It was about the regimen of government work—and security as compared to the private sector—though the security their fathers knew disappeared with the 1980s. He was short, heavyset, very Italian in complexion and demeanor, and had a comb-over most people were too polite to mention.

"I'd like a few minutes with your children," he said. "James and Jackie, correct?"

"Not Jackie," Mary said.

"It says right here, see." He said, showing her the numbered form.

"No—she goes by Jacqueline," Mary replied.

"Very formal," Ralla said.

"Not our decision. She is a very strong-willed, confident girl. She just prefers Jacqueline," Mary said amiably.

"And your son?" Ralla asked.

"You will talk with him, "David said. "You can decide. He is James here, but some of his teachers and friends call him Jimmy. Oh—and he is very protective of his sister."

"Is that a Costigan trait?" he asked.

"If you mean, do we look out for one another—yes, we do," David said.

"Your brother Brendan as well?" Ralla asked.

"Yes. He's my kid brother. Why?"

"Reads here like he's a bit of a hothead," Ralla said.

"What is that supposed to mean?" David asked.

"Brendan is a very emotional guy," Mary interrupted. "He sometimes opens his mouth before thinking, but he is a loving and loyal man. Jacqueline and James adore him."

"Just doing my job," Ralla said.

Mary excused herself upstairs. A few moments later, she returned with James and Jacqueline in tow.

"James, Jacqueline, this is Mr. Ralla. He's going to spend a few minutes with you and ask you some questions," Mary said.

"James. Jacqueline," Ralla said, introducing himself.

"Is this about Veronica Polino coming to live with us?" James asked.

"As a matter of fact, it is," Ralla answered.

"She needs a family to love her and a big brother to watch over her," James said with the seriousness of a funeral.

"And a sister too," Jacqueline said.

Kathy smiled at the two children and then at their proud parents.

"Where, um?" Ralla asked.

"The dining room? Is that private enough?" Mary asked.

"Perfect," Ralla said, escorting the children into the other room.

Kathy rose and moved from the leather armchair to the couch. She sighed with a kind of relief as she sat.

"Some coffee?" Mary asked her.

"If it's no bother," Kathy answered honestly.

"Of course not," Mary said.

The three sat in the living room, discerning only part of the dining room conversation. Kathy sipped on her hot coffee as she read the file in her lap and made notes.

"Is there anything in the way of danger we should be aware of?" Kathy asked.

"Danger? What do you mean, danger?" David asked.

"Well, if you were a convicted felon, for example, you might associate with an element that, let's say—well, you know."

"Nope, no felonies here," David joked.

"It could be if you were a policeman. Nothing wrong with that, but a policeman can have many enemies," Kathy said.

"I am an ER doctor," David said, "and Mary is a mother. There are no unusual dangers here."

"No, Kathy," Mary said, less defensively. "We have no dangers in our life such as that. It's all quite ordinary."

"It is what I imagined, but we have a protocol we have to follow."

Ralla sat on one side of the table, directly adjacent to the children. The conversation began with the expected pleasantries around school friends and favorite television shows. This too was very formulaic. Peter Ralla was not one to deviate from the appointed script and conducted every granule of the interview by the page and by the playbook. Still, he was a human being and also needed to draw on his experience and instincts.

Part of Children's Services training included several symposiums on psychology and the identification of the warning signs they were taught to look for. The children were both naturally quiet but were nonetheless social, as their parents raised them to be. Jacqueline was more deliberately talkative than James and was more apt to offer a wide range of information, including boys, the schoolyard social hierarchy, and music. James, though social in his own right, tended to answer the questions he was asked without a great deal of embellishment or editorial comment. Ralla was trained to look for natural personality traits, screening out aspects of the interview that only exemplified those traits.

There was also the science of body language, and though a relatively new component of the process, it was now considered integral in the evaluation. As they talked about the more mundane and everyday aspects of their lives, Ralla noted nothing which seemed unusual or concerning. He started the conversation with an understanding of the children's relationship and James' propensity toward a more paternal relationship with his little sister. That aspect seemed clear from the outset. James sat very close to Jacqueline, his hand touching her arm or shoulder as a means of comfort and safety. This aspect of his personality resonated with Ralla, in that he too had a younger sister whom he also protected—but in a severely dysfunctional family situation. Still, one thing they were drilled on in their training was to look for signs of potential sexual abuse of prospective adoptive siblings. He saw none of that.

"So, James," Ralla asked, "how do you feel about your parents moving ahead with the adoption of this little girl?"

"She needs a family. She needs a mom and dad," James said.

"So, you don't have any worries about her disrupting your family?"

"My grandmother says that love is not gasoline."

"I'm not sure I understand what that means," Ralla said.

"Me either," James said honestly.

"Hmmm," Ralla sighed.

Jacqueline squeezed her brother's arm. "Nannie says gasoline burns up, and you have to go out and find more. The love in our family never runs out. There's always more there. She said, "Jesus said that."

"Do you believe in Jesus, Jacqueline?" Ralla asked.

"Mom says He believes in me."

Ralla, a Catholic himself, noted Jacqueline's remark—more for his own edification than the interview.

"Is she scared?" James asked.

"What do you mean, James?"

"That's why you're talking to us, right? She's scared, and you want her to know she doesn't have to be afraid."

"Tell me more about that."

"Mom and Dad say, when she comes here, she's our sister—just as if she came out of Mom's belly like we did. So, she doesn't need to be scared. We will love her, and I will take care of her and Jacs."

"Jacs," Ralla noted.

"That's what I call Jacqueline," James said.

"I thought you preferred Jacqueline."

"Only James calls me Jacs," Jacqueline said in a matter-of-fact way. "He's the only one who doesn't call me Jacqueline."

"Is that okay with you?"

Jacqueline took her brother's hand and pulled it into her. If anything was readily evident to Ralla, it was the protective nature of this relationship.

"Of course. He's my big brother. He's called me that since I was a baby."

"But no one else does. Is that because of your mom and dad?"

"I don't understand," Jacqueline commented.

"Why is it okay he doesn't call you Jacqueline, but everyone else has to?" Ralla asked.

Jacqueline looked at the man across the table, her eyebrows furled, as she stared at him, not fully appreciating the question. She then looked at her brother, and Ralla could instantly see the fluent non-verbal interaction between them.

"Do you understand the question?" Ralla asked.

Still silent—and again, she looked at her brother.

"She doesn't understand what you're asking," James interceded. "I am her brother. No one else is."

"And what if Veronica wants to call you Jacs?" Ralla asked.

The two children assumed almost identical facial expressions. Their countenance was less anger and more of a kind of confusion. They looked at each other—a realization that was more than just a measure to assuage Veronica's fear.

"Then she does," James said.

"That doesn't concern either of you?"

"She'll be my sister," James said. "That makes her Jacs' sister. I think she ought to call Jacs if she wants."

"Would that bother you, Jacs?" Ralla asked.

"You're not my sister," Jacqueline said. "Only she and James can call me that."

Ralla smiled. He knew the signs of a healthy, loving family versus one of abuse and dysfunction.

"No, of course," Ralla smiled. "I need to respect you and call you Jacqueline."

The children looked at each other, as though they had triumphed in a game or contest. Ralla smiled, understanding the nature of joint sibling competitiveness versus sibling rivalry, the former being nurturing and productive; the latter being hurtful and destructive.

"I just have one more question," Ralla said, making notes inside the folder opened on the table. "What do you think will be the hardest thing about Veronica coming to live with you?"

The children looked at each other, confused by the question. Ralla too was a bit confused, in that he had not considered a different or simpler way of asking it. An uncomfortable silence ensued, which certainly seemed longer than it was. Ralla tapped his pencil eraser onto the table, wanting to make sure this question was in fact asked and answered.

"Are you worried about anything when Veronica comes to live here?" Ralla asked.

James and Jacqueline looked at each other, as though he was asking an obvious—if not naïve—question. They both smiled, and those smiles morphed into quiet giggles.

"What?" he asked jovially, trying to get to the answer. "You guys obviously know something I don't."

"You're a grown-up, Mr. Ralla," James noted. "You don't get kids, I don't think."

"Well, it's been a while since I was your age. Maybe I don't. Can you help me?"

"You're better at helping grown-ups, James," Jacqueline said more seriously.

"Yeah, sometimes they just don't get it," James laughed.

Ralla shrugged his shoulders and opened his palms as a kind of surrender. He placed his pencil gently on top of the folder and folded his hands, awaiting his education.

"Kids aren't like grown-ups," James started. "There are some mean kids and bullies, but mostly we're just kids."

"Okay," Ralla said, well lost at that point.

"I have some friends at school whose mom and dad don't live together anymore," James said.

"You mean divorced?"

"Yeah. Well, I try to help them when they're sad."

"How so?" Ralla asked.

"They feel like old toys that aren't important anymore. Their mom and dad are always fighting and using the kids or finding a new girlfriend or boyfriend who really doesn't want the kids around anyway."

"You talk about that?" Ralla asked.

"I don't know why grown-ups don't remember being kids. They think we don't know anything, or we don't hear everything."

"So, what do you know that you think grown-ups don't think you do?"

"Everything," James said, holding his sister's hand more tightly.

"So, in this house, what do you know they don't think you do?"

"That my mom and Granny Elizabeth don't really get along, and Granny Elizabeth wishes my Aunt Rachel wasn't Jewish."

"And you think your parents don't think you know all that?" Ralla asked, speaking even more softly.

"They think if they pretend, they fool us," James said.

"You mean about your grandmother and your mother?"

"Well yeah," James laughed, looking at Jacqueline. "Just like we know what kids don't like other kids, we know who doesn't like who in the family."

"And is it just your mother and grandmother?" Ralla asked.

"What do you mean?" James asked.

"Are there any other family members who don't like other family members?"

"Only Mom and Granny Elizabeth."

"But what about your Aunt Rachel?"

"I've heard Granny say she wishes she didn't love Aunt Rachel so much."

"You mean the Jewish thing?"

"Yeah, but then she says Jesus was a Jewish man. Did you know Jesus was a Jewish man, Mr. Ralla?"

"Yes, I did, James," Ralla smiled.

"Do you like Jewish people?" James asked.

"I, um…" Ralla stammered. "They are just like everyone else, you know?"

"But if Jesus was a Jewish man, and he was King of the Jews, like we learn in CCD, why don't Jewish people believe in him?"

Ralla's eyes blinked rapidly, completely befuddled by James' questions. Still, part of his training was to engage the children and not dismiss or ignore anything.

"I really don't know," Ralla said honestly. "I don't think it's that they don't believe—I think they don't believe he is the Son of God."

"My dad says we are all God's children. If I am God's child, why do we say he only has one son?"

"I, um… You know, that's a good question for CCD and Sunday School, James. So, are either of you worried about anything?"

"I'm worried about my friend Kristen," Jacqueline said. "She is going for her tonsils this week."

"You mean to have them out?" Ralla asked.

"What?"

"Her tonsils," Ralla said.

"I know," Jacqueline said.

"Is Veronica coming here worrying you?" he asked again.

James and Jacqueline again looked at each other, astounded by the question.

"I think you should ask Veronica," James replied.

"Why?"

"We have everything we always had. We just got a new sister. Veronica's mom died, and she has to go to a new place to live. I think she is afraid," James explained.

Ralla stared at the boy, mystified at his insight.

"You really are a thoughtful young man," Ralla said. "Your mom and dad must be proud of you."

"We're Costigans," James said.

David, Mary, and Kathy were just chatting socially when Ralla reentered the room. He told David and Mary how impressed he was with both children and how compassionate he found them to be. Kathy explained they were not at liberty to comment on the decision process specifically but did suggest they saw no readily apparent red flags. She also told them Veronica would need to come to Brookline as part of the assessment so they could see the entire family together.

"So next Thursday around two o'clock?" Kathy asked.

"That's perfect," Mary replied, closing the door as they departed.

David sauntered back into the kitchen, while Mary stood in front of the now closed door. She finally turned and joined her husband in the kitchen.

She sat down next to him, resting her head on her outstretched arm.

"Boy, that is tiring," she smiled. "You need to make this whole Youngstown thing go away." She insisted. "I have mentally adjusted myself to the impending arrival of our new daughter. Please don't let this get screwed up."

"I won't, Mary," David said, placing his head next to hers.

Mark Lockland always loved the downtime a urinal can provide. It was a momentary reprieve from the incessant pleas from one person or another—not to mention the political dances one had to do in his position. The men's room was recently renovated, and was still clean and shiny, the glass and steel fittings sparkling from the sun shining through the windows, no longer encased in wire.

The door opened behind him. He made note of the sound and the footsteps moving in his direction. He didn't give it much thought, other than his sanctuary was now disturbed. He finished and shook himself, as he had been taught to do as a child. As he zipped up, he felt something hard pressing against the center of his back. He froze.

"This is either a joke or really bad judgment," Lockland said.

"Not a joke," a voice responded with a Virginia twang.

"You know, this is the Justice Department. Not a particularly smart place for a holdup."

"Holdup?" The man laughed. "This is not a holdup, Mark."

"You know my name."

"I know your name, and knew you were going to take a piss," the voice said.

"How's that?" asked Lockland. "And only my friends call me Mark."

"Cocky. Some people like that. I don't. Just not a very dignified way to carry oneself."

Lockland turned and was staring into Covey's face. He knew it was him from the Virginian's first utterance, but looking into that famously malevolent face gave the moment an even darker dimension.

"What do you want, Covey?" asked Lockland. "How about I wash my hands?"

"Please," Covey grinned. "Not a fan of Yankee piss-hands."

Lockland, a non-confrontational man—being just astute enough to max out at his level—wiped his hands and tossed the paper towel into the trash.

"Don't you think my office might be a better place to talk?" asked Lockland.

"Sure."

The two men walked down the aisle formed by the four-foot cubicle walls, taking up most of the gray carpeted floor. Heads popped up over the walls as the two men made their way through. Lemuel Covey was well known across the Justice Department agencies. Some looked at him as a kind of "Clint Eastwood" type, doing the job without being a slave to the rule of law; while others saw him as a man who learned how to curry political favor to allow him to operate outside the boundaries of normalcy and ethics.

They reached Lockland's office. He instructed his forty-something admin to hold his calls and visitors and closed his office door after Covey entered.

"Sit down," Lockland said, placing his dark-framed glasses onto his face.

Covey slid his dark trench coat off and flipped it onto the other side chair. Lockland looked at his striped seersucker suit, complete with a multi-colored bow tie. *What a cliché*, Lockland thought, as Covey lowered himself into his chair and crossed his legs.

"Aren't you cold, Lem?" asked Lockland. "It's winter."

"You don't like the way I dress?" Covey asked.

"I didn't want to take us down a fashion rat-hole. What is it you want?"

Covey smiled. His goatee stretched across his face, giving him an almost "Jokeresque" look. "I like that," Covey said, his smile never relaxing. "A man who gets right to the point. No wonder you have climbed the ranks so gracefully."

"What do you want?" Lockland insisted.

"You know, I am pretty well connected," Covey reminded him.

"Yes, I know. Everyone knows."

"So, when I ask for help or a favor, one will always do well to comply."

"You mean what you did to Elizabeth?"

"Oh, that was a small thing. I never put her in harm's way."

"Whatever," Lockland said in a dismissive tone. "What do you want?"

"I want the file on a Youngstown attorney named Rushton."

"Why?" Lockland appropriately asked.

"Why?" Covey echoed, his eyebrow raised as if to suggest Lockland already knew the answer.

"Yes, why? There are still rules and constitutional protections."

Covey uncrossed his legs, pushed himself out of the chair, and leaned back to stretch out his lower back. He walked over to an oak, four-shelved open bookcase on the far side of the picture window. The top two shelves housed pictures of Lockland's wife and children, and several honorariums and awards he had earned over the years. Just to the right of his wedding picture was a round, gold award for bravery—an award Covey felt he had been deprived of. Covey reached into the shelf and drew it out. He stepped back, studied it, and looked back at Lockland.

"What's this for?"

"Can't you read?" Lockland asked disrespectfully. "Never got one, huh?"

"It's a bullshit award, so bureaucrats like you can fill bookcases."

"No, it was for saving a mother and daughter who were kidnapped outside of Clinton, New York."

"Really," Covey responded.

"Yes, really," Lockland said, relishing the moment. "I took out the perp and saved the mother and daughter."

"I suppose I should be impressed," Covey chided, putting the award back onto the shelf.

"I don't give a rat fuck whether you're impressed," Lockland said in an unusually combative way. "Why do you want that file—if there is one at all?"

Covey strolled back to the chair and re-seated himself, re-crossing his legs.

"Of course there is. There's a file on every law firm in the US."

"That doesn't answer my question, Lem."

"Only my dearest friends call me Lem, and that would not be you."

"Look, enough already," Lockland grimaced. "Give me a reason or get the fuck out."

Covey made a "tsk-tsk" sound and shook his head. "Such brevity, Mark, from such an austere man as yourself."

Lockland shot up from his high-backed seat. Covey raised his hand, suggesting a calming of the situation.

"Year-end is coming. Reviews, promotions, disciplinary actions— all of it," Covey said. "You don't want me asking the AG—a good friend of mine——to make some negative phone calls to the Director. Do you?"

"Is that a threat?" asked Lockland.

"Interpret it as you like."

Lockland's countenance softened, and the tension in his face subsided. He always got the Bureau's politics, whether he played the game or not. *What does it matter to me?* he thought. His career was built on compromise and passivity. He expressed his concerns to Elizabeth Chase when learning of what Covey forced, but it went no further than that. He turned and looked over at the open bookshelf—specifically, the medal of bravery award Covey had trivialized. That day was maybe the proudest of his life. His ascendance to department head had marked the beginning of placation and compromise. He was sick of it. He had left Elizabeth Chase in a position of such vulnerability and disrepute. He stared at the award, as if summoning strength from its power.

"Hello?" Covey snickered. "You going Walter Mitty on me, Mark?"

"Don't call me Mark," Lockland replied, his top and bottom teeth pressing tightly together. "No."

"No? No, what?" Covey laughed, trying to intimidate the FBI veteran.

"No, you cannot have the file. You want to go and make a stink about it with the Director, the AG, the President for that matter—you go ahead. But you can't have it."

Lockland knew he was sticking his hand in the cobra jar, but what he allowed to happen to an honorable agent and friend was unconscionable. It was time to stand up again. I feel strong again. Call truth to power.

Covey ripped his coat from the adjacent chair and stomped toward the door to the office.

"You fucked up, Mark!"

"Such nasty language from a cultured man—and don't call me Mark."

Covey threw open the door, allowing it to collide with the doorjamb on the wall. "You will regret this," Covey threatened.

"Not so much," Lockland smiled, knowing there might well be hell to pay.

He rose and made his way out of the office. A hundred sets of eyes, scattered about the modular floor, were fixed on him. None knew what the confrontation involved, but they knew Lockland had challenged Covey in a way many could not—or would not.

Lockland caught sight of Esther Chase and realized he had not yet had his first cup of the day. He moved toward her, a sense of pride lifting him as he acknowledged the other eyes across the floor.

"What happened?" she asked.

"Covey happened," he replied.

"Yes, I saw…"

"He demanded something he has no constitutional right to have."

"And?" Chase laughed. "That would be a first?"

Lockland poured the hot liquid into a cardboard cup and added a single sugar. He stirred it and studied the swirling motion inside the receptacle.

"He threw my medal of bravery award in my face," Lockland said, still staring at the spinning liquid.

"What did he want?"

"A file. A file on a law firm in Youngstown, Ohio."

"A file?" Chase squinted. "There are fifteen ways to obtain a file. You know that, Mark. Why would you pick a fight with the Grim Reaper over something he'll get anyway?"

Lockland picked up his cup and raised it as far as his chest. He looked at Chase but did not reply. Chase waited for a response and wondered if her boss had not considered that simple reality. She studied his face and realized that was not it at all.

"God, you did it for me, didn't you?"

Lockland continued to look at his subordinate and friend but said nothing.

"I have to be honest, Mark," Chase confessed. "I'm not sure that was all that smart. Covey is a vindictive little man. He can cause a world of shit for you. Nonetheless, I am impressed and grateful."

"No need for gratitude, Elizabeth," Lockland sighed. "Nothing will ever make up for me letting you get hung out like that."

"Cut yourself a break, Mark," she replied. "I wear big girl pants. I could have told him to go fuck himself. I hung myself on that clothesline, not you."

She reached over and touched his shoulder in a collegial way, then turned and walked back to her cubicle. He watched her walk away and then turned and walked back into his own office.

Rachel Nilson pulled open the file drawer and meticulously placed a manila envelope in the appropriate slot. She closed the drawer and returned to her immaculate, OCD desk. She carefully lifted a tiny piece of lint from the desk blotter, its presence making her anxious.

The phone rang. She answered it with a cold affirmation.

"Who?" she asked. "I don't know a Marie Vachon. You mean Aiden Vachon's wife?" She paused, awaiting the reply. "Show her in—and no chit-chat."

She stood, pressed down her pressed brown dress, and feathered her manicured hair.

A moment later, a knock came at the door. Normally she would bark out an order to enter, but knowing she had a guest, she herself walked to and opened the door.

"Marie Vachon, this is Rachel Nilson, our administrator," a young, well-intimidated aide said.

"Thank you, Andrea," Nilson said in an unusual way. "Can we get you a cup of coffee, Mrs. Vachon?" Nilson asked.

"Black," Marie Vachon said.

Youngstown Ohio was famous for a number of things—namely Aiden Vachon, organized crime, cookie tables, and steel. To some, Marie Vachon seemed the consummate trophy wife, a woman clearly in the shadow of her husband. Neither was a reality. Marie Vachon, born Marie Colangelo, was the daughter of a renowned thoracic surgeon known internationally for his work at the University of Pittsburgh Medical Center. Marie was a deadly serious, competitive child, who was as ethical as she was ferocious.

She interned with Aiden's father while pursuing her MBA at Ohio State. There she met Aiden—the Vachon empire apprentice who never shied away from telling people he loved her the moment before they met. Marie, not so easily smitten, was far more interested in the fruits of her internship than Aiden's romantic pursuits. The one immediate place they synchronized was around *The Mahoning Trumpet*, an organization Aiden was as passionate about as his grandfather and father had been.

Growing up on what was then elegant Fifth Avenue in Youngstown, the name and reputation of the Vachon family was not foreign to her. In fact, when their first date finally occurred, her father expressed deep disapproval. Never dissuaded by either of her parents, Marie assured her loving father she could handle herself and had the recognized Colangelo judgment instilled in her from birth.

Aiden and Marie kept their personal relationship quiet for some time—both understanding the potential perception of impropriety. Marie often laughed about the dichotomy in the Vachon family between decorum and the more unsavory elements of the empire. In the end, their relationship became public, and for a time, they were the Youngstown equivalent of Prince Charles and Lady Diana. But it was in the planning of their very notable wedding that Marie established herself as a thoughtful, frugal, and determined leader of that aspect of their impending family. One story made its way to the Cleveland, Pittsburgh, and Philadelphia newspapers, as well as the regional television networks, centered on Marie's engagement ring, wedding dress, and tiara.

After accepting Aiden's marriage proposal at the Nemacolin Resort in central Pennsylvania—and the three-carat marquise-cut ring—Marie lovingly and gently suggested the expense of the ring was unnecessary, and they both selected one less gaudy. Her journey with the heir apparent to the Vachon empire was extraordinary. Where others either cowered or challenged him, Marie understood who he was as a man first and a Vachon king second. She insisted the difference in price be put directly into *The Mahoning Trumpet*.

"A whole lot of children can benefit from the thousands of dollars endowed through this," she said. Her humility and grace became a kind of paradoxical joke in Youngstown, given people's perception of the Vachons.

Her wedding dress was her mother's, and she decided she would invest not one penny more than four hundred and fifty dollars in its redesign. Her stunning and sparkling tiara was purchased for eleven dollars at a downtown Youngstown thrift shop, also a consistent recipient of charity from *The Mahoning Trumpet*.

Aiden's father was enamored by Marie from the moment they met—not in an inappropriate way, rather like a mentor and father. He confessed years later he hoped Aiden would someday find a woman like Marie—never imagining it would be her. Their marriage also produced a decent relationship between Jerome, Marie's father, and Ernest Rushton. The three men were occasionally seen golfing together—and of course, at many of *The Mahoning Trumpet*'s charitable events.

When the next generation of Vachon heirs entered the world, Marie and Aiden very thoughtfully decided she would focus on three things: the raising of their children, the management of their household, and their devotion to *The Mahoning Trumpet* and its mission.

Another woman might have seized the opportunity to languish in the wealth of the empire. Marie Vachon saw only the good this wealth could do for a still-injured community and region. She became an avid and overt spokeswoman for women's rights in the region, the country, and the world. So eloquent and sensible, people the likes of Hillary Clinton, Bill Gates, and Dianne Feinstein frequently called upon her for help and support. She saw the continuing fight for women's and girls' rights and safety as an almost holy crusade. Never using money as a leverage point, she worked closely with Bishop Murray, the Bishop of the Youngstown Diocese, on this cause. In a speech given to the Youngstown Catholic Women's League, she said, "The Catholic Church has evolved like a bad child, who has now grown up." Under the auspices of Pope Francis, the first Franciscan Pope, she said the Church was beginning to realize its power to do Christ's original mission on Earth.

The aide returned with a black coffee in a paper cup. She handed the coffee to Marie.

"We do have coffee mugs, don't we, Andrea?" Nilson asked in a nasty tone.

"I am..." the aide stammered.

"This is perfect, Andrea," Marie said, making sure to note the young woman's name.

"Please sit down, Mrs. Vachon," Nilson said, taking her own seat. "What can I do for you? You can imagine how surprised I am."

"I'm quite sure you are, Mrs. Nilson."

"Oh, please call me Rachel," she replied.

"No, I think we'll keep things less informal," Marie said, sipping from the cup.

"Okay..." Nilson said, uncertain of how to respond.

"So, I should tell you—I came in through your back door. Through your kitchen."

"You did?" Nilson said, even more taken aback. "Why?"

"The front door is always what is best. The back door is always the worst," Marie continued. "Your kitchen, and for that matter your common room, is filthy. I daresay, some of the people have been there since the morning—and it's two o'clock."

"I'm sure that is not accurate," Nilson said, becoming a little agitated.

"I beg to differ," Marie said in a sarcastic tone. "From my perspective, this place is a disgrace."

"I understand who your husband is, but I don't need to be berated by anyone, including you. We do the best we can with what we have, Mrs. Vachon. I would challenge anyone to do better."

Marie reached down and pulled an envelope from her purse. She withdrew a thick document and flattened it on Nilson's desk, with the print facing the administrator.

"What's this?" Nilson asked.

"You challenged me to do better," Marie smiled. "Okay."

"What?"

"I assume you can read but let me help you. As of nine o'clock this morning, Vachon Enterprises own this nursing home."

Nilson looked down at the document, a red hue rising from her neck. She picked it up and stared at it. A small bead of sweat rolled down from her hairline and across her forehead. She drew in an anxious breath, calculating both her thoughts and words.

"I wasn't privy to any of this," Nilson said. "I need a moment to digest it."

"Certainly," Marie said. "I'll just go and get another cup of coffee."

"Andrea can get that for you."

"She's not a maid. I'm capable of getting my own coffee."

Marie excused herself, while Nilson perused the complicated legal document. She set it down on the desk, laid her chin into her hand, and stared out the window. A moment later, Marie returned, a new steaming cup of coffee in her hand. She reclaimed her seat and crossed her legs with a noticeable style.

The two women sat silently for the better part of a minute, Marie sipping the hot liquid.

"So, 'What does this mean for me?'—you must be thinking," Marie started.

"I was first going to ask about our staff," Nilson said.

Marie delicately placed the cup on the desk and retrieved the document. She glanced at it and then folded it, returning it to the envelope. Without urgency, she placed the envelope back into her purse. She picked the coffee cup back up and took a sip.

"I'm not a cold woman, and my husband is not a cold man. Giving you the benefit of the doubt—you really do the best you can—we're willing to give you a chance to turn things around here."

Nilson looked at Marie Vachon, her eyes as wide as quarters; her surprise broadcast as she stared.

"I, um, I appreciate the opportunity," Nilson said. "It will require funding."

"Of course it will. So, I've secured the services of a consultant who will work with you on an operational plan."

"A consultant?" Nilson asked.

"Yes. Although we both understand money is required here, we need to make sure we spend it wisely—and, as importantly, assess whether a turnaround is even feasible."

Nilson continued to stare, and Marie derived no pleasure from the administrator's discomfort.

"Well, I think we're done here for now," Marie said.

"And the staff?" Nilson asked.

"One of the first things our consultant will do is determine qualification requirements and match them to the existing staff. We'll have to deal with the unqualified staffers appropriately."

"I understand," Nilson said humbly.

"I hope you do," Marie replied, standing and pulling on her coat.

"I can show you out," Nilson said, also standing.

"I'm not leaving," Marie said. "There's someone here I need to see."

"See who?"

"Not that it's any of your business," Marie said in a casual way, "but Joseph Brady."

"Joe Brady? Why?"

"Let's make sure we understand something," Marie said in a more definitive tone. "You work for me now. I don't need to advise you if I'm dropping by, and I can see whoever I like. Do we have an understanding, Mrs. Nilson?"

"Yes."

"His room is?"

"To the left, and halfway down the hall," Nilson answered.

Marie knocked twice and pushed the door open carefully. It creaked as she pushed it.

The old man was sitting to the left of the dirty window, facing the exquisite landscape. Marie stood for a moment, consciously trying not to startle the man.

"Well don't just stand there," the man said, only his mouth moving. "Come in."

She walked through the door and pushed it closed behind her. Walking over to him, she took her place between him and the window.

"You make a better door than a window, dear," he said.

She stepped to the side and stood adjacent to his bed.

"May I?" she asked.

"Please. Sit."

She did as he suggested, pulling off her coat behind her.

He finally turned his head and looked at the visitor. He smiled and pointed his bony finger at her.

"I know you," he said. "You're Marcel Vachon's… um…"

"Daughter-in-law," she said. "I'm Marie."

"Oh yes. You're married to Aiden."

Marie smiled. Very few people call Aiden Vachon *Aiden*, and most would never think to be so casual.

"How is the boy?" he asked.

"Aiden—um, Aiden—is fine and sends his regards."

"What brings you to my palatial abode?" he joked. "Better hush, or Medusa will turn us both to stone."

"I just left her office," Marie said. "I wanted to visit with you and tell you she works for me now, Mr. Brady."

"Mr. Brady was my grandfather," he smiled. "I'm Joe; and I don't understand."

"My husband's company acquired this place, and he's asked me to oversee the changes."

"Changes?" he said more seriously. "Starting with firing that leather-faced bitch? Excuse me, Marie. I'm not accustomed to watching myself."

"No apologies necessary," she smiled. "But I don't have anyone else to run things right now, and maybe she deserves a chance to turn herself around."

"Maybe Mussolini deserved a chance to turn himself around, but they shot the bastard and hung him upside down. I have no godly use for that woman."

Marie reached over and set her hand onto his.

"Things will be different around here, Joe. Besides, we are moving you out of this place."

"Out, where?"

"Pinecrest, in Poland."

"Pinecrest? Deary, I appreciate the thought, but I don't have the kind of scratch the people there do."

She squeezed his hand affectionately. "Aiden feels just awful he's not paid enough attention to your situation. Vachon Inc. has owned Pinecrest for several years now. Henri Vachon would be mortified at your situation."

"I never made the money Henri and Frankie did. That is my cross. I haven't taken two bits of charity once in my life. I appreciate the thought, but I can't accept that."

Marie maintained focus on Joe Brady's eyes. He looked back at her with the same compassionate focus.

"This is hardly charity, Joe. We take care of our own—always."

"But I'm not your own. I'm not a Vachon or Costigan or Rushton."

Marie smiled and tightened her grip on his hand ever so slightly. She placed her free hand onto his arm and gently rubbed his desiccant skin.

"My apologies, Joe."

"You don't need to apologize, dear. I told you; I appreciate the thought."

She increased the intensity of her smile and shook her head slightly.

"No, I am apologizing for telling you—you *are* family. Henri loved you as a brother. You don't get to opt out of that because of pride. Aiden and I respect that—and you, of course—but family is there for family, and we don't debate that."

Unusually, Brady had no quip, comment, or comeback. He simply nodded and returned Marie's clasp in kind.

Marie looked out the window, contemplating the next comment. She recollected the stories her father-in-law told her of the three friends who became inseparable from their days in boot camp until their passing. Joe, the least financially successful of the three, was far too proud to accept help of any kind from his friends or their families. She understood the enormity of his acquiescence, despite her own self-awareness of how compelling she could be.

The question of when this transition would occur loomed in their conversation. He was aged and infirm. Moving out of this place—as decrepit and abusive as it might be—was not trivial. One's home is just that, despite its extreme failings.

"I understand this is not an insignificant move, Joe," she said softly. "We will need to decide when you are comfortable making it. I know you are settled here."

"Now. Today!" he exclaimed.

"Joe?"

"It's a fucking shithole, dear. I appreciate your concern over my hesitation to change. If I had a shit in my pants, would we be debating when the right time might be to change them?"

Marie chuckled and nodded. He was too old and too direct to parse his words. She liked that. He reminded her of herself, without the locker room imagery.

"You, Aiden's grandfather, and Frank Costigan were brothers—maybe more so than genetic siblings," she said. "Aiden will be so happy he can help you the way you and Henri helped Frank when he needed it."

She remembered hearing for the first time the story of the plan to convert Francis Costigan into Ernest Rushton, and the role Aiden's great-grandfather played in that. She remembered learning the genesis of the plan came from Joe, who could not understand Francis' anguish and his helpless acquiescence to it. At first, Francis and Henri thought Joe's idea was a joke—and then a ridiculous solution to a problem that had one clear solution: go back and live his life as he wanted. But they came to realize the significant flaw in that thinking.

In time, the three men dug into the details of the plan and solicited the help of the Vachon family patriarch, Marcel Vachon. Over just a matter of weeks, the plan took shape and form. Marcel funded both the plan and the political favors necessary to implement it. Joe, according to Marcel Vachon, struggled deeply with both the notion of Francis abandoning his family and the extinguishing of his own dreams.

Marcel architected the solution. Elizabeth Costigan would have to be part of the plan, in so far as she would know there were but two options. Francis demanded the continued financial support of his family. That meant Elizabeth would know she had a benefactor. Marcel Vachon suggested that it be anonymous. However, Francis was an eternal paradox if nothing else. He needed her to know he did not die in Anzio, and he also did not abandon her.

Marie always viewed this as a kind of upside-down, rationalized chivalry. So, Elizabeth Costigan could accept the reality of it, and Francis would somehow continue to financially support the family—or two, Francis would vanish, dead on that Italian beach forever.

Being a sanguine gambler and student of human nature, Marcel calculated Elizabeth had no choice. She could go theoretically to the authorities, but she had no idea who Francis was becoming or where he was. This was not the twenty-first century, and the tools available to law enforcement and the government were primitive by modern standards. No—if he closed that door, that would be that.

Marcel's other calculation was the children. Elizabeth was a mother first, and Marcel gambled on her need to protect them, thereby trumping any other impulse. Marie, of course, knew Marcel's assessment and calculation was on the money, and Elizabeth did exactly what he expected.

Marie understood there was a kind of insidiousness to it all, but she was a realist about the world she was marrying into. There was much about it that was distasteful to her, but like the Catholic Church, she saw the maturation of the family leading it away from their more nefarious endeavors. It was also one of the factors making her so passionate about being a force for good. It was an uneasy balance she struck in her own mind.

"And your daughter—Anna, isn't it? She is looking out for you?"

"She came with her spoiled butt-wiping kids for Christmas," Joe lamented. "She came for a whole hour. Can you imagine? A whole hour. What a loving daughter I raised."

"She is in Columbus, isn't she?"

"Toledo," Joe replied. "She married her wet rag of an architect. You know what he does?"

"No."

"He makes plans for McDonald's when they want to go into a strip mall. Well, I suppose someone has to do it."

He turned toward the window, a slight grin on his worn face. He pointed his finger out toward the landscape, trying to compose his thoughts.

"We were something, the three of us; during and after the war," he said, fighting back the emotion. "Three men couldn't have loved each other more. We put most blood brothers to shame." He looked over at her. "I would have gladly died for either of them. Now how often do you see that? Do you ever see Ernie's grandson, John?"

"I do—we do," Marie answered. "He's an attorney downtown."

"Yes, I'm aware. My body is pretty well trashed, and I am getting uncomfortably close to lunch with Jesus, but my brain is what it was in '42. I know who he is."

"I don't mean any disrespect, Joe," Marie apologized. "I didn't know if you knew."

"I sometimes think my life would be happier if I had gone daft like some of these poor fools. Then I'd be in La Land and not know all I lost."

"In order to lose something, you had to have had it," Marie said, removing her hands from his. "Memories are tough things. They can sustain us, and they sadden us too."

"How the hell did Aiden ever land you?" He laughed. "You are a smart one."

"I try."

"Now my Linda," he sighed. "God, she was one gorgeous woman. I fell for her the second I laid eyes on her. Know how we met?"

"I don't."

"USO dance in Cleveland—right on the lake. I was a shy little putz. Some GI bumped into me, spilled a beer all over my new clean uniform. Next thing I know, Linda is wiping it off with a damp rag, talking a mile a minute at me. She was so far out of my league. But she liked this galoot, and we were married before I shipped back out. I met her five days before we got hitched. You understand five days?"

"I understand."

"When I got back stateside, Anna was already born. I kissed Linda hello and didn't leave her side for sixty-five years." He started to cry. "When she up and left me, Anna couldn't take me in, so she and her lame-brain mate put me here. I'm so ready to be with Linda again."

"I can't imagine," Marie said, "but sixty-five years with the woman you love."

"Linda, Ernie, Henri—what more could a man pray for."

The fire captain barked out orders as the engines surrounded the flames coming from the warehouse. The alarm sounded just twenty minutes earlier, but the Boston Fire Department was among the finest in the land.

It was a strange thing. Costigan Iron Works had a perfect safety record in every sense. Patrick was a stickler for that. This was inexplicable. The fire started at the south end of the warehouse, in a place with the least flammable products.

Patrick pulled his car well short of the engines, so as not to interfere. Jumping out of his SUV, he heard his name being called.

"Bobby," Patrick said to the fire captain. "Man, oh man."

"You said it, Pat," the captain replied. "Lucky, we got here as fast as we did. We prevented real loss."

"I can't imagine what the hell happened," Patrick said.

The captain pulled Patrick off to the side. He wiped the sweat off his upper lip and looked around for anyone who might hear him.

"Do you have any enemies, Patrick?" he asked.

"Enemies? Why?"

"You know, arson is usually something people try very hard to mask. Usually takes my investigators to figure it out."

"And?" Patrick asked.

"Whoever did this, didn't try that hard to hide it, or do anything to mask it."

"You mean—you think this is arson?"

"I *know* it's arson. That's what I'm telling you. Any of my first-year rookies could see that."

"How?"

"Without getting too technical, there's an ignition fuse connected to the combustible materials. This was set to be a slow burner."

"I don't understand," Patrick said.

"In a wooden structure or house, you want a fast burner, because basically everything burns. In a warehouse like this, a fast burner will likely burn itself out. A slow burner drives all the metal heat to its failure point. The real giveaway is the fact your fire protection alarm has been disabled."

"Then how did you—?"

"Your son Brendan," the captain interrupted. "He installed a state-of-the-art, internet-based, independent system. Our arsonist is behind on the latest technology."

"I didn't know he did that," Patrick said.

"Would you have understood?"

Another car came around the far corner of the warehouse, farthest from the fire. The car squealed to a stop. Tom Costigan jumped out of the driver's side, and Brendan out of the passenger door.

"I got Anne's call and called Brendan," Tom said. "Hello, Bobby."

"Tom," the captain said.

"What happened?" Tom asked.

"They think it's arson," Patrick replied.

"Um, we pretty well know it is," the captain interjected. "In fact, I'd stake my career on it."

"Jesus. Why?" Tom asked.

The captain moved in front of the three men and led them a few feet farther from the others at the fire.

"Look," he started, "there are going to be questions."

"Questions? What kind?" Brendan asked anxiously.

"I've known you my whole life, Pat" the captain said, "but these things have insurance implications, and well—you know."

"What the fuck?" Brendan exclaimed. "You think we tried to burn it down for the insurance?"

"Take a breath, son," Patrick said in a level way. "Bobby's just doing his job. Do you know anyone who might have a reason to do this?"

Brendan looked at his father but hesitated to reply. Patrick looked over at the captain, concerned about his son's reaction.

"Do you know, son?" the captain asked.

"No," Brendan said, trying to sound convincing.

"Really," Patrick said in a condescending manner.

The captain excused himself and returned to his men, who were extinguishing the last remnants of the fire. Brendan and his father were accustomed to the smell of heated steel—just not outside the building.

Motioning Brendan to accompany him, David walked toward his car. Clicking his key fob, the lights of the SUV flashed, followed by a high-pitched beep.

"Get in," he ordered.

Brendan complied, anxious about what his father would press him for. The two men closed their respective doors, and David started the engine to generate some heat.

Looking over at the warehouse, the two men could see the myriads of icicles hanging from the gutters of the building. Smoke continued to stream from the broken windows along the side of the factory. Patrick gripped the steering wheel, trying to force out his anger before uttering anything. He looked over at Brendan and was decompressed with a few long breaths.

"You know, I haven't been successful for not having half-decent judgment and instincts," Patrick said. "Strange coincidence this happens after you boys start your jaunts to Ohio, and the McGough kid gets killed."

"I don't know, Dad."

"I think you do, but my Mac and Myer sons don't seem to want to let me in on whatever the hell is going on. Do you have your phone?"

"Yes."

"Get your brother on it."

"It's midnight, Dad," Brendan said anxiously.

"I don't really give a rat's ass. Call him. Now."

Brendan complied and hit speed dial three. A moment later, a ring—and a moment after that—David answered.

"Uncle Tom just called me," David said. "What's going on?"

"I'm here with Dad. He told me to call you."

"About the fire?"

"About who might have set it," Brendan answered.

"Definitely arson?" David asked.

"No question. I—"

"Give it here," Patrick barked, taking the phone from his son.

"My house. Tomorrow morning at eight o'clock. And don't be late by a minute. You hear me?"

"I have a shift at the hospital," David replied. "Can we do it—"

"Did I ask?" Patrick interrupted. "Call them and tell them whatever you have to. Whatever is going on with you two and whatever you've gotten into, it is now spilling over into all our lives."

"What makes you think this has anything to do with Brendan and me?"

"I don't know. The fact that I am not an idiot. Eight o'clock, David—or I'll come and get you."

"All right, all right, Dad," David acquiesced. "I'll be there."

Chapter 9

Paying The Piper

The sun was just peeking up over Mill Creek as the three black cars pulled up to the ornate iron gate. Mark Lockland was the first to step out of the black Lincoln SUV, followed by several men, each wearing heavy blue jackets with "U.S. Marshal" on the back.

A burly man in an awkward brown fur coat approached the gate from within. Two of the marshals placed their hands on their sidearms, but Lockland motioned to them to relax.

The man was wide awake, well-shaven and groomed, obviously on the job for a while.

"Federal Marshals," Lockland said. "We have a warrant to search the property."

"Warrant?" the man asked. "For what?"

"I won't ask you twice to open the gate," Lockland demanded.

The man, undaunted by the visage of law enforcement, pressed the intercom and explained what was happening.

A voice responded, indicating to let the men in. The burly man complied.

The marshals and Lockland got back into their vehicles and drove fifty yards to the front door. As they exited again, the front door opened. Aiden Vachon stepped out onto the large stone porch, his hands on his hips. A moment later, Marie Vachon appeared.

"Call John Rushton," Aiden asked his wife politely. Without a response, she faded back into the house.

"I'd like to see that warrant," Aiden said. "What is it you're looking for? What is your probable cause?"

"You obviously know the lingo," Lockland said. "Sure, read away."

The men moved up the stone stairs and past Aiden Vachon.

"Have fun, boys," Aiden said, knowing that arguing with them was futile.

Starting in the living room, the marshals toppled over end tables and couch cushions. Aiden sensed their enjoyment with the whole process but kept himself very calm. That is, until the children began to make their way downstairs for breakfast before heading off to The Ursuline Academy, one of two well-regarded Catholic schools.

"Rocco!" he shouted.

From the kitchen, Rocco Donofrio emerged, wearing a flowered apron better suited to a smaller frame and different gender. He stopped in the hallway adjacent to the living room where the marshals were rummaging and waited until they became aware of him.

"Nice apron, pal," one of the marshals laughed.

"I'll shove it up your ass, you—!"

"Rocco," Aiden said calmly. "Let the nice men do their work. Can you take the kids to Bob Evans or Rachel's for breakfast and then to school? I really don't want them here."

"What's going on, boss?" Rocco asked with an uneasy lilt.

"Not to worry, Rocco. It's all good. I promise."

Rocco took off the apron, hung it on the back of a kitchen chair, and mustered the kids. Marie and Aiden kissed them goodbye, and out the door they went.

The Donofrio family was an institution in Youngstown. In fact, by some accounts, they represented twenty percent of the population of Lowellville—an exclusively Italian, blue-collar town just East of the city. One could find a Donofrio alongside a Vachon going all the way back to Marcel. The relationship between so many in that area transcended boss and employee and who served whom. It was a kinship that was as much a family construct as blood—even more so.

A football defensive tackle and star at Lowellville High School, Richard Donofrio, better known as Rocco, received several Big Ten offers to come and play football for them. Feeling academically overwhelmed, he opted not to pursue that course. However, Aiden's father pushed him to advance himself and grow. So, Rocco attended Stanford University on a football scholarship and was a two-year starting guard for them. He finished his degree with honors and returned home to pursue a master's degree in American History at Duquesne University in Pittsburgh.

Subsequently, he went to work for Aiden's father and alongside his own. After taking over the business, Aiden felt Rocco sold himself short and brought him even further into his inner circle. Rocco Donofrio was a complicated man. Clearly intellectually potent to those who were close to him, the casual observer saw a hulk of a man—blessed with intimidating physical attributes and lacking substantive intelligence.

As Rocco pulled away, another car pulled onto the property and parked in front of the door. John Rushton stepped out of the driver's side, while a very attractive, middle-aged woman clad in a dark overcoat stepped out of the other. The two passengers hurried to the front door to escape the frigid Lake Erie wind. Aiden and Marie, both standing at the foot of the stairs in the foyer, turned to look as if the two entered the house.

"John," Aiden smiled, moving to shake his hand.

"Aiden, Marie, how are you?" he said, shaking Aiden's hand and kissing Marie on the cheek.

"Very good, John—well, except for…" He motioned to the marshals, who had now made their way to the den and office. Aiden, do you know Judge Linda Cullin, Third Appellate?" John asked.

"Actually, I do," Aiden replied. "How are you, Linda?"

"I'm well, Aiden. I'm sorry for all this," she sighed.

"Why are you sorry?" Aiden laughed.

"I swore out the warrant," she admitted.

"You did?"

"Kind of a *fait accompli* when requested by the Justice Department."

"Well, this is awkward," Marie laughed. "Hi Linda. The last time I saw you was at your election fundraiser."

"Marie," Linda replied. "Much preferred that. May I take off my coat?"

Linda Cullin was the consummate professional. She was about five feet five inches tall, very feminine, hourglass build, impeccable taste in clothing, and dark blonde hair that flipped under perfectly at the shoulder. On that day, she wore a red skirt suit, with a jacket sporting black lapels and wristlets. It was a perfect color for her.

She was in her second term as an appellate justice, and her election was only a year away. Aiden and Marie Vachon were major and steadfast donors; they brought a lot of what was left of old Youngstown money to the table.

"So why are you here with my attorney, Mrs. Cullin ?" Aiden asked.

"To do something that can easily have me removed from the bench and disbarred."

"I'm usually pretty quick," Aiden said, crossing his arms over his chest, "but I am lost here."

"Please, can we find someplace more private?" she asked.

Aiden nodded and motioned her and John to the far side of the foyer.

"Coming, Marie?" Aiden asked.

"Think I'll take a pass on that. This is just too messy for me."

Cullin motioned for Aiden and John to hold whatever thoughts they had. Both men were openly confused about the situation but knew there had to be a damn good reason for this *entendre*. Aiden had an uneasy though functional relationship with the Justice Department. Esther Chase and he worked well together, and she worked for Lockland. None of this made any sense. Now Cullin was here—the judge who issued the warrant. Even in the Vachon sphere, things didn't get more inappropriate than this.

Lockland pushed open the French doors, entered the room, and closed the doors behind him.

Aiden shook his head, even more confused and frustrated than before.

"This must all seem surreal and odd, Aiden. I understand that" Cullin explained.

"You know, Linda," John interjected, "this has all the markings of a conspiracy—but an upside-down one."

"How so?" Cullin asked.

"You're conspiring right in front of us. I could file a strong complaint with the State Judiciary Ethics Board and the Justice Department. You both might well be asking, 'Fries with that?' a couple of months from now."

"Yes," Cullin replied starkly.

"Yes, Linda?" Aiden asked.

Lockland positioned himself in front of Aiden and John. Both men clearly had a lot to say; however, Lockland motioned them to temporarily refrain.

"Maybe I can provide some clarity here," Lockland explained. "This was all Esther Chase's brainchild."

"The one who…?"

"Yes, she's the one. Don't be too hard on her. Lem Covey is an obsessive dick and an asshole."

"So, what is all this?" Aiden asked.

"Theater," Lockland answered.

"Theater?" Aiden shouted. "That's a real warrant, yes? And an invasion of my home. Linda, I need a reason not to go scorched Earth."

"Reason, Aiden? The reason is—it is necessary. Director Lockland came to me a few weeks ago and explained what was happening, and this loose cannon Covey—and two open murder investigations," Linda explained.

"Our government and even our law enforcement institutions are imperfect," Lockland interjected. "One obvious flaw is how a man like Covey can amass such power and influence."

John pushed himself off the couch and sat between Cullin and Lockland.

"This is all a show for Covey?" John asked.

"It's a show to make him believe he has forced an action against the Vachon family and buys us some critical time to euthanize that power."

"And these agents?" Aiden asked.

"They need to believe this is just a straight warrant. I trust these men, but Covey's tentacles are deep," Lockland explained. "We need this show to appear authentic. Telling you this is risky, but you have a right to know."

"Normally, yes—but as I said, *fait accompli,*" Cullin added.

John walked around the corner. Lockland was grimacing, as one of the marshals indicated they had found nothing. Lockland felt nervousness coming from his personal albeit limited encounter with Covey and the fact his charge was, in fact, to find something. He cleared his throat and walked cautiously over to Aiden Vachon.

"I'm sorry, Mr. Vachon," he said with sincerity. "This should not have happened. Politics and the law make horrible bedfellows."

"If my inclination is to be litigious, there's a hell of a civil suit here," Aiden replied, picking up on the theater in which he was participating.

"I hope my apology is enough," Lockland said. "It is necessary."

David answered the phone on the third ring, startled by the unexpected call.

"Hello?" he fumbled, not awake.

"Do you get the idea, Doctor Costigan?" the voice asked in a familiar and disturbing southern twang.

"Covey?" David asked, fumbling the phone.

"What was that?" Covey asked.

"It's the middle of the night," David replied. "I dropped the phone."

"I advise you to hold on to it more meticulously. I am growing impatient with this little dance of ours."

"Look, I have a busy schedule. I don't know what you really want from me," David said.

"Sure, you do," Covey replied. "You and that Youngstown lawyer just haven't done it, so I've provided some incentive, yes?"

"You mean killing an old lady and a young kid, who had nothing to do with anything?" David said. "I'm more awake now."

"I am not one who loses well, David," Covey said, with a note of superiority. "I thought we were friends and understood each other. Now I am wondering if I can count on you."

"You know, have you considered there is nothing there? The Vachons are not doing anything wrong."

"That isn't relevant to me," Covey said. "Between you and that lawyer, there's something you can find. I don't much care what."

"I'm not a secret agent, Covey. I went there. I tried. I don't know how to do this."

"Then you have a problem, Doctor," Covey insisted. "I can't hold your hand. You have to figure it out, or there'll be more accidental fires."

"Leave my family alone," David exclaimed. "They did nothing to you."

"You still don't really get the rules of this game," Covey laughed. "You don't get to decide who is and isn't on the game board; I do."

"You fuck......!"

"Now that's the vigor you need to get this done. Atta boy!"

David did not respond. Instead, he embraced the uncomfortable silence.

"I didn't hear you," Covey said.

"I didn't say anything."

"I want to hear you're on board," Covey insisted.

"What the hell!" David exclaimed.

"I want Vachon—and any way I can get that son of a bitch," Covey exclaimed. "I'll burn down more than just that shit-ass company of yours. Now you do what you must, or someone you really care about is going down."

"I know what to do," David said.

"Good. Do it."

David turned off Broadway the way he did a thousand times before. Today things felt different. South Boston was always home, and there was that certain familiar safety in being here. He regretted ever going into that attic and finding those letters. He regretted pursuing any of it—and most of all, was distraught over dragging his family into this mess.

He pulled up to the curb and noticed Brendan coming around the corner from the other direction. The air was beginning to warm, now that spring was nearing. He waited at the bottom of the steps for his brother. Brendan reached him but didn't utter a word. All they did to try and find the truth—while keeping it all from their father— was coming apart. They should have known how far over their heads they were, but that was hindsight. As their father taught them, "you have to live in the world that is, not the one you wish it was."

They climbed the stairs silently, each dreading this conversation. Patrick was neither a patient nor outwardly gentle man. He was angry, and mincing words was not going to work here. Still, neither had an effective plan in mind. Their father could not know the truth—but they had no strategy to ensure that.

The door opened as they reached the entrance. Anne opened it and rushed them in against the cold.

"Hurry, you'll heat the neighborhood," she said, planting a kiss on both her sons. "Just throw your coats over that chair."

"Is he in his office?" David asked.

"What's going on with you two and him?" she asked. "I know he's upset about the fire last night, but it's more than that."

"He wants to talk with us, Mom," David said. "I'm sure everything will be fine."

"I've never seen him like this, boys. Whatever it is, fix it—and fix it fast."

They walked across the dark wooden hallway to their father's office. Through the closed French doors, they saw him standing, back to them, on the telephone. Instinctively, he turned and motioned them in. They would have never contemplated just walking into his office—or even interrupting him by knocking.

"All right, I appreciate it. We can talk tomorrow?" Patrick said, finishing up his call. "Say hello to your wife."

He hung up the receiver and motioned for his sons to take a seat. He remained standing and moved several feet to face them.

"So, boys, we have a problem," he said. "I'd like to know everything you know, and I'd like to know it now."

"Dad," David started. "There are things I, um…"

"Not the time for bullshit or secrets, David," Patrick said. "Now is the time to clean off the plate and fess up."

The brothers looked at each other, not having any idea how to respond to their father. He waited a few more uncomfortable seconds.

"Since you two—especially you, David—started your trips to Ohio, things have happened. I don't believe for a whisky minute the fire is a coincidence, so I need to hear from one or both of you. What is happening?"

"Dad," David said, "I wish—I really wish—we could tell you everything. You have to trust us; we can't. We just can't."

"Can't? You can't? Why can't you?"

"You need to let us manage this and trust us," David said.

"Trust you." Patrick smiled, now taking a seat in his great-grandfather's high-backed chair. "Do you even know what you're doing—and who you're playing with here?"

"We do," David said confidently. "We have it under control."

Patrick leaned forward, his elbows on his thighs, his chin in his hands. He began to laugh—just a chuckle at first, and then outright laughter. A moment later, Anne came to the door and opened it just a crack.

"Well, I like that sound," she said, immediately closing it.

Patrick slapped his hands onto the walnut desk and sat back on his chair. He pointed at David and smiled.

"You're protecting me, aren't you?" he asked. "This is about me."

"Dad?"

"You know, you and I haven't always seen eye to eye," Patrick said calmly. "We've had our moments, yes?"

"Yes."

"But you are my sons. I love you, and I have done my best. I am so proud of you. You're both pursuing your own paths—and damn good at it, each of you. But neither of you, especially you David, know when to ask for help. This time, people have died."

"What?" David asked, not certain what his father was saying.

"Youngstown Ohio." He said, shaking his head. "This is about my father?"

"What?" Brendan interjected. "Your father?"

"I suppose I should consider myself lucky—neither of my sons are very convincing at acting stupid."

The brothers looked at each other.

"Maybe some truth in a family rife with layers of secrets might be a healthy thing. What do you think?"

He stood and walked over to the roll-top desk just behind his main one. He rolled up the top, pulled out three glasses and a bottle of VO. He placed the glasses on the desk, opened the bottle, and filled each glass halfway. He put down the bottle, not saying a word, and handed one glass to each of his sons.

"Not one time in either of your lives have we ever had a drink together. Not like this. You're both men now—and it's about time. To be a Costigan!" he said, raised his glass, and took a drink.

The boys followed suit.

He sat back down and rolled the short glass on the inside of his fingers. He studied the glass and the liquid, understanding the profound significance of this conversation. Not knowing what to expect precisely, the brothers innately understood this also. Patrick took another mouthful and put the glass down on the desk. He folded his hands on his lap and sat back.

"When I was sixteen," he started, "I found some things in the attic that were troubling. I think you know what I am talking about."

Neither of the brothers acknowledged their father but sank in the notion they had no idea the depth of the Costigan deceit.

"I agonized for weeks, not knowing what to do with what I found. I couldn't go to your grandmother's. What would I say to her? Call her a liar?"

"What did you do?" Brendan asked, overwhelmed at what his father was revealing.

"I did what you did. I went to my brother."

"Uncle Tom?" David asked.

"Uh huh," Patrick said. "And we went to your great uncle Billy."

"What did he say?" David asked.

"What do you think he said?"

"Did he know? Did he try to hide it?" Brendan asked.

"No, but he was devastated that we found out. He and my mother wanted to make sure we never knew."

"So, what did Uncle Billy do?" David asked.

"Took us on a camping trip," Patrick answered.

"What, camping? You hate camping," Brendan asked.

"In Connecticut, or so everyone thought. The three of us actually went to Youngstown."

"You went to Youngstown?" David asked.

"We did," Patrick answered without any hesitation. "We spent a day with my father and Henri Vachon."

David rubbed his face with both hands and sighed. He could not easily process what he was hearing. Everything that happened until this point seemed ironically dwarfed by what his father was now revealing.

A knock on the door startled the brothers, though Patrick expected it. Tom Costigan opened the door and entered the room.

He closed the door behind him, taking note of the glasses sitting on the table.

"Drinking without me?" he smiled.

"You know where it is," Patrick said.

Tom stepped to the roll-top desk and took out the last of the short glasses. He moved to the desk, picked up the bottle of VO and poured himself a drink. He raised his glass.

"Better late to the party than not at all." He gulped the liquid in one fluid motion.

"Take a seat," Patrick said.

Tom complied, as Patrick rose again to his feet.

"So," Patrick resumed. "I wasn't sure you boys ever wondered why Tom was satisfied in his role and didn't aspire to something more."

"It crossed my mind, but I figured it was his decision," Patrick said.

"Well, sort of," Patrick replied. "We also met Jennie Goodearl and some other interesting Italian guys when we were there. Up until then Billy was the link between the two worlds."

"Okay," David acknowledged.

"One of us needed to be the new go-between, and we realized it was not a part-time kind of thing."

"So, Uncle Tom took that on?"

"Yes, and goes to Youngstown a couple of times a year. Covering for him is easy. Brendan, did you ever wonder?"

"No," Brendan replied.

"But when I met John Rushton, he didn't know anything," David said.

"Of course not," Tom interjected. "Just like you and Brendan, it was important he be protected from this."

"Well, that's out the window," Brendan said.

"I imagine it is," Tom replied. "None of us created this mess. Our father did, but we have to make the best of it."

Brendan flipped his glass back into his mouth and emptied it completely.

Patrick walked over to the door, making certain Anne was not in the vicinity. He turned and leaned against it. He looked down at the glass, swirling the liquid around the interior.

"I suppose I should thank you, David," his father said. "For trying to protect me; as flawed as your thinking was."

"I would have done anything to keep you from finding out, Dad," David said.

"I suppose I underestimated you," Patrick said, swallowing. "I've always underestimated you and maybe have a little chip on my shoulder about your choices."

"You mean becoming a doctor?" David said.

"That, and moving out of Southie, to name a couple."

"I'm glad I am the good son," Brendan laughed, grabbing the bottle for another drink.

"Good is not the word I'd choose, but okay," Patrick said.

Patrick walked over to his eldest son and put his hand on his shoulder.

"You weren't wrong about protecting secrets. You just had the wrong one."

"Dad?" David asked.

Patrick looked over at his brother and nodded affirmatively. Tom came around to the front of the desk to talk as softly as he could.

"Here's the thing," Tom started. "My mother—your grandmother—doesn't know…"

"But she does, Uncle Tom," David interrupted.

"Let me finish, David," Tom said. "Of course, she knows about her husband. It would kill her if she knew your dad and I knew the truth—and worse, were involved."

"That secret goes to the grave, boys. Understand?" Patrick demanded.

"Okay, Dad," David said. "By involved, you mean the money and…"

"He means involved, David," Tom said. "I don't consider myself a blithering idiot, but compared with your father…"

"I think I am the idiot," Brendan said. "I have no fucking idea what any of you are talking about."

The other three men turned and stared at Brendan—and then burst into full-blown laughter. A moment later, Anne pushed open the office door, smiling as wide as a mile at the favorite men in her life. She took note of the VO on the desk and folded her arms, feigning displeasure.

"Keep an eye on my baby," she smiled. "He thinks he can drink. He can't."

"I'll make sure he gets home safe, Mom," David said, wiping the tears from his eyes.

She closed the door as she left, understanding nor wanting to understand all the commotion. As she entered the kitchen, she turned and looked down at the long hallway toward the front door. She smiled. David stood in the hallway, his loosely fitting overalls hanging from his skinny frame, his baby brother tugging on his pant leg, their father standing behind them, three baseball gloves piled in his hands. David was looking down at his brother, stroking the top of his head. Her eyes met Patrick's, and they acknowledged the success in raising their boys. The three faded into the flowered wallpaper as she drew a peaceful breath and continued into the kitchen.

Patrick picked up the receiver of the desk phone and dialed a number. He raised the earpiece, waiting for something specific. A moment later, he pressed the speaker button and returned the receiver to its cradle. David shot to his feet when he heard what he could not believe. Brendan jumped up too, and the two younger brothers listened:

"Leave my family alone." David exclaimed. "They did nothing to you."

"You still don't really get the rules of this game." Covey laughed. "You don't get to decide who is and isn't on the game board; I do."

"You fuck.......!"

"Now that's the vigor you need to get this done. That a boy!"

Silence, then...

"I didn't hear you." Covey said.

"I didn't say anything."

"I want to hear you're on board." Covey insisted.

"The most vulnerable assholes are the ones who think they're smarter than anyone else." Patrick said.

He pressed the off button on the phone, and the voice was silenced.

David looked at Brendan, a vacancy in his stare. Three months ago, the fabric and realities of his family were intact and absolute. A few months later, that foundation weakened, though there remained some absolutes. The father, his father, oblivious to all David and Brendan discovered. Looking back, and knowing his father better than anyone, he recognized how naïve, if not foolish, it was to assume anything about him.

He knew Patrick Costigan was smart. He knew he was savvy enough to play in the Massachusetts bidding playpen and be successful at it. He knew he took a successful business built by his grandfather and turned it into a top ten Boston company. He knew all that about his father, and yet he was now confronted by the realization: he didn't know his father at all. A man who not only knew the whole truth all along—but was protecting his children, not the other way around?

"Shit!" Brendan exclaimed. "Does that mean you know about Doreen Tarmy?"

"The high-pitched screams don't muffle well from the basement, son," Patrick said, not entirely amused. "Thank sweet Jesus your mother didn't know."

"Dragged me down to Flannery's that night," Tom laughed. "He couldn't stop saying, 'Little Bren has a woody.'"

"Jesus Christ!" David scolded. "Do we have to talk about that?"

"Embarrassed about my getting it?" Brendan chuckled.

"Where did you get that?" David asked nervously, pointing at the phone.

"From your conversation, of course," Patrick replied.

"You know what I mean, Dad," David insisted.

Tom jumped to his feet, inserting himself between his brother and his nephew.

"Do you think for a minute we'd consider trying to protect this whole clusterfuck without being very connected?" Tom said. "It's the Costigan version of the Bat Phone. Don't you think we knew when you and your brother were meddling down there?"

"No, I didn't think anyone knew," David replied.

"That's where you have to learn to open your eyes, son," Patrick said, in a more conciliatory tone. "You know I am an optimist, and I believe there to be a lot of goodness; but there are a lot of very dark places as well. Ignoring them, or trying to convince yourself they aren't there, is like walking back into a house on fire."

"I'm not sure I get the point, Dad," Brendan said.

"When my father made the choice to do this, you know he gave my mother one chance to agree, or he would vanish."

"I know. Aiden Vachon told us that," David said.

"Yes, but what he didn't tell you was this set some very dark and scary things in motion. Things your uncle and I have spent a lifetime keeping away from the family."

"Dark things?" Brendan asked.

"Not by intention or design, but by virtue of who the Vachons are—or more appropriately, were."

Patrick told them about the early days of this deception, and the nature of the Vachon family at the time. Marcel Vachon was a very different man than his grandson and ran the family business like any other of the competitive criminal families in Cleveland, Indianapolis, or Chicago. It was a cold, hard, cutthroat world, where power, money, and death were essential and indiscernible. There was less law than code, and the code was loose in those days. Betrayal—or even the suspicion of betrayal—would most certainly result in someone face down in either the Mahoning River or Mill Creek. If that wasn't the result, then a car bomb was the preferred and nationally notable form of Youngstown execution.

Marcel Vachon was one of few non-Italians who led a business far more a syndicate than an enterprise. He was, as most of his ilk of that day, a paradox of a man: dutiful to his family and others who were close, and malevolent toward those who wronged him or who he perceived as a threat. This was the world Francis Costigan walked into, and a world he saw clearly as he entered it.

The two brothers sat in awe as their father described a city not building a roadway to the future, but a kind of mausoleum built on a single and vulnerable industry—steeped in union and organized corruption—that existed as a perennial house of cards for the first half of the twentieth century. He described the metamorphosis of Francis Costigan to Ernest Rushton, not just in terms of name, lineage, and profession, but his immersion into this world of scandal, bribes, payoffs, and execution. Yes, Ernest Rushton became a doctor who served the community well, but he also became a piece of a broader and nefarious world around him.

Patrick described how the channels between Jennie Goodearl and Billy Costigan were created and managed. He described how even at a young age; he found his mother becoming more aloof and less engaged by the day. Before his sixteenth birthday, he chalked it up to a woman made a widow by war. After that, he understood being made a widow would have been far less agonizing than the truth she needed to shelter her children from.

He reiterated his trip to Youngstown at sixteen, seeing his father for the first time in a decade, and what he described as the rape of his innocence—now part of this terrible illusion and having to pretend, maybe for the rest of his life, that it wasn't so. Francis told his son he loved him, but this was the last time the two would see each other. Patrick cried and begged his father not to do this thing, but Francis—now Ernest Rushton—told his son this was the way of things now, and his job was to protect his mother from ever knowing what David now knew, and to take over the Iron Works when Robert either died or retired. Ernest then made young David swear on his mother's soul and the souls of his yet unborn children he would keep this oath forever. Otherwise, he would have to cut off all contact and financial support and disappear into nothing.

As wonderful a man as Ernest Rushton was, and as much as he gave to Youngstown, it was impossible for either David or Brendan to fathom how any father could knowingly do such a thing to his own child.

Hesitantly, Patrick agreed to what he thought was an unholy covenant that would one day come back and destroy everything. Patrick now feared that day would come, and everything in both Boston and Youngstown lay in the balance.

"The Vachon family—Aiden in particular—has worked hard to separate himself from those elements I described to you," Patrick said. "One can only do the best we can, and it is impossible to eliminate those things completely. That leaves the door open to men like your Lemuel Covey."

"Dad, how—I..." Brendan asked.

Patrick raised his palm, cutting his younger son off. He looked over at Tom and nodded.

Tom slid over to the other side of Patrick's desk and leaned against the front of it.

"It's been an odd life," Tom said, staring at his shoes. "I accepted the underachiever, lazy label because of what that son-of-a-bitch did."

He crossed his arms and grew sullen. He turned and looked toward the window, but he was not looking at anything at all. He shook his head, as though debating with himself.

"It's for my mother," he said, snapping out of his daze. "I'd like to kill the bastard were it not for the inconvenient fact he's dead."

"That's not what—"

"I'm getting to that, Brendan!" he interrupted.

"The connection with the Vachons is tight and perpetual," Tom explained. "Like you and your brother, the Rushtons are guarded, protected. Just as your father never wanted you to know, the Rushtons could know nothing." He paused and looked over to his brother.

"The one colossally dumb difference is, no one other than Ernest Rushton and a select few know any of this."

"Until now," David interrupted.

"Well, yes. Until now," Tom replied. "You see the cascade your father and I have been fighting to avoid all these years? Do you see why this is a full-time—and sometimes full-time-plus—job?"

"That still—"

"You boys are impatient," he said, cutting Brendan off again. "I talk with someone in the Vachon sphere at least two times a week normally. I know what they know, and they know what I can provide. My father wanted it that way. We knew about Covey from the time of your dinner at that pizza place."

"That was the very start," David said.

"Yes, it was."

"Dad, and you are tied into all of it?" David asked.

"I told you," Tom interjected. "Channels and contacts."

"Contacts?" David asked. "You mean Aiden Vachon specifically?"

"Well, yes. Aiden sometimes—but more often Rocco Donofrio and Jennie Goodearl," Tom answered.

"You know them?" Brendan asked.

"Listen!" Patrick said, flicking the back of his younger son's head.

"This might sound idiotic, but I feel a little better. Our worries about Covey are minimized, because it's out in the open," Patrick said.

"Really?" Patrick grimaced. "He killed Jennie Goodearl and that kid and nearly burned down our business. Nothing about him is minimized. He's worse even than Marcel Vachon—and has the weight of the Justice Department behind him."

"What do we do?" David asked.

"That is in the works," Patrick said, "but it's very tricky. Covey is still connected, and there are plenty of others in Washington and Ohio who'd like to see the Vachon family pay the piper."

"I need another drink," Brendan said, standing and grabbing for the bottle.

Patrick continued to unveil what he and Tom knew; how they had connected themselves through Rocco Donofrio and sometimes Aiden Vachon directly. He described how, until his sons became involved in this escapade, how he first heard the name Covey once. It was in passing and not conveyed with any anxiety at all.

He told them that in 2002, he attended a *Mahoning Trumpet* fundraiser in Youngstown and met Marie Vachon for the first time. Marie, of course, had little idea who Patrick Costigan was, though she had heard a few snippets from her husband. This was something coveted by both Patrick, Tom, and Aiden Vachon, out of respect for Ernest Rushton—but most of all, to protect the myriads of interwoven secrets even John Nash (*A Beautiful Mind*) would have difficulty managing.

Then he grew more somber, and talked about his mother's anguish, and he and his brother's helplessness to alleviate it. His father had created a nightmare, and in many ways, the family would have been better off if he had disappeared or died. The irony was, Francis Costigan's impossible goal of undertaking two paradoxical pursuits: the first to fulfill an ambition he believed could not be achieved in Boston, and the second to somehow continue to support his family from behind the shadows.

Patrick lamented over the notion of his father trying to assuage his own guilt or lessen his sins by providing his financial support. With further irony, Elizabeth and her boys would have been fine without Francis' support. The Works prospered in the war, so financial concerns were more Francis' own concoction. It was pure Irish guilt.

"I don't get it, Dad," David said. "You really didn't want me to be a doctor, but I did. Why didn't he just do it?"

"That's a good question, Son," Patrick replied. "I'm sure we'll never know the answer to that."

Patrick undid his watch and placed it on the bureau as he did every night. He did the same with his wallet and keys. He walked into the renovated master bathroom, changed, washed his face, and walked over to the bed, where Anne was reading yet another book about the Catholic Church's child sex abuse scandal. As she often did, her head shook side to side, along with a troubled "tisk-tisk."

"Why do you do that to yourself?" he asked his wife. "I have never seen someone love something and hate something so much at the same time."

She rested the book face-down on her chest and removed her stylish reading glasses.

"This is not what he wanted," she said.

"He who?"

"Jesus. He didn't want this gargantuan, ornate church. He certainly didn't want the church the Romans created. Can you imagine what he would say if he came back?"

"As you recall, we are Roman Catholic, " Anne reminded him. Still, I suppose he'd be unhappy about the whole stinking mess," he said, as he climbed under the covers.

"What's wrong, honey?" she asked, putting her arm around him.

"Oh, nothing," he lied. "Just work and, well, all that."

"It was nice to see you all together in your office." She smiled, placing her chin against the back of his neck. "A lot of laughter. That's good."

He rolled toward her and, very uncharacteristically, pulled her into him. He squeezed her in a way she rarely saw. He was not an overtly affectionate man, though she understood his heart and ability to love. She had no doubts about being his priority.

"And don't lie to me. Is it one of the boys? Tom?"

Patrick pulled himself into a sitting position, not letting go of his wife. He looked at her—really looked at her—deeply into her eyes.

"Will you always love me? No matter what?" he asked.

"Well, unless there is another woman in all of this, then yes, of course. There isn't anything you can't tell me."

"This is bad. Out there, you know?" he said, half smirking.

Anne straightened up, readying herself for bad or even catastrophic news. She intertwined her fingers into his and squeezed.

"Whatever it is, David, I'm here."

He cleared his throat in a way one does when they must relate something horrid.

"Go ahead," she said lovingly.

He recounted the Costigan story—his father's heroic death. She nodded, as one would expect, given the staleness and commonness of the family tale. He reminded her of how opposed both Robert and his own mother were to his pursuing his dream, and how Joe Brady's plan grew into what became the staged death of Francis Costigan and the miraculous birth of Ernest Rushton.

He told her about the Vachon family, their evolution through the syndicate mob years to Aiden Vachon's efforts to fully legitimize the business and the family. He told her about the complicity of his Uncle Billy and his mother, and the burden his father placed onto the family. He told her about his trip to Youngstown at sixteen, and the horrible revelation that accompanied it.

He described how Tom became the intermediary—or more appropriately a kind of Templar—in protecting the web of secrets wrapped around the Costigan, Rushton, and Vachon families. And then he told her what he dreaded most: how David found the letters in the attic, and how he and Brendan set out to find the truth Tom and he tried so hard to protect. He told her about Lemuel Covey, the renegade Marshal, and what he already did in his obsession with the Vachons.

Anne gasped, slapping her hand over her mouth. Her eyes snapped open, and tears formed at their bottom. Patrick grabbed her and again pulled her into him. She began to cry but inexplicably seemed to draw back the sadness and replaced it with that maternal strength he saw so many times over the course of their marriage.

"Our boys are in danger, along with us and their families," she said calmly. "That is the first order of business, Patrick. I don't care what you must do, but you get them somewhere safe until this is resolved.

He looked at his wife and realized that if he told her this long ago, much of his life's anguish could have been averted. This was not the first time he had this kind of revelation with his soulmate.

She placed her hand behind his head and rubbed him in a nurturing way. Then a quick, half-joking slap.

"You know, we could have done a hell of a lot better job figuring this out together, rather than you and Tom playing *Mission Impossible* all these years. Now our sons are involved. I should give you another slap."

"Please don't, Anne."

She leaned back onto her pillow, crossed her arms, and furled her brow. Without exception, if there was any time something needed to be figured out—a problem to be solved or a difficult question to answer, Anne assumed the same position. Through the course of their marriage, Patrick learned to give her time and space to think, and her solutions were more sanguine than his.

She relaxed her arms; her thoughts coming together in a visible way. She looked at him.

"First of all, I think putting this all on your father is wrong."

"I—"

"Let me finish," she interrupted. "Your mother is not just a victim here. She is complicit."

"She had no choice, Anne. He—"

"Please, Patrick, let me finish," she demanded. "She had two choices. You just can't see them. You are not a woman or a mother. She could have either supported her husband, rather than diminishing him, or rejected this idiotic conspiracy."

"I don't see what real choice she had," he said defensively.

"You were sad when David wanted to pursue his own course, but you didn't crush him. Neither did Mary. She supported her husband."

He looked at his wife, and she saw the wheels turning behind his eyes. It was such a simple, logical notion, and one that eluded him all these years. He always thought of his mother as the helpless victim in need of protection. He never contemplated her complicity in all of it. He pondered on her view of spousal loyalty and her refusal to support her husband. All *this could have been avoided if she had just done that.*

"Maybe this was to her liking, Patrick," Anne said carefully. "I know you don't want to hear that, but did she love him? Did she love him the way I love you, or Mary and Rachel love our sons?"

The wheels kept turning. It was hard to change his sensibilities, having lived in this paradigm so long. Was his mother really a cause in addition to being a participant? Was this possibly the best outcome for her? She retained his financial support, while not having to feign an affection that was never there at all. This was such a dramatic shift in thinking, he struggled to ask the question, let alone seek the answer. Then he settled, took an easy breath, and smiled.

"Okay, wife," he smiled. "What do you think I should do? Should I confront her with this?"

"You are the man of my dreams, Patrick," she said. "But you are such a man. For all your mother's quirks and failings, she is still a mother. Protecting you, Tom, and the boys from this is in her DNA. You need to leave that alone."

"Then what is the sense of this re-evaluation?" he asked.

"Maybe to give your father a break, and though no one can really excuse this, understand what he was doing and maybe why."

"He abandoned his children in the ways that matter. Tom and I grew up without a father."

"And what kind of father would he have been, if he was consigned to the Works, in a life he hated?"

"We would have had a father!" he insisted.

"True," Anne said, consoling him. "But I would think about what that could have been like. I would at least consider how miserable it could have been. Was your life that miserable?"

"Knowing he was down there raising his new family was hard for me."

"Then try and find some good from it and give that to the boys," she suggested. "You can't change the past, but maybe you can change the future."

Linda Cullin was a bit of an enigma in the world of Youngstown Ohio law and politics. Trained as an attorney, she practiced in Mahoning, Columbiana, and Trumbull Counties. Her first foray onto the bench was winning a seat on the Mahoning County Civil Court. A few years later, she ascended to the coveted Court of Appeals—one of three justices, the only Republican, and the only woman.

She was enormously respected in the community, by Republicans and Democrats alike. She was often heard to say, "This robe is solid black. It's not red or blue." She believed that—and acted as such. Though very active in the Ohio Republican Party, she conducted herself with grace, integrity, and competence.

Part of her enigma too was her judgeship in urban Mahoning County and her life on the farm, some twenty-five miles south in the city of Columbiana; a farming community ascending in popularity and value.

She and Aiden Vachon maintained a cordial though careful relationship. She understood all the Vachon family had done for the Greater Youngstown community, while being mindful of the family's nefarious roots—starting with Marcel, who grew the family's power and influence during Prohibition and a time when unions, especially those tied to the steel industry, themselves grew in power.

She was an articulate "country gal" who could, at one moment, sport a flowered Kentucky Derby hat and the next, work the dank hallways of the Youngstown, male-dominated political machine.

Aiden understood how valuable he and Linda Cullin were to each other. Fortunately, she too understood the importance of their relationship.

Mark Lockland removed the key from the ignition and pushed himself out of the vehicle. A moment later, John Rushton pulled into the driveway next to Lockland, Linda Cullen in the passenger seat beside him.

Cullen's tan skirt suit was neatly pressed and accented a body unusual for most women her age. As they moved toward Lockland, the front door of the 1950s sprawling white stucco ranch opened. Rocco Denofrio stepped out onto the cement stoop and moved one or two feet back away from the door. Aiden Vachon emerged a moment later and he moved away from the door too. Esther Chase then stepped out onto the stoop, and Lockland paused his movement toward Rushton and his companion.

"Chase!" Lockland grimaced. "What are you doing here?"

"All to be explained, Mr. Lockland," Vachon commented, moving toward the three visitors.

All except for Esther Chase were already acquainted.

"Rocco Denofrio and Dominic Stagno, these are my guests," Aiden said, introducing them one by one. "Everyone knows Esther Chase, I presume, but if not—Esther works for Mr. Lockland and has a bit of an unwilling history with Lemuel Covey."

Lockland stared at Vachon, understanding both the truth and the credibility of the present situation—and how accurate he was about Esther Chase. He put his hands in his pockets and looked over at the heavy set Lockland.

"Not my decision," Lockland said. "You're in charge here. I want that on the record."

"Director, can you excuse us for a moment?" Linda Cullin asked.

Lockland nodded and stepped outside onto the stoop.

"Let's stop chipping at the edges here," Cullin said. "Perhaps there is a mutual best interest for all concerned. Rather than throw us into what will undoubtedly be a Justice Department meat grinder, what if we deal with the real problem?"

"Covey," Donofrio stated.

"Covey," she confirmed.

"Can this Lockland be trusted?" she asked.

"I don't see a choice, Linda," John replied.

"Rocco, get him back in here," Aiden ordered.

Lockland looked around the room, understanding he needed to decide who to trust. Covey was, in fact, the problem. What he allowed to happen to Elizabeth Chase was inexcusable. Not only that, these four people were presenting him with a possible way out. *"I should at least listen,"* he thought. It was time to pick a side.

"So, why am I here?" Linda Cullin asked. "Haven't I already risked enough?"

Aiden was across the room pouring cognac into several shot glasses arranged on a circular, crystal tray. He picked up the tray and walked over to where the group was standing.

"Please," Aiden said. "This cognac was bottled in Quebec while Washington was surveying the Western Reserve."

"Thank you," Lockland said. "But I am on duty."

The rest of the group looked over at him with a kind of dismay.

"Perhaps this one time." Lockland smiled.

Aiden distributed the small glasses. John raised his glass first.

"To Youngstown," John said.

"So, why am I here?" Linda asked again, sipping on the savory liquor.

Aiden put down his glass and motioned everyone to sit. His office was large—walnut and steel. Two Cherry floor-to-ceiling bookcases were replete with a myriad of English, French, and American nineteenth-century classics—many first editions. Two long leather sofas sat in the center of the room, positioned at ninety-degree angles, just inches apart at the corners. Two additional high-back leather chairs were placed adjacent to the open ends of the two sofas.

"This has become a malevolent attack on David Costigan and his family," Aiden began.

"Costigan?" Linda asked. "That family isn't even in Youngstown."."

All of them found a seat and turned their attention to Aiden Vachon. He began by recounting the long history of Lemuel Covey's obsessive pursuit of the Vachon family, beginning with his grandfather Henri, his father, and now him. He described Covey's extortive demand of Elizabeth Chase and subsequent engagement with David and Brendan Costigan, and how it quickly transmuted from aiding them to now extorting them. He told her of two murders—one a harmless old woman in Youngstown, and the other of a young man in Boston, having nothing to do with any of this.

"Why would he kill these two people?" Linda asked.

Aiden glanced over at Rocco and nodded.

"A dead fish wrapped in newspaper," Rocco said.

"Excuse me?" Linda asked.

"Messages," Rocco replied.

"You have to help me here," Linda insisted. "I am not up on my Michael Corleone slang."

"What he is capable of. How far he will go to get what he wants," Rocco replied.

"And he wants you, Aiden?" Linda asked.

"My family," Aiden replied.

Linda uncomfortably recrossed her legs, looked down at the red Oriental carpet, and shook her head.

"I still don't get it," Linda said.

"Perhaps if I may?" Elizabeth Chase asked.

Aiden nodded.

"Covey knows now he's hit another dead end—and he blames David Costigan. He sees Costigan's obstinance as a betrayal. He's reset his sights on that family."

"Why?"

"Why?" Esther winced. "He's an obsessive sociopath. If he can't get Aiden Vachon, someone needs to be punished for what he views as a personal transgression."

Rocco rose, walked across the spacious study, and retrieved the bottle of cognac from the cherry desk. He walked back across the room and freshened everyone's glass. This time Linda didn't sip. She tilted her head back slightly and poured the liquid into her mouth. She extended her arm, and Rocco again filled her glass.

"If all this is true, why haven't you worked inside the Justice Department and let that process deal with Covey?"

John, seated next to Linda, placed his hand on her forearm and affectionately applied some pressure. She looked over at the renowned Youngstown attorney and raised her brow. She drank down half of her glass and again glanced around the room.

"It seems I am the only one out of the know here. What am I not understanding?" she asked.

"Lemuel Covey is a protected child—well-connected at the highest levels of the Department of Justice, as well as a handful of "patriotic" senators and congressmen," John explained.

"You mean the Justice Department—*all* of the people there—are afraid of this guy?"

"Early in his career, he became something of a folk hero in the department," Lockland intervened. "His methods were always questionable, but he was the department's equivalent of Clint Eastwood—Dirty Harry, to be exact. Operating just outside the generally accepted boundaries were tolerated, even admired. By the time the powers that be realized the monster they created, it was too late. Every incoming AG already knew of him. Even several FBI directors had unofficial hands-off directives."

"But murder? Threatening and extorting?" Linda asked.

"Like I said—blind eye is the marching order when it comes to Covey."

Linda finished her drink. Rocco raised the bottle toward her, and she waved him off.

"So again—why am I here?" Linda asked.

John motioned to the others to refrain from commenting. He looked at her with an affable stare.

"You are not just a judge, Linda. You are a highly respected member of the community—by both Republicans and Democrats. These days, that is as rare as the Hope Diamond."

"That doesn't answer my question, John," she said.

"We need a Judicial sanction, or some type of warrant."

Again, she frowned and stared back at him as though only the two of them occupied the room.

"John, I am a state and county judge. There are other judges— some connected more closely to the Justice Department. Why me?"

Aiden leaned forward onto his thighs. John sat back, and Linda turned her attention toward Aiden.

"Because of who Covey is and how deep his tentacles run, this needs to be above reproach—buttoned up with no legal gap Covey can squirm out of," Aiden said. "You are a trusted servant of the law and the bench and have no dog in this fight. Questioning the efficacy of this action will be difficult."

Linda smiled with discernible sarcasm. She glanced at everyone in the room.

"I am an appeals court justice. My authorizing whatever action is proposed will itself be viewed as highly unorthodox. That alone may jeopardize whatever it is you are planning—not to mention any reelection ambitions I might have."

Aiden rubbed his palms together and nodded.

"Or it will be the shining star of a very long and effective career," Aiden said, never taking his eyes off hers. "Reelection? You will hold this position as long as you like. What is Youngstown, if not the underdog who never gave up? You'll be as ubiquitous as George Washington and the Western Reserve."

"I see that possibility, but…"

"And you are a steward and protector of the community?" Aiden interrupted.

"Yes, but…"

"The community is under attack," Aiden elucidated. "You are the most ethical and trustworthy public servant I know. It is neither unorthodox nor unwarranted."

"So, what is the action you want to undertake?"

"Not to sound melodramatic, but it's a sting," Rocco interjected.

"A sting? How?"

"Covey is himself planning an action against the Costigan family. We need to open that door and invite him to step through it. When he does—well, there it is."

"There it is," she said sarcastically. "And if the Justice Department or the AG himself comes after me?"

"They can't," Aiden interjected.

"And why not?"

"Two reasons," Lockland said, stepping in.

Linda tilted her head and motioned for him to continue.

"One—it's all by the book and above board. Covey is a menace and a murderer. Everything here and in that writ is and will be factual," Lockland explained.

"And?" Linda asked.

Lockland pulled himself forward on the sofa, extending his head out beyond the others.

"They want it," he said.

"Come again?" Linda asked.

"From top to bottom, the Justice Department wants Covey gone. His very existence is a daily ass boil to those who have enabled this fucking jagoff—pardon my language. They're more likely to award you a medal of merit than pursue any course of discipline."

"Really, Mr. Lockland?" Linda asked.

"You'll be added to the Avengers™—Disney permitting— group of superheroes, Linda." John smiled.

Linda thought for a moment and turned her attention back to Mark Lockland. "You're okay with all this?"

"I am. This must end. Besides, I owe Liz. I knew about his fucking extortion and I played safe politics instead of doing the right thing and standing up for her."

"The United States Government? Covey *is* the United States Government," Linda insisted.

"So am I," Mark Lockland said with unusual confidence.

Chapter 10

Connecting the Dots

Aiden Vachon was a shrewd businessman, understanding better than most how to successfully straddle the paper-thin line between authentic negotiation and just the right degree of arm-twisting. Aiden had supreme trust and confidence in Rocco—not only in getting the job done but in never applying more than the minimum encouragement necessary. He did not threaten or browbeat any of the individuals he was tasked with persuading. Rocco was himself a brilliant man and more often looked to oratory urging versus physical leverage.

At one point, there was an ongoing competitive war among the larger private sanitation companies in the Youngstown area. The feud was not only creating disruption and anxiety in the community, but it was also beginning to affect Vachon Enterprises financially. Though he had no direct concerns in the sanitation industry, Aiden owned stakes in two large trucking companies in the region. Also owning many properties in the metropolitan area, he was dependent upon the smooth operations of the companies now at war with one another.

So, Aiden tasked Rocco Donofrio with bringing this "nonsense" to an end. Representatives from the three sanitation competitors were encouraged to attend a Vachon-sponsored luncheon at the Youngstown Country Club. Somewhat tongue-in-cheek, Rocco instructed the various owners that this was an offer they couldn't refuse. At the arranged luncheon, Rocco presented a simple set of ground rules crafted by Aiden. Rocco told the representatives of each organization, "Agree to these terms now, and Vachon will stay out of all your local markets. Continue to fight, and Vachon Enterprises will enter the sanitation market with a half-billion-dollar startup budget.

"We will take crushing volumes of commercial and residential customers away from all of you. You all know Aiden, and so you know he doesn't bluff."

Whatever these companies thought of Aiden Vachon, there was never any doubt: Rocco Donofrio was a deliberate and direct man. If he said it, it was.

State Senator Rufus Clairborn of Beaver Local raised a myriad of concerns about the creative, unorthodox way the crisis was solved. As quickly as he announced his trepidation, he sank back into the scenery, as though a profound epiphany swayed him. "It was like magic," John Rushton was heard to comment on the senator's enlightenment. This was not the first time local politicians "came around."

The Youngstown sanitation wars, as reported in *The Vindicator*, the premier Youngstown newspaper and website, ended with no fireworks or fanfare. Aiden Vachon once again saved the city and its people. The "Youngstown Garbage Wars" were over.

Patrick looked up from his desk to see Tom coming around the corner, his phone pressed to his ear. As Tom entered his brother's office, he was saying his goodbyes. He pressed the phone with his thumb and deposited it into the holster clipped to his belt.

"It's started," Tom said.

"So, we need to move."

"Yup—and probably quickly," Tom said.

Patrick leaned back into the old wooden desk chair—the chair his grandfather had sat in a thousand times—and flicked his pencil onto the ink blotter on the desk.

"You think he'll definitely come after us?" Patrick asked.

"Rocco's worried about it, so yeah, I do. Everything is ready, and the 'should-have-been-just-in-case' bags were packed a week ago.

Patrick shook his head and sucked in a lungful of the smoky air. "I suppose this all has to be done."

"Either that, or we'll all be looking over our shoulders forever."

The dark Ford van pulled up in front of the Brookline home. The driver, Rocco's Uncle Dominic, jumped out, motioning Mary and the kids into the van. Dominic was a normally nervous guy, but he maintained the image of calm like an Olympian.

Mary burst out of the house, a small suitcase in one hand, Jacqueline's hand in the other. He told them both his hands would likely be full, so they would have to help carry odds and ends. James followed closely behind, a mystified—if not confused—look on his face.

Mary looked up and down the neighborhood, awaiting whatever terrible experience was now underway. She thought about the first time they looked at this house and how enormously different her reality now was. She wasn't sure what to feel. She was afraid—mostly for her children—but also angry that David didn't leave well enough alone. She knew that was wrong and remembered she supported her husband. She owned this as much as he did.

Then there was her husband's motivation and ethics. He didn't go down this road for profits or glory; he did it because he could not cope with the notion that his life was a lie, and not knowing the truth. Still, there was the idea of discretion and judgment. He should have considered his family, but how could he possibly have known his efforts would lead to this?

"And what about this other family in Youngstown?" she thought. Were they also living in a fabricated world, and was all this thrusting them into a new reality they were no better prepared for? Then, as she so often did, she steadied herself. She was made of stern and steady Irish Catholic timber. This was not about her or her husband. This was about her children and their well-being.

She recalled the many times Elizabeth Costigan schooled her in the paradigm of playing the hand you are dealt—or don't. This whole mess created by Francis Costigan years earlier had inconceivable tentacles, reaching from Boston to Washington to Northeast Ohio. It brought into focus, for her, a city and a people she had no recollection of ever considering. It also reminded her of Veronica Polino, and she thought, "This can't be a coincidence. This is all somehow tied together."

This was for later, however. Right now, the priority is getting the children to safety and hoping this will go away.

"What about my sister-in-law and her kids?" Mary asked Dominic as she stepped up into the van.

"Same drill," Dominic said. "There's another van like this one at their house."

"And Anne and Elizabeth?"

"Anne is with your sister-in-law. Can't say about the old lady."

Dominic slid the side door closed, climbed into the driver's seat, and sped away toward Coolidge Corner.

David pushed open the door, knocking as he entered.

"Granny Elizabeth?" he asked entering the house, as he always did.

Not once in as long as he could remember had he ever stepped through that door without reflecting on his life and the Costigan legacy. This time it was even more profound, and the usual feelings of comfort, safety, and love were different. He still loved his grandmother, but her South Boston home of more than sixty years felt—and even smelled—differently.

"Is that you, Billy?" her voice rang out from the other room.

"No, Granny. It's David."

"David!" She smiled as she entered the kitchen with another huge, hard-covered novel about either the Pope or JFK. "This is a surprise," and she hugged her grandson, who now towered over her.

"Would you like some coffee or some tonic?" she asked.

"Maybe some water."

"What's the matter?" she asked, filling a glass from the refrigerator door. "You seem troubled. Does this have anything to do with you and your brother gallivanting here and there?"

"Yes, kind of," he said, sitting down at the table.

She too sat down—her hair, blouse, and slacks impeccable, as if she were going out to Davio's or Turner's.

"What's the matter, David?" she asked, rubbing his cheek with her hand.

David looked at her, not sure if he was more anxious about her ire or her sadness. He was also not sure of his own feelings toward the woman who was one of his rocks. He took a mouthful of the sweet Quabbin water. He tapped on the table—his old childhood quirk. Elizabeth moved her hand over his and squeezed it in a loving rather than disciplinary way.

"So, what is it?" she asked.

"Granny, I wouldn't be here if I didn't think you might be in some danger," he said.

"Danger?" She laughed; quite sure this was his usual wit.

David looked at her, his face as firm as an un-ripened pear.

Her smile collapsed back into a sullen gaze.

"You're not kidding," she said.

"No."

She placed the large book directly in front of her and wiped it with her hand as though both thinking and cleaning.

"Well, you best get to it, lest I reach the end of my days before you finish."

David smiled, as he always did, at the way his grandmother thought and communicated.

He asked if she remembered the day she found him coming down from the attic. She did—and remembered not being all too happy. As he began to retell the story slowly and chronologically— starting with the attic letters from his grandfather—her body seemed to slouch down ; her hands tightened around the hardcover novel on the table; and her eyes narrowed and began to glisten.

He went on to tell her about Aiden Vachon and how he revealed the real story to him, Brendan, and John Rushton. And of course, he told her about Lem Covey—the only reason he would ever have broached this with her. When he finished, Elizabeth just stared down at the back of the novel she held, her head and hands both shaking.

"Granny, are you all right?" David asked.

"All right?" she stammered, as if physically dazed by a fall or impact. "No, I probably wouldn't suggest I am okay."

"You can't stay here," David said. "I don't know what he's capable of."

"I would have thought you'd think I'm getting what I deserve," she said in a deprecating way.

David put his hand over hers, as he stared toward her.

"I'm not sure about all this yet, but I do know what an amazing grandmother you've been. You must've had your reasons. How could I ever judge you or question your motives? I wasn't there. This was a very different time. What have you always told me, "Judge not, lest you be judged'? That's been a kind of golden rule for me."

"I wish someone had," she sighed. "And now you and your brother are swept up. That was the one thing—well, and your dad—I was not going to let happen."

"What, Granny?"

"Finding out the truth, of course," she said. "Now look at this mess. Your father?"

David thought for a moment and then smiled.

"He doesn't know," David lied. "At least I don't think he does."

Elizabeth gripped the book with her perfectly manicured fingernails, the redness in her knuckles deepening. She stared down at the back of the book jacket, her thumb rolling over the photo of Doris Kearns Goodwin. David was not ignorant of his grandmother's way of thinking and how she processed information. He knew to give her adequate space and time to take it all in.

"I can't even try to explain all of this to you," she said. "I did have my reasons, though I think you'd be hard-pressed to understand them."

"Did you really feel like you had a choice?" David asked.

"I was young myself then," she said. "Two young children. Your great-grandfather was a dominant and unrelenting man. Not to mention my own father, who thought me far better off without Frank. But did I have a choice? I wish I could go back and talk with that young girl."

"What would you say?" David asked.

"Oh sweetheart," she sighed. "A woman's heart is a well of mystery and secrets. I never wanted to hurt you. I love you too much."

"You can't hurt me, Granny," he said, pulling one of her hands off the book. "You were a great mom to my dad and Uncle Tom, and I could not have had a greater grandmother."

Elizabeth looked at David as he squeezed her hand. She raised it to her mouth and kissed his fingers.

"You do know how much I love you and Brendan?"

"Of course."

"Well, you are not a child anymore," she said. "Let me tell you a story."

Elizabeth told David how she met his grandfather, and her story was consistent with what he had been told growing up. She described the tension between her and her father, and his disappointment over her marrying someone like Francis Costigan instead of someone with a pedigree he approved of.

She told him about his grandfather's initial secret dream of medicine, and how that became less of a secret over time. She also painfully told him how no Costigan or McGowan thought much of Francis's fanciful whim—including herself. She looked to be in great pain as she relayed what seemed to be one of her most ardent regrets.

She described Francis in an almost desperate way, regarding his dream and the prospect of a life in the iron works.

"I was his wife," she exclaimed. "A wife is supposed to stand by her husband and support him."

"Maybe you didn't—"

"I did," she interrupted. "I knew he could do it. Your grandfather was one of those men who could do literally anything he set his mind to."

David continued to listen, though nervous about the Covey situation. Elizabeth talked about how quickly they planned the wedding, and all of this was against the backdrop of what was happening in Europe and the Far East at the time. Then she stopped and grew very pensive.

"The speed of our wedding wasn't because of war, David," she said. "I had no choice."

"That figures" he thought to himself. "Great, now I find out my Granny was knocked up, in addition to everything else."

He rubbed her fingers with his thumb, remembering it was not his place to judge.

"Well, you would have gotten married anyway—just later," he said.

"Oh really?" she said, almost sarcastically. "What if I told you that was unlikely? Would that change how you see me, and feel toward me?"

"No, Granny." David lied again.

"So, how could I knowingly agree to this unholy situation? That's what you really want to know, isn't it?"

"I never used the term 'unholy,' Granny," David retorted.

"But it is an abomination, for Christ's love," she said regretfully. "He was married to me and another woman in Ohio at the same time. I believe she was spared the truth. I was not."

David stared at his grandmother, now feeling a sense of remorse and sympathy, rather than anger.

"Did you love him?" David asked.

"My father used to tell me, don't ask a question that might give you an answer you don't want to hear," Elizabeth said. "Is this an answer you can hear, David, no matter what it is?"

"We've come this far, Granny."

She leaned into him, who by all evidence loved her dearly. She squeezed his hand a bit tighter as she organized her thoughts.

"I thought he was strikingly handsome—the same black hair as you, and those crystal blue eyes. Things weren't as free back then as they are today. Understand?" she asked.

"Yes, Granny."

"That didn't mean our desires weren't the same, you know?"

David squirmed in his chair. For him, trying to conceive of his Granny as a young, attractive woman, complete with all normal desire, was like trying to visualize his mother on a stripper pole—just not possible.

"So, I found myself succumbing to those feelings, and we didn't have the number of options you have today. No... then there was your dad."

David had no earthly idea how—or if—to respond.

"But you don't want to hear that," she smiled. "The truth is, I never loved him. And I think I was angry about that more than anything."

"Granny, is that why you didn't support him, and not because you really believed it?"

"This is why Mary is a lucky girl," she said. "You don't require crayons."

She went on to tell him it was a perfect plan for the two of them. She had the children she always wanted, her husband would forever be heralded as a hero—and a dead one at that—and she would be free to find a man she loved, after the appropriate grieving period.

"But you never did," David said.

"I miscalculated two things."

David nodded, awaiting the rest of her point.

"I miscalculated that there were two to three women for every returning GI—and most of them without two kids already."

"And the other?" he asked.

"Sin."

"Sin?"

"I told you—I walked willingly down that road. I knew there was a wife and a family in Ohio who knew nothing of me. He went before God and pledged himself to another woman. I was so afraid of cursing this family. Maybe this Covey fellow is that retribution."

"Covey is not divine retribution, Granny," David said. "He's an obsessed sociopath and certainly has nothing to do with God."

She rubbed his hand and nodded affirmatively. She looked about her kitchen, smiling as her head turned from side to side.

"I remember like it was yesterday, you and Brendan making a ruckus here, and my yelling at you. Lord, I miss that so much. You really have to get James and Jacqueline here more."

"I know, Granny, but Mary isn't very patient with that kind of behavior. Anyway, Jacqueline is a girl."

"Oh, flying fudge cakes," she laughed. "Kids need to be kids."

David stood, walked to the sink, and refilled his water from the tap. He sat back down, running his thumb up and down his glass.

"The day you found me coming down from the attic?" he started. "Was it because of the letters in the trunk?"

"Of course it was. There are other things you didn't find—thank God."

"Why didn't you just throw them away?" David asked.

"I don't know. I just couldn't. I probably should have."

"My dad could have found them."

"Your father was the perfect child," Elizabeth said in a naïve way. "He was told to stay out of there, and he did. I'm a little surprised your Uncle Tom never did."

"Well, it's good neither of them did," David said.

Esther Chase knocked. Mark Lockland looked up and nodded to her. She stepped in and closed the door behind her.

"Covey's gone dark," she said, expecting this to not be new news—and it wasn't.

"I'm sure he has," Lockland said.

"What do we do?" Esther asked. "Is there a move we could or should make?"

Lockland tossed his pen onto his desk and removed his reading glasses. He swung his chair around and looked out the window, across the mall. He stared out into Washington, then swung his chair back toward Esther.

"I think we're way past that. Don't you?" he asked.

"That depends."

"What—on how many people get killed in the meantime?"

"I, um…"

He raised his hand, halting her mid-sentence. He looked down at his desk and nodded.

"We're both bureaucrats, you and I," he said. "That doesn't mean we can't do the right thing—and maybe what our jobs are supposed to be."

"I'm not sure I understand," Esther said.

Lockland opened the lower drawer of his desk and took out a large manila envelope. He placed it on the desk and slid it over to where Esther was standing. She leaned over, picked up the envelope, and opened it. From inside, she withdrew a manila folder. She placed it on the desk and opened it. Inside was an e-plane ticket and accompanying boarding pass.

"Boston?" she asked.

"First thing in the morning," he replied.

Under the two travel documents was a letter, and she could see the Justice Department letterhead at the top. She picked up the letter:

TO: Esther Chase, JD Agent, E412A

FROM: Mark R. Lockland, Director, United States Justice Department

CC: The Honorable Linda A. Cullin , The Courts of the US 6th Circuit of Courts

In the matter and investigation of Department Agent Lemuel Covey, Agent Chase is heretofore authorized to employ and use any and all resources available to her, to return Agent Covey to the U.S. Department of Justice, under guard or immobilized.

This action co-signed by The Honorable Linda A. Cullin , 6th Circuit of Courts, and Mark R. Lockland, Director, United States Department of Justice.

You should consider this action as an immediate and sensitive undertaking. Employ your best judgment and maintain all safety protocols in the process.

Order executed by:

Mark R. Lockland, *Director, U.S. Department of Justice*

Linda A. Cullin , *U.S. 6th Circuit Courts*

Esther read the letter—and then she read it again.

"Mark?"

"Your get-out-of-jail-free card, Esther," he said.

"Where's your cover, Mark?"

"I'm not interested in cover. Go there and do whatever you have to. Oh, Joe Lawlor is the commander of the Massachusetts State Police. He and I were roommates in college, and we're still good friends. Here's his card." He handed it to Esther.

She took it and placed it into the folder along with Lockland's letter.

"You know, if this goes south, Mark…"

"Don't worry about that. Just get the bastard," he said.

"Do you think that's where he's headed?"

"I'm guessing, soon enough."

Claire Wilkins was the consummate chief of staff: smart, savvy, well-spoken, and attractive. Washington was a hornet's nest by all accounts, and it was particularly hard for young, ambitious women. The city and political environment, though changing with the rise of more and more female legislators and cabinet members, was still a laboratory of men behaving badly.

Greg Harrison, the moderately popular U.S. Attorney General, sought Claire's advice and counsel more than almost anyone—except his own wife and Assistant Attorney General Cletus Morgan.

Greg Harrison was a supremely ethical and honorable man. Some Democrats, including the president, also saw that as a contributor to his perceived naïveté. His biggest blind spot was that he could never quite get his arms around how low and deceitful some of the "highest and mightiest" could sink. That's where Claire came in. She was both his eyes and ears—and the one who often instructed him to either duck, stand back, or hit.

At a time when the Justice Department was under scrutiny and pressure to deal more effectively with the Russian and Romanian syndicate—bold and ruthless, particularly in Chicago, Dallas, and Philadelphia—Lem Covey was a kind of godsend. He was afforded the chance to head up this organized crime field unit. Covey's impact came quickly, along with reports of excessive force and a cavalier attitude toward Miranda and suspect abuse.

Almost immediately, the media began reporting on the success of the unit, and Harrison received most of the credit. They either missed or ignored the slew of constitutional violations—including the use of banned restraints, torture, and occasional "accidental" deaths.

She tapped on his doorframe and stepped into his office. He was reading, his bifocals down at the end of his nose.

She cleared her throat, and he took off the glasses and smiled at her.

"You have a call," she said.

"A call? From whom?"

"Rocco Donofrio."

"Who?"

"He's Aiden Vachon's right-hand guy. You met him last April at a law enforcement symposium in Columbus, Ohio."

"What does he want, Claire? Can't you manage this?"

"You need to take the call, sir."

He thought for a moment and shook his head.

"Put it through."

Elizabeth watched David intently as he ate the homemade stew, which she was so proud of. He added a jolt of vinegar—that always improved a good Irish stew for him. Trying not to slurp as he ate, the broth tasted so delicious and was right on time in the emotional comfort category.

He set down his spoon and wiped his mouth with the cloth napkin Elizabeth had set out for him.

"We need to get going, Granny," he said.

"Go? Where?"

"Ogunquit," he said.

"Maine? Why Maine?"

"It's where Mary, Rachel, and the kids are headed. It's not safe here."

David knew convincing his grandmother to leave would have its challenges, but he didn't anticipate outright refusal. The more he pleaded and argued, the deeper she dug in her proverbial heels.

"If your Mr. Covey wants to come here and shoot me, I suggest he get about that and spare us all the drama."

"For the love of God, Granny!" he shouted. "Do you really want me and Brendan and the kids to be the descendants of a murdered grandmother?"

Elizabeth frowned, as if David had employed unfair tactics in his efforts.

"I have never been one for running away, David," she said. "But I will do anything for you, your brother, and your families. What about your father?"

Elizabeth asked the one question David hoped she wouldn't. Yet there it was, tossed up like a bad softball pitch.

"Dad is safe," he said, hoping that would be enough. It was.

He flicked the silver butane lighter, raised it to his mouth, and lit the thin cigar. He puffed on it until the tip glowed a sharp red. He drew in a mouthful of smoke and exhaled a smooth, straight stream. Being conscious of the people walking behind him in both directions, he read the inscription on the memorial to the Massachusetts Fifty-Fourth Regiment—the first Black unit in the Civil War—under the command of Colonel Robert Gould Shaw. Covey shook his head in a dismissive way, unappreciative of the contribution these brave men made. He was, after all, descended from generations of slave-owning Virginia planters.

He made his way through the Boston Common, across a busy Boylston Street, and into a small sandwich shop on the corner of Summer Street. He arrived to find a crowd nestled up to the counter, but a lone man sitting at one of the few tables in the shop. He walked over to the man, the cigar still in his mouth.

"Hey, you can't smoke in here, pal," a man in a white kitchen apron said from behind the counter.

Covey looked over at the man—nary a hint of expression. He turned and flicked the cigar across the breadth of the shop, barely missing a pedestrian as they passed.

"May I sit?" Covey asked.

"Please," the middle-aged, balding man said, focused more on the menu than his guest. "The pastrami here is great. A little mustard, and you're in business."

"I'll have whatever you have," Covey said, eager to get to their business.

The balding man jotted something down in a small notebook he carried, tore out the page, and held it out toward the end of the counter. A young man—maybe twenty—opened the waist-high door at the far end of the counter and took the note from the man.

"Just be a few minutes, Mr. F," the young man said, stepping back behind the counter.

On the table was a bottle of Pepsi and two paper cups. The man opened the bottle—sharp hiss as the carbonation escaped. He filled each glass halfway and slid Covey's over to him.

"You shouldn't have picked such an opulent place," Covey snickered.

"Hey, this is all on your nickel," the man said. "You aren't paying me for my fine dining expertise."

Covey smiled, as the young worker stepped through the small door and placed the two hot sandwiches on the table.

The bald man picked up a half sandwich, blew on it, and took a small bite.

"Hmm!" the man moaned. "Now that is a sandwich."

Covey also took a bite, though not as enamored as his tablemate.

"So, you understand the nature of our arrangement?" Covey asked in his usual Southern twang.

The man took another bite, wiped his hands on a paper napkin, and took a sip of his cola.

"I find them, tell you where they are, and we're done. Right? Well, except for that other thing."

"As long as they are where you tell me they are," Covey smiled. "I'm not used to doing business with people I don't know intimately."

"Don't I come with good recommendations?" the man asked.

"Yes, you do—but I haven't gotten to where I am by being careless."

The man leaned in toward Covey, while also assuring no patron was within earshot.

"We agreed on twenty thousand, right? Half now and half when I find them."

"Half now, and half when you get me to them," Covey replied.

"Splitting hairs, aren't we, General Lee?"

"Bostonians!" Covey snarled. "You think you're all that. I have news for you—the rest of the country doesn't think so."

"Really?" The man smiled, taking another bite of his sandwich. "We may not say 'y'all' or 'good day,' but we also win. We don't fuck around with bullshit. We tell it like it is and get on with it. So—I get fifty percent now, and fifty percent when I tell you where they are. They will be where I tell you they will be."

"Very well," Covey said, pulling a white legal envelope from the inside pocket of his coat and handing it to the balding man.

The man reached out and took the envelope. "I assume it's all there."

"Of course," Covey replied.

"Now—I won't do business with a man whose name I don't know," Covey insisted.

The man took another bite of his evidently delicious sandwich and smiled.

"Fiaschetti," the man said, extending his greasy hand. "Tommy Fiaschetti."

"Mr. Fiaschetti," Covey said, reluctantly shaking his hand. "Our friend in Washington thinks highly of you. I will look into you. Never too careful, you know?"

"Feel free. I'm a ghost, but you probably know that." Fiaschetti smirked.

"I like working with ghosts. No one bats an eye when I turn them into pâté."

Fiaschetti looked up and stopped chewing.

"Relax. I'm joking. But you will come through, correct?"

"Never missed on a job yet."

"Do we have an estimated target?"

"It isn't a perfect science, but I'd guess inside of a week. You can't hide a half-dozen people that easily."

Covey took a last bite of the sandwich and tossed it down onto the table like so much garbage.

Fiaschetti looked at him as he rose from his seat. "You know, people wait in line for those sandwiches."

"I suppose if you sell it right, people will wait in line for a bag of shit."

Fiaschetti nodded and savored the cured meat, nonetheless.

"A week," Covey said as he turned toward the door.

"Thereabouts." Fiaschetti smiled as he consumed the sandwich.

Covey walked through the patrons in his path and disappeared into the passing Boylston Street pedestrians.

As he finished, a young Hispanic busboy began cleaning the side of the table vacated by Covey.

"How's the sandwich, Mr. Stagno?" the boy asked.

"Fiaschetti, Armand!" Stagno cautioned.

The young Armand jerked back, embarrassed at his gaffe.

"¡Dios Mio!" Armand exclaimed. "I am sorry, Mr. Stagno."

"Dominic. It's Dominic when we're alone. In situations like this, it's Fiaschetti—Tommy Fiaschetti."

David pulled his car into a space beside Brendan's. He jumped out and ran around to the passenger side. As he helped his grandmother out of the car, the front door of the blue-sided Cape Cod home opened. James and Jacqueline ran down the front brick stairs, waving their arms wildly.

"Granny!" James yelled, almost knocking his great-grandmother over.

He wrapped his arms around her waist, followed almost immediately by the other two children. Elizabeth rubbed their heads while she laughed loudly.

"My babies," she said.

"C'mon kids," David said. "Let's help Granny Elizabeth into the house."

A moment later, Brendan and Dominic appeared in the doorway.

"Hi, Granny," Brendan said, stepping forward, helping his grandmother up the final step.

"Who's this?" Granny asked, her governor was gone at her age.

"Rocco Donofrio," Brendan said. "He's a friend."

"Donofrio—that's Italian," she said.

"It is, ma'am," Rocco said.

"That's okay," she smiled as she passed him. "Not everyone can be blessed to be Irish."

"No ma'am."

Inside, Mary and Rachel all walked into the main living area to greet Elizabeth.

Hugging and kissing ensued, though no reference to the reason for this impromptu getaway was made. The awkwardness of not referring to the present situation was obvious—not to mention the absence of Patrick and Tom.

"Rachel is making her stuffed cabbage," Mary said.

"Wonderful," Elizabeth said sincerely. "Jewish stuffed cabbage is like Irish chopped liver."

Everyone stopped, not sure how to reply to that comment or whether to take it seriously.

"That was a joke, children," Elizabeth said.

The group forced laughter, and David helped Elizabeth to the kitchen table.

"Something to drink, Granny?" he asked.

"Some hot tea?"

A bedroom door opened, and Anne stepped out into the living room.

"Hello, Granny Elizabeth," she said, walking over to the table and giving Granny a kiss.

"Hello, dear."

Anne sat down at the table, and a moment later, Rachel joined them.

David stood at the far end of the open living area, uneasy about both the obvious threat and the weave of intrigue inside his family. Who knew what? Who did not? Who was to be protected—and from what? He looked out to the front door he had walked through so many times in his life and thought about Bob Seger's lyrics: *"Wish I didn't know then what I didn't know now."* He never thought his life was simple, but like so many of us, the past always looks and feels less complex. The fact is, it was not—but retrospect carries with it the beginning, middle, and end. The future is not yet unfolded and therein lies the anxiety.

David jumped from the Subaru wagon, his small legs clicking in the river stones as fast as he could move them. Granny Elizabeth and Uncle Billy stood on the stoop, waiting for him to reach them. Her hair was darker, she was thinner, and most of all, she was infallible.

Anne and Patrick helped Brendan out of his harness as he galloped to see his grandmother and great uncle.

David jumped into his grandmother's arms, her laughter echoing across Ogunquit Beach.

"Did you make choco-chip cookies, Granny?" he asked, as she patted his head.

"Was I supposed to?" she asked.

David looked up at her, a vacant and confused stare on his face.

"Well of course I did, little one," she smiled, Brendan slamming into her from the other side.

"Bluefish are running," Uncle Billy said, as Patrick and Anne reached the stoop.

"That Evinrude been tuned?" Patrick asked.

"Two weeks ago," Billy smiled. "Tommy did it for me."

Brendan walked over to Billy, the awkward waddle of a toddler. As he so often did, he walked into him and looked straight up into Billy's round Irish face.

"Well, hello there, buddy," Billy said, looking down into his great-nephew's face.

"I fish, Uncle Biwy," Brendan said with the seriousness of a New Orleans funeral.

"Yes, you do, little man."

Elizabeth pulled two metal cookie trays from the new oven and placed them carefully on the two racks she had positioned on the counter. She leaned over, inhaling the comforting sweet aroma.

"Perfect."

David and Brendan saddled up to her instantly, waiting for the delicious cookies she never failed to make, when the boys were coming to either Southie or Ogunquit. She handed them each a plate with two cookies for each of them. She poured two glasses of milk and set them on the table adjacent to the plates.

Neither David nor Brendan were all that compliant with their grandmother, but the advent of chocolate chip cookies and milk made them as dutiful as monks in a monastery.

"David?" Anne's voice broke through after the fifth time calling it out.

David took a breath and turned.

"Mom?"

"Your father is on the phone."

David walked over to his mother, took the receiver from her, and gazed over at the aging, well-used oven. He smiled, catching his reflection in the front glass panel.

"Dad?"

"Is everyone there and safe?" Patrick asked.

"Everyone but you, Uncle Tom, and Uncle Billy," David said.

"We're fine. You just keep your wits about you and your eyes open, okay?"

"Okay."

Tommy Fiaschetti sat at the back of the Wood Island diner as Covey walked up the five steel stairs to the door. The bell clanged as he opened it and looked about the small restaurant for his new partner. Fiaschetti raised his hand nonchalantly, gaining Covey's attention. Covey walked around the few patrons in the narrow diner until reaching the table.

"Fiaschetti. I bet I'd beat you here," Covey laughed.

"Sit down," Fiaschetti suggested.

"Just for a moment. So, you have both of those things for me?"

"Of course I do. That is why I come so highly recommended," he sneered.

"Well?"

Fiaschetti withdrew an envelope from the breast pocket of his blue blazer and handed it to Covey. Covey opened it and read.

"Ogunquit?" Covey smiled. "This is the actual street address?"

"That's the one."

"And the other thing?" Covey asked.

Fiaschetti reached down into his coat pocket, pulled the automatic pistol out, and handed it under the table to Covey.

"Untraceable?" Covey asked.

"Of course. And fingerprint-resistant tape on the handle. You could shoot someone outside the state police barracks, and there is no way they can link the gun to you."

Massachusetts, unlike many southern and western states, has some of the most restrictive gun laws in the nation. Certainly, Covey was legally able to carry as many firearms as he chose, but these were some connected people. He was too smart to take a chance on something as stupid as a traceable handgun or bullet.

"I have a lot of sources," Covey said. "But this kind of thing, well, takes someone like yourself. No offense."

"None taken, Mr. Covey," Fiaschetti smiled. "I am a market-driven guy. There is a market for my unique services."

Covey smiled, looking at the pistol under the table.

"What are you, ah, going to do with those people?" Fiaschetti asked.

"Is that material to you?" Covey asked. "Our agreement and your price never included knowing any more than I tell you. Correct?"

"No sir," Fiaschetti said, holding up his hands. "That's your business."

"Yes, it is, Mr. Fiaschetti. You best remember that."

Covey slid the weapon into his coat pocket, picked up the envelope, and stood up. He buttoned his black trench coat; his eyes fixed on Fiaschetti as he fastened the garment. Fiaschetti too maintained a vex on Covey—a kind of vacant stare.

"Nice doing business with you," Covey said, his Virginia drawl starkly out of place here on the Massachusetts shore.

"Pleasure's mine. I will expect my money, when?"

"By the end of the week. Is that acceptable?"

"That will be fine," Fiaschetti smiled, as Covey made his way to the end of the diner and out the door.

Outside, Covey looked at the weapon, the handle wrapped in fingerprint-resistant tape. He looked around and bounced the gun in his hand, feeling its weight. He smiled, carefully placed it inside his jacket, and started walking. He smiled again. He liked winning and considered obtaining the information from Fiaschetti a victory. He could not have asked for anything better. They would all be in one place, making it that much easier.

His immediate plan might not lead to bringing down Aiden Vachon, but he prided himself in never being successfully crossed. There would always be another plan and another day for Vachon.

For now, he had business to attend to.

Chapter 11

Bridges

Dominic Stagno exited I-95 at the Portsmouth traffic circle. He moved around the roundabout—or the rotary, as it was called here—until deciding to pull into an all-night Denny's. He turned off the ignition and pushed the "Bluetooth" button on his steering wheel. The female voice asked for a name or number.

"The boss," he said, as the speaker sounded a quick tone and then a ring. It rang again.

"Dominic?" the familiar voice said.

"I'm about an hour away," Stagno said. "I'm stopping for a cup of coffee."

"Very good. I guess you have a few hours yet."

"I don't want to push it, but I want to get there before the sun comes up."

"It must be beautiful there."

"I wouldn't know," Stagno laughed. "It's just black, and I'm not at the ocean yet."

"Maine lobster, Dom," the voice said. "You should try and get one before you head back."

"Just might do that."

Patrick paced the floor of his office, clicking the pen cap in sync with his steps. Tom sat in the plush desk chair, watching his brother deal with stress the way he had all his life. Every few moments, Patrick gazed over to the phone, walking even faster each time he did.

"You're going to need a new carpet if you keep that up," Tom said.

"Can't just sit here," Patrick replied. "My whole damn family is up there."

"They'll be fine, Pat. I know how tough this is. That's my mother too."

Patrick took a bottle of Tanqueray from the desk bar and poured a glass. He raised the glass to Tom, but Tom shook his head from side to side. Patrick took a large mouthful and swallowed it with a loud "Ah."

He walked over to the window, pulled down one of the blind slats, and peered outside.

"So quiet," Patrick said.

"It's three-thirty A.M.," Tom laughed. "Not even the paper boys are out yet."

"Remember Charlie Tomkins?" Patrick asked.

"Sure," Tom said. "I remember being half asleep and hearing the clanking of the milk bottles."

When they were boys, it was common to have milk delivered in glass bottles to one's home. Most houses sported a gray, metal, insulated box on the stoop. Fresh milk was magically placed there at ungodly hours in the morning, and the discarded bottles were retrieved. It was a tradition and business long gone, just like physician house calls. It was a simpler time, though no sane person ever really wanted to go back.

Patrick smiled, thinking about those days. This was a time before his first visit to Youngstown, when the reality of his world was simple and untainted. Things were different now, and Patrick lamented over his sons and their families being drawn into this mess.

The phone rang, and Patrick leapt to answer it.

"Hello!" he said anxiously.

"Tom?"

"No, it's Patrick."

"Patrick, it's Aiden Vachon. You, okay?"

"Depends on how you define 'okay.'"

"It's all going to be good, Patrick. You just need to relax. You sound stressed."

"You think?" Patrick said sarcastically.

"Sometimes you just have to trust," Aiden said calmly.

"That's not your family up there, Aiden."

"No, it isn't, but nothing will happen to them."

"How do you know?" Patrick asked.

"I just know."

James sat cross-legged in front of the television, with his video game control in his hand. Jacqueline sat on her great-grandmother's lap, her mother and grandmother on either side of them. They were watching a Miley Cyrus concert, a favorite of Jacqueline's.

"I hope she keeps her clothes on," Anne said.

"I think she's past all that," Mary laughed.

David walked over to James, knelt down, and kissed his son on the top of the head. James looked up at him and smiled.

David stood quickly—an unfamiliar sound from the kitchen.

"What is it?" Mary asked.

"I thought I..."

Like an apparition, he turned and saw a man standing just inside the threshold. He could make out a silhouette and instantly grabbed for his son. He pulled James to his feet, the game control flopping onto the area rug and then the hardwood floor.

"Jesus Lord!" Elizabeth exclaimed, moving Jacqueline to Mary's lap.

The man stepped out into the light. He wore a long trench coat and skullcap, but the white beard and white hair were unmistakable. It was Lemuel Covey.

"Jesus isn't in Maine today," he said in his Southern twang.

His arm was partially extended, an automatic pistol pointing into the living area. David placed himself between Covey and his family, looking back at them, their faces masked with a terror he had not seen before.

"Easy does it, Mr. Costigan," Covey said. "I'm a very good shot."

"What are you doing here?" David asked. "My family has nothing to do with this."

"You crossed me," Covey said. "You brought this on. Now sit down."

Covey sported a malevolent grin, clearly enjoying the fear he caused. David carefully complied and sat down on the arm of the sofa. Covey moved to the front of the room, never taking his eyes off David. He stood still and silent, immersing himself in the terror of the moment. He looked down and to his right, catching a brief glance of the television.

"Miley Cyrus," he snickered. "No, I like her father. Nice Southern boy."

"What is it you want, Covey?" David demanded.

"Well, for one thing—or maybe two," he laughed, "I want your father and brother out here. Now!"

"My father isn't here."

"That's a lie. He wouldn't send you all up here to Maine without him."

"That's just exactly what he did," David said.

Covey cocked back the hammer of the pistol and pointed it at David. He froze for a moment and then turned the gun toward Mary.

"All right, all right," David said. "Bren, please get up here, before he hurts someone."

"Who?" Brendan's voice came from the basement.

"Just get up here!" David shouted.

"Be right up," he replied.

A few moments later, the sound of pounding footsteps arose from behind the basement door. It opened slowly. Brendan stepped out, noticeably shocked.

"Get over here with the others," Covey said.

"Easy," Brendan said, moving over toward the couch, his back carefully turned away from Covey.

"Well," Covey said, "most of the clan is here. I can deal with your father later."

David stood—not in a provocative way, but the way a man readies himself to talk to another.

"What possible good could come from this?" David asked. "You gain nothing."

Covey laughed and slapped his free hand onto his chest. He looked about the room and shook his head.

"You don't get it," he smirked. "That is why I am standing here, and you are all there."

"Get what?" Brendan asked indignantly.

"I don't pretend to understand all the details of your family and the Vachons, but there's something."

"So what?" David asked, looking over at Mary.

"Do you think he'll just stand by after… well, after?"

"You're looking to draw him out," Brendan said. "You want him to come after you."

"And I thought you were the dumb one," Covey said.

"He'll kill you," Brendan said.

"No, no, I don't think so. I have the US government behind me."

"You have shit!" David shouted.

"David Costigan!" Elizabeth scolded.

Covey laughed almost hysterically and nodded his head.

"Now that is ironic," Covey laughed.

"What is?" Elizabeth asked. "You don't know the first thing about it."

"About what, old woman?" Covey asked snidely.

"Life, family, truth; honor."

"She is kidding me?" he asked.

"I'm afraid not."

"Truth, honor—these are manufactured to elevate people we want to elevate." He paused. "We can send men in to slaughter a whole village because there's oil under it. But if we call them heroes and call the slaughter a battle… Well, that's how it works."

"No, Mr. Covey. That is not how it works. There is truth and honor, and sometimes the good guys do win."

"In the movies," Covey laughed.

"Do you like movies?" David asked.

"What?"

"Do you like movies?"

"Whatever," Covey said impatiently. "Yes, I like them."

Dances with Wolves, David said.

"What about it?" Covey asked. "The one with the Indians?"

"Yes, that one."

"All right, I'll play along," Covey laughed. "I have all the time in the world."

"In the early part of the movie, the character Timmons is taking Kevin Costner to his new post. Remember?"

"Kind of," Covey replied.

"Well, there they are, their first night at the campfire, when after slogging down some food, Timmons bends, farts, and laughs."

"And?" Covey asked, feigning indifference.

"Costner is narrating, as he scribes in his journal. He says, *"This may be the foulest man he has ever met."*

"And so?"

"Well, that pretty well sums up how I feel right about now," David said in a challenging way.

"David!" Mary said, pulling herself halfway to her feet.

Covey shifted around, pointing the gun directly at Mary.

"Easy does it there, ma'am," Covey said, as Mary settled back down.

He stared at the frightened woman for a few more moments and then turned back toward David. He nodded slightly and smiled.

"Now I ask myself, why would he goad me? Why would he talk gibberish about some movie from the nineties?" Covey asked.

"Ninety," David specified.

"Now this is what I mean. It doesn't fit, unless you are trying to stall me for some reason. Could that be it?"

Just then, the basement door swung to a fully open position. Confused, Covey turned slightly toward it, his weapon rising a bit higher.

Covey's head bent back as Esther Chase came out from behind the brown hollow-core door. She was dressed in jeans and a loosely fitted U-Penn sweatshirt. Then she stepped to the side to make room for Rocco Donofrio, who emerged.

Taken aback, Covey looked over at David, his anger visible through the veins in his neck. He turned the gun back toward Mary, noting that neither Esther nor Rocco had a visible weapon.

"No matter what happens, I will shoot your wife," Covey said.

"You won't shoot anyone," another voice rang out from behind the basement door.

Covey turned. A look of utter shock, confusion, and anger took over his countenance. It was Dominic Stagno.

"Fiaschetti! You fu—"

"Language, please. There are kids here—and you, such a proper gentleman."

"I had a feeling about you, Fiaschetti," Covey scolded.

"Stagno. Dominic Stagno, actually."

Covey's jaw dropped. He was now noticeably shaken, confused, and angry.

"It's over, Mr. Covey," Elizabeth Chase said. "You haven't killed anyone yet. Well, not here anyway."

David and Elizabeth's eyes met. Disbelief sang out from both.

"Did he just say what I think he did?" Brendan asked.

"That's what I heard," Elizabeth half-chuckled.

"What the Christ is this?" Covey exclaimed, turning the weapon back toward Mary. "I will shoot her. Don't be stupid enough to think I won't. You think this is funny?"

"No, you won't," Dominic sneered.

"Yes! Yes, I will!" Covey shouted, his demeanor was now jittery and anxious.

"No, I mean you won't shoot anyone—not that you wouldn't try," Dominic said.

Covey wheeled the pistol around, aimed it at Dominic, and pulled the trigger. *Click*—but no gunshot.

Both Esther and Rocco immediately pulled pistols from their backs and pointed them at the shocked Virginian. He pulled the trigger again; the result was the same.

"So, here we have a guy with a gun, terrorizing this family," Rocco said. "Well within our rights to put him down."

Covey pulled the trigger three successive times, then threw the dysfunctional weapon at Rocco, who ducked, as Covey turned to run.

The crack of a gunshot pinged about the house, as Esther fired her Glock-9. The bullet struck Covey in the side, midpoint in his rib cage. He fell to his right, slammed his shoulder on the wall, and fell across the end table, the bluish glass lamp breaking onto the floor. David moved his head emotionlessly, as Covey rolled onto the carpet.

"Ooh, that's got to hurt," David said, watching Covey's blood leak out onto the light blue rug.

Dominic pulled his cell phone from his jacket pocket and dialed.

"Yes, my name is Dominic Stagno, from the Ohio State Police on special assignment. We need an ambulance at 22 Rollins Drive in Ogunquit. There's been a gunshot, but the intruder has been disarmed."

David and Brendan looked at one another and then both turned toward Rocco. Rocco shrugged his shoulders and smiled.

"He's a cop?" David asked.

Dominic smiled and took a small faux bow. He returned the cell phone to his jacket and crossed his arms with exaggerated pride.

Esther walked into the kitchen and returned with a dish towel. She pushed Covey back and applied the towel to his wound. She took his hand and placed it onto the towel.

"Advice, doctor?" she asked David, without looking at him.

"No, you're good," David said, squeezing in between Mary and the kids.

Elizabeth got herself up from the couch and walked over to Covey.

"Granny!" Anne shouted.

"It's fine, dear," Elizabeth said, as if she were getting a cup of tea.

She stood over Covey, now reeling in considerable pain, her arms folded across her chest.

"Know what your problem is, Mr. Covey?" she asked, not expecting an answer. "Ego. You think you're smarter than everyone else, and you're cocky about it. Better hope that the ambulance gets here soon. That's quite a puddle collecting."

Stagno signed the clipboard and handed it back to the detective. David walked over to him, uncertain of what was happening.

"Esther Chase set this all up," Dominic said. "Covey came across several state lines, so the FBI and Justice are within their authority. I needed a special waiver to cross into Maine."

David nodded, extended his hand. Dominic squeezed hard and patted David on the shoulder with the other.

"I'd love another slice of that T-Anthony's Pizza while we're here."

"Oh no, we are going to Santarpio's in East Boston," Brendan interrupted. "Maybe some fire-grilled lamb too."

Dominic smiled and nodded.

"Dominic?" David said. "What if Covey had figured out the gun you gave him didn't fire?"

"You really want to know?"

David nodded.

"There is a tiny GPS tracking chip in the handle, thanks to Ms. Chase. If he had a different gun, he would have been dead before he touched that back doorknob. Lucky him, huh?"

Mary walked over and put her arm around her husband. The two paramedics stabilized Covey, his hands cuffed to the gurney. Esther walked over to David and Mary and pushed her black hair off her forehead. Mary looked at her up and down.

"She is pretty," Mary said.

"Thank you, Mary," Esther said. "Having one to manage is more than enough, thank you."

Mary laughed. "Thank you, Ms. Chase," she said.

"My pleasure, Mrs. Costigan."

"Mary, please," Mary said, extending her hand.

Esther took Mary's hand in kind. The two women looked deeply at one another's eyes, as only women can.

"How did you know the gun wouldn't fire?" Mary asked David.

"Uncle Tom called Bren and told him everything. He was the one who told us to leave the back door and the bulkhead unlocked."

"Couldn't we have spared the kids?" Mary asked.

"I guess," David said. "I thought of everything I could."

Brendan and Rachel walked over to where David and Mary were standing, the flashes of blue and red light danced in the cool Maine night. Brendan put his hand on David's shoulder and squeezed. They both watched as the paramedics loaded Covey into the ambulance, accompanied by a large, humorless Maine State Trooper.

"Think he'll make it?" Brendan asked.

"Don't really give a shit," David said.

Chapter 12

Sunshine Through the Fog

Ernest Rushton had a saying about Northeast Ohio weather: "It is unpredictable and can be harsh, but I'll stack a Youngstown Spring against anywhere." This was one of those perfect spring days. The one undeniable upside to the demise of the steel industry was the air. Once sooty and rife with the smell of ash, it was clean and sweet today. What was once a gray and brown sky was now so blue, it hurt one's eyes just to look at it.

The crowd gathered in front of the re-fitted building at the corner of Mahoning and Glenwood Avenues. The yellow ribbon stretched some thirty feet across the front doorway, a man in a suit holding a bronze plaque with gold lettering. There was a short, wide wooden stage, with a banner hanging to the ground, bearing the letters YB&GC, an acronym for Youngstown Boys and Girls Club.

In the crowd, two families stood compacted together, about fifteen feet separating them. On one side, Leesa Rushton stood with her mother in law, her children, along with Marie Vachon and her children. On the other, Brendan and Rachel stood on either side of Elizabeth, with Tom, Patrick, and Uncle Billy to their right. To their left, Mary stood with her three children at her side.

A moment later, a dark black step van pulled onto Mahoning Avenue and eased its way adjacent to the curb, where the thousand or so onlookers were gathered. Rocco Donofrio jumped from his driver's side perch, ran around to the side, and opened the sliding door. Rachel Nilson stepped out onto the ramp Rocco had drawn down from the van, turned, and started pulling the wheelchair down the ramp. James Costigan's head was turned halfway around his shoulders, mesmerized by the mechanics of getting the heavy wheelchair down the ramp. Marie Vachon looked across the crowd and caught Mary's eye. She smiled, and Mary returned it sincerely.

Marie motioned behind her, and the two women watched Rachel Nilson do her work.

She reached the sidewalk, rolled the chair off the ramp, and turned it. Joe Brady desperately scanned the crowd until he found Marie Vachon. She raised her hand in a subtle, feminine way, and his smile exploded like paint on a canvas.

Marie looked over again at Mary and now Elizabeth. Elizabeth turned to look behind her and instantly recognized the man she had not seen in decades. He motioned for Nilson to take him there. She traversed the crowd, a constant "excuse me" as she turned and twisted through the throng.

"Joseph," Elizabeth said, leaning down to kiss his cheek.

"Hello, Liz," Joe said, patting her hand. "You are as ravishing as ever."

"If I were an over-ripened tomato, maybe," she laughed. "How are you, Joe?"

"Dandy, now," he said, looking up at "Nurse Cratchit," who remained employed by Marie Vachon—but in a rather different capacity. "I wanted to call you so many times, but I promised…" He began to cry.

Elizabeth put her hand on his shoulder. "It's okay, Joe," she said compassionately. "I know you made him that promise."

"I only just now found out you knew. I thought the money went up to William, and no one was the wiser," Brady said.

"Funny thing about deceit and conspiracy." She smiled. The emotion of it all, long since departed—or so she thought.

Rocco Donofrio stepped up onto the makeshift stage, Aiden, John, and David taking positions behind him. He took a step into the microphone.

"Today is not only the day we open this new Youngstown Boys & Girls Club, but also a day we honor a man and a tradition. But it is not for me to say." The crowd laughed. "Please give it up for the Chairman of the Mahoning Trumpet Endowment, Mr. Aiden Vachon."

The crowd cheered the man they knew had risen from a rather colored and nefarious legacy, but a man who had helped to keep a city afloat in its darkest hours.

Aiden shook Rocco's hand and stepped into the microphone.

"We have had many dedications in these years since nineteen seventy-seven," he started. "But this one has a very special meaning. Today, we honor men who served the community and city in its most desperate hour".

Next, John was called up. This was an important and historic moment, and not merely because of this opening. This was the first time in over sixty years Costigan, Rushton, and Vachon families stood together.

"My uncle, Francis Costigan, left Boston to keep us safe, while Youngstown provided the steel which led to the Axis' ultimate demise. So, it is my deepest pleasure and honor to hand these scissors to my cousin, David Costigan, to cut this ribbon."

Dozens in the crowd exchanged glances, their expressions brimming with curiosity and mild confusion. To most—perhaps to all—the name Costigan rang unfamiliar. Yet, despite the obscurity of the connection, they seemed willing to embrace the idea of this unintroduced cousin, as if the moment itself demanded a quiet acquiescence.

David stepped up, took the scissors, and embraced Aiden. He stepped down the few steps but turned away from the ribbon. He cut through the crowd until he reached his father. No words exchanged; David stared into his father's eyes. Patrick looked sternly at his son, but that sternness melted into a gentle smile. David held out the shears. His father reached and took them from his son. Aiden began to clap, and the crowd followed suit. The applause and whistles echoed down to Federal Plaza and up through Mill Creek Park.

Patrick and David moved through the crowd, Patrick working to stave off his emotions. Finally, they reached the ribbon. They looked up over the double glass doors. Just above the granite keystone, a flat black quartz square sat keenly out of place from the brownish granite blocks. Carved into the quartz:

The Ernest Rushton

Memorial Boys & Girls Cub

Of

Youngstown

What was a cacophony of cheers was now an eerie silence. Only the sound of cars moving along Route Six-Eighty and the distant echo of Youngstown State University soccer broke the stillness. A thousand heads followed Patrick's, gazing up at the memorial to a man who, by all accounts, was an American hero. Patrick contemplated that himself as he looked up at the name, and understood it was his father's name after all. He smiled and wondered: *What is the measure of a hero?* This very building was a testimony to that.

He positioned the scissors around the bright ribbon and pressed the handles. The fabric split, and two sides floated away into the light spring breeze. The crowd exploded. John walked over to the double glass doors and symbolically opened them to signify the dedication.

The crowd settled down as Aiden stepped back up to the microphone. He waited for the last voice to still. Then he spoke.

"This is a miraculous day. I see so many friends and family out here, commemorating this building that will help so many of our young people. But we also commemorate hope, optimism, and selflessness."

He looked down at Joe Brady. The two men smiled at each other. He continued.

"I see generations. My children, me, John, his wife and children. September Nineteenth, Nineteen Seventy-Seven is regarded by most as the blackest day in our city's proud history. I suppose it is." He paused, breathing in the clean air, trying to contain his emotions. "It, however, was also the genesis of the amazing coalescence of a resilient community, retaining their pride and looking toward a more optimistic future. My grandfather, John's grandfather, and other people of vision created *The Mahoning Trumpet*. This is just the latest result of that commitment."

The crowd cheered again.

"Thank you," Aiden said, trying to quiet the crowd. "I think it is probably appropriate to bring up three honored guests who will help us invocate this miraculous achievement. Please welcome Bishop Darren Hruska from the Youngstown Diocese, Reverend Mark Gullard from Grace Lutheran Church, and Rabbi Frank Miller from Beth Shalom Synagogue."

The crowd applauded as the three men climbed the few stairs and encircled the microphone.

"God is smiling on Youngstown," the bishop said.

"Amen," Gullard echoed.

"We ask God to bless this edifice and the heroic and blessed people responsible for it," Hruska continued. "The Holy See of our church has called upon us to be our brother's keepers and tend to our less fortunate brethren. I think he would be excited about our great community."

Miller stepped into the microphone.

"In Jewish tradition, we use the word *Mitzvah* to describe an important sacred moment or event. This is certainly a joyous moment. *Mazeltov!*"

The crowd roared with applause. The three men of different faiths signified the essence of Youngstown. Very much un-gentrified, Youngstown remains an ethnic community, with its pockets of Eastern European, Italian, and Greek communities firmly in place. It also signified the spirituality of the city—most evident in its loyalty and optimism about the community. Others might consider the city a little sister to Cleveland and Pittsburgh; people in Youngstown certainly do not.

Aiden shook all three men's hands, gave the bishop an additional pat on the back, and returned to the microphone.

"Before everyone goes inside for the tour and goes home, I cannot in good conscience end this dedication without thanking the two men most responsible for this and many other treasures of our city. I am, of course, referring to Henri Vachon and Ernest Rushton—two men who saw a tremendous need and delivered. We miss you. God bless you all."

John and David stepped to where Aiden was standing, each taking one of his hands. Four hands raised up, as if victorious in some renowned sporting event. The crowd applauded for the last time—a collection of whistles, screams, and claps. The three men moved off the stage to join their families. Many people stopped John or Aiden, and each politely negotiated his way through the dense crowd.

David hugged Mary, as John hugged Leesa. John took Peter and Annabell's hands and walked them over to where all the Costigans were standing. Leesa moved toward Mary directly; shyness was not part of the Youngstown DNA. The two women engaged in a careful albeit sincere hug.

"It is so nice to finally meet you, Mary," Leesa said. "This is Peter and Annabell."

"This is James, Jacqueline, and Veronica," Mary said proudly. "These are your cousins, Peter and Annabell."

The children were shy at first—standoffish. Then, as kids did, they teamed up and headed into the club, leaving Mary and Leesa to chat.

David walked over to Joe Brady's wheelchair and extended his hand.

"Good to see you again, friend," David said.

"I have to thank you for what you did," Brady sighed, hating his relegation to this wheelchair.

Patrick followed, closely trailed by Elizabeth, Tom, and Billy. The five Costigans encircled the failing old man, who was once the strapping and dashing soldier attending one cold South Boston Thanksgiving, during one of the greatest examples of carnage in human history. Each one touched the man, as though his age and wisdom bestowed some miraculous sanctification.

"I remember as if it were yesterday, sitting at the table in South Boston before we shipped out," Brady said. "You were just a little boy," he said to Patrick.

"I remember my uncle talking about you, and what a good friend to my father you were," Patrick said, looking at the sky, grasping the irony of what he said.

"We were at that," Brady smiled, looking out toward the YSU stadium.

Marie walked over, all the while smiling at Rachel Nilson.

"Nice to see you, Rachel," Marie said. "And you, Joe."

"Yes, ma'am," Nilson said.

Slowly, the Costigans, Rushtons, and Vachons slid into the unopened club. On the other side of the round oak matriculation desk was a small conference room. As one or more of the three families crossed the main desk, he or she was hailed into the room.

David and Mary were the last. When they entered, the small room was already crowded. At the front was a whiteboard the height and length of the wall. Against it leaned Aiden and John. They motioned to David as he came into view. David kissed Mary on the eye and joined his two friends at the front.

Food, beverages, and dessert lined a rectangular white buffet table off to the side. Most of those in the room had already retrieved their meal when David joined the other two. Peter, Annabell, James, Jacqueline, and Veronica naturally coalesced at one of the smaller dining tables set about the room. Mary, Leesa, and Marie also found their way to a single table, while Elizabeth, Anne, Aiden and John's mother, Tom, and Billy established themselves at the table farthest from the door.

This time it was John who stepped up at the front of the room. He looked around, stopping for a moment at each person's face.

"Eighteen months ago, many of us didn't know each other. Now we are a family."

Elizabeth stood from her seat and began to clap. One by one, the Costigans, Rushtons, and Vachons took their place, as the clapping got louder and louder. Mary, too, wrapped her arms around Leesa and pulled her closer. The room was packed, and people spilled out into the foyer. The guest list was kept to two-fifty. Trying to fit a thousand people into this re-fitted building would be impossible. As a matter of fairness, after the families and dignitaries, tickets were awarded on a first come basis.

"You realize we have no shopping here," Leesa said.

"That's okay. We do in Boston," Mary replied. "Maybe we can plan a visit."

David walked across the room where Aiden, John, and Patrick were standing. He sipped on a beer, then raised his glass.

"Are you doing okay, David?" Aiden asked.

"I am Aiden, but I have a question about Covey."

"You're not sick of all that?" Aiden asked.

"Sure, I am, but why didn't you do something like this years ago? You didn't really need us."

Aiden smiled and took the glass of wine Marie brought over to him. He motioned David to the corner of the room. Patrick joined them there and turned to make sure they were alone.

"It didn't matter," Aiden said. "So, it wasn't worth the risk."

"This is much more your area than mine, but isn't the risk pretty much the same now?" David asked.

"He wasn't directly threatening my family until now," Aiden replied. "For years, it was more like a "Pink Panther" movie. He fumbled around, but we were always a few steps ahead of him."

David stared at Aiden, uncertain of how to comment. He looked down at his beer, swishing the liquid around the inside of the cup.

"You didn't even know me eighteen months ago," David said.

Aiden laughed.

"What's so funny?" David asked.

"I've known you all your life, David."

David cocked his head, as a dutiful Doberman might do.

"My family and yours are eternally linked," Aiden said. "Once Covey threatened you, that was it. His time was running out."

"How did you…?"

"You know, David," Aiden interrupted. "Becoming completely legitimate doesn't mean not connected. My epiphany, around my twenty-fifth birthday, was that when it comes to power and influence, the line between legitimate and illicit is blurry."

"So, what's the difference?" David asked.

"The difference is what you do with it, and how you use it. Now I want to get to know that family of yours."

David carefully looked about the room.

"I'm still worried about Covey," David said.

"He's going to jail," Aiden explained.

"Yeah, but someone like him doesn't just give up."

"Oh, I don't know," Aiden smirked. "Maybe sometimes his kind need a little help."

David looked at Aiden, not sure he really wanted an interpretation—perceiving the threat to his family to still be very alive.

"And you can help him?" David asked.

"Jail is a tough and unforgiving place," Aiden said, taking a sip of his wine. "Do you know how hard it is to protect someone in that environment?"

"Not really."

"Unless you keep a guy in absolute—and I mean absolute— isolation *forever*, it's just a matter of patience. There's always an unfortunate accident around every corner."

David pushed his eyes toward Aiden, feeling some involuntary complicity. Aiden met his eyes and raised his wine glass. David tapped his cup against it and smiled.

"Well, Cuz," John said, walking over to where David was still standing. "Worlds collide, hey?"

"You aren't kidding, John. When I think of life before all this..."

"Miss it?"

"Not a bit," David said, rocking on his heels. "I didn't know you even existed. Now *that* is depressing."

Just then, Elizabeth walked up on them.

"Granny," David said.

"Mrs. Costigan," John said.

"Granny Elizabeth, John," she suggested.

"Okay," he smiled.

Granny, David, and John talked for more than thirty minutes. Once she was negative toward Francis or regretful about their short life together. Instead, she focused on what she gained through David's efforts over the past year and a half. Granny talked to the cousins about family, what it means, and how it can be both complicated and painful at times. David and John nodded in an accepting way, keenly attuned to Elizabeth's wisdom.

David looked about the room and thought how amazing this all was. Francis could not have predicted all this unfolding as it had. He could not imagine the likes of Lemuel Covey and how, in his malevolence, would bring three families together in such an unprecedented way. His efforts to fulfill his own dreams, while not utterly forsaking the duty to his family, created a world that would not have otherwise existed. The very idea of right and wrong dissolved into a reality that was something miraculous. Had it not been for what some might perceive as selfishness, the generations of Youngstown children lifted by the Trumpet would not have been.

So, in the end, judgment of the man who died as Francis Costigan and was reborn as Ernest Rushton was, at its core, misplaced at best.

Epilogue

Only a few "die-hards" remained on Carson Beach as the summer sun sank into the western horizon. David watched the tiny waves lap up onto the mid-tide beach, the sound of the rolling stones and splashing water echoing into the South Boston evening.

He looked out toward the Boston skyline, thinking about who he was, and how that very sense of himself changed over the last year. Fatherhood had taken on greater meaning with the arrival of Veronica into his family, and the closeness with his own immediate family deepened—though his relationship with his father remained tense at times. Add to that the Vachon and Rushton families, and he was now part of something greater than any of its previous, disparate parts.

Then he was startled by a tap on his shoulder, and he jumped back. Patrick was standing there, apologetic for scaring his son. It was not his intent to surprise David, but he could see how engrossed he was.

"Mary thought you were down here," Patrick said.

"Nothing quite like looking at the city across this water," David reflected.

"You know I'm proud of you, right?" Patrick said.

"I thought you'd be pissed at me for starting this whole thing."

"I'm not thrilled about putting our family in danger, David," Patrick said, "but the rug we piled our family crap under was about up to the ceiling anyway. But that's not what I mean."

"Dad?"

"You taught me a lot through all of this, David," Patrick said, as compassionately as he had ever spoken. "But I'm proud of you—for all of it."

David looked at his father, the only sounds now from jet engines at Logan Airport and the rolling stones disturbing the quiet.

"You're way smarter than me, Dad," David said. "I'm not sure—"

"Your life, son," Patrick interrupted. "Your decision about medical school, who you are as a father, a husband, and a man. How could I be anything but proud of you?"

"So, what have you done with my father?" David laughed, sucking in his emotions.

"I guess I deserve that. I've been harder on you than Brendan." He took off his Red Sox cap and scratched his head. "It's hard for an old coot like me to admit—but it's because you and I are the same. You also sometimes perceive things in me that aren't there."

"Dad?"

"C'mon David. We're both stubborn Irish bastards when we want to be." His eyes welled up. "But I love you and your brother more than my life. God, if anything—"

"It didn't, Dad," David said, putting his hand on his father's shoulder.

David turned toward the street. Brendan was just then hopping down from the boulevard wall and started toward them. Both men wiped their eyes and assumed a nonchalant stance.

"Am I interrupting something?" Brendan asked.

"Nope," Patrick said.

"Mom, Mary, Rachel, and Granny are in their Progesterone zone. I felt like a Martian on Venus," Brendan laughed.

"Then I'm glad you came down," Patrick said.

"Mom kind of suggested it."

"Glad you're here, little brother," David said, clasping his brother behind the neck.

"I'm thinking there was some serious male bonding going on here. You two, okay?"

"Never better," David said, glancing back at his father.

Patrick maneuvered himself between his sons and put his arms over their shoulders. He said nothing at first. Instead, he closed his eyes, and for the first time in his life, thanked God for the two blessings standing under his proverbial wing.

David and Brendan leaned forward just a bit and stared at each other. Two generations of Costigan men were now the last people on Carson Beach as the sun fell away to the west. At that single, precious moment in time, nowhere on Earth were fathers and sons more thankful and content to have one another.

The Bluish school bus turned off the main road and drove the one hundred yards or so to the Allenwood Penitentiary gate. The driver exchanged paperwork with the guard, and the bus proceeded past the first open gate, and then the second.

The bus came to a stop in front of a huge stone archway, which evidently led into the prison itself. In the front of the bus, a burly and humorless officer stood and barked out for the men to stand and file off the bus.

The men were clad in blue jumpsuits with the acronym DOC stamped on the back. Each man was shackled at the wrists and ankles, and there was a central chain binding them together. One by one they clanked off the bus and onto the dusty and partially paved staging area.

Two more guards came from behind the arch and, without an utterance, lined the men up shoulder to shoulder.

One of the prisoners made a comment to the man on his right. The guard from the bus walked over and placed his face an inch from the prisoner's.

"One more word, and your first night here at the Pennsylvania Hilton will be the worst night of your fucking miserable life."

Third to last off the bus came a frail specter of a man—shoulder-length white hair clinging to his skull like cobwebs, beard tangled and forgotten. He shuffled forward, barely more than a shadow among the others.

The burly guard began his slow march down the line, clipboard in hand, ticking off names with mechanical precision. But when he reached the third man from the end, he stopped cold.

"Covey. Lemuel Covey?" he said, voice flat.

The old man lifted his eyes. There was no defiance in them— only the hollow gaze of someone who had already surrendered to fate.

"I said, Lemuel Covey?" the guard barked. Third to last off the bus came a frail specter of a man—shoulder-length white hair clinging to his skull like cobwebs, beard tangled and forgotten. He shuffled forward, barely more than a shadow among the others.

The burly guard began his slow march down the line, clipboard in hand, ticking off names with mechanical precision. But when he reached the third man from the end, he stopped cold.

"Covey. Lemuel Covey?" he said, voice flat.

The old man lifted his eyes. There was no defiance in them— only the hollow gaze of someone who had already surrendered to fate.

"I said, Lemuel Covey?" the guard barked.

"Yes," came the reply, thin and trembling. "I am Lemuel Covey."

The guard glanced around, then leaned in close, his breath hot against Covey's ear.

"Don't fret too much, Agent Covey," he whispered. "Your suffering here will be very short-lived."

He straightened and moved on, leaving Covey frozen in place, the words echoing like a death knell.

Covey didn't blink. Didn't breathe. Just stared ahead, as one final thought clawed its way to the surface.

Checkmate.

And somewhere, deep within the prison walls, a door slammed shut.